RENEGADE MAGIC

STAR BANDITS: UPRISING
BOOK 1

JENNIFER M. EATON

Renegade Magic: Star Bandits: Uprising Book 1
© 2021 Jennifer M. Eaton
R4

Published by Galactic Razor
Series Cover designs: Art4Artists and Covers by Julie
https://www.art4artists.com.au/ | www.coversbyjulie.com

In outer space, there is no right or wrong...unless you get caught.

Cal commandeers a smuggling vessel to escape a death sentence for a crime he didn't commit. When a galactic law enforcer lands far too close, Cal's new crew kidnaps her hoping they can prove his innocence.

Hey, what could go wrong?

Dania, a powerful mage enforcer, is on a mission to eliminate a human trafficking ring. When a small team of criminal buffoons grabs her instead, she's honor bound to exterminate them despite their pleas of innocence.

The *Star Renegade* crew is guilty and must be punished for their crimes. However, they use their smuggling profits to feed the hungry. Dania will face her own execution for not enforcing royal edicts, but how can she execute people breaking the law for all the right reasons?

Star Bandits: Uprising *is Guardians of the Galaxy meets Firefly and Robin Hood.*

Jump on board and start your inter-galactic adventure today!

For my kids.
When I started writing, you were all barely out of diapers.
Now you are young men, launching your lives.
Shoot for the stars, and be happy wherever you land.
(As long as you land within driving distance of your mother.)
[Insert all-knowing Mommy glare]

CHAPTER 1

DANIA

A HINT of fuel emissions and aged metal filled the air, but it would soon smell like blood if Dania had any say in it. The small skipper craft that had transported Dania and her men from her cruiser lifted off the docking platform, the hum of the engines rattling the metal gangway.

Workers scurried about, doing their best not to look in her direction.

Nothing unusual. Most humans tried to avoid enforcers at all costs.

Her communication bracelet pinged, announcing a transmission from her team on a nearby moon.

The voice of one of her lieutenants rose from the band. "General, the twenty-three accused colonists have been detained in the center square."

Dania nodded. "And you've ascertained their guilt? They are the ones who vandalized the king's gardens?"

"Without a doubt, General."

"Fine." Dania grimaced.

Trampled flowers. Such a waste of life.

"Show them mercy. No pain. Execute them quickly and

return to the ship." She closed her eyes and breathed deeply. Why humans continued to break laws when they knew the consequences confounded her.

A few paces ahead, her primary medic and protector, Alexander, stepped off the gangway. The artificial illumination made his opalescent uniform sparkle, and his long, nearly white hair flowed through the air, pulsing with primordial energy and shimmering with a light all its own.

He held out a hand to her, and she stepped down, taking her place beside him.

Their new mission would be fulfilled by gaining undetected tactical advantage. Still, allowing Alexander to walk so close, like she were a fragile crystal that might break, grated against her resolve.

Yes, she'd instructed Alexander to look like he was shielding her, but the truth was, she was the one that *others* needed protection *from*.

He cocked a brow at her. "You aren't bulletproof."

Dania heated over his intrusion into her thoughts, but this was nothing new. "I can run faster than a bullet."

He pursed his lips. "You can't outrun a weapon you don't see."

Dania sighed. Alexander's excessive warnings of caution grew tiresome, but unlike Kile and Miguel, walking far ahead of them, Alexander cared whether or not she survived. His regard for her was some consolation when they were in battle. This wasn't a battle, though.

"Not yet, it's not," Alexander whispered.

As usual, he was right. But Dania was more than capable of fulfilling this mission on her own.

A group of humans bowed as they passed, an unnecessary gesture, but fitting. This station, and all of Earth's galactic territories, had been signed into the protection of the Banes thirty-eight years ago, after the Carteks had swooped in from the Camian galaxy and started decimating Earth's holdings. The treaty had put Earth and her territories under the king's protection.

There was an adjustment period for the humans as they learned the king's law, but all agreed that bowing to the will of the Banes, and their enforcers, was a better option than allowing the Carteks to strip all of Earth's worlds of their natural resources.

Her boots thumped on the metal grates covering the ventilation system as they caught up to the others. Per their plan, she took the weaker position in the rear of the enforcers' formation. Dania steeled herself against the need to stride forward and take her proper place at the head of the diamond. She'd proven that she belonged there. Anywhere less mocked her station.

This was her own plan, though. And it would work. She just needed to convince the humans she was the weakest enforcer of the four.

Kile strode before them with his head held high, his short, opalescent hair gleaming in the space station's murky light. He was doing well, feigning authority. Miguel kept a step behind him, dwarfing Kile in both heights and shoulder width. The two could not be mistaken for the weapons they were.

Several people raised cameras, probably sending messages to the criminals her team were here to find. Within moments, the trappers would know what Kile and Miguel looked like, believing they were the ones to be avoided.

Little did they know the one they should fear was the

younger woman in the rear. It would be this lapse of judgment that would be their undoing.

"As long as you don't get shot first," Alexander said over his shoulder.

Sometimes, her friend had a ridiculously one-track mind. She narrowed her eyes at him. "Keep out of my head."

He snickered and returned his attention forward. She had to work with him on breaking protocols. They needed to be alert, especially for this mission.

They were here under orders of the king to stop the most heinous of crimes against their kind.

The insolent slavers who'd taken refuge here in Midway Station had been abducting weakened or novice enforcers for over a year. At first, the royal family had believed the attacks to be politically motivated—until they'd discovered their elite police force had been deemed valuable collectors' items and were being sold on the black market as exotic *pets*.

Dania gritted her teeth. For a time, it hadn't been personal. But two weeks ago, Matara, an enforcer apprentice from another team, had disappeared.

The girl had been only in training for four years when Dania had taken her under her tutelage. Two years later, Matara had excelled, turning stronger than any of the men on that team. And they'd noticed.

Dania had known they would. Dania herself had once fought for every last bit of her own training as her power had manifested, and she refused to see another woman struggle because of men's bruised egos.

Under Dania's guidance, Matara had grown fierce. Smart. Ready to take a high place in the enforcer ranks.

But now she was gone.

Dania's stomach soured. Matara had disappeared before the galaxy got to see her shine. She hoped to find the girl alive, but Matara's chances of survival waned with each passing of the moons.

Dania quickened her pace. For all she knew, the girl could be being tortured at that very moment.

She needed to end this threat. Now.

They moved farther into the facility, to where the docking bays emptied into a massive high-ceilinged space. Grime-coated walking paths connected tables manned by vendors shouting and holding up everything from partially ripened fruit to reclaimed ship parts.

Trade, refueling, and human entertainment were the core proficiencies of Midway Station. Too bad the criminal element made this a frequented stop for the galactic enforcers as well.

A shot rang out, and several women screamed. Alexander bolted in the direction of the shouting before Dania could order him to stop.

He knew better. He was supposed to be pretending to protect her.

The instincts of an enforcer were strong, though. She couldn't begrudge him doing his duty.

Kile and Miguel raced after a man running for the rear exit. So much for following her plan to the smallest detail.

No matter. The more commotion, the greater the chances of the trappers swooping in, hoping to take advantage.

Kile and Miguel certainly didn't need her help to handle one criminal, so Dania headed after Alexander. She pushed through a small crowd gathered around a human female cradling a man's head on her lap.

Tears streamed down the woman's face as she swept back her cropped, pink-tipped hair. "Doc… Peter, hold on. I'm here."

A red bloom of blood spread across the man's white shirt. His short, dark hair stuck wet to his forehead as he reached up to her. "Alanna?"

"I've got you," the woman, Alanna, said. "I'm not going anywhere."

Alexander knelt beside them. "What happened?"

Alanna's eyes widened, and her lips parted, trembling. "W-We were just getting supplies." She shook her head. "I don't know what happened."

"Stray bullet," a bystander said. "Not all that uncommon in these parts."

Dania frowned as a tear from the woman's cheek dripped onto the dying man's forehead.

Stray bullets should never be *common*. This needed to be dealt with expediently—once their current orders were carried out, of course. No one should die needlessly in a market.

She blinked, the programming of her mission pushing out the extraneous thoughts.

Stray bullets were irrelevant to their operation. Catching trappers was the current priority, which Alexander had seemingly forgotten. Again.

Past the shops and tables, toward a rear exit, a man cried out. His voice elevated to a screech and then gurgled to a stop. Apparently, Kile and Miguel had caught up to their target and passed a swift judgment.

"Hold him still." Alexander pulled the man's shirt apart

and placed his hands on the patient's crimson-stained chest.

The air about them vibrated and warmed. Alexander's hair floated, pulsing with the power of the Banes. Around them, citizens gathered, shoving to get a better look as a small fragment of metal slowly rose from the man's chest.

The blood flow increased. The woman sobbed before Alexander placed his palm over the hole.

Dania had seen this countless times, and it never failed to impress her. Prince Geron had spent a considerable amount of time making Alexander an efficient healer. It made her friend a liability in battle, always working to help others rather than pressing forward to achieve their goal. However, he'd saved several of her soldiers from inconvenient deaths when their arrogance had gotten in the way of their sense of safety. She supposed all skills had their place.

Alexander removed his hand and wiped away the blood. Fresh, new skin graced the man's chest.

The woman gaped. "Doc?" She reached for the clean skin but then drew her hand back.

The patient looked down at his chest before meeting Alexander's gaze. "I-I don't believe it."

Kile appeared over Dania's shoulder. He glared at Alexander. "We will get nowhere if you stop and heal every commoner we find. Get up."

Alexander sighed and mumbled, "We'll have no commoners to serve if we let them all die."

The girl, Alanna, grinned at him, probably a reaction to Alexander's polished angles and long, shimmering white hair rather than his trite comment.

As he made to stand, the girl grabbed his wrist. She

held him for a moment, staring at him. "Hey, thank you. I mean, really."

"It's nothing." Alexander motioned to his patient. "He should lie still for a few days. His internal organs still need to heal. Keep him quiet."

Her eyes brightened. "I will."

Dania tugged Alexander from the crowd of smiling merchants and shoppers. "Can we catch the people committing atrocities now?"

He smiled. "You aren't fun anymore, Dania."

Had she ever been fun? Certainly not during a mission. There were at least a dozen criminals on this space station. Once they were eradicated and she'd found Matara, then she'd be able to rest.

She pushed forward. "No more stunts. You're going to make yourself look weak."

A child of maybe seven years stood along the edge of the road, a bloody gash on her forehead.

"I hardly look weak." He drew his finger over the child's laceration, and the cut disappeared.

Dania scoffed. No, maybe it didn't make him look weak. In many ways, he was the strongest of them. Too bad his affinities were all toward helping others or she'd be able to put those talents to better use.

Still, caution was necessary. Alexander looking less aggressive might make him a more appealing target, which would ruin days of planning.

As they turned toward the center of the market, a woman cried out, "Stop! Thief!"

Dania smirked. She hadn't anticipated such a short wait for the next crime.

Kile looked over his shoulder at her. "Are you ready?"

She nodded. A thief was exactly what they were looking for, and this was a much more public place than the side alley the previous criminal had run to. They couldn't have planned this better.

A man whipped around the corner. His eyes turned to saucers when he saw them. The criminal skidded to a stop, dropping several orange and yellow fruits, and ran the other way.

Kile raised his hand, and the man rose off his feet and floated back to them. The people in the streets covered their mouths, wide eyed.

Odd, how the power of the enforcers was the stuff of legends, yet anytime a commoner saw their strength first-hand, they always seemed surprised.

The crowd moved closer as Kile placed the condemned on the ground before them. Also odd, how humans were as fascinated with executions as they were with healings.

The man fell to his knees. "Please." He held up his hands. "I only did it to feed my family. They're starving."

Kile towered over him. "So, you admit to breaking the king's law?"

The man looked at each of them. "Yes, but for a good reason…"

"There is never a reason to break the law." Kile turned to her. "Dania?"

She stepped forward. Several people in the crowd were already on their phones, relaying the spectacle.

Statistically, at least five of these people were connected to the trapping ring in some way. She needed to appear weak and untrained. This would solidify her as a potential victim. The sooner one of these miscreants tried to kidnap her, the sooner she could find and execute the leaders and be done with this.

She stood before the weeping thief.

Behind her, Kile said, "This man has committed a crime against our king and must be punished."

The criminal struggled against the air holding him in place. "No, I didn't do anything to the king. I stole some fruit from a vendor." His lower lip trembled. "Please. My daughter has scurvy. I can't afford vitamin supplements. I did this for her."

Dania's hands shook. This crime deserved a quick blow. Something painless. Maybe breaking his neck and then burning the body to cinders. A merciful death.

Tears lined through the dirt on the man's face. "Please. They can't survive without me."

"Your judgment?" Kile asked Dania.

Dania flinched at the sound of his voice. Her decisions were normally swift and definitive, but she needed to fumble this one to solidify that she was a novice, uncentered in the king's law. However, she ached with the desire to end this man's life to make sure he never broke the rules again. The people gathered around them needed to see and understand that the law was absolute.

She grimaced. It shouldn't be so hard to do the wrong thing. Criminals broke laws every day.

"Dania?" Kile growled, kicking the back of her leg.

He was playing his part, but she'd make him pay for that later.

She took a deep breath and released it slowly. She hunched slightly and turned to her supposed leader. "His children were hungry."

Kile's expression remained placid. "Inconsequential."

"Is this my judgment, my decision?" she asked.

"Yes."

She turned back to the man. "You need to find honest work to feed your family." She cringed over the idiocy of the statement. All criminals knew this, but they chose to break the law rather than abide by the rules of the king's society.

"I've tried," he said. "No one will hire me."

Of course they wouldn't. Who would want a criminal under their employ?

Dania pulled a silver *shaila* out of her pocket and handed it to him. That single coin was worth a month's ration of fruit, more than enough to save a sick child. "I want you to take this to the station staffer. Tell them that House Bane wants you employed. If they do not accept this, I will visit them and make sure they comply."

The man wrapped his fist around the coin. "Y-You're not going to execute me?"

Like a muscle memory, every fiber in her body screamed to reach out and end this thief's life. One less criminal made the galaxy that much safer.

She drew in another deep breath. "Not today, but there will be no leniency if you commit another crime. If you want your children to grow up with a father, you will obey the law."

Miguel shifted his feet. She hoped he wouldn't snap and sever the man's head. Then again, if he did, justice would be served, and Dania had already done her job and marked herself as an easy target.

Still clutching the coin, the man ran for the nearest exit. It would be interesting to know if he actually took the coin down to the staffer, or if he'd spend it on food—if he'd been telling the truth and there was a family that needed to be fed.

Kile grabbed her wrist and pulled her toward an alley. She could easily twist around and break his arm. All her training pushed her to carry through, but her commander was only following her orders.

He stopped just inside the partition between two shops, enough to feign privacy, but also giving a full view to anyone who wanted to eavesdrop.

"The king does not grant mercy to criminals," he told her. "That man will steal again."

"But he said…"

Kile slapped her across the face. "I don't care what a criminal says."

Dania stumbled back and fell. She rubbed her cheek, sensing the bruise forming beneath. Her commander was taking his role far too seriously.

She tried to make her eyes seem innocent of all the criminal blood she'd spilled over the years. "But it doesn't seem right to…"

Kile raised a palm. She tensed, remembering not to defend herself as a sparkling bolt of energy left his hand. Pain exploded up her nerves. The ends of her silver hair smoked as she hit the ground.

Before she could take a breath, another jolt hit her, this one from Miguel—slightly more tentative, but equally painful. The third assault blasted around her in a bolt of bright light. She cried out as her blood heated from within, then instantly cooled. Icy fingers spread through her, extinguishing the fires and relieving the pain.

Alexander.

He'd hidden a healing inside his punishment. She

glanced up at him. She should rebuke him for disobeying her orders, but she appreciated the gesture. She'd forgotten how painful even a small admonishment like this could be.

Kile turned. "Leave her. If she is worth our efforts, she'll find her way back."

Dania let her hair fall in her face to disguise her grin. She'd done almost the same thing to him when he'd disobeyed her orders once. That had been the last time he'd ever questioned her command.

Alexander frowned as he looked back to her.

Go, she mouthed.

They couldn't waste time worrying about Dania when Matara could be out there dying.

He hesitated another moment before heading out after the others, leaving Dania alone and vulnerable.

She stood slowly. Alexander's healing stroke had helped, but her muscles still screamed in defiance with each movement. If anyone came for her now, it wouldn't be hard for her to pretend to be injured.

Dania flinched, pushing away the thought. When the trappers attacked, she wouldn't be at her best. That was what she wanted, though, to be taken back to their lair so she could dispose of the leaders.

It was a good plan, but she didn't expect to feel so alone as the shadows began to close in on her.

CHAPTER 2

CAL

CAL LEANED toward the empty co-pilot's station as a yellow light flashed in his face. *That can't be good.*

Outside his ship's main view pane, the dock workers darted between the other freighters loading and unloading cargo. At least no one was shooting at him. Not yet, at least.

Every few minutes, a taskmaster would stop, look up at Cal's ship, and make notes in their ledger, probably wondering why Cal hadn't checked in any cargo.

As long as the workers made notes and didn't ask questions, everything would be fine.

Cal grimaced as the light on the other console continued to blink.

Why did stuff always go wrong when his maintenance guys were off-ship?

He tapped the blue communication button, calling his crew out in Midway Station. "Ty, that yellow light is flashing on your dashboard again."

Static filled the line before Ty's voice answered. "Come on, boss. I warned you about that."

Of course he did. "How about you warn me again?"

"Tap it three times."

He was joking, right? Cal tapped the button, and on the third tap, the blinking stopped.

"Did it work?" Ty asked.

"Yeah." Cal really wanted to tell him *no*. As usual, though, Ty knew every last quirk in the ship. "Are you guys going to fix that anytime soon?"

Ethan's voice joined the call. "I'll get on that if you want me to put the oxygen diffuser on the back burner."

Cal laughed. "I'm quite fond of breathing, so as you were." He glanced at the light again. "This flashing isn't the sign of a bigger problem, right?"

Ty snorted. "As long as it doesn't flash orange, it's okay."

"What's orange?"

"Just call me if it ever turns orange."

Great. One day he'd force Ty to sit down and explain every last modification he'd made to this ship.

"The flashing is just a short," Ethan said. "I checked it last week."

Cal rubbed his eyes. "Roger that."

This was just one more thing on the long list of repairs for the *Star Renegade*. Too bad "Bessie," the cadaver Doc Sanders had picked up in last week's trading run, couldn't be used as an extra set of deck hands. Then again, Bessie could stay right in the med bay where she was. The last thing Cal needed was any more dead weight on the bridge. He filled that spot enough for all of them.

He ran his palms over the pits and grooves behind the dashboard. If this little ship hadn't saved his rear end so many times, he might have thought of trading her in for a newer model, but in a galaxy where any semblance of creature comfort was hard to find, she'd become home.

"How's it going with supplies?" Cal asked. "You've all been gone too long."

"Patience is a virtue," Ethan cooed.

Cal fought against making a fist. He spent half his time wanting to slap that little piece of space trash upside the head and the other half thanking him for saving their lives. Ethan was lucky he was a competent engineer.

Cal checked the readings on the command panel. So far, the false docking codes he'd provided were still green. If anyone ran the markings on the hull, though, or recognized his crew, they were all toast. He'd used this ship on far too many smuggling runs for her not to be on every local law enforcement's radar.

Luckily, most station security officials could be bought. However, he didn't want anyone playing hero and turning them in for one of the many rewards out for their hides.

The communicator flickered. "Boss, you're not going to believe this," Ty said.

Cal tapped the button. "What's up?"

"A band of the king's enforcers just landed in Section Twelve."

Ice flooded Cal's veins. He glanced at their docking location: *Section Twenty-Seven*. Still, that was too close.

He leaned closer to the panel. "You're sure? It's not just similar uniforms like on Neptune Nine?"

"No, I'm sure. They have that freaky silver hair that sways around like it's alive."

Cal's shoulders tightened. He stood and stared through the window. A trader raced to one of the ships, closing the ramp as soon as he'd boarded. Another man dropped a package as he dashed for a different ship, not even bothering to pick the box up.

Cal certainly didn't blame them. The enforcers were supposed to be an interplanetary police force, but they were more like murderous vigilantes.

He slammed his fist down on the comm button. "Get back here. Now. All of you."

If the enforcers had found him, they had precious little time to get away. He glanced at the instruments. He could start as much of the prelaunch as possible until everyone was back on board.

He tapped into the station's public communications archive and checked for royal data extractions. The enforcer ship had done some basic searches on an illegal trading ring of some kind and an analysis of when the most people would be in the market area, but nothing else. *Strange.*

What were the chances that a band of enforcers had landed here by coincidence?

He shivered. It wasn't worth the risk to even hope.

Cal had made a vow to keep at least a million miles from the closest enforcer, and sometimes that hadn't been enough. He was wanted for killing an aristocrat with close ties to the royal family. It wouldn't matter that he didn't do it. He'd be executed for the crime, and the enforcers would move on.

He'd seen it before...the shiny white uniforms appearing out of nowhere...people screaming...blood running through the streets.

Cal shuddered. Enforcers didn't care if you were falsely accused. They killed anyone who even *might* be guilty, and they moved on.

He leaned closer to the glass, checking every entrance to the receiving docks for his people. Where were they all?

He punched the comm button again. "Call in. I want everyone back on this ship immediately. I'm starting preflight."

"Doc and I are on our way," Alanna's voice answered. "You're never going to believe what just happened."

"Yeah, tell me when you get here." Cal checked the instruments again. "Ty. Ethan. Answer me."

Static filled the line. "Boss, you're breaking up. Ethan and I are going to do some recon and see if we can figure out what the enforcers are doing this far away from the Bane home world."

Were they out of their minds? "Ty, get your ass back here now. That's an order."

"Sorry, boss, I can't hear you." The line cut out.

Dammit! If those idiots got caught, they might all be screwed. Cal would be executed for murder, and the rest of the crew, even if they found a way to avoid the smuggling charges, would be killed for just being on the same ship with him.

Cal gripped the edge of the console. This couldn't be happening to him again.

It had been sixteen years, but it seemed like yesterday when the enforcers had taken his father away.

Cal shook away the memory of the screaming, the blood. His eyes blurred and refocused on his fingers, white from clutching the console. He took a deep breath and wiped the sweat from his brow.

You couldn't negotiate with an enforcer. They killed without mercy. They were like robots, and his crew knew that.

Cal scanned the area outside his ship. Alanna and Doc entered the docking bay and held up their access cards to the chip readers on the security gates. Cal breathed a sigh of relief before his hands dampened on the console.

Alanna looked over her shoulder twice, her eyes wide. Doc's hair stuck to his forehead, looking like he'd just run a marathon. A single bag hung over Alanna's shoulder, too small to be holding all the supplies she'd gone out for.

Doc's hands were free. He didn't have his usual box of medical supplies and mad scientist gadgets.

The man never came back empty-handed.

Cal's stomach sank. Doc held one hand over his chest as he scanned his access card, while Alanna kept a palm on his back.

Worry creased her brow.

Something must have happened. Cal focused on the fact that they were alive. Right now, nothing else mattered.

Cal checked the area behind them and then scanned the security feeds of the hallways leading to the receiving docks. Traders and local guards passed the cameras, but no enforcers. At least no one was following them.

Once they got past the gate, Alanna moved beside Doc, placing his arm over her shoulder so he could lean on her. He'd definitely been hurt. But how? If it was enforcers, they would have been in pursuit.

The yellow light flashed on the console. Cal tapped it three times and it stopped.

Alanna and Doc were almost to the ship. Whatever had happened, he'd deal with it once they were safe.

Right now he had to get this ship ready to take off as soon as everyone was on board. With enforcers on the station, every second might mean the difference between living one more day and dying as part of some sick public spectacle.

He hit the comm. "Ty, Ethan. Come on. I know you can hear me. Please, do the right thing and come back to the ship."

Cal closed his eyes, breathing slowly as silence answered him.

Quiet was deafening at times, like the heartbeat of a twelve-year-old boy, drenched in blood, limping home to tell his mother that her husband had been stolen—murdered by the very people tasked to protect them.

The only thing Cal knew with any certainty was that the galaxy, with all its size and grandeur, was nowhere near large enough to hide in. In time, they always found you. He just didn't want to bring the rest of his friends down with him.

Cal straightened. They still had a chance to get away. All he could do was hope that Ty and Ethan wouldn't be foolish enough to go anywhere near those enforcers.

CHAPTER 3
DANIA

DANIA FEIGNED A LIMP, which wasn't hard since both legs still tingled after the blasts of power from her men. They were supposed to make her appear disabled—not *actually* disable her, but no matter. She'd trained for this her entire life. She'd follow through with the plan, whatever the circumstances.

She just hoped this meant victory, and not the defeat Alexander was so fond of warning her about.

The air about her hummed with energy as she scanned the crowd. There were eyes on her. Human. Male. One watched from the side, while another followed her.

Perfect.

Human males, from the beginning of time, had been known to prey on women in establishments that served mind-altering beverages. She made her way toward a tavern called "Gwen's Brewery." Her new shadow followed as Dania made her way into the poorly lit chamber and sat on one of the raised stools lining a long countertop at the far end of the room.

The shadow took the seat beside her and ordered a

beverage before he turned to Dania. "Do you need a drink?"

She smiled at him. He was young, maybe a few years older than her. Golden highlights in his sandy brown hair glinted in the overhead lighting. He was handsome in his own way. A perfect face to put a frightened, lonely girl at ease.

He turned to the man behind the counter. "Why don't you get the lady a Virillian Dancer and put it on my tab?" He turned and held out his hand to her. "Hi. My name is Ty."

An introduction? This was unexpected. She took his hand and shook. "Dania."

"Nice to meet you, Dania." He slid her drink toward her as it appeared on the counter. "You look like you could use this."

"What makes you say that?" A bead of water dripped down the outside of the glass, and small bubbles fizzed through the light-pink drink.

He shrugged. "I saw what happened earlier. You're an enforcer, right? And I'd guess from the crappy way they were treating you, you're a new recruit."

Interesting. He was working at gaining her trust. She'd figured they'd be more direct, shooting weapons and hurting the innocent, doing whatever it took to capture her.

She wiped her finger up the glass, erasing the drip. "Sometimes I wonder if I can handle this. The king's law is hard."

Ty nodded. "Do you think his laws are right?"

Dania closed her eyes. Lying wasn't part of her programming. Enforcers needed to be truthful in every way. She looked at him. "In most cases, yes. Criminals should be punished." She looked back to her glass.

Ty's drink appeared, and he took a sip. "For what it's worth, I think you did the right thing. If you took that family's father away, all the children and the mother might have turned to crime. By sparing one life, you probably saved the others."

She shook her head. "It wasn't the right thing to do. The commander made me very aware of that." She gripped her glass more tightly. This small talk grated on her nerves. She preferred a straight-on battle.

Ty frowned. "Yeah, well, if you ask me, he was an asshole."

One of the cubes of ice shifted in her glass, freeing a fizzy sparkle of bubbles.

"Why did you become an enforcer?" he asked.

Dania blinked. *Why?* It wasn't like there was ever a choice. This was what she'd always been. One of her earliest memories was her sponsor's smile and his warm embrace.

However, humans were not born to their vocations. They chose their own destinies. This was one of the many things that made judgment easier for Dania, knowing that these people chose to be criminals despite knowing they would die for it. That left the onus of their deaths on themselves rather than on the enforcers entrusted with keeping the peace.

Still, this trapper needed an answer, and she needed to continue to feign weakness until he made his move. "I suppose I wanted to stand up for what's right. I wanted people to feel safe in the galaxy."

"I guess that's as good a reason as any." He perused his

glass. "Do you think people have the right to a trial, like on Earth—to be proven guilty before punishment?"

What an odd question. "Only the guilty are punished."

"Yes, but enforcer punishment tends to come quickly. Have you ever seen someone executed and then found out the enforcers were wrong?"

He was right that judgments were passed quickly, but she wasn't aware that any mistakes had been made. Then again, what enforcer would admit to being wrong?

"I'm just saying," Ty continued, "that sometimes the evidence might not always tell the whole story. Maybe you need to look at things from all perspectives before executing people. Or maybe have different levels of punishment."

She looked at him. "Would you rather have a galaxy filled with prisons? The king's law is meant to bring order. If you don't want to be executed, then don't break the law."

She cringed. She was supposed to be making herself appear weak, but sometimes it was hard not to speak the truth when presented with such ignorance.

"Then again," she continued, "I am not upset about the judgment I passed on that man." But only because it had led Ty and his trapping ring right to her. She just wished he would make his move so she could confirm he was her target. The sooner he led her back to the ring leader, the sooner she could eradicate the threat and be done with it.

Ty's expression changed as a slight smile touched his lips. He turned back to his glass and took a drink before returning his gaze to her and letting the smile break free.

Good. Hopefully, he was done with this ruse, and they could both finish what they'd come here to do. First, though, she needed to get herself to a quiet, remote area. There was no reason to put any civilians at risk.

She'd allow herself to be taken, and when they brought her for processing, she'd drop her charade and eliminate the threat to her kind at the source. She'd stand proudly before her king, vanquishing the threat to the Banes' law in Prince Geron's name.

She pushed her glass back. "Thank you. This has been nice."

His eyes widened. "But you didn't touch your drink."

She glanced at it. Could the beverage have been drugged? She hadn't considered that. Maybe they would not even try to take her unless they thought she was further weakened? She picked up the glass and pretended to take a sip.

Ty smiled. "It's been nice meeting you, Dania."

She clenched her teeth against the response she wanted to give and headed for the exit.

Outside the tavern, she walked down the dirt street. Odd, how much filth could accumulate on metal floors after so many years of use. This supply station didn't feel much different than walking on a real planet.

Pulling up her sleeve, she hit a few buttons on the communication band on her wrist.

Alexander's voice spoke directly into her ear. "Are you okay?"

She continued walking, and whispered, "Yes. I just met with a trapper. I think he'll try to take me tonight."

"I still don't like this."

She glanced over her shoulder but kept walking. "Alexander, we've discussed this in depth. Now is not the time."

"My readings show you in sector four. You're near the aviary. Meet me there."

"I can't meet you. We need to…"

"The aviary is secluded, and probably empty this late in the day. We can meet and then I can leave you to be taken. I can at least watch to make sure you aren't harmed."

He was always the one to look for the safest way to obtain their goal. Even when they'd caused chaos in the palace as children, he'd always planned out their escape. It was probably why Prince Geron had added him to the team. Alexander was supposed to be the voice of reason, while the rest of them were programmed to get the job done as expediently as possible. She certainly couldn't fault him for being what her sponsor had engineered him to be. Still, it could be annoying at times.

"I'll be there in four minutes," she said.

"Good. I'll be there in three."

A few moments later, she slipped into the aviary, inclining her head to the woman at the *Reception and Questions* desk. Fortunately, the aviary was considered part of the king's arts program, which received funding from the royal family, so no one, no matter their financial situation, would be turned away. Not having to pay made it easier on her, and on the trappers.

The lights were fading inside, simulating the pending dusk that would be equated with the time of day registered at the station. The tall ceiling replicated an actual sky, apart from the seams in the metal framework.

A man and child exited as she stepped onto the pathway between two strips of simulated sod. This left her mostly alone, with the exception of a tall, silver-haired enforcer pacing beneath a spotted elm tree.

"You shouldn't worry so much," she told him.

Alexander gave her a hug. "How can I not worry? You don't need to be the one to sacrifice yourself."

"I'm not sacrificing anything."

He cocked his head. "You're the closest thing to family I have. If anything happens to you…"

"Nothing's going to happen, and our prince is the only family we need."

He looked down, then away. His long, silver hair shifted despite the lack of a breeze. He seemed tentative and cautious, even more so than normal.

She reached for his arm. "You're acting oddly. Do you need to be fed?"

He tried to pull away. "You're about to go into battle. You need all the strength you have."

Alexander…always thinking about others first.

She gripped him tighter. "I may be gone for some time, and Kile can't feed you. Unless you expect to return to Prince Geron anytime soon, you need this." She grabbed his other arm.

He looked away again.

"Alexander." She pulled him to her. "Let me feed you."

His arms moved around her, and he nestled his nose into the side of her neck. Tightening her grip, she closed her eyes and called on her strength. The warmth came from her core, eddying up and filling the cells just beneath her skin. She held still, building the heat, before she willed the power out and into her friend.

Her skin cooled, and a chill raced over her as the strength passed from her to him. His hair whipped up into the air, his body coming back to life.

A small moan escaped his lips as he drew away. His

silver-blue eyes sparkled with renewed strength. "You're too good to me."

She tapped his chest. "Just don't tell Kile or Miguel you had an extra feeding. They might get jealous."

His lips thinned. "You'll be weaker now. You shouldn't have done that."

She waved her hand. "When I'm done, I'll return to Geron and he'll feed me enough to take care of all of you. I'm still more than powerful enough to take care of a few dozen simpering humans."

"Yes, but what if it's more than a few dozen?"

Several birds flew from one side of the aviary to the other, disappearing into the treetops. Strange, when they had been silent before.

Dania closed her eyes, calling on her senses and searching for...*there*...two heartbeats not far from where the birds had taken flight.

"Two men," Alexander whispered.

"It probably looks like we're being intimate to them." The trees where the men were hidden were still now, but she knew her stalkers were there. "Back me against the tree. Make it look like you're using me."

"Me *using* you? You'd melt my face off."

She reached up and kissed him. "But they don't know that."

He backed her against the base of the elm and fumbled with the fasteners of her uniform before he pushed her pants down her thighs. She furrowed her brow over how easily he'd done that, but before she could question him, he'd unfastened his own pants. In one swift movement his lips covered hers, and he simulated the motion of pounding into her.

Men's voices whispered, but Alexander's breathing was too loud to make out the words until he stopped and eased away.

She fell to her knees and mustered up tears. "Wait. Where are you going?"

He backed off, buckling his pants. His eyes showed concern before they hardened. "I got what I wanted. If you know what's good for you, you won't tell anyone."

She blinked. That was harsher than she would have expected from him, but effective, as the whispering voices hushed. She covered her face and pretended to cry as Alexander stomped away. He slowed at the doorway, glanced back at her, and then disappeared.

Careful. His last word exploded in her mind before he broke the connection.

She'd expected him to stay, maybe watch from a safe distance. Their impromptu public display had made that impossible, though.

Dania was alone.

Well, almost alone.

She could feel the human gazes on her, their minds whirling, wondering when to strike. The faint scent of Ty's cologne hung in the air, along with a tinge of oil and sweat from his cohort. She could smell their eagerness, their anticipation.

They underestimated her in every way, and it would be their undoing.

ALANNA'S KEYCODE signaled on the main screen, and Cal watched as she closed the door behind her. She ran down the hallway toward the bridge. Thank the stars at least one of his people understood the urgency of the situation. Doc limped slightly as he followed.

Cal grimaced. Hopefully, whatever had happened wasn't too bad.

That damn yellow light started blinking again, and no matter how many times Cal tapped it, it kept flashing in his eyes as he tried to get clearance to take off.

For some odd reason, half the space port requested clearance to leave the second an enforcer ship landed. Imagine that?

Alanna stormed onto the bridge. "Peter's been shot."

Cal jumped to his feet. "Doc, what the heck?"

Peter 'Doc' Sanders walked in behind her, rubbing the center of his chest. Red stains covered his shirt.

Doc held up a hand. "I'm fine."

"You should've seen it," Alanna said. "An enforcer saved his life. It was like magic!"

Magic? Cal cringed. "Are you out of your minds?"

"It's not like we asked for help." Alanna folded her arms. "Doc was bleeding to death, and the enforcer just appeared."

Holy stars over Venus. Was she even thinking about what she was saying? "Listen, I'm glad you two are okay, but you're damn lucky they didn't scan their databases and find your faces on someone's most wanted list."

Alanna shifted her weight. "I guess I hadn't thought of that."

Of course not, because she hadn't seen what a ticked-off enforcer could actually do. "That's about as close as I want any of you to get to the king's guard. We're leaving. Now."

Alanna tapped the blinking light three times and it stopped.

How'd she do that?

She waved her fingers over the pad on her console. "You know Ty and Ethan aren't on board yet, right?"

The two of them were always at the wrong place at the wrong time.

Cal scanned the screens, hoping to see Ethan's red hair. If those idiots had gotten themselves caught, he'd kill them himself, he swore it.

He tapped the keys to open a comm link. "Ty? Where are you?"

"Boss," Ty whispered. "Don't be mad."

"I'm plenty mad. We're leaving. With or without you."

"That's going to be a little hard without your engineer and first mate," Ethan whispered.

Not really, when he had Alanna on board. "Why are you both whispering? Please tell me you're not doing something stupid."

"Stupid? Us?" Ty asked.

Cal closed his eyes and took a deep breath. Somewhere in the record books, he was fairly certain it was documented that stupid actually *was* Ty's middle name. "Ty, please come back."

"Boss, I think I've found a way to clear your name."

What? "It better not have anything to do with those enforcers."

Ethan snickered in the background. "I told you he'd blow a fuse."

Cal's stomach bottomed out. "Ethan, I need you to drag Ty back here now. That's an order."

"What's that?" Ty's voice drowned in static again. Odd, since that the line had been clear a moment ago. "Sorry, boss, I can't hear you."

Cal slammed his fist on the dash. "Dammit, both of you, whatever hair-brained idea you've come up with, it won't work. Stay away from those enforcers and get back here now."

The static hissed at him before the transmission ended from their side.

"Dammit!"

"Maybe they heard you and are on their way back?" Alanna said.

Cal dragged his fingers through his tightly cropped hair. Ty and Ethan both knew enforcers were dangerous, but neither one of them had seen firsthand how quickly one of those automatons could pass judgement.

If they tripped or fell and broke something in the station they could be convicted of vandalism and executed on the spot. He'd learned long ago that there was no gray area where the enforcers were concerned.

Everything was black and white: guilty or innocent. And any crime, according to the king's ridiculous law, was punishable by death.

But Ty was insane enough to go and try to talk reason with them, and Ethan was impulsive enough to follow along for the fun of it.

Of course, they all thought Cal overreacted when it came to the enforcers. Maybe he did, but being on the king's most wanted list made a guy jumpy. Not to mention waking up night after night, screaming, certain there was a man with long, silver medusa-like hair standing over his bed ready to slash his throat.

He took a deep breath and released it. He needed to remember that his crew was usually right. He did overre-act, and sometimes he needed a calmer head to reel him in. Luckily, the coolest head he knew was standing right next to him.

He turned to Doc. "What do you think?"

Doc snorted. "They're going to get themselves killed."

"But wait," Alanna said. "The enforcer who helped us was really nice. I mean, he saved Doc, and he didn't have to. Maybe Ty is onto something. Maybe our enforcer might listen?"

Our enforcer?

Doc snorted again. "Alanna also might be a little smitten. I have to admit, the guy was ridiculously good looking."

How could these two be so trite about this? "That enforcer would not hesitate to use the same power that healed you to snap both your necks for the laundry list of crimes you've committed if he'd known who you were."

Cal knew this better than anyone. His dad hadn't even

committed a crime, but he'd been punished for being with someone who had.

The enforcer had been large enough to blot out the sun, looming over his father's body before the behemoth simply walked away, not caring that he'd destroyed Cal's world as his father's blood had pooled on the ground around them.

Closing his eyes, Cal pushed away the pain building in his chest. Every time he thought he was over this, the hole in his chest opened back up.

Cal should have fought. He should have stood between his father and the silver-uniformed man. Of course, if he had, he'd be dead, too.

He lowered his arms, and both his hands curled into fists. He needed to stop blaming himself. He'd only been twelve, and you couldn't change the past.

But maybe, just maybe, he could stop the same fate from happening to anyone else he cared about.

Cal turned back to the comm. "Ty, please. Don't be foolish. Come back and use that silver tongue of yours to get us departure clearance."

More static.

"Blast it!" He grabbed his gun belt from the back of his chair. "I need both of you to keep prepping the ship for departure. Alanna, do your best to get clearance. Lie if you have to."

"Where are you going?"

Wasn't it obvious? "I'm going to drag them both back here before they get themselves killed."

CHAPTER 5
DANIA

THE HUMAN MEN whispered in the dark somewhere in the bushes off to the right as Dania adjusted her uniform. Most Earthans didn't realize that enforcer hearing was better than a human's. In most cases, she could pick out a conversation in a crowded room if she concentrated hard enough.

She stood, wiped away her feigned tears, and stumbled to the doorway. She didn't have to act. Her legs still ached from the beating she'd received. It didn't take much to look vulnerable.

The man from the bar, Ty, stepped out in front of her. "Are you okay?"

A human woman would be embarrassed or angry if she'd been taken advantage of. Dania decided to act somewhere in between the two emotions. "I don't want to discuss it."

She attempted to pass him, but he placed his hand on her arm.

"I sort-of wanted to talk to you about something else," he said.

Of course he did.

She looked down at his hand and then back to his face.

He smiled sweetly. He'd seemed so kind in the bar. How many young enforcers had fallen prey to that fetching grin?

Dania looked forward to slowly removing those lips, so he'd never be able to take advantage of anyone again.

His smile turned to a frown. "I'm sorry."

She narrowed her eyes. She was sure he wasn't sorry, but he *would be* before she was done with him. The other man moved behind her. His coppery hair whisked about as she pretended to struggle.

Ty grabbed her and the other man pulled her arms behind her back. Fifteen years of instinctual training kicked in. Her knee came up and caught Ty in the groin. He shouted a typical human expletive and backed away just as the other man managed to click something around her wrists.

Cursing again, Ty straightened, his face red. "I told you I just wanted to talk."

Dania twisted away from the other man. "Then what are these?"

She sent a trickle of energy through the restraints, testing their resolve. She'd allow them to think she was captured, allow them to think they'd won, and then…

A deep cold ran up her arms. She sent another jolt of power to the restraints, and the sizzling energy ebbed away, lost as if it had never been there.

Dania's breath caught in her throat. The restraints had been fashioned from Palian steel.

These atrocities were manufactured for a single purpose: to drain the energy of an enforcer, making them more like a human.

The king had destroyed all deposits of this steel years ago. These trappers must have purchased these shackles illegally, probably from this very facility.

Once she'd executed these miscreants, she'd need to come back and deliver a slow and painful death to whomever had sold them these blasted monstrosities.

The shackles hummed, tingling her skin, drawing in her power. Her stomach turned, imagining a new enforcer, trapped, feeling the energy granted to them by their royal sponsor drained away to nothing…wasted.

Dania's skin beneath the bindings chilled slightly. Within hours, she'd be at a fraction of her strength. Fortunately, even at a quarter of her power, she'd still be able to decapitate these imbeciles with a flick of her wrists.

This narrowed her window of opportunity, though. She needed to get free as soon as possible.

She twisted, calling up tears, trying to appear as helpless as possible. "What's happening? It hurts." She fell to her knees. "What have you done to me?"

Ty got down on one knee and placed a hand on her shoulder. "It's not permanent. It's just to make sure you don't freak out and kill us while we're trying to talk to you."

She twisted away from him. "Please don't hurt me."

Stars, she wanted to strike these men down and make an example out of them. Maybe Alexander had been right. He may have been a better target. His first reaction was never to execute a criminal.

Dania worked to slow her breathing. In order to do the job her prince had assigned to her, she needed to quell her base instinct to eradicate all lawbreakers, but it was hard when every ounce of her screamed for justice.

A tall man ran into the aviary, a gun in one hand, a tracking device in the other. He wore the thick, odd blue material on his legs so many humans seemed to covet, and a tight black T-shirt that appeared to be real cotton imported from Earth. Expensive—the type of garments worn by people who profited from the sale of sentient beings.

His pale blue eyes widened, and his warm skin tone paled when his gaze fell on her. A gamut of emotions erupted on his face. Fear. Hate. Anger. Loathing. This man had come in contact with this uniform before, and it hadn't been a pleasant experience for him. Which wasn't a surprise if he spent time in the company of trappers.

Something about his sharp, angular features seemed somewhat familiar as his face twisted into a sneer.

"Are you two out of your star-brained minds?" The newcomer pointed to the man behind her. "Ethan, get those things off of her."

The man who'd shackled her, *Ethan*, apparently, backed away. "Cal, if we take these things off now, we're goners. We need to explain first. She'll get it and then we'll be home free."

Get it? Get what? Humans grew more perplexing every time she encountered them.

The newcomer slipped the tracking device into his back pocket and dragged his hands through his overly short hair. Her memory focused and centered.

Eyes, nose, lips...match.

He'd changed his hair, cut his dark locks short to avoid detection. Smart, but not smart enough.

Calvin Espinoza: wanted for the murder of Prince Geron's best friend, Filluck Palogivan.

Her skin heated, tingling with power. Up until a few days ago, Calvin Espinoza had been the top target for every one of Prince Geron's enforcers. Their directive was to kill him slowly and painfully, and then place his head, and only his head, at the feet of their prince to prove justice had been served. Geron wasn't normally a vengeful prince, but he hadn't taken lightly to his friend being slaughtered.

Had Espinoza added sentient trafficking to his long list of crimes?

Ty held up his hands. "I swear, I've talked to her before. She'll listen. I think we can get you off the hook."

Off the hook? If anything, she'd draw him in more quickly. Luckily for them, her prime target was not Espinoza at the moment. First, she needed to eliminate this trafficking ring. She'd allow them to bring her back to their leaders, and after she'd executed them all, Espinoza would feel her sponsor's wrath.

Dania was already Prince Geron's general, his most prized enforcer. When she brought back Espinoza's head, no one would question why her prince had selected her to lead his guard.

She stared at Espinoza and held back her smile, imagining Geron's delight to finally see justice served for his friend. Geron deserved that closure, and she'd gladly give it to him.

Dania tested the restraints again and her arms cooled. She shivered at the thought of sacrificing more of her power. She needed to find a way out of these monstrous restraints before she had no more strength to fight.

CAL'S HANDS clenched as he stared at the handcuffs holding the enforcer on her knees before them. That wild, silvery-white, living hair floated about her face as tears streamed down her cheeks.

Bile built up in the base of his throat. This wasn't who he was, terrorizing a helpless girl. But he needed to remember that this woman was not really all that helpless, and the second she got those cuffs off, she'd be gunning for them.

He couldn't believe Ty and Ethan would do anything so foolish. At the same time, he was damn impressed they'd managed to get handcuffs on a trained killing machine.

The cuffs glinted in the low lighting. He needed to figure out how to…

Wait a minute. Were those made of…Palian steel?

He pointed to the cuffs. "Where in the name of Jupiter's moons did you get those?"

Ty smirked "You know me: Mr. Resourceful."

Yeah, but this time, his resourcefulness might get them all killed.

"Please let me go." The silver-haired girl sniffed. "I promise I won't hurt you."

Was she serious? "That's not going to happen." Because they'd be dead before those cuffs even hit the floor.

Her eyes darkened like a cornered predator before the expression whisked away again. She looked like a scared girl underneath that mass of swirling hair and opal white uniform, but they all needed to remember what she really was.

Cal grabbed Ty's shoulder. "We have to let her go." The question was, how?

"Can we at least try to talk to her?" Ty asked.

He had to be insane if he seriously thought this woman was capable of seeing past any of their crimes.

A blast of light shot past Cal's head. Heat seared across his skin as one of the trees exploded in flames. Cal grasped the girl in one hand and Ty in the other and pulled them out of the way, shoving them behind the brush. Another blast hit where Ty had been standing, and Ethan leapt toward them, rolling behind a tree.

"What the heck?" Ethan's red hair glowed as another laser bolt exploded not far from their hiding spot.

Cal peeked out from behind a bush as at least a dozen armed mercenary-types flooded into the dark. They flared up laser pointers. They probably had night vision, too.

The girl seemed oddly calm, but Cal kept her close anyway. "Were you guys gambling again?"

Ty shook his head. "No. I swear."

They ducked as lasers scanned over their heads.

"Then what do these guys want?" Cal whispered.

Ty looked at the girl and cursed.

"What?" Cal asked.

"I've heard rumors." Ty peeked through the trees.

Was he seriously going to leave it at that? "Are you going to elaborate?"

"They say there's a black market for enforcer slaves." He looked down at the handcuffs. "I think that's what those shackles were actually created for."

Enforcers? As slaves? Everyone in this galaxy had lost their minds but Cal.

The girl's jaw dropped. She looked at Ty, then Cal, then in the direction of the guys with the military tech. Any other time Cal would have wondered what she was thinking, but he had worse things to worry about at the moment.

Ethan army-crawled to them and pointed to a simulated tree painted on the wall. "We need to get over there. That's a maintenance entrance."

"Are you sure?" Cal asked.

Ethan shrugged, but at the moment, that was all they had. They bolted for the painting. Ethan ran his hand along the edge.

"Hey. Stop!" a voice called.

Ty pressed against the outer line of the inked leaves before a flash ignited, blasting a hole in the door and lighting Ty's shirtsleeve on fire. Ethan slapped the fire out with his palm, and then spun to the door.

"Let's go!" Cal pushed the enforcer forward through the smoking opening. She twisted in his grip, but the shackles must have been working because she wasn't fighting with anywhere near the vigor he would have expected.

"They're after the girl?" Ethan looked over his shoulder as they sprinted down the hall. "Then leave her."

Cal glared at him. "And condemn her? You idiots made it so she can't defend herself."

Ethan stopped, pulling out a key. "Then let her go."

The wall behind them exploded in flames.

"Come on!" Cal grabbed the girl's arm and dragged her down the hall.

By now, Alanna and Doc would have the ship prepped for departure. They could get to the *Renegade*, let the girl go, and then blast out of there.

The enforcer would be too busy fending off the mercenaries attacking her to turn that power on Cal and his crew. By the time she'd eliminated her own problem, the *Star Renegade* would be long gone.

It was a haphazard plan, but it was something. There wasn't time to come up with anything better.

Cal handed his gun to Ty, and his first mate shot over his shoulder in rapid bursts. Hopefully, any civilians had run for cover by now.

The enforcer scowled at Ty, but she continued to run. Cal guessed she'd decided they were the lesser of two evils. Too bad that realization probably wouldn't save them once they set her free.

"Almost there," Ty called.

They rounded the corner, and there she was, the *Renegade*, already moved into position for takeoff. When he got on board, he was going to give Alanna a long overdue raise.

Crews stepped back, letting them pass, while others shouted expletives. Not that he cared all that much. He didn't plan on coming back to this hole anytime soon.

Shots came from behind, and the dock workers leapt for cover. Hopefully, Alanna would see her crewmates running toward her and lower the entry ramp.

Another shot flashed right in front of Cal's face. He stopped short as another blast crossed their paths. What was happening? The bad guys were behind them, not out here.

"Ambush!" Ethan ducked behind a different ship.

Several meters away, the *Renegade's* landing platform began to lower. Doc stood at the entrance with a particle distributor in his hands.

Damn, that was overkill, but at least Cal knew no one was getting on his ship without permission.

Ethan made for the ramp. A blast sliced across his jacket, and he fell, rolling. Doc shot, covering him as Ethan crawled up the platform to safety. Good. One down.

"Go!" Ty called, covering Cal with several shots into the flanking attackers.

Cal looked down at the enforcer, then back to the dozen or so attackers entering the docking bay, and the several points of fire coming from behind the storage containers.

His ill-conceived plan to free her had required a key, but the key had just made it to the ship with Ethan.

Another shot blasted over their heads.

The easy thing to do would be to leave her, to toss her to the wolves and make his escape. After all, she was most likely all they wanted. The enforcer stared back at the people firing at them with an unnerving coldness in her eyes. She was probably calculating all the wonderful ways to kill them. Heck, she was probably including Cal in that list.

If he left her there, though, stuck in those handcuffs, they'd take her. She was only a year or two younger than Cal, and there were just too many. If Ty was right, and these people were going to sell her as some kind of expensive party favor—well, he just couldn't do that to another person, even if she'd execute Cal either way.

Ty jumped on board, and he and Doc fired out, trying to clear a path for Cal to join them.

There were far too many weapons discharging to get through to them, though.

Ty yelled something to Doc, and Doc disappeared into the ship, probably to help prep for departure.

That was probably a good call. Cal would need Ty for liftoff, but for now, Ty was a far better shot than the doctor.

Cal wiped the sweat from his brow. This was a no-win situation. Bringing a restrained enforcer on board would put a target on the *Renegade* bigger than Jupiter. But leaving her to slavers was out of the question.

Cal took a deep breath and gripped the girl's arm. He hoped they'd all live long enough to regret this.

DANIA DUCKED as an intensified honing beam exploded over their heads. Alexander had pointed out an annoying number of times that no matter how strong she was, a well-placed shot with any number of weapons could disable her. And multiple hits would kill her if she wasn't healed in time. She dearly didn't want to prove him right.

She pulled against the bindings. If she could only break free of them, she could eliminate dozens of trappers in minutes. That would leave the leaders free, though, and her goal unattained.

Another shot rang out, and Espinoza ushered her farther along the wall of shipping containers they'd hidden behind.

She was still baffled that these men who'd subdued her weren't the criminals that she'd been sent for. Why would Espinoza's men want to bring an enforcer right to him? Did they want to overthrow their captain and take the ship for themselves?

Espinoza pulled her down as another blast shot over their heads. The bindings itched behind her back. Did any of these men filling the hangar bay know where Matara was? Did it matter?

Her jaw ached and Dania loosened her clenched teeth. She wished she could unleash her power and take down all these people who had been responsible for the suffering of dozens of young enforcers. They deserved death, and she'd give it to them in time.

First, she had to allow the plan to progress as far as possible. By now, news of the ruckus must have reached Kile. He would come and at least *pretend* to rescue her. If only there was a way to tell him that she wasn't with the real trappers. That way, he could deal with the fifty or so criminals raining fire on the innocents in this chamber while she took care of Espinoza herself.

She'd have to hope she'd trained her men well, and that they would realize what was going on. She'd be more than happy to give her commander the glory of stopping the trapping ring because deep down, executing Calvin Espinoza was far more important to her sponsor, no matter how many enforcers the royal family had lost.

Of course, she and her people had to comply with the king's decree, but in private, her prince had deemed Espinoza's death to still be his top priority, and she would see it done.

Three of the trappers came out from behind the storage containers, guns raised. When Espinoza looked back to his ship, she turned slightly, balled her fists, and sent a wall of energy at the attackers.

Dania winced and unclenched her hands as a blast of searing pain stung through her arms.

When the wall of energy she'd conjured hit its target,

the trappers flew back into the barricades, and one of the containers exploded into shards.

She closed her eyes as the burn in her arms deepened. She'd slowed them down, but at what cost?

Over the years, she'd discounted the power of Palian steel, believing that the ensnared enforcers were simply weak. Nothing could have prepared her for the truth of the material's power.

Sweat beaded her brow as she considered sending out another blast to solidify their escape route. A shiver raced across her skin, and her hands fell lax beneath the bindings. As the sting settled deeper, burning from within, she understood the plights of all those taken before her.

The steel had done its job. She wouldn't use her power again unless absolutely necessary.

She pushed down the lump building in her throat. She'd never been vulnerable, even from her earliest memories as a child. A deep ache formed in her chest and she pushed it away.

She *would not* be afraid. She refused.

Trappers screamed as another canister exploded.

Heat billowed over their heads as Espinoza grabbed her. "Time to go."

Her head spun slightly. She had never been at anyone's mercy, and she refused to succumb now. She needed to find a way out of the shackles before they did irreparable damage.

Dania stumbled as Espinoza dragged her across the floor to the entrance of a timeworn ship several levels high. A smuggling vessel, no doubt—big enough to carry freight but small enough to be maneuverable and faster than most local police ships.

When they reached the base of the platform, Ty reached down and grabbed her, dragging her inside. A loud *boom* echoed between the metal walls. She faltered and tripped up the incline as a blast seared a hole in the deck near her boot.

A few inches to the left and she'd have lost a foot!

"Come on!" Ty grasped her arm and yanked Dania to her feet.

She stared at the singed tips of the man's blond hair as he pulled her with him down a long hallway and into what appeared to be a small command deck. Two chairs stood centered over unique consoles spread evenly between a large observation window.

A third, occupied chair farther to the right seemed placed between two smaller screens flashing what appeared to be navigational coordinates. The woman in the chair turned, her chin-length hair and cropped bangs bouncing about her face. Dania took in her pink highlights as the woman's eyes widened.

Interesting. This was the woman who'd held Alexander's patient when he'd removed a bullet from the man's chest. What a fascinating web of intrigue she'd stepped into.

"What in *all that's good and right in the galaxy* is that?" The woman pointed at Dania.

Espinoza pushed past them into the room. "Don't ask questions. Get us out of here."

The woman spun her seat back to her console and pointed to one of her screens. "We're in line, but we don't have clearance."

"Do I look like I give a damn? Get us out. Now."

Ty attached Dania's shackles to a hook in the center of

the rear wall. "I'm sorry about this. We really aren't going to hurt you. We just want to talk and explain things."

So he'd said. Oddly enough, after all that had transpired, she was interested in why they'd take such a chance. Dania was still going to kill them all—once she got free from the Palian steel—but first she'd humor them to quell her curiosity.

Espinoza hit several buttons on the control panel. "It's useless trying to reason with her. For now, the plan is to save her life and then drop her off somewhere where she can wait for a ride home."

A yellow light flashed. He cursed then hit it three times before the blinking stopped.

Dania pushed against the wall. Did he actually think she'd let him leave her anywhere, let alone fly away with his head still attached?

Ty put a small device into his ear. "Control, this is the *Star Renegade* requesting clearance for immediate take off."

"Are you insane?" a voice said from the speaker. "We're on lockdown. No one is—"

Ty slammed his fist onto a button, cutting the person off. He pointed out the window. "They're closing the gel filters."

Espinoza stared out the window. "Alanna?"

"I need a clear line of sight. I can't jump us from inside."

Espinoza tapped Ty on the back. "Do your magic."

Ty smiled. "Here we go!" The ship rose into the air and throttled toward the rapidly shrinking gel filter. The clear, green film shimmered and darkened as it solidified.

Were these people insane? Once the gel hardened, it would be like hitting the side of a mountain.

"Ty?" Espinoza shouted.

"Close your eyes, boss."

Dania clawed at the wall behind her until she found and grabbed the hook she'd been attached to.

The gel turned a deep, forest green, almost solid. They weren't going to make it. Yet Ty only pressed the controls to go faster.

If she were outside the ship, she'd let this happen and dispose of the whole lot of them at one time. She wasn't outside, though. An explosion of that caliber would incinerate all organic matter onboard, even her.

Dania squinted, sending a bolt of her power forward to explode into the bio-gel. Her vision blurred as another icy lance stabbed at her from beneath the bindings. Her arms seemed leaden as the ice roared through her muscles and exploded behind her eyes. Her vision skewed and she clenched her teeth against a scream until the pain began to abate.

They'd been taught that Palian steel drained more power if the victim tried to use their abilities while restrained. She almost wished the infernal metal would have taken all her strength to keep her from doing that to herself again.

When her power hit, the bio-gel lightened, sparkling with her primordial energy seconds before the ship made contact. They slipped through the light-green matter, slowing slightly in the suction map before they skated past the protection layer and blasted into space.

"Woohoo!" Ty punched a fist into the air.

Espinoza slapped Ty on the back again. "How did you pull that off?"

"That's good, old-fashioned flying right there, boss!"

Dania held back a laugh. She didn't bother telling them that they'd all be dead if she hadn't helped. Still, she leaned against the wall and closed her eyes, breathing slowly as the icy pain subsided. She didn't relish the idea of leaving her life in the hands of these fools any longer than necessary. She needed to find a way to get the cursed steel off her wrists.

Espinoza looked over his shoulder. "Alanna, get us out of here."

The ship jolted, wrenching Dania's shoulder.

"What was that?" Espinoza asked.

"We're taking fire." Ty pointed out the main viewing pane again.

"You think?" Espinoza fell back into his chair as another charge of sonic fire rocked the ship.

"Those are warning shots," the pink-haired woman said. "It's station security. They're asking us to cut our engines."

"Why the heck do they care what we do?" Ty asked.

Espinoza leaned over his console to look up through their main viewing pane. "Because they know we were involved in the mess in their hangar bay."

A huge ship sunk into view, filling the window.

"Bite me." Ty pointed. "Royal insignias."

Espinoza turned to look at Dania. "Friends of yours?"

She smiled at him. The terror on all their faces warmed her, but this wouldn't do.

Her ship could squash this vessel with no more effort than flicking a bug off the wall. Twisting, she tried to access the communication band on her wrist, but she couldn't see the screen with her hands still fastened behind her back.

She couldn't have her people concentrating on this

crew, though. She could handle these imbeciles. Her enforcers needed to focus on the king's requested targets: the trappers back on Midway Station.

Dania closed her eyes and sent a gentle trickle of power out, then tensed for the pain. The bindings chilled, but the sensation quickly abated.

Good, so little strokes of energy were manageable.

She sent another small wave of power out. It was a simple gesture, one meant to calm her soldiers after an altercation. Kile should read that as a sign that she was fine. If he backed off now, he could still apprehend the few dozen trappers in the docking bay before they dispersed.

"What was that?" The pink-haired woman spun, wiping her arms as if trying to get something unseen off of her.

Ty stood and faced her. "Alanna, are you okay?"

The woman—*Alanna,* apparently—shivered.

Odd. The energy Dania had sent out should have been barely discernible to a human.

Alanna blinked and nodded. "Sorry. I think I just got creeped out."

Dania's ship shot a spray of power over their bow.

"Holy crap, they missed." Ty returned to his seat. "This must be our lucky day."

Either that, or they're letting you get away. How simpletons like this ever eluded local law enforcement was beyond her.

The screen before them lit up with a fireball.

Espinoza clutched the console. "Incoming!"

The ship balked and Dania's knees slammed to the floor, wrenching her arm again. Pain seared through her shoulder.

Her stomach churned. She needed to get off that hook

and out of the bindings before she ended up needing a medic.

Fire spewed from the navigation console. Ty pulled Alanna back, shielding their eyes from the sparks.

"That shot didn't come from the royal cruiser. Someone else is out there." Espinoza reached for the controls, banking the ship down. "Let's keep away from whatever just hit us."

Alanna tried to smother the flames on the navigation console with a silver-colored rag. One flame went out, and another flared up.

Ty returned to his position. "Either way, we can't outrun that royal cruiser."

"If we play our cards right, we won't have to." Their captain hit a button on the panel. "Doc, get up here. Now."

Espinoza turned and walked over to Dania. She rose to her feet as he grabbed her wrist, snapping off her communication band.

"What are you doing?" She scowled as he flipped the bracelet over in his hand.

"Getting us out of here."

The door slid open, and a man entered—the one Alexander had healed. "Someone hurt?"

The man scanned the room, checking the crew before his gaze settled on Dania. He startled, his mouth forming an 'O' as he faced her. His lips formed several words that he didn't actually speak before turning toward Espinoza.

The man pointed at Dania, as if that simple gesture and his wide eyes summed up everything he needed to say.

"Ty," Espinoza said. The word sounded more like an explanation than a name.

The man shook his head. "Figures."

"One problem at a time. Those ships are after the enforcer." Espinoza held up Dania's band. "This belongs to her." Espinoza checked the screen, then moved closer to the newcomer. "You still got the cadaver?"

"Bessie? Of course."

Espinoza pressed Dania's communication band into the man's hand. "Let's send her for a ride."

The man stared at the band before a smile spread across his lips, as if he'd just been let in on the galaxy's biggest secret. "I want to be you when I grow up."

Espinoza turned. "Yeah, fine. Let's just get out of this in one piece first."

Dania yanked against the bindings. "That's mine. I need that."

Espinoza didn't even look at her. "You'll have to get over it. Right now, if any of that stray artillery out there hits us, you get blown up, too."

Dania gulped. That, at least, was true.

Her heart throttled. Other than her power, or being close enough to make a mental connection with Alexander, the bracelet was her only means of communication with her people. Cutting her off meant she *was* actually alone.

When she'd planned on being taken by trappers, she hadn't anticipated the illicit steel. How could she have been so foolish, believing the foul material had all been destroyed?

She made one more useless tug against the hook holding her to the wall. If she couldn't get the bindings off, she was trapped with these people.

Espinoza stormed back to his console while Alexander's former patient left the bridge with her bracelet. Losing her means of communication would be problematic, but no matter. She could deal with a small crew of miscreants with or without help from her soldiers.

Not having her link left her unsettled, though. She needed to make sure the ship, and its systems, remained intact so she could use it to return home when her job was done.

"Looks like they dropped the gel barrier." Ty pressed the earpiece tighter to his ear. "We have mass exodus from the hangar bay." He grimaced. "Half of them are running, but the rest are headed straight for us. Guns blazing."

"No doubt our new buddies, looking to get chummy with your girlfriend," Espinoza said.

Ty looked over his shoulder at Dania. "He didn't mean that. Well, the girlfriend part, at least."

"Can we focus on the ships shooting at us, please?" Espinoza stared at the cruisers becoming bigger in the viewscreen.

He was right. There were too many of them.

Their ship spiraled around the small vessels spraying bolts at them that weren't much more than an annoyance, meant to wear down this smuggling ship's shields, rather than do any real damage. The trappers were being cautious because their target held precious cargo—namely, Dania.

If Espinoza's ship was boarded, Dania would have to break free from these bindings in order to remove the threat. She needed to find a concentrated particle transducer, or possibly a fully charged light refractor. She'd seen them in medical bays and also used as lightweight handheld weapons. Either one would melt through Palian steel at close range. She'd just need to figure out a way to not dissolve the flesh off her hands in the process.

"Here we go." The man they'd called *Doc's* voice sounded over a speaker.

A *whoosh* filled the chamber, and a small pod ejected from the ship, hurtling into space.

Espinoza pressed a button and spoke into a microphone, probably disseminating his voice to all the crafts outside. "You want her, take her."

He banked the ship up, then right, barely missing Dania's cruiser.

Kile broke off his pursuit of the trappers, heading away from them all, chasing the ejected pod. Why was he going after that piece of junk?

The firepower of all the smaller ships turned toward the royal cruiser as the trappers pursued them like starflies shadowing a fuel tanker. What was wrong with them all?

Ty slapped his hand on the arm of his chair. "Holy smokes, it worked!"

"We're showing a perfect woman's signature out there," Doc's voice said from the speaker. "That communication band sealed it, Cal. They all think Ty's new girlfriend is on board that escape pod."

What? Dania turned back to the screen. All the ships, including her own, chased down the small metallic cylinder.

Her bracelet...they all actually thought she was in that pod. The idea was so deviously simple, and ridiculously effective.

Ty kissed his own hand and tapped Espinoza's face. "I freaking love you, man."

Espinoza stared as the last ship skipped past their port bow, leaving a clear shot at open space. "Love me later. Alanna, do your thing."

"On it." The girl raised her palm, and a circle of blue light formed in the air. "Prep for jump."

Dania cocked her head. What were they doing?

The ship shook as the stars in the distance grew fuzzy.

Alanna pressed her finger into the circle of light. "Three, two, one…"

A small skipper craft flew in front of them.

"Abort!" Espinoza shouted.

But the stars blurred, forming lines. The ship jolted, clipping whatever had flown in their way. Their ship spun, the stars and reality whipping around her. Dania's gut twisted, and she retched. Her head swam until the ship stopped, facing Midway Station.

She blinked, wishing she could rub her eyes. They were almost a league away from their last position. The faint glint of the space station was barely visible through the stars.

Dania straightened, staring at the navigator. How had they traveled so far? What had the woman done?

"Sorry!" Alanna spun the blue dial of light floating in the air.

Espinoza pressed a sequence of buttons, and the screen zoomed in on Midway Station as a hoard of ships turned on them.

Espinoza cursed under his breath and hit the communication button. "Ethan, we're in trouble up here."

A voice cut through the static. "Oh, really? Didn't anyone tell you guys you're not supposed to hit things?"

"Cut the lip and get us moving."

"Already on it."

A spray of fire shot up and over the window.

"Their aim is going to get better when they get closer," Espinoza warned.

Two of the smaller ships exploded in the distance, becoming fireballs before the cold of space winked out the light.

Good. Kile had finally decided to do his job.

Maybe scans showed one of the trapping ships was giving commands. It didn't matter who dealt the fatal blow to the trappers as long as her king's directives were achieved.

"Hold on!" Alanna pressed the center of her blue light dial again, and the stars blurred once more before they settled.

Dania gasped. They were now more than two leagues away.

"Shoot!" Alanna said, once again spinning the dial of light hanging in the air.

"We've got a problem." Ty stared into a raised section of his dashboard. "That royal cruiser is heading right for us, and they're driving like they're pissed off."

A small vein in Espinoza's temple drummed as he turned to Ty. "They must have realized that Bessie was not who they thought she was. What about our other friends?"

"It looks like they're all headed our way. The slavers must have figured it out first because they have a good head start on the enforcers."

Espinoza slammed his fist on the console. "Ethan?"

"Working on it." He fumbled with something on the other side of the line. "This is one of those times when the beautiful pink-haired damsel is supposed to be saving the useless men in distress."

Alanna continued to work her fingers through the airborne dial. "I'm trying!"

Dania's cruiser bared down on them. Not to mention the smaller trapping vessels that would no doubt reach them first.

Espinoza's ship needed better shields, or they'd be ripped to pieces. Dania scanned the deck and the walls. If she were free, she could protect the ship easily.

The bindings burned, almost like they were tightening on her wrists. She called up enough power to charge herself, and the icy sting of the Palian steel sliced up through her spinal column and exploded. Her blood boiled, searing and burning from within.

She gritted her teeth, unsuccessfully thwarting a whimper. Her hair stuck to her temples as she lifted her gaze to the screen, struggling to catch her breath.

For the first time she could remember, she was powerless. If the trapping vessels reached them, there'd be nothing she could do.

The ship rocked. A new spray of sparks shot from the ceiling.

Alanna shielded her eyes. "They're getting too close."

That, Dania had to agree with. The last blast was dead on. Someone had good aim, and when they got closer, that happy trigger finger might break through the airlock. Dania could live several hours floating in space. But that was without Palian steel leaching away her strength. Was it even possible to survive the vacuum of space without a shield around her?

The royal cruiser got larger on the screen.

Ty glanced at Dania, then to his captain. "Okay, boss,

maybe taking an enforcer on board wasn't such a good idea."

Doc's voice came over the speaker again. "I might be able to scramble their systems."

"Do it." Espinoza stared down Dania's ship as Kile took out another one of the trapper crafts. "Ethan, even a little bit of power would be nice."

"Tell me about it. I'm working with a flashlight down here."

Five more trapper vessels flew past them, leaving Espinoza's ship alone.

"Did they just go by us?" Alanna asked.

Ty looked into his console. "They're turning around."

The ships crossed back over them, attacking Dania's cruiser head on. Blasts riddled the hull and a line of ice crystals streamed from her ship as the air escaped into space.

Dania's lips parted. What was happening? Her ship was nearly impenetrable.

Ty pointed at the screen. "Are you all seeing what I'm seeing?"

"They're venting air," Alanna said.

She was right. That shouldn't have been possible.

With Dania's ship looking at least temporarily disabled, three of the trapper vessels turned and headed right for Espinoza's ship.

Alanna spun the light dial again. "I don't know where we're going, but we're going." She punched the center of her dial, and a white cloud filled the room. The floor beneath Dania's feet trembled.

"What the blazes, Alanna?" Espinoza yelled through the fog.

"Sorry, hold on."

The room shook. A screech filled the air like a million *Entrogian* scalpers screaming at the same time.

Then silence. They jolted to a stop. The fog sparkled and faded away.

Ty leaned over his console. "Where are we?"

"Scans?" Espinoza asked.

Ty gaped. "I think that's the Trillian Cluster out there."

Espinoza checked the readings. "I think you're right."

It wasn't possible for them to be within a hundred parsecs of the Trillian Cluster. Not even the king was capable of bending that much space, as far as Dania knew. Then again, why would he even have a reason to try?

They both looked at Alanna, as did Dania.

The woman's pale skin hinted at a greenish hue. "I think I'm gonna puke."

She stumbled, and Ty grabbed her, easing her to the floor.

Espinoza tapped the communication button. "Doc, Alanna passed out again."

"On my way."

Again? Interesting.

Dania slipped to the ground. She'd seen the high prince bend space half as far as this once before. However, he was one of the highest-ranking Banes on record. For a commoner to have that kind of power was unthinkable. Even Dania couldn't manipulate space like that. She'd have to conjure a singularity of some kind.

Doc appeared and placed a cloth on the girl's head.

Dania stretched, trying to look around them, but the blue circle of light was nowhere to be seen.

"Keep scanning," Espinoza said. "Those trappers don't

know what happened to us, but they can probably at least figure out which way we went."

Ty returned to his console. "If they had a jumper of their own, they would've been on top of us already."

A jumper? Dania glanced back to the woman again.

"If they do have a jumper, the trail will only last three minutes. We need to be ready, just in case."

Ty reached up and turned off the emergency lighting, casting them in darkness.

An interesting ploy. Most non-military scans would look for interior lights in the dark of space. Most enforcers would look for power signatures as well, though. Of course, it didn't look like Dania's ship would be searching for her for quite some time.

The doctor pulled out a small personal lamp and set it beside the woman, casting a reddish glow over her face.

Espinoza looked back to the sparking equipment. "Let's make what repairs we can, as quickly as we can. I have a bad feeling they're not going to give up that easily."

Unless, of course, the damage to Dania's ship was only minimal, and Kile was already rounding up all of the trappers. By now, he'd have sent out individual ships, and all of her pilots were more than capable of destroying multiple targets, even if the main cruiser had been disabled.

However, Kile's actions had seemed odd, almost disjointed. Could he have panicked?

Dania knew Alexander would be concerned for her, especially if they'd figured out that she hadn't been taken by her intended targets. Kile should be more in control of his emotions, though.

She wished she could get word to them both. If

anything, so she could let Kile know to back off, at least for now.

Dania looked back at the woman, still pale and looking like she was asleep. There was something very interesting about this crew, and only part of it had to do with their murderous captain.

THE FLOOR to the bridge hummed lightly as Cal knelt down beside Alanna. The back of his neck itched, which had everything to do with the eyes of the enforcer still throwing daggers in his direction. She'd been blessedly silent, but that wasn't enough to keep her presence from encompassing the room.

That didn't matter, though. Cal had more important things to worry about.

He smoothed back Alanna's hair as Doc placed a thin strip of metal onto her forehead. "Is she going to be okay?"

Doc nodded. "She knows better than to try to pull the ship that far, but she'll be fine."

Alanna blinked and smiled at them. "Stop looking at me like I'm dying. I just took a little nap."

Cal pursed his lips. "Right here on the floor of the bridge?"

She sat up, rubbing her nose. "Well, the floor was here, and I was tired, so why not?"

Cal tucked back her pink-edged bangs. "You don't have

this jumping thing down pat yet. You need to be more careful."

Alanna pushed his hand away. "And we also need to be alive. It's nothing I can't handle." She shielded her eyes as sparks crackled over the co-pilot's panel. "Stars, I go to sleep for a few minutes and the whole place goes to heck."

"I'm handling it." Ty pinched off the sparking wire and flames ignited beside him. He cursed before smothering it with a rag.

Alanna pulled herself to her feet. "Let me help before you melt the whole system matrix."

Cal grasped her shoulder. "Is she cleared for duty, Doc?"

Doc shrugged. "I guess. She looks good to me." He nudged Alanna. "Take it easy, girl, or I'm going to have to start treating the captain for high blood pressure again."

Cal glared at him. He'd never been treated for high blood pressure. Although this crew had driven him to drink on more than one occasion.

Doc placed his stuff back into his bag and headed toward the door. He took another look at the enforcer, shook his head again, and left the deck.

Cal certainly couldn't blame him. He'd leave if he could, too.

He hit the communication button for the engine room. "Ethan, you okay down there? Any fires?"

"Fires. No. Do you have any fires up there?"

Another flame shot out from the panel. Alanna and Ty swatted it with towels.

"No fires up here," Ty said.

Ethan snorted through the intercom. "Alanna, are you up there to help Ty?"

She chuckled. "Yeah, I'll keep them from doing irreparable damage."

The enforcer sighed, shaking her head like the crew were children, not worth her time.

The one who'd killed Cal's father had acted the same way, stomping through the blood in the streets like they'd inconvenienced him.

It was like this woman couldn't drop the attitude, even though she'd been chained to a wall.

She was far from incapacitated, though. That, he was sure of. Cal needed to remember to treat her like the caged animal she was.

Cal flipped a switch on his control panel. "Ethan, if you're stable down there, would you please come up for a minute?"

"Be right there, boss."

Cal took a deep breath. They all seemed so calm. Either they'd almost died so many times that this was no big deal, or they all had bigger balls than he did. Of course, they might all be insane for being part of his crew from the start. Unfortunately, that was the more likely scenario.

The enforcer pushed up onto her knees, her arms still bound behind her and wrenched at an odd angle. Death irradiated from her eyes.

He rubbed his forehead. Yesterday he would have given almost anything to keep as far away from the enforcers as he could, and now there was one tied up on his bridge. Cal didn't know who was crazier…him, or his crew.

At this point, it really didn't matter. They needed to deal with the problem at hand. He strode toward the enforcer. "You're welcome, by the way."

The girl blew a strand of that freaky opalescent silver hair from her face. "For what?"

"For saving your life."

Her lips parted slightly as she stared at him. "Saving my life? You kidnapped me."

His T-shirt stretched as he folded his arms. "For your own safety. Those guys back there would've sold you into slavery."

She twisted, showing her cuffs. "You put these on me before they even got there. Without them, I could've handled myself." She smiled as sweet as acid. "How about you take them off, and we can have a more proper conversation?"

Did she think he was a complete idiot? "Don't hold your breath, sweetheart."

Cal pushed through the door into the hallway, pacing atop the worn imprint in the flooring. He'd done the right thing. He couldn't have left the enforcer back there. Now, though, he wasn't sure what to do with her.

Ethan rounded the corner. His eyes widened. "Whoa. You look like you're about ready to blow a gasket."

Cal held up a finger, silencing him. "First of all, I saw you take a hit out on the station. Are you okay?"

Ethan's mouth formed an 'O' before he turned, showing the burn-line seared into the back of his jacket. "Just a scratch. I didn't feel a thing. Luck of the Irish, my friend."

"Good. In that case..." He shoved Ethan against the wall. "What were you thinking? I expect this kind of idiocy from Ty, not you."

The engineer stared at Cal for a moment. "Are we talking about the pretty platinum blonde in the handcuffs? Because I thought she was totally your type."

"This is *not* funny." He pointed in the direction of the bridge. "That is an enforcer."

Ty stepped out into the hall. "And that's exactly why she's here. Think this over, boss. She has the ear of the royal family. She's one of their own. They trust her."

"This is not making me feel better." Cal glanced at the closed door. "And did you actually leave Alanna alone in there with her?"

"Alanna can hold her own, and the enforcer is shackled to the wall, anyway."

Hopefully, the energy-draining properties of those handcuffs were as strong as everyone said they were, because an enforcer didn't need their hands to destroy everything in their immediate vicinity.

Ty looked at the door to the bridge. "I talked to this girl in a bar, of all places. She's not a blank automaton like the others. I think I can get her to listen to reason."

Was he daft? "She's not going to listen to reason. She's a cold-blooded executioner-in-training."

"The key words there are *in training*." Ty held up his hands. "I'm telling you. She still has feelings and she'll listen. I saw her grant a criminal mercy and she admitted she'd do it again. Whatever they do to brainwash them into not caring or having any remorse hasn't happened to her yet."

He hoped so, for all their sakes. Cal rubbed his face. "Are all the fires out?"

Ty nodded. "Alanna is starting on the electrical work."

"Good." He turned to Ethan. "How long will your repairs take?"

"An extra few hours if we keep running dark, but I think five at the most."

Five hours as sitting ducks, and a woman on board who was probably already planning all the possible ways to kill him and his crew.

Cal supposed this was just another day on the *Star Renegade*. "All right, let's get to it. I'd rather be mobile in case anybody looking for us finds a way to track Alanna's jump."

Ethan gave a thumbs-up and headed back down the hall.

"And the girl?" Ty asked.

They really didn't have much of a choice. "We'll give your plan a try, but then we'll drop her off at the nearest habitable planet and then we do what we do best."

"Run like hell?"

Cal nodded. "Run like hell."

THE PINK-HAIRED WOMAN glanced in Dania's direction before she leaned over the control board, tucking a wire that she'd spliced together into the panel. She moved to the next set of wires and barely seemed to look at them before she'd twisted them together and moved to a third set.

There was more to this Alanna woman than maintenance skills, though. She'd pulled this ship through space, something no human should be able to do. She was a conundrum Dania very much wanted to figure out, but she needed to handle this delicately.

Extracting needed data without injuring someone was Alexander's forte, but she'd seen him sweet talk information from people enough times. All she needed to do was pretend to be nice.

How hard could it be?

"You're fast with repairs." Dania did her best to keep her voice smooth and warm.

The woman glanced at her again. "Yeah, well, we get banged up a lot. I guess it's the nature of the business."

Dania shifted, hoping to look only partially interested. "And what is that business?"

The woman's eyes widened. "Trading, of course. Nice, run-of-the-mill, legal trading."

Dania held her expression steady, sure that their trading was anything but legal. On top of the murder charge, Espinoza was wanted in three systems for smuggling illegal foodstuffs and several types of contraband machinery.

However, Espinoza wasn't her chief concern at the moment, now that they'd left Dania alone with the most interesting member of their crew.

"Back there, when we were being attacked by those horrible men…" Dania cringed at the weak sound in her voice. "The ship suddenly went so fast." She feigned a slight smile. "That was you who got us out of there, wasn't it?"

The woman kept working. "Yeah."

Dania considered the blue circle that had appeared in the air as if Alanna had willed it into being. When she'd seen the high prince skip a ship from one star system to the next, he'd drawn in the air, but she hadn't seen anything like the blue dial of light this Alanna woman had used.

"How did you do it?" Dania asked. "It looked like magic."

Alanna raised a brow. "This, coming from an enforcer who can make a bullet rise out of a man's chest and then heal the skin over."

Technically, Dania couldn't do that. Healing wasn't one of the gifts granted to her by her prince, which was fine, since he'd given Alexander enough healing power to care for her entire squadron of enforcers.

"Healing doesn't seem like much compared to making a ship move so fast."

Alanna continued to tinker. "It's just something I've always been able to do. Cal says it's called 'jumping.' It's not common, and I've had to learn on my own."

Interesting. If it wasn't common, that meant there might be more like her. Dania wasn't aware that humans had the capacity to harness that kind of power. Even on the Bane home world, only the most powerful of the royal family had such gifts. The high prince, the king, one of the princesses, but few others, at least on record. Alanna's warm coloring showed no signs of the rich blue hue of the Banes, though.

This was an enigma indeed.

Too bad this woman could be tied to smugglers and at least one murderer. Dania would have liked to study her, but she doubted she'd have the time before Alanna would have to be executed with the rest.

The door slid back open. Ty and Espinoza reentered.

"How are the repairs going?" the murderer asked.

Alanna dragged her fingers through her straight-cut bangs. "I think I have all the supplies I need, but it's going to be a few more hours."

"Okay, good. Keep it up."

Espinoza and Ty turned to Dania. They both folded their arms.

The captain was older than Ty by at least three years, she'd gather. Espinoza dwarfed Ty in both height and muscular definition, probably a result of the murder's background as a miner. Ty didn't show up in any of her memory scans, so he must have been skating in Espinoza's shadow for however long they'd been accomplices.

The younger man pushed his shoulders back, trying to seem taller. Espinoza simply glared, flexing his large arms.

Any other day, she might have considered breaking his humerus bones for the impertinence.

"Are you ready to give yourselves up?" she asked.

Espinoza puffed out a laugh, turning to Ty. "See?"

"Hold on." Ty walked toward her. "Listen, I told you I wasn't going to hurt you, and we haven't."

Her wrists tingled beneath the bindings. She wasn't really sure if these miscreants could hurt her or not, at this point. Dania could still use her power, but how much, and how long she'd still have control were the questions.

She could kill them all, but she'd probably pass out from the pain, and when she woke, she'd still be stuck in the shackles. And it was only a matter of time before the steel sapped what remained of her strength. Her best option was to trick them into taking them off.

"Things aren't what they seem," Ty said.

Dania tried not to laugh, and failed. "Then what exactly are they?"

He pointed at Espinoza. "Cal didn't kill anyone."

Cal? Short for 'Calvin,' apparently. It had always annoyed her how humans had the tendency to shorten their names. "He's already been convicted."

Espinoza narrowed his eyes. "So you *do* know who I am?"

"You're the man who killed Filluck Palogivan."

The murderer held out his hands. "Why would I kill him?"

She lifted her chin. "Because he refused to give you money."

"That's not true," Ty said.

Espinoza shook his head. "I'm telling you, you're wasting your breath. She isn't capable of hearing the truth."

What was he implying? "The truth has already been decided."

Espinoza leaned toward her. "Can you hear what you're saying? The truth *has already been* decided. Even the way you phrased that shows that there might be another version of the truth."

"Impossible."

Ty crouched beside her. "Would you at least hear us out?"

Dania pulled on her bindings. "It's not like I have a choice."

A dull ache simmered just beneath the metal. The restraints were still draining her power, although not as much as when Ty and the copper-haired man had first put them on her. Still, she needed to get them off. Soon.

She checked her captor's hips. Neither man wore a sidearm. There had to be weapons somewhere, though. The med bay might be a better place to look. If they had a doctor, they might have surgeon's tools as well.

"Tell her what really happened," Ty said to Espinoza. "We've got nothing to lose at this point."

Espinoza sighed and looked at the floor. "It was a drug deal, from the looks of it. Your precious Filluck Palogivan seemed to be the money man."

Dania cocked her head. "Are you saying he was involved?"

"I'm saying he was more than involved. It looked like he was running the damn thing."

"Impossible."

"Anyway." Espinoza turned from her. "There was a kid there, at the wrong place at the wrong time. He tried to get away, ended up with a gun, and accidentally shot your friend."

Interesting, how he took for granted Filluck Palogivan was her friend. She'd only met the man once, and while he'd seemed afraid of her, a telltale sign of a criminal, she'd disregarded it. Filluck Palogivan was Geron's friend, and her prince would never associate with someone who'd break a law.

"What I *do* know," Espinoza continued, "is that Filluck Palogivan was not an innocent bystander like everyone said."

"If a child committed the crime, why would you have been accused? You ran from the scene."

The murderer slipped his fingers into his pockets. "I knew that kid would never get out of that situation alive. When the guards came, they accused me, and I didn't argue." He lowered his gaze. Somehow, it made him appear smaller. "I was already wanted for other crimes. One more wasn't going to make my death sentence any worse."

That part, at least, was true

Espinoza started pacing like a feral lion. "Not only that, I had a knack for getting out of bad situations. That kid didn't have a chance of leaving that station alive."

Dania narrowed her eyes. "I find it hard to believe anyone, even a known criminal like yourself, would want to add homicide to your repertoire of crimes. Murderers rank higher on the king's target list."

"Like I said, I had a way to escape, and I'm good at disappearing."

As so many criminals were, but Espinoza wasn't going to fade into the stars this time. She'd see him punished for his crimes. "There is no possible way that Filluck Palogivan was involved in an illegal activity. You are a murderer and a liar."

"You're wrong," Ty said. "This is one of the most giving, generous men I've ever met. There's no way he would have killed someone."

"Then I suppose he has you fooled. His list of crimes is long."

"That's true," Espinoza said. "And since I do run around in those circles, I see and hear a lot." A vein in his right biceps bulged as he folded his arms again. "Filluck Palogivan had his hands in everything from drugs to slavery to prostitution."

"Impossible."

"You need a new word," the murderer said. "That one is getting old."

She glanced between the two of them. "You are both criminals and would say anything to save yourselves."

Ty held up his pointed finger. "The Hitus Four drug explosion. Filluck Palogivan was there."

What was this fool getting at? "He left two days before that happened."

Ty held up a second finger. "The hydro-influxed heroin on Neptune Nine."

"What about it?"

"Filluck Palogivan was also there."

Dania searched her memory but couldn't recall.

Ty held up a third finger. "The trafficking of children from the Aravai colony."

Dania shuddered. Filluck Palogivan had frequented that colony seven times that year. Geron had mentioned that to his friend, who'd just talked around the subject. She'd never had a good feeling about that.

"And there are more examples," Ty said. "It's more than a coincidence, you have to admit."

Dania frowned. This was troubling, but she wasn't about to condemn a dead man. There was no reason to soil his name, especially if he was Geron's friend.

"I didn't kill him," Espinoza repeated.

But he'd already been convicted. The law stated he had to die. Her own prince had asked for his head.

Her stomach twisted.

"Can you at least admit that there is a possibility that Cal is telling the truth?" Ty asked.

Maybe not, but Dania was intrigued by Filluck Palogivan's association with so many crimes. This, at a bare minimum, piqued her interest. "Let me make you a deal. Free me so I can research your claims."

"You think I'm an idiot?" Espinoza asked.

If he were an idiot, he would have been caught years ago. "I make you a promise, on the honor of my prince, that I will not kill you today."

"What about tomorrow?"

"You have already admitted to a list of crimes. I can make no guarantees about tomorrow."

Ty shrugged. "Hey, it's something."

"There's no way I'm letting her loose. She thinks she can solve all the problems in the galaxy by murdering people."

"But she said she'd look into it, and she won't kill you today. Lock her back up tomorrow."

Dania kept her expression placid. This simpleton actually thought he'd be able to get these shackles back on her if she didn't comply?

Espinoza reached past Dania and unclipped her bindings from the bolt she'd been fastened to. He unhooked one, and before she was able to register that she was partially free, he'd refastened them in front of her. An interesting skill, but maybe not so surprising, knowing the depths of his criminal dealings.

He released her, and Dania's bound wrists fell to her waist before he walked over to the captain's station centered in front of the large viewscreen. "I'm keeping those cuffs on because there are four people other than me that you could kill, and I'm a bit protective of my crew." He hit a few buttons. "What I'll let you do is search the archives. Gather as much information about large-scale crimes as you want and then crossmatch them against travel records for Filluck Palogivan. I think you'll be very interested in what you find."

Dania walked toward the computer station. "I expect to find that you are just as guilty as the law states."

She sat in Espinoza's soft recliner chair and called up the screen. The bands tugged at her wrists. It would be difficult to research with her hands bound, but not impossible.

Sliding her hand over the keys, she checked the communication module, but the ship was running dark. No messages could be received or sent.

Espinoza leaned over her shoulder and swiped the screen, closing off the already useless access to the ship's communications. "I'm not that dumb."

She never said he was, which made the thought of

removing his head all the more satisfying. "I promised not to kill you today, and I will make good on that."

He straightened. "Hopefully, when you're done here, you'll be nice enough to give me tomorrow, too."

86

CHAPTER 10

DANIA

SMOKE ROSE out of the panel Ty worked on. He shouted an expletive before Alanna leaned over and tapped on a button. The smoke stopped.

Dania hoped they knew what they were doing, or she might have to use the last of her strength to create a containment field so the ship didn't blow up before she could execute them all. It would be hard to present Geron with Espinoza's head if it were frozen in a vacuum of space —or if she, herself, were dead.

Dania sifted through a download of the royal databases. Since the information wasn't live, it was entirely possible these people had manipulated the data for their own gain. When she checked a few of Espinoza's known smuggling runs, though, the information all showed correct to her recollections. Why would they manipulate data concerning Filluck Palogivan's business dealings while leaving clear evidence of guilt for their own offenses?

She breezed over the information: travel schedules, flight patterns, criminal movements, arrests…

The Hitus Four drug explosion, the hydro-influxed

heroin epidemic on Neptune Nine, and the many times before the breakup of the child trafficking cartel targeting the Aravai colony. Filluck Palogivan had been on record in all these places, and many more entries with red hazes over the records, showing the intensity of criminal activity. Once or twice she could overlook as coincidence, but this many times?

"How is the wiring coming?" Espinoza asked his crew.

"It would be better if Ty would stop frying things," Alanna said.

Ty jumped as sparks shot out of his panel. "Hey, that wasn't my fault."

This was an odd crew of miscreants. Dania couldn't imagine how they'd eluded capture for so long.

A file popped up on her screen that had been flagged red by Espinoza. Each member of the crew had tried to access it but had apparently failed.

"What is this?" Dania asked.

Espinoza leaned over her shoulder. He smelled of machine parts and a hint of a spicy scent that was oddly reminiscent of Alexander. "We pulled that file from Europa Nine."

Europa Nine, the Jupitorian moon station where Espinoza had killed Filluck Palogivan. "Why?"

"Doc thinks it's a camera feed, but it's encrypted. We've all tried to break through, but whoever locked that thing sealed it iron tight."

Interesting. Dania's fingers flew over the keys, only partially encumbered by the bindings. The file beeped twice and then opened.

Espinoza cursed under his breath. "How did you do that?"

"Royal passcode." The screen scrolled before her, men mulling through the hallways.

"There." Espinoza pointed. "That's Filluck Palogivan."

Dania blinked. He was correct. Filluck Palogivan's blue Kever skin stood out as he moved down a stark white hallway, flanked by two armed human men.

"You got it open." Ty watched over her other shoulder, while Alanna moved to Espinoza's other side.

Filluck Palogivan met with another human, and they spoke.

"Can you get any sound?" Espinoza asked.

Dania shook her head. "The recording doesn't appear to have any audio."

The conversation turned heated, before one of the men to Filluck Palogivan's side raised his gun and shot the other man. Alanna gasped, covering her mouth.

Dania stared at the screen, waiting for Filluck Palogivan to protest, but he simply stepped over the body and continued on his way. She clenched and unclenched her hands, her skin itching to kill something. Filluck hadn't pulled the trigger, but ignoring the crime made him guilty by association.

Her stomach clenched. This would make her prince very unhappy. He and Filluck had been close, which was one of the reasons Espinoza was such a wanted man.

The last thing Dania wanted was to crush Filluck's memory, but this was information the royal family needed to know.

The screen flashed to the next camera in the hallway and then to a third in a larger, dimly lit room. Commoners walked about, unaware that a crime had just been committed.

Hadn't anyone been monitoring these feeds? Where was the local law enforcement?

The two men with Filluck Palogivan raised their guns and fired. But at what? A child of maybe ten years ducked his head, and Filluck Palogivan seized the boy, holding the child in front of him like a shield as people scattered and more guns fired in his direction.

Dania's skin heated, wishing cowardice was a crime. Palogivan was knowingly placing that child in harm's way.

"There you are, Cal." Ty pointed at the screen, where Espinoza screamed something at Palogivan before ducking his own head down.

"They started shooting out of nowhere," Espinoza said. "That kid just got caught in the crossfire."

One of Filluck Palogivan's guards fell, and the child squirmed away, picking up the man's gun. Espinoza ran for the child, but the boy turned toward Palogivan.

Dania cringed as Palogivan grabbed for the gun, and he and the child spun before a flash erupted between them. The child backed away, dropping the gun as Palogivan slipped to the ground. A dark pool spread over the white floor beneath the aristocrat's body.

Dania's veins chilled as Espinoza grabbed the child and pointed at the door. The unheard word on his lips was unmistakable. *Run.*

The child complied as three local law enforcement soldiers ran into the room. They skidded to a stop, several yards from where Espinoza stood over the body.

They called to him, shouting, but Espinoza darted out the opposite door he'd sent the child through. Two of the officers chased Espinoza out of the frame, while the others worked on crowd control. The other one of Filluck Palogi-van's guards was nowhere to be seen.

The feed faded to black, and Dania took in the dark screen of nothing. She'd always wondered how in a high security compound, that no cameras had captured anything but Calvin Espinoza running down a hallway and evading capture.

She'd been over all of the evidence from this case twice since her prince had called for Espinoza's head, yet she had never seen the actual footage of the murder until now. How was that possible?

She turned to see all attention had centered on her. Ty's brows lifted expectantly.

Dania took a deep breath. "It would seem that your captain didn't kill Filluck Palogivan."

Ty slammed his fist on the back of his chair. "Damn straight."

Espinoza rubbed his chin. "Does anyone else find it odd that the only file with a hundred percent irrefutable evidence was sealed, and only she could open it?"

Dania nodded. "That is troubling. There is an additional crime here. The crime of hiding evidence." She looked back to the dark screen. "Whoever has done this will be executed for it."

Ty leaned away. "You are way too into all this execution stuff."

"Shut up, Ty." Alanna smacked his shoulder before turning to Dania. "Since you were able to open it, do you know who sealed it to begin with? I mean, that was a crazy seal. I've seen Doc break into government databases, and even he couldn't get through."

"Alanna," Espinoza hissed.

The woman widened her eyes. "Oh! I mean completely legally, of course. They, umm, hired him to try to hack in as part of a security protocol."

Alanna's temperature elevated point zero zero seven nine points with each word she said, but she didn't need that confirmation to know a lie when she heard one. Still, Dania reviewed the inscription on the lock: an intricate flower burst inside a rounded-edged star.

"Do you recognize that?" Espinoza asked.

"Yes." Though she hated admitting it. "It's royal." Meaning someone in the royal family, or extremely close to them, had seen this file and chosen to seal it. But if they'd wanted to hide something, why not just destroy it?

Ty leaned against the wall beside a series of flashing red lights. "Well, I guess this is a perfect time to point out that things are not always so black and white. You thought you knew the truth, but now you've seen the *real* truth."

Dania stared at the screen. *The real truth.* What did that even mean?

Her stomach churned. How could the details of this murder have been so clear only a few hours ago, and now be so muddled?

She looked up at Espinoza, the face of the man whose head she was still bound to sever and bring back to her sponsor. She couldn't deny a direct order. The conundrum was, would she hand her prince the man's head and then say, 'Oh, by the way, Espinoza didn't actually do what you thought he did,' or would she take another path?

She blinked and looked at the floor. Could she belay the order and ask for clarification?

A stinging pain started at the base of her neck and carried through to her fingers. It had been years since her programming had sent her a harsh reminder of her vocation.

She swallowed and took a deep breath. The royal family's commands were absolute, and their enforcers were physically incapable of not following through on their orders. Her prince had been quite adamant. Espinoza needed to die, no matter what.

Ty moved back beside her and leaned close, as he had in the tavern. "Do you see now how it might be possible for people to do things that are illegal, but for good reasons? I mean, if this truth was wrong, how many others are wrong as well?"

An interesting question. However… "It's never right to break the king's law. Rules are there for a reason, and those who break the law need to be punished."

Ty shook his head. "Maybe she just needs to see a little righteous lawbreaking in action before she'll understand." He and Alanna folded their arms, staring at Espinoza.

The captain's lips twisted into a sneer. "You can't be serious. We are not bringing her with us."

Dania cocked a brow. Now, *this* sounded interesting.

"Why not? Let's give her a visual. We just got you off the hook for murder. Now let's work on the rest of us."

Only, Espinoza was *not* off the hook. True, he had not committed the crime of murder, but her prince's orders had been specific: 'Bring me back Espinoza's head.'

Prince Geron had not asked for the head of Filluck Palogivan's murderer. If he had, she would be looking for that child now.

Espinoza walked toward the observation window. "As soon as we're safe to fly, we're taking her to a colony somewhere and dropping her off, just like we planned."

Ty and Alanna smiled at each other. "No, we're not."

———

The crew mulled around Dania, continuing the repairs as she scanned more data feeds, looking for anything to distract her as she tried to soothe the roiling in her gut.

Filluck Palogivan had been Geron's good friend. Could her prince have come across this file? Had he sealed this evidence himself to save his friend's name? And if so, why ask for the head of an innocent man?

She cringed. Espinoza was far from innocent, but still, she needed to execute him in the name of the correct crime. Smuggling, yes, but not murder.

She rubbed the bridge of her nose as she'd seen so many humans do. It didn't help.

Dania needed to consider the possibility that her beloved prince may have broken his own father's laws.

But that wasn't possible. Geron wouldn't do that. Certainly, he had his faults. He was every bit the womanizer the rumor feeds said he was. He was more interested in his own personal pleasure than the law that his station called him to abide by, but he never broke any laws that she was aware of, and he'd never overlook the law being broken, even if by a friend.

A tone sounded, and a voice came over the speaker. "This is your friendly neighborhood doctor. How's it going up there?"

"Slowly, but we should be up and moving in an hour or so," Ty said.

"Awesome. Do you think we're clear from trackers? Can we turn our instruments back on?"

Espinoza looked at a time meter on the wall. "Yeah, we are more than in the clear. If they were following, we'd be dead already."

"Okay, then if it's all right with you guys, every book I've read on medical protocol says that a foreign entity should be checked out by the medical team before they're allowed on your ship."

"What?" Ty said.

"Well, I happened to notice you had a non-human tied in the corner of the bridge. I think that would qualify as a foreign entity."

"He's right," Espinoza said. "We should get her checked out."

"Checked out for what?" Dania asked.

"You know, the regular." Ty fiddled with a few wires sticking out of a panel. "Microorganisms, viruses, sexually transmitted infections..."

Alanna slapped him. "STIs? Seriously?"

"Hey! My mother taught me it's important to check."

"Focus, people." Espinoza stepped between them, holding back a smile. "Bring the power up slowly so we don't catch on fire again."

"Got it, boss." Ty saluted before walking over to Dania and pointing at her chair. "May I?"

She stood, relinquishing the captain's station.

Espinoza gave Dania a gentle tug. "Come on. I'll walk you down to the med bay."

The med bay...could she get so lucky? She'd seen doctors use surgical instruments. If she tried hard enough, she might be able to discern one that might be able to cut through the steel around her wrists. And with her hands now bound in front of her, she might have a better chance of not burning off any fingers.

The door slid open, and they stepped into a dark hall. The lights slowly rose as the ship's systems came back online.

"I don't have any diseases," Dania said.

He guided her down the hall. "Probably not, but you of all people should understand the rules."

Dania certainly couldn't argue with that.

Thick, metal ramparts rose around her. The ship was old but sturdy, meant for versatility rather than comfort. She stopped, staring at a scorch mark on the wall. "Is that from an ion blaster?"

"Yeah, that wasn't the greatest of days."

A few feet away, another burn mark mottled the wall. It seemed this ship had seen as many battles inside its walls as it had attacks from the outside.

They curved around several bends. The ship was tight, compact, and much larger than it looked on the outside. With its multiple floors, it could easily house a much larger crew. Either that, or ridiculously large and illegal amounts of cargo.

A doorway slid open, and they walked inside.

The man who had been shot earlier in the day clapped his hands. "How is my patient doing?"

Dania pursed her lips. "I should be asking you the same question."

He pulled open his shirt, exposing dark, curly hair covering a slight pink mark on his chest. "As good as new. Please give your friend a big hug for me next time you see him."

"Can we cut the crap and get to it, Doc?" Espinoza asked.

The doctor leaned toward her. "You have to excuse Cal. He has no bedside manner." He tapped her bindings. "These need to come off."

Espinoza shook his head. "No way. They stay on. She's too dangerous with them off."

Which was true…unless the blasted shackles had already drained too much.

The metal hummed around her wrists again, and she grimaced. Every hour or so, they'd warm or sometimes cool. The temperature didn't matter because each time, more of her power ebbed away. Hopefully, that was temporary, and she'd be more than ready to do her job once she got them off.

She had to believe that. The alternatives were unthinkable.

The doctor placed his hands on his hips. "How do you expect me to give her a proper examination?"

"They stay on."

"Whatever." The doctor tapped a gurney board. "Jump up here, please."

Dania sat on the hard steel and waited while he ran several scanning devices over her. None of them looked strong enough to cut through Palian steel. More instruments lined the walls behind clear panels…probably sterile holding chambers. Nothing she couldn't break through, even restrained.

The doctor frowned, looking into the device. "How old are you, sweetie?"

Sweetie? "I'm not actually sure. We don't count our ages like humans do."

"Hmm. What is your earliest memory?"

Her earliest memory…

Opening her eyes, and her sponsor, Geron, smiling at her, holding out his hand.

The sense of love and belonging.

Prince Geron bringing Alexander home to play with her a few days later.

She smiled. "I grew up in the palace with my sponsor and his family. What does that matter?"

The doctor pulled the cap off a small white container. "Just curious, making conversation." He ran the scanner over her again, then he poked her finger with something sharp. A bead of blood formed, and he squeezed it into the container.

"Ow." She drew her hand away, shaking her finger.

He tapped her shoulder. "Sorry, sweetie. That was the worst of it."

Espinoza paced like a rabid beast looking for an opportunity to strike. "You have that look on your face, Doc."

"I'm just getting some perplexing readings, but that's not unexpected."

Dania straightened. "What do you mean?"

"Well." The doctor sat on the edge of her gurney. "No one has ever done any medical research on an enforcer. I mean, people have written papers, but they're mostly supposition. I'm actually deliriously excited to look over these readings."

What an odd man.

Espinoza continued to pace. "Did you run that doohickey over her enough times to clear her to board the ship?"

Doc waved his hand in front of his face. "For heaven's

sake, yes, she's fine." He turned back to Dania. "But I'd love it if you could stop back tomorrow morning. This might be my one and only chance to make history."

By scanning her? Ridiculous, but that would give her more time to find a light scalpel, or maybe even something stronger.

She jumped off the gurney, and the room spun.

The doctor grabbed her. "Are you okay?"

She pulled away. "Of course I'm okay. Why wouldn't I be?"

He held up his hands. "My mistake."

Blinking until her head cleared, she followed Espinoza from the room.

What had happened in there? She looked down at the shackles. It couldn't be the illicit metal causing *that* much weakness.

Was she ill? Had she contracted some sort of disease from these humans?

The ship hummed beneath her feet as they stepped back into the hall. The lights flickered.

"Are we moving?" Dania asked.

Espinoza hit a few buttons on the wall. "Ty, what are you doing?"

"You said you didn't want to hang here like a bunch of sitting ducks, right?"

He rubbed his face. "Yes, but where are you going?"

"To Agenica. Carl says he has a package to pick up."

Espinoza licked his lips, glanced at Dania, and then back to the wall. "All right. Let's make it quick."

"You got it, boss."

———

Dania stood beside Alanna on the main bridge, watching as Ty and Espinoza met a lone man with long, dark braided hair in an otherwise deserted docking port just outside their ship. They shook hands and slapped each other's backs in the way human men frequently did. She'd never understood the strange greeting customs of Earthans.

Espinoza opened a small container and showed it to the man. The hairs on the back of her neck stood as she imagined what might be inside that package.

"What new larceny are you up to this time?" Dania asked.

Alanna glanced at her, then looked back out the window. "No larceny. We deal with Carl all the time. This is a perfectly legal trade."

Dania was sure it wasn't, although the woman's temperature remained neutral. After more talking, the man, Carl, apparently, pushed three large containers out. Ty opened them up and rooted around inside.

"What's in those?" Dania asked.

"Just normal, legal supplies. Nothing for you to worry about."

Dania gritted her teeth. She needed to worry about this. She was bound by her prince to stop anyone breaking a law, yet she stood, rapt. The cargo might be illegal, but the trade looked fair enough. It didn't even seem like the men on either side had guns.

They wouldn't be foolish enough to break a law right in front of her, though.

But maybe that was why she was up here, where she could not see what was being traded.

Unless it actually *was* a legal trade.

Her mind whirled and she blinked. Why was she having such trouble focusing?

As Espinoza shook Carl's hand, Ty pushed one of the three containers toward the cargo ramps below them. Dania would have to find out what they were bringing on board. The containers would probably be stored in the lower levels with countless other kinds of contraband. Once she saw the contents for herself, she could decide who was guilty on the ship and who, if anyone, was innocent.

Espinoza's voice rang over the communicator in the wall. "Alanna, everything still okay?"

She glanced at Dania. "Yeah, we're just having some girl time."

"Good. Bring her down to the brig area."

Dania stiffened. If they locked her up, how would she be able to get more information? Even worse, she wouldn't have the opportunity to pick up a forgotten tool that might free her.

"Is that necessary?" Alanna asked.

Dania mustered half a smile. Somehow, she'd gained an ally in the woman. She needed to keep it that way.

"We all need some sleep," Espinoza said. "I need to know she's contained for everyone's safety, including her own."

Dania scowled, sure he had no concern for her safety whatsoever.

She rolled her shoulder and winced against the ache from having her wrists fastened behind her back earlier. Maybe a short sleep would do her good, but she'd need to get out of her cell as soon as possible.

She grimaced at the shackles as they cooled on her skin.

The now all-too-familiar tingle set in as more of her power drained away. She turned her back to the woman and pulled against the steel bindings, but they only seemed to constrict. The illicit metal was every bit the horror she'd been told it would be.

This was all the more reason to try to get back to that med bay to look through the instruments housed in glass. There had to be something in there that would cut through Palian steel. She could do so when the humans fell asleep.

First, she'd have to break out of the confinement cell Espinoza was about to put her in, and she'd probably have to do this without her powers. It had been a very long time since she'd had to rely on her skills of body and mind, rather than primordial energy.

She was about to find out just how resourceful she could be.

CAL WAVED his hand over the panel in the hallway, and the door to the infirmary slipped open. Doc stood behind his lab table, leaning over a microscope window.

"You wanted to see me?"

Doc looked up. "Yes. Thanks for coming down."

The seriousness in Doc's voice sent a chill running over Cal's skin. "What is it?"

"I've found some strange things in the enforcer's blood." He frowned at the scope. "It's like there are pathogens living inside her red blood cells."

"Pathogens? That's bad, right? Are we in danger?"

Doc shook his head. "I don't think so. They aren't attacking her platelets. It's more like they're in some kind of symbiotic relationship."

Cal moved closer. "I don't know what that means."

Doc tapped his lips with his fingers. "Well, they seem to be coded to her, for one thing. I gave them a drop of my own blood, and they just ignored it." He looked at Cal. "That means it's not contagious. They'll only affect the host, but that's not the most interesting thing."

"Are you dragging this out on purpose?"

Doc smiled before looking back to the microscope. "They've completely mutated her blood, but beneath all that, she's human."

Cal balked. "That's impossible." There was no way that psychotic killing machine was human.

Doc motioned to the scope. "Do you want to look and see for yourself?"

Cal narrowed his eyes. Doc knew Cal would have no idea what he was looking at.

Anyway, it was going to take quite a bit more than a self-taught doctor to make him believe that the woman locked up in his brig was human.

"Look at her. She has that silvery hair that flies around on its own, and enforcers can do all that crazy stuff like making a bullet rise out of your chest." He pointed at Doc's heart. "You saw that firsthand, up close and personal. The only thing worse than running from an enforcer is running from someone in the royal family themselves."

Cal considered the woman's nearly lifeless silver-gray eyes. None of that was human.

Doc started to pace. "When we first saw her on the space station, her hair was flying around all medusa-like. The enforcer who'd healed me had the same crazy, living hair. It was like they were standing in a windy room, but the rest of us weren't."

"Your point?"

He held up his palms. "Her hair isn't flying around anymore."

He was right. When Cal had locked her in her cell last night so they could all sleep without worrying about her trying to strangle one of them, her hair had been flat, nearly normal-looking, except for the shimmering silver color. "It was flying around when we were trying to fight our way out of the station. I saw it."

"Yes, but not anymore, right?"

Cal looked at the ground, thinking over the last few times he'd seen her. It had seemed to lessen after that battle, and now the movement was pretty much gone, or so slight, he hadn't noticed.

"I've watched the pathogens split apart and fade in the blood sample she gave me. I think they're dying off."

"Could it be because you removed the blood from her body?"

"I don't think so, but I want to keep researching." He looked down.

"What aren't you telling me?"

Doc's lips thinned. "I'm far from an expert on enforcer physiology, but from what I can see, the relationship between her blood and the pathogens is so symbiotic that I'm not sure she'll be able to survive without them."

Well, that didn't sound good. "Is she in immediate danger?"

Doc shook his head. "I don't think so. It will probably be months before all the pathogens are all gone." He pointed to a different screen. "But I'm going to keep researching to see if I can find a way to replicate them because there is a possibility that these pathogens are the source of all the ridiculous power the enforcers fling around to terrorize people."

The source of their power? He had to be joking. The enforcers were feared throughout the universe for their seemingly unlimited magical power. They were second only to the king, from what Cal had seen. And in wielding that power, they culled the universe of anyone they even *thought* might commit a crime someday.

If this power was something that could be given and taken away, that would put everyone on a more level playing field. And one thing Cal loved was a level playing field.

He centered his attention back on Doc. "Do you need anything from me?"

"I'll let you know."

The ship hummed beneath Cal's feet as he moved into the hallway. They must be slowing down.

Cal hit the comm button on the wall. "Ty, are we here already?"

"Dropping into orbit, boss. Do you want us to land?"

"Call ahead and make sure they're ready to see us. I want to stop, trade, and then get out as fast as we can." The enforcer was still locked in the brig, and those confounded cuffs seemed to be doing their job, but the last thing Cal wanted to do was be caught anywhere near a pirate colony.

"Roger that." Ty cut the comm from his end.

Alanna came around the corner, rubbing her eyes. "Good morning."

"It's a little early for you, isn't it?" Cal asked.

"Ty pinged me that we were landing soon, and I wanted to make sure our new friend in the brig got some food."

Cal shivered. He hadn't even considered that. "Do enforcers eat?"

"She certainly looked happy to see the plate. And it's 'Dania,' by the way."

Cal cocked his head. "What?"

"Her name. It's Dania. She's actually pretty nice."

"When she's not threatening to execute you."

Alanna shrugged. "That's kind of her job, right? And isn't that why we're taking her with us, to show her that we're not bad people?"

Why did they all assume this would be easy? "I'm still not on board with all this. I want to cut her loose as soon as we can."

Alanna's eyes widened. "Not on Cannis Proper, though, right? I mean…the pirates."

Cal shook his head. That would put the girl right into the hands of the slavers they'd tried to save her from in the first place.

This was another reason he wanted to get in, trade, and get out as soon as possible. If any of the unsavories on this planet found out that they'd busted out of Midway Station with an incapacitated enforcer on board, the *Star Renegade* would have a target on its hull the size of Jupiter.

Ty's voice sounded over the comm. "We have clearance, boss. They're waiting for us in landing bay twenty-seven."

Cal hit the button on the wall. "Okay, set us down ridiculously close to the door, like close enough that we could crash through the damn thing if things go bad."

"Expecting trouble?"

"On Cannis Proper? Always."

———

Cal stepped off the landing platform while Ethan maneuvered the three floating cylinders of remanufactured transistors they'd procured from Carl out of the *Renegade's* cargo hold. Above, Ty and Alanna watched from the bridge, ready to give Cal cover fire, if needed.

It wasn't that Cal didn't trust Christopher Columbus.

Well, no, that was *exactly* it. He didn't trust Christopher Columbus at all. For one, that wasn't even his name, obviously. Like all pirates, he'd chosen a new name to do business under.

He was fairly certain that his first name was actually Chris, since he'd used that name years ago when they'd first met as teenagers. In fact, if smooth-talking Chris hadn't been stowing away in the same cargo container, Cal may have never made it off his home planet to begin his illustrious life of crime.

Christopher walked toward him and flashed a smile that had probably broken a dozen hearts. It was likely meant to put them all at ease, but Cal knew better.

Chris wore an all-brown flight suit that looked far too much like military fatigues, with enough pockets bulging in his cargo pants that he could have been hiding dozens of weapons.

Cal tensed. Under normal circumstances, he'd want Ty and his silver tongue down here to work out the negotiations. Today, though, Cal wanted his best pilot with his hands glued to the controls, just in case.

"Espinoza." Chris shook Cal's hand, looking past him at the *Renegade*. "It looks like you've taken some fire recently."

Cal glanced over his shoulder at the scorch marks across the hull. "You know us, always begging people to use us as target practice." All things considered, they'd gotten off Midway Station with minimal damage. The real question was, did Chris know they'd barely gotten out of there alive, and if he did, did Chris know who was in Cal's brig?

Chris laughed. "And we wouldn't have it any different."

He waved at Ty and Alanna up in the window. "Ty tells me you have transistors?"

Ethan pushed up one of the canisters. "Three full cases."

He opened the lid, and Chris barely looked inside. "Very nice. I'd like to have my techs sift through them. Do you want to invite your crew onboard for some breakfast while you wait?"

So he could send spies into Cal's ship to see what else they had, or find a helpless silver-haired woman in their brig? Not a chance.

"You know our stuff is good. I'm not going to screw you." The last thing Cal needed was Chris and his pirate buddies after him, too.

Chris looked him over. "You guys in a rush for some reason?"

Cal kept his expression placid. "We're always in a rush. You know that."

Chris walked up to the second container and tapped on it. "Let's see this one."

Ethan glanced at Cal, then complied. Thank goodness, he was keeping his mouth shut as instructed. Ethan's sarcasm could get them killed in a trade like this.

As Chris picked up a few transistors, Cal scanned the walls, checking each point that could hold a sniper. All but one of the spaces was dark, so at least eleven guns were pointed at them.

The hairs on his arms rose. After Chris had gotten him off that merchant ship eight years ago, Cal had helped Chris get a job as a miner in the NGC 2899 Beltway. Chris wasn't much for honest work, though, disappearing in the night a few weeks into the job.

Two years later, Chris had used his pirate connections to smuggle Cal off of Europa Nine after Cal took the blame for Filluck Palogivan's murder.

He and Chris had a history of good trades since Cal had been on the run, but the guy was still a pirate. Most enforcers would disagree, but there was a big difference between a pirate and a smuggler. Chris was willing to cross lines Cal refused to even fly near in order to get what he wanted.

"Do you have what we agreed to or not?" Cal asked.

Chris pretended to keep rooting through the stuff and whispered. "I'm supposed to give you a fake one."

Cal tensed. Ethan glanced up to the dark corners. He'd been taken unaware by snipers one time as well. Once was enough to make you never forget.

Cal held up a transistor like he was trying to sell it. "I take it they can't hear what we're saying?"

Chris took it from his hand. "Nope."

Okay, good. At least he knew Chris was on their side. For a pirate, he was a good guy, most of the time. Sometimes, though, someone else was pulling the strings. Cal just needed to know what kind of strings were being pulled. "Is there any chance of us getting out of here alive with what we came for?"

Chris smiled. "Nope."

Great.

Just great.

A bead of sweat formed on Ethan's brow. "Boss?"

"Relax." Cal folded his arms. "I'm sure my old buddy Chris is telling us this for a reason."

Chris reached into the cylinder to grab another transistor, and as he did, a small metal octagon slipped out of his sleeve.

He looked at Cal and then Ethan to make sure they noticed before he picked up a transistor. "Are you sure this is the same grade as in the first canister?" He walked back toward the first.

Cal darted a look to Ethan and then to the tiny octagon Chris had dropped as Cal walked to join the pirate.

"They're all the same. My engineer checked them all before we landed," Cal said.

Behind them, Ethan palmed the octagon into the pocket of his jacket.

Chris held the two transistors up together. "Yeah, I guess you're right." He waved to a dark hallway, and a woman in a brown leather jacket and thick, black pants walked out and handed Chris a box not much larger than a serving platter.

Cal flipped the box over, and his trained eye instantly drew to the small re-soldered seal. The box was too light. This was an outer casing, a shell to what they'd agreed to. The priceless part was the brain, which they'd no doubt removed and re-soldered to make the unit appear intact.

This was the type of thing you needed to worry about when dealing with pirates. Chris was usually honest with him because they gave each other repeat business.

He wasn't really sure who these people in the background were, or what they had over Chris, but it seemed none of them were in a good place right now.

"It looks good, right?" Chris raised a brow.

Cal glared at him, but Chris kept his face stony.

Was Cal supposed to pretend he thought he was getting a fair deal? He could pick up an empty casing on any trading world for a fraction of the cost, probably because empty casings were frequently unloaded from the victims of bad deals like this.

Ethan's hand appeared on Cal's shoulder. He looked into the case. "Wow, that's a pretty nice one. Is that last year's model?"

"Two years back," the woman said.

Ethan whistled and then looked her up and down. "Definitely some nice goods there, boss. I can shine that up and we can get a fortune for it."

Part of him wanted to punch Ethan for eyeing up a woman who was probably packing enough firepower to take them both down before they could blink. The other part of him also wanted to punch Ethan for getting involved.

Ethan nudged him. "Take the deal, boss."

Chris's eyes darkened. "Take the deal, Cal."

There was ice in the pirate's gaze. The men in the shadows shifted.

Ethan had shoved the small octagon into his pocket. Did his engineer get a chance to see it? Was Ethan telling him that whatever Chris had given them was worth it?

The woman flinched and then held her ear like someone was talking into a comm implant.

She looked at Cal, then at the boarding ramp of the *Renegade*.

Stars, this deal was going south fast.

"We're good." Ethan took the box from the woman's other hand. "Thanks." He grabbed Cal's shoulder. "Let's go."

Cal glanced at Chris. His friend mouthed the word, '*Run*.'

Yeah, Cal didn't have to be told that twice.

Above, in the observation window of the *Renegade,* Ty's eyes widened. The ship's engines came online as Cal and Ethan started to sprint.

A laser blast echoed through the room. Ethan cried out, falling forward. The empty box sprawled across the floor as he hit the ground. Cal ducked a sniper shot, racing back to Ethan.

The engineer pointed. "No, the box."

"It's worthless."

"No, it's not."

Alanna ran from the ship and grabbed the engineer's arm. "Ethan!"

"Hey, beautiful, I didn't know you cared." He coughed, wincing.

Three shots blasted at their feet. How in the blazes were they missing?

Across the room, Chris held a small device in his palm, tucked beneath his jacket. Red lights flashed—a particle beam disruptor. That's why the pirates' aim was so bad— Chris was refracting the beams. Maybe the guy was still an ally, after all.

"Get the box," Cal told Alanna as he put Ethan's arm over his shoulder.

As she reached for it, a blast got through, slicing a line through the arm of her jacket. She hissed but still clutched the box. "I got it. Let's go."

The landing plank had already started to close. Cal ducked and slid the rest of the way in before dropping Ethan unceremoniously to the floor and hitting the comm button. "We're in. Go."

The ship rumbled to life. Blasts hit their hull. Cal grabbed the side of the ship as Alanna knelt beside Ethan.

"Get up there," Alanna told Cal. "I've got Ethan."

Cal nodded. He really needed her on the bridge, too, but he didn't have any idea how bad Ethan had been hit.

He punched the door-release pad and bolted down the hall and onto the bridge. "Status?"

"Same old, same old."

That was never good. Cal touched the blue button on his dashboard. "Doc, you have incoming. Ethan's been hit."

"How bad?"

"I don't know. But send Alanna up here as soon as she gets him to you."

"Got it."

A *boom* jolted the bridge, and the ship rocked.

"That didn't sound friendly," Cal said.

Ty scowled at him. "These are freaking pirates. I don't want to think about what they're pointing at us. Did you at least make the trade?"

Cal seriously hoped so. "Can you blast through the doors?"

"Blasting." Ty hit a round into the frame of hulking metal. Nothing.

"What the hell?" Ty repositioned the weapons grid.

"They must be shielding."

"Did you screw them or something?"

Cal shook his head. "I think they found out about your girlfriend in the brig."

Ty cursed under his breath. "Then let's hit them with all we got."

Risky, but better than being dead. "Go for it."

Ty slammed his fists down on several buttons. The ship rocked.

Alanna ran through the door. "I see we're doing just as well as ever."

"It pays to be consistent," Ty said.

"Cut the banter, people. Let's get out of here alive first." Cal checked the power levels, and Ty hit the door with another spread. "Can we get any more power?"

"Not without an engineer."

Dammit! Why couldn't he have taken Doc out there instead of Ethan?

He cringed. Because then Doc would have been shot, and he was the only one who knew how to treat any sort of injuries.

Cal couldn't second-guess himself. He needed to trust that Ethan had brought the ship back up to full operational capacity, which was about a hundred and fifty times stronger than was legal for a ship this size.

Cal closed off the power to the lower levels and sealed off the med bay, then the bridge. He stared at the compartment Dania was confined in, hesitated, then sealed her off as well.

Alanna took her seat. "What are you doing?"

"I'm diverting power from everywhere but the brig, med bay, and this room and transferring it into the weapons systems."

He signaled Doc. "You're sealed in. Do *not* try to open your door until I give you clearance. Do you understand?"

Doc cursed. "Got it."

Cal glanced at Alanna and Ty. "Go."

Ty turned forward, and a blast of light flew from their

ship. People outside jumped back, a few of them on fire. Ty hit the panel again, and part of the wall disintegrated.

Cal pushed the controls, slamming the ship through. Metal screeched against metal until they were out in open air.

"Check the hull integrity."

"On it," Alanna said.

Three small ships dropped down on them, firing.

Alanna's hands flew over her console. "Returning power to the shields."

Ty swept over the ships with another blast of fire, and the first attacker careened to the ground. The second backed off, while the third headed straight for their window.

"You want to play?" Cal shouted. "I'll play."

He ignited the engines, racing toward the other ship.

"Hull integrity good, if anyone is still worried about it." Alanna held on to the ends of her station.

Ty grabbed on to the panel, screaming a creative expletive as the impact alarms shrieked through the bridge.

Cal gripped the controls. "All power to the front shields."

"Done!" Alanna cried.

The ship veered up, just missing them.

"Punch it!" Cal called, and the *Star Renegade* blasted out of the atmosphere and into open space.

"We have incoming," Ty said. "Oh, crap, there are at least a hundred ships coming out from behind their moon."

Ambush. They'd definitely found out about Dania.

"Alanna?"

But his navigator already had a small circle of blue light dancing in the air before her. "Do you care where we go?"

"Not particularly."

The stars around them flashed and elongated. Space evaporated into blinding white light before the ship jolted to a stop.

"Ow." Alanna clutched her head.

Cal ran for her, grabbing her shoulders. "You okay?"

She slumped onto her chair. "Never better."

Ty whooped, turning in his seat. "That was freaking awesome!" He stood. "Did you at least get what we came for?"

Cal glanced at the door. Down in the med bay, Ethan was being patched up. The stars only knew how bad his injury was.

"I have no idea," Cal admitted. And it was the truth.

They got…*something*. He just didn't know what.

Whatever Chris had slipped them, he hoped it was worth them all nearly getting killed.

THE SHIP RATTLED AROUND HER. Dania stared up at the camera monitoring her cell. She could tap into the wiring to access the computers and find out what was going on, if she wanted to.

Bumbling as this crew seemed, though, they must be somewhat competent to have garnered the reputation and the high ranking on the king's wanted criminals list. Chances were they could get out of a small trading spat.

The shaking finally stopped, so Espinoza must have managed to outrun whoever had been chasing them.

Boots tapped in the hallway, and Dania approached the glass wall of her cell.

The pink-haired woman smiled at her. "Hello."

Dania raised a brow. "I get the feeling you aren't here to exchange pleasantries."

A bandage showed through a burned hole in the woman's shirtsleeve. *Interesting.*

Alanna shook her head. "Back at the supply station where we first picked you up, your friend saved Doc's life."

Yes, much to Dania's chagrin. Not that she'd known the doctor was a criminal at the time, rather than the innocent Alexander had thought him to be.

"Can you do it again?" Alanna asked. "Can you heal someone?"

Ah, so Dania had been correct about them being in some sort of a fight. "I don't have the skill to heal bullet wounds like my friend can."

Her eyes saddened. "It's not a bullet. He was hit with a particle beam."

What a horribly painful way to die. "Was it Espinoza?"

She shook her head. "Ethan, our engineer."

The copper-haired man who'd managed to get the shackles on Dania's wrists? She should leave him and allow the particle acceleration to sear through his flesh like acid. A criminal was a criminal.

At least, that's what she would have thought before seeing those encrypted files.

Providing any assistance to these people was wrong. However, she hadn't been able to free herself from this cell without using the primordial energy the bindings stole at every turn.

At the moment, she was trapped here, and helping him would mean leaving this cell and seeing more of the ship again. If they could trust her and continue to take her along on their nefarious expeditions, she would have a long list of places to return to and destroy once this little game had played out.

Maybe helping save another of the crew would ingratiate her enough in these humans' minds for them to grant her free run of the ship long term.

She nodded. "I'm not a healer, but I might be able to help."

Hope sprang in the woman's eyes. Could she possibly have feelings for this engineer?

Dania had taken for granted that the woman had been paired with the doctor from her reaction when the man had been shot on Midway Station, but this might be something else.

The woman wiped her damp cheeks.

Dania's chest clenched. Friendship was one of the few human behaviors she understood. Dania would die before she allowed anyone to hurt Alexander.

Could human feelings be so strong? Would any of the men's deaths affect Alanna so deeply?

The woman pressed a few buttons on the wall, and the glass doors split apart.

Dania smiled. This one, out of all the crew so far, interested her the most. Alanna didn't seem so much like a criminal, but more like someone who had gotten mixed up with the wrong sort of people.

And then there was her odd ability to bend space to jump the ship out of danger. Dania hoped to ferret out that little mystery long before she had to end this crew's reign of larceny.

When Dania and Alanna entered the medical area, Espinoza's eyes flared. "What is *she* doing here?"

"I asked for her." The doctor pushed past him. "She'll help?" he asked Alanna.

"I can try." Dania held up her bindings. "Can you remove these?"

That was more of a challenge to Espinoza than anything else.

The captain shook his head. "It's not going to happen."

The doctor turned on him. "Boss, Ethan is dying. I can't stop it."

Espinoza's gaze remained lanced to hers. "She will kill every last one of us if those cuffs come off."

True, but not right away. "What if I make another promise not to kill anyone?"

He shook his head. "How about you explain how particle beams work so Doc can treat him on his own?"

She sighed. "That will be a very long seminar that your engineer will probably not live through."

The doctor pointed at her bindings. "Are those absorbing all of your power?"

An interesting question that they should have asked earlier.

"No." There was no use in denying it. She needed to gain their trust.

"Can you at least try with the cuffs on?" Doc asked.

Of course she could, but it would be painful.

She glared at Espinoza but acquiesced. This wouldn't be the first time she'd risked herself for the good of a mission.

The engineer was strapped stomach-down to a table, his orange hair sticking to his scalp in thick clumps. Blankets covered him to his hip, leaving his back exposed to the bright examination light above him. His skin pocked and oozed as the particles ate away at his flesh. She crinkled her nose at the stench of impending death.

"Who shot him, and why?" Dania asked.

Espinoza folded his arms. "We're traders. Sometimes trades go bad."

"Legal trades rarely go bad."

"Just tell her what she wants to know!" Alanna's eyes

reddened as she picked up a carton the width of a meal platter. "Ethan might die for this piece of trash, and I don't even think this is what they went out there for."

Dania very much wanted to take a look in that box, but first she needed to gain a little trust. She considered the severity of the man's wounds. She'd seen something similar before.

On Teseon Minor, Miguel had allowed himself to be distracted and had been hit with a particle beam. Alexander was engaged in the more important task of healing a small bruise on Prince Geron's shoulder, so Dania had been left with a fully grown man in tears as his flesh blistered down to the bone. After knocking Miguel out, she'd surveyed the situation, and while she couldn't heal him, she could at least stop further damage.

She held her still-shackled hands over the engineer's wounds and released a small burst of power. Her sight wavered as the skin stretched and started to bubble.

The engineer's rusty-haired head jolted before his eyes sprang open. He screamed until the doctor gave him an injection.

Espinoza pushed her back. "What are you doing?"

Her power shot back into her. The shackles began to chill. She braced for the pain and released her breath when it didn't come. Next time, she might not be so lucky.

Dania lifted her chin. "Do you want me to save him or not?"

Alanna held her captain's shoulder. "Cal, please, let her try."

Espinoza muttered something as he stepped back.

Dania raised her hands again, then drew them back,

licking her lips. Another release of her strength might invoke the pain. Was saving this man worth the risk?

Alanna's eyes were beseeching.

Both the doctor's and Espinoza's grim faces were turned to the prone engineer.

To them, this man's life was worth a sacrifice. To gain their trust, she needed to believe the same.

Taking a deep breath, she released a surge of cooling energy to counteract the particles.

The engineer whimpered. Even in his unconscious state, the pain must have been unbearable. The doctor monitored him as the bubbling in the patient's skin intensified.

Espinoza took a step toward her, but Alanna pulled him back again.

Smart woman. More importantly, the captain listened to her. She cataloged the information for future use.

"Do you have something to safely store the particles in?" Dania asked.

The doctor quirked a brow. "How would you get the particles out?" He stared at her before his eyes widened, as if suddenly remembering who she was. He scampered to a storage unit and returned with a gray-tinted flask. "Is this big enough?"

"Is the polymer reinforced?"

"Yes."

Dania flicked her wrist. The particles rose from the body like a stream of clear, pure water and fountained into the flask. When the last drop disappeared inside, the doctor placed a stopper on the bottle.

Dania stepped back, wiping her brow with her sleeve.

Her stomach roiled. "I don't have the capability to heal,

but I believe you can now treat him for severe burns." She swayed and steadied herself against a table.

"Is he going to live?" Cal asked.

The doctor scanned the patient several more times. "Yeah, but he's going to be a very unhappy camper for quite a while."

"Do your best." Espinoza eyed Dania's shackles. "That was a lot of magic for someone handcuffed with Palian steel. What more are you able to do?"

This man's suspicions were endless. It was probably the reason he'd lived so long.

The room spun. Dania blinked hard, bending over the table so she wouldn't fall.

Alanna steadied her. "Are you okay?"

Dania grabbed her head. The answer was *no*, but she wouldn't admit that to a human.

Espinoza took a step, reaching for her, then drew away, frowning.

Had he almost helped? Nonsense. Dania must have imagined it.

However, it wasn't going to be hard to look unthreatening when the world seemed to press in on all sides. "That shouldn't have bothered me. I feel like..." What did humans normally say tired them? "I feel like I've run a marathon."

Alanna eased her over to a gurney. "Here, sit."

"She's playing you," Espinoza said.

Dania wished he was right. The king was correct to try to eradicate Palian steel from the universe. This metal shouldn't be allowed to exist.

Her vision skewed again, and she grabbed the edge of

the gurney. "I just saved your man, as requested. Should I send the particles back into his skin?"

Espinoza's nostrils flared, and Dania trembled.

This man, this normal *human* man, now held her life in his hands, and there was nothing she could do about it. She felt herself cower under that gaze, and hated herself for it.

"Lay her down," the doctor said. "I wanted to run a few more tests on her, anyway."

More bothersome tests. She had to admit, though, that the doctor wasn't a completely annoying companion, and if he could negate any of her symptoms, she certainly wouldn't complain.

Alanna helped her onto the cot.

As Dania started to lie down, the room spiraled again. Flashes of light ignited throughout the medical bay. She gasped, clutching the gurney.

"Whoa!" Alanna grabbed her. "Hold on there."

The room fogged. The shackles iced as a tingling jolt ran up her arms.

"What happened?" The doctor's voice. "Crap, she's pale. Well, pale-*er*."

The bindings tightened. Dania grimaced, lifting her wrist. "Hurts." She wanted to say more, but no words could encompass the sensation of ice and fire battling within her.

"You have to get them off," Alanna said.

"No way." Espinoza's voice lingered like a beacon of doom. "*They-do-not-come-off.* Period."

Dania clenched her teeth as another jolt ran up her arms. Her blood scorched her, boiling from within.

This was it. She was going to die here, and no one would ever know what had happened.

A shriek echoed through her ears. She didn't realize it was her own scream until her throat burned.

The fog deepened before something pinched her neck.

Her eyes sprang open. "What did you do?"

The doctor stepped away, holding a needle as darkness crept in from all sides.

CAL SAT beside Ethan on the gurney. He couldn't believe what a relief it was to see his engineer sitting upright.

Ethan rubbed his head. "Have I really been unconscious for three days?"

"You got pretty banged up." Cal just hoped it was for a good reason. He held up the small octagon Doc had found in Ethan's pocket. "Can you tell me what that is?"

Ethan took the metal device, grimacing like the small movement hurt. "It's a frame relay transducer. A damn nice one, too."

Cal hated it when his crew made him feel dumb. "And what would one do with a frame relay transducer?"

Ethan smiled. "Whatever we wanted." He looked over his shoulder and winced. "Did we get the casing they wanted to trade?"

"Yeah, but it was worthless. They'd spliced it already."

"Yeah, but when I add this, it won't be." Ethan held up the octagon. "The casing will allow us to add the transducer to our shields or pump our engines to ridiculous levels." He closed the octagon in his fist. "Or we could *not* attach it to the ship and do the humanitarian thing, instead."

Across the room, Dania startled. Cal swore sometimes she could hear them, even when they were whispering. Doc gave her a drink, which she guzzled down.

"What are you thinking?" Cal leaned closer to Ethan.

"I'm thinking that any of the dome colonies would be damn happy to get a backup system to bolster their oxygen supply."

Seriously? There was no possible way they'd gotten their hands on that kind of tech. "The pirates wouldn't have given something like that up."

"But they didn't." He held up the tiny device. "Your buddy knew we were about to get screwed, and he gave you something better. Actually, you probably owe him one."

Great. The last thing he needed was to be indebted to a pirate.

Ty entered with Alanna behind him. "You wanted to see us, boss?"

Cal stood. "I didn't call you."

Doc walked up. "I did. There's something I need to talk to you all about."

Across the room, Dania fell off the gurney and slammed to the floor.

Alanna cried out and ran to her. "What happened?"

Cal bolted toward the fallen woman but hesitated. Dania had been pretty much incapacitated for the past three days, but who knew when she'd be back to threatening them all again?

Now, though, she lay limp and not moving, her shock of pearly-silver hair completely covering her face. The high and mighty enforcer wasn't a threat to anyone at the moment.

"That's my fault," Doc said. "I gave her enough sedative to take down an elephant, just in case."

"In case what?" Cal reached down and helped Doc heft her back on the gurney.

Doc pulled the bars up on the sides of the bed so she wouldn't fall off again. He pressed a few buttons beside a screen in his wall and called up a zoomed-in picture of blood cells.

"I ran a genealogy on our enforcer friend and confirmed what I suspected." He tapped the screen twice. "She was born human."

Cal tensed. This wasn't news to him, but he still wasn't buying it.

"What?" Ty walked toward him. "That's impossible. Enforcers are some sort of unknown species."

"Not this one." Doc changed the picture to a young human girl with dirty blonde hair, maybe ten years old. "Meet Dania Rain. She was the daughter of a merchant on Kellis Nine when she got sick."

Cal looked into the eyes of the little girl, seeing no resemblance to the woman who'd threatened him countless times.

Doc continued. "The colony doctors took a blood sample for testing and must have uploaded it into the archives. Two days later the Banes showed up."

"They took her?" Alanna asked.

Doc nodded. "After that, she dropped off the grid, never to be seen again. A tidy sum of eleven million *tigara* was deposited into the merchant's accounts, and he moved his family back to Earth and retired."

"Are you telling me that the Banes bought her, like actually paid money to her parents?" Ty asked. "Isn't that illegal?"

Cal's shoulders tensed. Nothing was illegal if you were a Bane.

Doc moved to a records page. "It was documented as an adoption. The royal family has been known to seek out children they deem special. In many cultures, it's considered an honor to have a child taken, and the families are always rewarded highly."

Ethan limped over and sat slowly into a chair. "Yeah, like *eleven million tigara* highly. That's insane."

"It's hush money," Ty said.

Doc called up side-by-side pictures of red cells. On the left, the cells trembled. On the right, they flowed more smoothly. "Whatever they did to her, she's not human anymore. These pathogens they placed in her body made her something else."

"Something lethal," Cal said.

Doc tapped on the screen. "But like I told you, she's slowly devolving and becoming more human every day. However, her body is so degraded, she might not be able to survive as a human anymore."

Cal walked over to the enforcer and brushed the hair back from her eyes. Could it be true? Could she have actually been just a regular girl once?

She looked so peaceful when she was asleep. So normal.

Cal turned back to Doc. "Is it something you can fix?"

Doc paced, tapping his fingers against his lips. "I was hoping I could come up with something to replace whatever it is they did to her." He shook his head. "But that would be nearly impossible. This pathogen is a complex microorganism. Creating something with technology would take years, far longer than she has."

Ty laughed. "So that means this is your new top priority?"

Doc's grin beamed. "I do love a challenge." He turned to Cal. "You need to know something, though, and I don't think you're going to like it."

Great. "What?"

"After they took Dania from her family, she was taken to the Bane home world. Soon after, she was documented as Dania DuBane, ward of the king. A few weeks later, the king gave her to his son as a gift." Doc turned to Cal. "Prince Geron."

Cal gripped the metal bars surrounding Dania's bed. Geron was the prince who had personally called for Cal's head. Filluck Palogivan had been that prince's best friend.

Cal glared at Dania, making sure she was actually asleep. If she hadn't mentioned this, it was probably because she was still bound to Geron Bane's orders to kill him.

His veins iced. He'd actually felt sorry for her, but her supposed weakness had all been a ploy to get his guard down.

Once an enforcer, always an enforcer. They meddled, they connived, and they killed. She was no better than the one who'd killed his father.

"Wait. It gets worse." Doc pointed at the monitor. "From what I was able to extract from the royal archives, Dania DuBane took to her calling with flying colors, becoming the youngest and most lethal enforcer in recent history." He turned from the screen, looking at each one of them individually. "We are not dealing with a novice, but a full-blown general."

Alanna gasped, stepping away from Dania's bed.

Ty narrowed his eyes, moving closer to the unconscious death machine. "That's impossible. If that were true, those cuffs wouldn't be able to hold her."

"Could she be faking it?" Ethan asked.

The ice in Cal's veins turned to heat. Yes, she could definitely be faking it. Enforcers were heartless. She was capable of anything.

Alanna rubbed her shoulder. "She was able to help Ethan, even with the cuffs on. Maybe there is more power there?"

Cal had to wonder, though...the way she'd screamed after helping Ethan, that hadn't seemed like an act. The steel was doing its job. Maybe too well.

He'd seen enforcers salivate, fighting over the honor of killing someone on the king's blasted dead-man list. If this woman were at her full power, his head would already be staring at them on a platter. Especially if the order had come from her own prince, a man who apparently owned her. Paid for her. Or, rather, had received her as a gift from dear-old-Dad.

Cal forced down the bile building in his throat.

Back on the supply station, Dania and the other enforcers must have been looking for him after all, and Ty had played right into an elaborate trap. Now here he was, harboring the very general he'd been running from all this time.

He considered the handcuffs still firmly clasped around her wrists. He hoped they were actually holding her, because if they weren't, the clock was ticking, and when she decided he and his crew were guilty of whatever crime annoyed her, she'd slit their throats and probably laugh about what fools they'd all been.

Ty pushed away from her bed. "Nothing's changed."

"What?"

Ty pointed at her. "She's still an enforcer, just a much more dangerous one. We can still prove to her that we're good people. We can still clear our names."

Alanna shrugged. "She *has* been nice."

"While she's been plotting all your deaths," Cal pointed out.

Ty raised his hand. "I still vote for bringing her with us on the supply run. All in favor?"

Alanna raised her hand, and then Doc did the same.

Ethan shifted nervously.

Good. At least one of them hadn't lost their minds.

"She saved your life," Doc told Ethan.

"But to what end?" Ethan asked. "I think I'm with Cal on this one. That silver hair scares me."

More than her hair scared Cal. He grabbed Doc's arm. "Have you done enough research to create a bio shield that would be able to hold her?"

"You want me to do surgery on her or something?"

"No. I want you to build something to contain her, just in case those cuffs stop working."

"Wow. That would be all kinds of illegal." Doc stared at her until a monomaniacal grin appeared on his face. "Sounds like fun. She'll kill me for it, though."

"I'll take the blame." Cal turned from the room. "Keep her sedated if you can. Let me know if she wakes up."

Because once she did, things were going to get messy.

CHAPTER 14
DANIA

A BRIGHT LIGHT stung Dania's eyes. She blinked and groaned as a deep pounding seared through her brain. She grabbed her head.

The pain was maddening. If this was what Matara had gone through when they'd taken her, would the girl have had the inner strength to survive?

"Are you okay?" the doctor asked, dimming the overhead lamp.

If she were okay, she wouldn't be grabbing her head. "What happened to me?"

"You passed out." He turned the lamp away. "I think you caught a small bug on Midway Station. I'm treating you with a broad-spectrum antibiotic. You should be better in no time."

His temperature increased slightly—a sign of deception—but she sensed no malice in his voice. It seemed the doctor truly wanted to treat her. If that were true, though, then why lie? Maybe he knew something he didn't want Dania to find out.

She held out her arms. Her uniform shimmered as if she'd just received it from the tailor. "My clothing is no longer soiled."

The doctor pointed at a machine on the far side of the room. "I have a laundry recycler. I usually use it for sterilizing sheets, towels, and gloves, but it worked like a charm on your uniform as well."

Which meant, he'd undressed her…

He rolled his eyes with over-zealous abandon. "Oh, please, sweetie. What kind of a doctor would I be if I didn't make sure you were clean?" He waved his hand at her. "Don't worry, all of the other guys were on the far side of the ship."

The room spun, and she scrunched her eyes closed.

"Whoa there," the doctor said. "Take it easy. Let the medicine do its work. You've had a rough night."

She rubbed her temples. "I've never been sick. I highly doubt I've caught something. I think you're wrong."

He sat beside her. "Well, you were sick at least once, when you were ten. That's how the Banes found you."

She lowered her hands. "What?"

"You had parents once, but the Banes showed interest in you, and it looks like your parents agreed to sell you into slavery."

Dania's hands balled into fists. "Ridiculous. I'm not a slave. The only family I've ever known is the Banes." She should kill him now for insinuating such a thing.

Espinoza leaned against the far wall. "Why didn't you tell me Prince Geron was your patron?"

Dania balked. She hadn't even noticed he'd been standing there. Her senses were normally much more in tune to her environment. What was wrong with her? "Who my prince is makes no difference. You are a criminal either way."

The smuggler stared her down and she fought not to look away. "Word has it that he personally asked for my head. Is that true?"

There was no reason to lie. "Yes."

"Then why am I still alive?"

Good question. Her desire to wreak justice had quelled of late. Yes, she still intended to execute all these people, but she wasn't in as much of a rush as she'd been in the past. She lifted the shackles on her wrists. Could these arcane devices have drained her too far?

It was more than that, though.

She sat up, and the med bay spun. A deep ache settled between her eyes, and she held her head as the ache started to drum.

Was this what her life was to be now—pain anytime she moved?

Espinoza still glared at her.

And they said *enforcers* had no empathy.

She leveled her gaze at him. "At first, I thought you were the trapper whom I'd been tasked to find and eradicate. Once I realized that wasn't true, I was intrigued to learn why you would take me on board when there was a price on your head." Her head continued to throb. She closed her eyes and rubbed her temples. "Then, of course, you provided that sealed evidence about Filluck Palogivan. I must admit, I'm intrigued. I want to know who sealed that file."

Cal pushed away from the wall. "Intrigued enough that you won't kill us?"

Lying would do her no good. Espinoza had proven to not be a fool. "That still remains to be seen."

"If I set you free right now, would you be honor-bound to kill me because your prince asked for my head?"

Would she?

If she rid the galaxy of this criminal, it would be unlikely for the rest of the crew to cooperate and show her where all their illicit trading spots were.

And there was still the issue of the sealed security records proving Espinoza had not committed the crime that had led to Geron asking for the man's head. Who'd sealed those files, and why?

So many questions, and not enough answers.

The ache deepened.

If she were free, if she no longer had this blazing pain in her skull, would she be able to stop herself from carrying out her duty?

She lowered her hands from her head. "I can't guarantee one way or another. I'm unable to ignore an order from my prince."

"That's probably the truth," the doctor said. "The pathogens running through her seem to control the compulsion centers."

Pathogens? Probably more nonsense about her being sick. At the moment, the only things causing her discomfort were the illicit steel bindings.

She steadied herself with a cleansing breath. "I would like to know who sealed the file that proved your innocence. Until that's clear, I will allow you to live."

"Only until you know who sealed the files?" The doctor frowned. "Even though you've seen proof that Cal is innocent?"

"He is only innocent of murder."

"It's all right, Doc." Espinoza walked toward the exit. "I'll take what I can get for now."

CAL HAD a woman on board his ship who didn't like him, and she'd all but admitted that she'd kill him if she decided it suited her on any given day. This trip just kept getting better and better.

Ty met him outside the door. "You know, it's perfect that she has doubts."

"Eavesdropping again?"

"Think about it, boss. She's getting more and more human every day. She's even starting to look more human. Her hair is turning more blonde, rather than the shimmering silver color."

That part at least was true. If this kept up, she might even be able to pass for human someday.

"All we have to do is keep convincing her you're a great guy, and she'll have her prince drop the charges."

Drop the charges? Why in the name of Jupiter's moons was he living in fantasyland? They were dealing with a Kever prince. The royal family had no feelings and no remorse. It was like dealing with sentient reptiles.

Cal stopped and shoved Ty against the wall. "Don't you

get it? It's not that simple. She's not just gunning for me anymore. She's gunning for all of you."

Ty smiled that grin that had gotten them out of so many slippery places. "We're all equally guilty of the smuggling charges. Once she sees what smuggling is really like, we'll all be off the hook."

"Don't count on it." Cal started walking again. "I still want to drop her off at the next waystation and make a run for it. Ask Alanna to rest up because she'll probably have to jump us."

"No."

Cal spun on him. "No?"

"We've all voted. We're taking her with us."

Cal pointed at his chest. "Ethan sided with me. We all agreed three votes wasn't good enough on this ship."

That annoying smile returned. "Alanna convinced him."

"That's playing dirty." He could still override them, though. This was a democracy, but this was still his ship. "In case you haven't noticed, we have a ton of highly illegal items onboard. If you want to convince this woman not to kill us, she can't stay here."

"Yes, she can. This is the perfect way to show her how you can do something good with something illegal."

"But what we have is a little more illegal than most things."

The compact power source that Christopher Columbus had given them could certainly be used for good, but out here, and knowing what kind of people they were dealing with, that little piece of technology could be turned into a major weapon.

They needed the money, but Cal wasn't sure if he could live with himself if this tech got into the wrong hands. For now, though, it was all they had to trade. They just needed to hope that the person they traded it to didn't have any disreputable intentions.

———

Cal wiped the sweat from his brow with the back of his hand as Doc lowered the landing ramp. They'd traded in tons of places. Some good, some bad. Most trading posts were a combination of the two. Port Walker, unfortunately, tilted more toward the bad side of the scale.

He led the rest of his crew from the ship with Ethan and Ty flanking Dania, still in handcuffs. When the bright, natural sunlight hit her hair, it was more obvious that her natural blonde tones were taking over the enforcer silvery-white. To anyone seeing her, they'd think she was a normal prisoner. There would be no reason to suspect she was anything different.

"Where are we meeting?" Alanna adjusted the small light refractor weapon at her hip.

"Room nine seven one," Cal said. "It's uncomfortably far back from the landing site, but it was all we could get."

This was one of those stations that saw a lot of trading, some legal, some far from legal. While many stations allowed transactions to happen in public spaces, as Cal preferred, this colony favored all transactions happening in private. He supposed that made things cleaner for the local government. Cal preferred being out in the open, though. It let him see what was coming. Then again, that hadn't helped him much in the last trade.

Dania's gaze kept flashing toward Alanna's weapon. Certainly a being who could pull molten particles out of a man's back without even touching him had no use for such a small sidearm. Still, Cal moved between them, keeping his eyes forward.

He would have rather left Dania on board, but the crew had agreed that she needed to see them complete this very illegal trade so she could understand the endgame. Cal could only hope that they all lived to see this through to the final trade on Kirato.

A guard held up a hand as they neared. "Pass?"

Cal held up a purple card.

"Violet, this way." He pointed to a door on his right.

"Ready?" Cal asked them.

"Let's do it," Ty said.

They slipped inside. In the rear of an oversized chamber, a man sat at a lone desk with a glowing stone centered on the old-fashioned wood frame. The overhead lighting glistened off his nearly bald scalp as he shifted his substantial girth and smiled.

Cal held his hands out to his sides. "Glenn, buddy, how are you?"

"Calvin Espinoza." Glenn stood, accepting the hug.

He smelled faintly of grease and...was that fried chicken?

Glenn sank back into his chair. "When I heard it was you, I thought someone was pulling my leg. It's been almost a year."

"Well, I haven't had anything good enough for you in all this time." Cal looked over his shoulder. He trusted Glenn, but there were a lot of shadows surrounding them, and too many places to hide.

Glenn's grin warmed as he held up a paper cup that

looked like it contained old-fashioned french fries from Earth.

"Where did you get those?"

Glenn chuckled. "A man always finds a way to get life's little necessities."

Only Glenn would think french fries were a necessity.

"So, my friend, did you bring what Tyler said you have to trade?"

Cal nodded. He could feel Dania's judgmental stare boring holes through his back. "Yeah, I got it. Ty said you seemed overly interested. What do you want it for?"

Glenn plucked a french fry out of the cup and waved it around. "It's not your concern once you've traded it."

But it was a concern, and Glenn damn well knew it.

They stared at each other until Glenn busted out in laughter. "Relax, my friend. I'm going to sell it, of course. That's our business, right?"

Yeah, but sell it to whom? "This isn't the kind of tech you want to send to the highest bidder."

Glenn's eyes widened. "Oh my, do you think I've taken up with terrorists now?"

"I hope not, but stranger things have happened lately." Like dragging an enforcer along on a trade deal.

Glenn snickered and swallowed another fry. "No worries, my friend. When you called, I found a buyer in minutes."

Cal stepped back. "Who?"

Glenn folded his hands. "The mayor of the Tigelan colony on Aster Nine just lost the main power supply for their asteroid shield, and they're using their backup. He's looking to get a replacement ASAP."

Ty moved forward. "That's not a rich colony. They can't

afford that kind of tech, unless you're selling it way below market value."

Glenn chucked again. "My, my, boy, are you worried about my financial stability? So kind of you."

But Ty was right. "It *is* concerning," Cal said. "You aren't really the charitable type."

Glenn sighed. "Cal, Cal, Cal...like you, I'm in this for the money, but the last thing I want to see on the market is a weapon that can kill children from miles away. It's bad enough that the royal family sends out those horrid enforcers killing everyone who forgets to say *God bless you* when someone sneezes."

Dania shifted behind him. Thank goodness her hair no longer moved on its own. Without that unique feature, no one would believe she was an enforcer.

Still, Cal held his breath. The uniform she wore was common enough. Several colonies' police forces had copied the style, probably because people were so afraid of it. Still, Cal wished they'd thought to change her clothes.

He trusted Glenn, but he didn't think even his friend would be able to resist the bounty on a captured and restrained enforcer.

Glenn leaned back. "I won my trade goods in a poker game, so I'm not losing any money at all. To be honest, I'm pretty happy to be rid of this stuff. It's a bear to store, and there's always the worry of a blasted enforcer showing up with a good nose sniffing me out."

That, Cal could understand. Some cargos were a lot harder to hide than others. "Okay, let's see the goods, then."

Glenn pressed a button hidden on the back of his desk, and a metal case hovered toward them. "As I stated, I have thirty cases just like this. All identical. If you don't trust me, you can have your people go through them."

Ty opened the case, and the smell of citrus filled the room. Cal's mouth watered as Ty picked up a large, round orange.

Dania growled from behind them. "Trading consumables, especially citrus, outside the main food stores is illegal. That fruit is probably stolen."

Glenn chortled, holding his belly. "Your prisoner better watch it, or she'll be in for worse than whatever you're sending her to." He narrowed his eyes. "Why *do* you have a young lady in handcuffs, Cal? That doesn't seem like your style."

"She's not your concern. Please have the crates delivered to my ship. Once they start loading, I'll give you the power source."

Glenn inclined his head. "I'll have them sent straight away. Should I call in for your immediate departure?"

"Of course." Cal checked the shadows again. "Like you said, no one wants to be caught with fruit on board. I want to unload these containers as soon as possible."

Glenn stood and shook Cal's hand. "Consider it done, my friend. Safe trading to you."

"And you."

They backed out of the room, and Cal handed the purple card to the guard.

"That went well," Ty said.

Behind them, the guard talked into his shoulder, seeming to forcibly muffle his voice.

A chill ran down Cal's back. Everyone knew fresh fruit traded like gold on Earth, and Cal was about to transfer a huge haul. Those cartons of citrus had been on this station for days already, though. If anyone wanted to steal them, they could have taken them from cryo-storage at any time.

Unless it was easier to snatch them when they were already on the way to the hangar.

Cal picked up his pace, grabbing Dania and dragging her along. "We need to get out of here. Fast."

"What's up?" Ethan asked.

"I just have a bad feeling, that's all."

Three men, clad neck to toe in black, turned into the hallway and pulled out guns. "There they are!"

Crap… Cal hated it when he was right.

"In here." Cal pulled them all into a side room as fire lit up the hall.

"Look for a back exit." Ethan pulled Dania and Alanna behind a metal partition. He winced, his face scrunching up.

The painkillers must be wearing off. It was dumb of Cal to have Ethan come out on this trade. *Shoulda, woulda, coulda,* as his mom used to say… There was nothing he could do about it now.

Alanna palmed her small sidearm and aimed it at the door. When it opened, she shot three times, and two bodies fell.

Ethan held up his hands. "Remind me to never piss you off, beautiful." His grin seemed half-hearted. He probably hadn't been anticipating a problem, either, or he might have opted to sit tight for a few more days.

Another blast came through the door, and a hole exploded in the wall just over Ethan's head.

Cal tensed. That was way too close.

"Over here!" Ty called.

Alanna and Cal gave cover fire as Ethan ran Dania

toward Ty's voice. Then they followed the others through a narrow hallway.

Cal gritted his teeth. They weren't running in the right direction. But not getting shot was their primary concern. They sped through the corridor, Cal taking out the lights, before Ty pushed through the last door into a small room. Tables lined a small gathering place with no exits.

Ice chilled Cal's veins. They were trapped.

Ty cursed, spinning toward them. "I'm sorry!"

"Take flanking positions," Cal said. "There are enough of us to defend."

Cal and Ty flipped over the metal tables and threw the chairs on the floor. They weren't much, but if they tripped a few of their attackers, it was something in their favor.

Dania eased behind one of the tables. Her expression seemed…bemused. Did she really want to see them all dead so badly?

A bolt of light blasted into the room. Alanna fired, and something thumped to the ground.

Ethan held up his palm for a high-five. "That's my woman."

Alanna pointed her gun at him. "I am *not* your woman."

"Yet." He turned his attention back to the door, wincing.

Only Ethan could be in that much pain and still manage to hit on Alanna.

Cal centered his sights down the hallway. "Could we please focus on not dying, people?"

Ethan looked over the partition and gasped. His face twisted again.

They should have left him on the ship. He was in no condition to be under fire.

Cal handed him a small pistol from his own boot. "Why did you leave the ship without a gun?"

He shrugged. "I'm a pacifist. And she's here." He pointed at Alanna. "And you have to admit, a babe packing iron is pretty hot."

Cal shoved the gun into Ethan's hand. "Shoot the damn thing."

The engineer leaned around Alanna and fired. A body thumped to the floor. *Pacifist, my ass.*

More bolts blasted over their heads.

"I'm running low," Ty called. His next shot glowed orange, not yellow. Not good.

"Me, too." Alanna sent three more bolts through the entrance.

The firepower suddenly stopped.

"Calvin Espinoza?" a voice called.

Cal jolted at the sound of his name. The crew looked at each other, gaping.

His ship was registered, but he hadn't left his name when they'd docked. That was protocol, giving traders and smugglers as much anonymity as possible.

There was no reason to deny their identities, though. Cal leaned up but kept behind the partition. "Whom do I have the pleasure of speaking with?"

"My name's Max. We have no beef with you. You're free to leave."

Cal looked at Ty. His first mate shook his head, and Cal agreed. No one expended that much firepower and then just let you walk away.

"The terms?" Cal asked, but he knew the answer. Thirty cases of oranges were a massive haul for any trader out here. It was a huge loss, but he'd give them up to save the crew.

"The terms are simple," Max said. "Leave the enforcer. Tie her to something so she doesn't give us any trouble, and the rest of you walk out of here."

Alanna cocked her weapon and whispered what sounded like *mother plucking cow-herds* as she pointed her gun at the door.

"I'm sorry." Ty wiped his nose with the back of his hand. "This is my fault."

"It's no one's fault." Cal ducked farther behind the panel, easing to the floor. "I need ideas, people."

Ty looked at Dania, his gaze drawing to the handcuffs. His lips thinned. He'd led them down this hall, and now Dania was right back in danger from the very trappers they'd saved her from in the first place.

Cal looked over both his shoulders. There had to be a way out of this light-forsaken hall!

"We're not giving her up." Ty spun to Ethan. "Give me the keys."

Ethan's eyes widened. "What keys?"

Ty's lips parted. "I told you to grab the keys to the handcuffs before we left the ship."

Ethan felt through his pockets. "I-I don't have them."

Behind them, Dania shrank closer to the floor. Her gaze darted through the room.

She looked more annoyed than scared. Maybe they were right about how powerful she was. Of course, they couldn't get the cuffs off to see. Hopefully, this wouldn't be the death of them all, because he knew his crew. They wouldn't sell their worst enemy into slavery, even if it was to save their own skins.

Dania caught him staring at her and smiled. "Quite the problem."

"Yeah," Cal said. "You do realize this crew won't give you up, and they're probably going to die defending you."

Her smile deepened. "Probably."

Cal sneered. "They're innocent in all this."

"They're far from innocent. They all committed a crime just minutes ago. Citrus trading, as I pointed out, is illegal without a license."

This was like talking to a computer. He pointed to his crew. "These people are about to be executed for the crime of protecting you. Can you live with that?"

She glared at him, unmoving.

Apparently, she could.

"Espinoza?" Max called.

"Hold on," Cal said. "We're trying to contain her." He got on his knees before Dania, setting his gun on the floor. "Those men are about to come down that hall unloading an arsenal over our heads. Please don't let this happen. These people are my family."

She held up her hands. "I can't help. I'm restrained." Her expression dripped with smugness.

If she kept this up, he might forget she was a woman and punch her in the face.

She wasn't helpless. She'd drawn ion particles out of Ethan's back with those cuffs on. She could do *something*, and something was more of a chance than they had now.

A sizzling sound filled the room, and a heavy object clunked to the metal floor.

"Bomb!" Ethan cried.

They all hit the deck before a low explosion and a

rumble filled the room. Smoke billowed up, surrounding them. Footfalls tromped through the fog.

Dania fingered a small hole in her uniform from a piece of flying shrapnel. "Now I'm annoyed."

Is that all it took? If Cal had known that, he would have ripped her clothes when all this had started.

Another small bomb sailed over their heads and landed at Dania's feet. Snarling, she snatched the round metal casing and threw it back at the advancing trappers. Several voices cried out before it exploded.

Ethan's brow rose. "Damn, that's my kind of woman."

Dania kneeled. "I tire of this." She pointed her chin at Ty. "You." Then at Ethan. "And you." She placed her hands on the floor, pulling the cables of the shackles tight. "Both of you set your weapons to laser, and hold them until they're expelled."

Ethan cocked his head. "That won't do anything. That's Palian steel."

Her lips rose in half a grin. Cal shivered. She obviously knew something they didn't.

"Do it," Cal told them, as the shouting started outside the door again.

Yellow light illuminated Dania's face as Ty and Ethan unloaded the last of their weapon's energy into the handcuffs. Ethan's weapon went dead and then Ty's, but the handcuffs remained.

A thousand curses came to Cal's mind, but none of them sounded harsh enough. They'd just wasted two guns.

He stared at her. "You've killed us."

Her half-smile became full. "Not yet, little smuggler."

Smoke billowed about her as she lifted her hands, and

the cables connecting her wrists melted into a puddle at her feet.

Ty cursed from within the smoke.

Cal shivered, barely able to move. They'd done it. They'd set her free.

He'd been flying through the galaxy with a virtual nuclear weapon on board, and now she was about to go off.

She stood and stared down the corridor, death in her gaze, before a beam of light sliced through the air, hitting her shoulder.

Dania fell back and growled. "That stung!"

Yeah, getting hit with a light razor did that.

She stood, only to get sliced on the other arm. She fell again, staring at one of the wounds.

As she tried to get up again, Cal pulled her back to the floor. "News flash, sweetheart. Guns can hurt you."

She glared at him. "Not me."

He pointed to her bleeding arm. "All evidence to the contrary."

Her brow furrowed.

She could deny it all she wanted, but those cuts had to hurt.

Her lower lip trembled. Was this pride, or blind dumb foolery?

Alanna slid to her side. "Please stay down. Why give them a target?"

Dania held up her arm. "They shouldn't have been able to shoot me."

"But they did." Alanna looked over her shoulder at the door. "We'll figure it out."

Dania stared at Alanna's gun. "How much of a charge do you have?"

Alanna looked down at her gage. "Twenty-five percent."

Dania held her wrists out, showing the metal bracelets the cables had been connected to. "Hit these with the entire charge."

Alanna leaned away, shaking her head.

Cal pulled Dania back. "That will take both your hands off."

Her gaze lanced him. "I'm incapacitated."

Was this supposed to be new information?

She snarled at him, holding up the bracelets. "I. Need. These. Off."

Cal got into her face. "If she blasts you, it will slice clear through your wrists. You'll lose your hands."

She lifted her chin. "Not if I stop her in time."

Despite the defiant stance, Dania's eyes quaked. For the first time since Cal had met her, the mighty enforcer actually looked scared.

"It's my choice," Dania said. "I'd rather have no hands than be taken."

Cal leaned back. If he were in the same position, he might feel the same.

He grabbed Alanna's weapon. She wouldn't be able to live with herself if she hurt someone by accident.

He met Dania's gaze. "Ready?"

A blast exploded over their heads. Alanna cried out as the table fell on her.

Ty and Ethan scrambled to free her.

"Now or never!" Cal said.

Dania took a deep breath and held out her wrists.

Cal steadied his aim and flicked the igniter.

He hoped this worked.

CHAPTER 16

DANIA

DANIA PULLED AWAY from the weapon when the melting bracelets stung her skin. The first binding dripped to the floor, and a hum filled Dania's mind as the visceral power she'd been cut off from reached for her.

Another explosion, and Ty pulled Alanna into his lap, slapping her face until she opened her eyes. He looked relieved when she took a breath, but they weren't safe yet.

The second bracelet dripped to the ground, the illicit metal carving a hole in the tiles as its liquid form ate through the flooring. Her wrists burned and ached, but the power of her prince—drained, but still tangible—returned to her.

"Dania?" Espinoza's gaze held concern.

His heartrate increased. He didn't want to die. This man was inordinately wary of her. Which she supposed wasn't odd for a smuggler. His distaste seemed more than that, though…something personal.

No matter. They'd freed her for a purpose. One she was more than happy to accomplish.

Dania reached for more power, but it didn't come. She was free, but she wasn't anywhere near her full strength.

Another bolt of light shot over their heads. She might not be able to save them all as the captain had obviously hoped, but she might be able to get a few of them out alive.

Taking a deep breath, she stood.

The copper-haired engineer cursed and rolled away from her.

"Here we go." Ty smiled at her then looked back to the door. Very trusting, for a criminal.

Alanna moved beside her, pulling out an old-fashioned bullet-loaded sidearm.

The woman blinked, as if dizzy. "I have a few rounds left. I can cover you."

"You were just unconscious," Dania pointed out.

The pink-haired woman's eyes narrowed. "I can still shoot better than any of these guys."

Dania huffed out a laugh, then caught herself. There was nothing amusing about this situation.

The woman still had her focus on the doorway, gun set, and appearing more than ready to make good on her promise.

Something about the woman's determination, the comradery, warmed her, but Dania shook away the thought. She'd never been backed up by a human before. The woman would probably be a liability, but she supposed Alanna was preferable to Espinoza.

Dania's skin tingled, coming alive after far too long as the essence of her prince reignited. She raised her hands to focus the increasing force. It wasn't the flood of energy she was used to, but the warmth still filled her like an old friend. She drew in a deep breath, reveling in the power. She'd never take it for granted again.

Nor would she allow these trappers to do the same to another of her kind.

Focusing on the doorway, she set the energy inside her free.

The warmth burst from her fingers, swirling up into a billow of yellow before her power shot through the door and exploded on the other side. The smell of scorched flesh rose over the trapper's screams. Several weapons discharged, one blast entering the room and exploding behind Dania's head.

She twitched, her chest clenching as the screams outside the doorway rose to a feverish pitch. She wasn't supposed to kill the trappers. The chances were slim that their leaders were out there, risking their lives alongside their men. She was supposed to let them take her back to their lair and then dismantle the entire operation from their core.

Instead, the criminals outside cried out in agony, hitting the floor one at a time as they took their final breaths.

Dania lowered one hand, rubbing her chest to soothe the odd ache. A direct order from her prince and her king had been broken. What she'd just done should have been impossible. One simply didn't disregard orders.

Yet there she stood.

Dania thought about the photographs posted on the smuggling networks of beaten and shackled enforcers, treated worse than animals in cages and placed on display for bragging rights. One day, Matara's photo would probably be among them. Especially now that Dania had quashed her chances of finding the leaders.

These trappers deserved death for the horrors they'd inflicted on her kind, though. They'd relinquished their right to live the second they'd committed a crime against their king.

Her prince's warmth eased through her, egging her forward to make sure none escaped. She needed to make sure the kills were clean. No survivors. That was the only way to see justice done.

A deep sense of satisfaction swept through her.

The doctor was wrong. Enforcers were not slaves. They were punishers, meant to tame the galaxy and make the stars safe for those who would bow to the king's rule.

Today, the galaxy *was* a safer place. She'd find Matara and take out their leaders another time.

The screaming stopped, and Dania drew back the remainder of her power. It returned in a fluid sweep, and she tilted her head back, savoring the strength.

Alanna gulped. "Wh-What did you do?"

The men gawked at her.

Dania tilted her head. "I eliminated the problem, as you asked."

Espinoza's cheek ticked. He looked to the doorway. The muscles in his back seemed to tighten under his shirt before he turned back to his crew. "She's right. It's no different than if we'd taken them all out with gunfire. Let's go."

He stood, and the others stared at her for a moment longer before following down the hallway. Alanna glanced over her shoulder at Dania. The woman seemed paler than when she'd lost consciousness. Weren't they happy to be safe? Wasn't that the goal?

Gray tendrils of smoke rose from the ashen remains of

the bodies that could still be identified as once human. Alanna sniffed as she stepped over one of the charred, smoking lumps. The smell was unpleasant, but it was far from bad enough for her eyes to water like that.

Alanna cringed, looking back at the remains of the men who certainly would have killed her, if they'd had the chance. Was she upset that they were dead? If so, why?

The engineer reached down and picked up a dropped weapon, then another.

Alanna hugged her shoulders. "What are you doing?"

"These things aren't cheap." He shoved a gun into his waistband. "And who says we might not run into more trouble?"

"He's right." Espinoza scavenged a weapon of his own. "These could be good in a fight, and no need to leave them here to get sold on the black market."

Dania stepped over a smoking, blackened torso. This was not the real reason for picking the bodies clean, but it was a good enough excuse for her to allow him to obtain a few of the more powerful—and illegal—firearms.

Espinoza picked up his pace once they cleared the trail of bodies. They sprinted down the hall and into the hangar bay. On the other side of the platform, the *Star Renegade's* docking plank was down, and workers slid the canisters of illicit fruit into the ship.

The doctor stood at the entrance, directing the movement of the goods. His eyes widened when he saw them, and he ducked back inside.

A man pushed the final canister up the ramp, then waved to Espinoza as he approached. "This is the last one. It's all on board."

So, they'd accepted their cargo of illegal food. If they

really had thirty cases, Espinoza was a rich, and very *dead* man.

"Skip." Espinoza stopped short. "If it's not all A1 prime merchandise, as promised, I'm going to come back to haunt you."

Skip held out his hands. "You bet it's all real. Do you want to check?"

A particle beam exploded over their heads.

Espinoza ducked. "Can't. Gotta go."

Dania spun, throwing up a shield of power between the attackers and the ship. Her hands trembled, and a few blasts sizzled through her defenses. A simple shield shouldn't have been so hard!

Her arms ached, as if the power had a weight she couldn't carry. The shield blinked, and her eyes grew heavy. The slices on both her shoulders burned, stinging like someone had cut her with a fresh round of knives.

She needed to stop expending so much energy so she could heal.

Espinoza ushered Ethan and Ty onboard, and the doctor leaned out and threw the captain a package.

Holding the shield with one palm, Dania snatched the bundle from the air. "What are you trading? What is worth thirty cases of illegal citrus?" The bigger question was... why was she still helping them?

Espinoza wiped his face with his hand as more trappers took cover, aiming at Dania's shield.

"It's a frame relay transducer."

He had to be joking. She ripped open the package with her teeth and palmed the tiny device.

The markings were clear. This simple piece of technology, in the wrong hands, was capable of putting a large hole in the side of a planet. Even holding such a thing was illegal.

Espinoza grabbed the octagonal tech from her and tossed it to Skip. "I'm trusting you to get that back to Glenn."

Alanna fired past the shield, and the advancing trappers dove behind a pile of large black containers.

Skip ducked as another blast came from the side and nearly hit him. "I will." He scooted out of the way of the fire.

A blast slammed into Dania's shield. She stumbled back a step as it faltered and fizzled out with a flash. She stared at her hands. Her shields never failed.

She summoned her strength, but nothing came. She had to have more power at her disposal than that!

Alanna pulled her down as the trappers opened fire on them.

The navigator fired over Dania's head. "Last time I checked, you aren't invincible." She pointed at Dania's wounds. "You need to be more careful."

Careful? Dania had never had to be careful, despite Alexander's constant warnings.

She ducked as another barrage of fire shot over their heads. The ache in her arms deepened. Dania bit her lip, regretting how harsh she'd been to her injured soldiers in the past. Cuts this deep actually *did* hurt as much as they'd said.

Beside her and Alanna, the ship roared to life.

Blinking out of her shock, Dania found Skip inching along the far wall toward a doorway. She couldn't allow a weapon with that much destructive power loose in the galaxy, even if it was earmarked to help a colony. She started after Skip, but Alanna grabbed her arm.

"We have to go," Alanna said.

"Not without the weapon." Dania pushed her back and raced toward the fleeing man, but a scream rang out behind her. Dania skidded to a stop as Alanna dropped to her knees, then fell to the deck.

Dania's chest clenched. Over her shoulder, Skip disappeared through the exit.

Espinoza's voice carried over the cacophony. "Alanna!"

Dania froze. Did she chase down the weapon, or help?

Back near the ship, the trappers advanced on Alanna's position. Espinoza ran to the woman, trying to get her up off the floor, but she didn't move.

Dania growled to herself. She needed to trust that Espinoza, and that *Glenn* person, would do the right thing with the illicit power supply. If she didn't give up on the weapon, Alanna wouldn't live to take another breath.

She ran back, calling up as much strength as she could muster and throwing up another smaller shield around Alanna and Espinoza. Several trappers slammed into the invisible wall. Blood coated their faces as they grabbed their noses.

Pressing her other hand into the air, Dania clenched her teeth as Alanna's prone form rose off the ground and floated. Dania grimaced as blood seeped from the lacerations in her arms as if she were using her muscles, and not her power, to move the woman.

Espinoza stumbled back, wide-eyed, as Dania floated Alanna into the ship.

He shook off his blank stare and waved Dania toward him. "Come on!"

She looked back to where Skip had disappeared. All her training told her to go after him, but part of her dearly wanted to trust that this smuggler wouldn't set something free on the galaxy that would do so much harm. Her stomach settled as if she'd convinced herself it was true. She needed to trust herself. She had no soldiers to assist her and few options that led to survival other than getting on Espinoza's ship.

Dania bolted up the gangway beside Espinoza as the doors started to close. Several blasts ignited against the metal, sparking as the entrance started to seal.

She slipped to her knees, shaking as she used the last of her strength to set Alanna's body on the ground.

Espinoza placed his palm on Alanna's forehead and looked past Dania. "Doc, you got this?"

"Yes." The doctor grabbed a bag from a compartment in the wall. "Get out of here."

Espinoza stood and flipped a switch beside the door before sprinting down the hall.

The ache in Dania's chest seeded deeper than the cuts in her arms as the doorway clanged shut. She'd just allowed an illegal act. She could have executed that courier and stopped the power supply from leaving the hangar bay.

Yet she hadn't. Instead, she'd saved the smuggler's navigator—a woman probably guilty of all the same crimes as her captain. She crawled to Alanna and swiped the hair back from the unconscious woman's face. Dania's stomach lurched as the doctor dropped to his knees beside them. Alanna lay limp, her lips parted unnaturally.

A weight built in Dania's chest and she reminded herself to breathe as the doctor fumbled with his bag.

Didn't he realize Alanna had been shot? Alexander would have healed her by now.

She punched the floor. "Hurry!"

The doctor jumped before steadying himself and injecting something into Alanna's neck.

The woman opened her eyes, lifted her head, and grabbed the blood-soaked slash on Dania's shoulder.

Dania bit back the pain and did her best not to pull away. This woman had stood beside her while the men had cowered uselessly. Dania wouldn't balk next to the woman now.

Alanna stared at her before taking two labored breaths, and easing her head back onto the deck. "Ouch."

Dania released her own breath, and her shoulders relaxed. She wasn't a medic, but Alanna's reaction had to be good. At least the woman wasn't unconscious anymore.

The doctor smiled down at his patient. "How many times have I told you to jump out of the way when someone is shooting at you?"

Alanna winced, grimacing. "Well, I guess you'll need to tell me one more time."

Dania sat and looked at the deck plates. Her eyes blurred and refocused as the weight inside her chest lifted. She rubbed the base of her neck, warding off the strange heaviness that had built there.

Had she been worried about a woman she didn't even know?

She glanced at the doorway as the ship hummed, lifting off the ground. If anything, she should have been horrified with herself for letting an illegal weapon loose on a trading station filled with criminals. But somehow she just... *wasn't.*

Beside her, Alanna turned and smiled at her. "Thanks."

Dania smiled back, nodding. Warmth flooded her—a sensation similar to sharing time with Alexander. She blinked and tried to refocus herself.

Why wasn't she more worried about the weapon?

Her reactions were off.

Wrong.

Human.

Dania's gaze trailed back to Alanna and then to the doctor.

What had these people done to her?

CAL SPRINTED ONTO THE BRIDGE, skidding to a stop before the front viewing pane. "Why aren't we out of the blasted landing area yet?"

"They aren't clearing us," Ty said.

"I don't give a rat's ass. Punch it."

His first mate shrugged. "You're the boss."

The ship banked up. Several people ducked their heads as they blew past the air shields and into the clear blue sky.

A mottled voice came over the comm. "This is border patrol. You have not been cleared for takeoff. Return to the landing platform immediately."

Cal had taken about as much as he could today. He grabbed the comm from Ty. "This is Captain Espinoza of the *Star Renegade*. We were just making a fair trade with Glenn and we were attacked without provocation. We're leaving whether you like it or not."

Cal hit the forward weapons array, and three bolts of energy left the ship, scattering the base's small shield. The shimmer of light faded...probably not from their blast.

Security was most likely afraid Cal would do damage getting out, and repairs cost far too much this far away from any engineering settlements.

The *Renegade* blasted through the atmosphere, but as soon as they reached free space, three enormous cruisers blocked their path.

"Double ambush." Ty adjusted the controls. "That's not border patrol. They knew we were here."

Yeah, Cal had the same feeling. That wasn't the way Glenn operated, though. Someone else must have tipped these guys off.

He hit the comm. "Doc?"

"Yeah, boss?"

"I kind of need Alanna up here."

"You're kidding, right? She's been shot."

"I get that, but we're all about to die."

The ship rocked. Ty banked down. Cal held on as his first mate swirled the ship between two surveillance pods and barely dodged a freighter that tried its best to lumber out of the way.

Alanna's frail voice came over the speaker. "I already tried to jump us. I c-can't concentrate."

The weakness in her voice made him feel like amoeba slime for even asking.

Several smaller ships left the big cruisers—high-end racers, the kind drug runners used...or trappers. The *Star Renegade* was fast, but it was only uncatchable because of Alanna. There would be no way they could outrun ships manufactured for speed.

"We are so screwed," Ty said.

Doc's voice came over the intercom again. "Ah, boss, the scary enforcer lady says to hold on."

A flash of light erupted in front of them, as if someone had just pointed them at the sun.

Ty cried out, covering his eyes. "There's a…" He squinted at the light. "I don't know what that is, but we're being drawn toward it."

Cal leaned toward the console. "And the other ships?"

Ty squinted, holding up a hand to the light. "It's hard to see, but it looks like they're backing off."

Cal called up his scanners and stared at the results. All the readings said the anomaly was a small black hole. *What the blazes?*

"Pull up!" he screamed.

"I can't." Ty's face reddened. "The controls aren't responding."

The trapper ships swarmed just outside the pull of the odd singularity, as if waiting for Cal to run so they could give chase.

Cal wanted to humor them. Facing the enemy you knew was much better than getting broken apart and smashed by a sinking chasm in space.

Doc started shouting obscenities, and Cal realized the intercom was still on. "What's wrong?"

The shouting continued.

Alanna screamed from the med bay, "What's going on?"

Cal had to hope that they were worrying about the same thing he was. The swirling vortex was about all he could handle at the moment.

Cal switched to the engine room. "Ethan, we have a black hole up here."

"A what?"

"You heard me. I need more power."

"Working on it!"

Ty glanced at Cal, sweat beading at his brow as he fought the controls sucking them in. "What's the plan, boss?"

Cal gulped, staring into the harbinger of their doom. The light filled every part of space, a blinding megalith that had sprouted out of nowhere.

No one had ever escaped a black hole once caught in its grip, and they were definitely caught.

He looked back to Ty and tried to put on a reassuring face. "As soon as the power comes up, we're both going to take the controls and then we bank down on the count of three. Full thrust."

"Will that work?"

Probably not, but they didn't have another choice.

Hopefully, they'd break free and then maybe they'd be able to outrun the trappers. They'd been in worse situations.

Well, maybe not worse, but some pretty bad ones.

The hole flexed and then shrank.

"Are you seeing what I'm seeing?" Ty asked.

Cal breathed a sigh of relief. They might actually make it out of this alive.

"Wait." Ty leaned closer to his instruments.

Cal ran another scan as the black hole stretched.

"What the…?"

The singularity shimmered, then widened, arching like it reached for them. The ship shook.

"Cal!"

"Hold on!"

The lights winked out in the ship. The black hole swallowed them, spinning the *Star Renegade* into its gaping maw. The stars swirled, flashing in reds, blues, and yellows. Cal's fingers dug into his chair as the ship vibrated.

"Hull integrity?" Cal cried out over the roar.

"Can't tell. Nothing works."

The galaxy sunk and rolled over them, twisting and distending until they slid out into the quiet of stars hanging in deep space.

Ty's heavy breathing filled the room.

Cal's hands gripped his chair. His ears rang like he was underwater.

It was like life had stopped, leaving the two of them hanging in space, trapped in the small, dark bridge area.

The lights flipped back on, and they both cried out.

Ty pumped his fist in the air. "Whoo! What a rush!"

Cal wiped his face. Yeah, it had been a rush, all right. He probably needed a new pair of underwear. "Where are we?"

Ty looked into his console. "This can't be right."

"What does it say?"

Ty turned to him. "It says we are seventeen quantums from our last location."

Cal turned back to the stars, looking for something familiar. The Brim Cluster shone back at him, and the Chupacabra Constellation. But that wasn't possible.

"Boss, we just flew about a week's worth of quantums in a few minutes."

Not only that, but they were right on their flight plan. That simply wasn't possible.

The doorway slid open, and Dania walked onto the bridge. Her uniform had been cut off at the shoulders, and a white bandage covered each of her forearms. Cal was too shocked to wonder why she was alone.

She smiled at them. "You're welcome."

Cal's knuckles whitened on his backrest. "You're welcome for what?"

ESPINOZA JUMPED up from his chair. He pointed out the window.

"You did that?" His eyes were wide. Manic.

Did he think the doctor had saved them, or maybe Alanna?

Dania tilted her head. "Of course it was me."

The skin along the edge of his dark hair glistened with perspiration. He actually looked surprised, like he had no idea how powerful enforcers could be. Maybe he had never encountered a full general before. Which made sense because if he had, he'd have been caught by now.

He spoke through clenched teeth. "You shoved us down the throat of a black hole."

To somewhere safer. What was his point? "I saved you."

"You could have killed us all."

But she hadn't. Why wasn't he happy with the result?

Dania glanced through the window. Holding the singularity should have been simple, yet she'd nearly lost control twice. Her hands trembled, and she wanted to sit, but she couldn't appear weak in front of these humans. Not now that she was free.

She *was* weak, though. She'd never had trouble focusing her primordial energy. She needed to get back home before she starved to death.

Espinoza advanced on her. "You will not put this ship and my crew in danger like that again. Do you hear me?"

"Your ship is fine." But he was right. If she'd lost control, they all would have been crushed.

Only Dania and one other enforcer—and the king, of course—had successfully called up a singularity for travel. It was dangerous, and she'd been warned to use the gift in an emergency only, and only when fully fed.

Dania's knees shook, and she backed up a step to support herself against the wall. She'd never felt so frail. The steel had done its damage.

Her sponsor could make her whole, though. Prince Geron always saw to her needs. He took care of all of his enforcers.

Espinoza's eyes softened slightly. "Are you okay?"

She nearly spat at him. How dare he insinuate there was something wrong?

"I'm fine." She pushed away from the wall. Her head spun, but she kept herself upright.

Ty jumped to his feet and grabbed her arm. "Are you sure you're okay?"

She shook him off and flopped into Alanna's chair.

Ty and his captain stared at each other and then looked back to her.

"Maybe we should bring you down to see Doc," Ty said.

"No." Now that she was seated, she was fine, and they had

serious issues to contend with—topics far more important than her being tired. She turned to Espinoza. "That power supply you just traded away could be turned into a weapon."

"I know. That's why I traded with Glenn. He doesn't want to see innocent people suffer any more than I do." He rubbed his eyes. "I trust him to get it to a colony that will use it for the right reasons."

There was no change in the smuggler's temperature, no sign of a lie. Both statements were true: that he didn't want to see anyone hurt, and also that he trusted Glenn.

Still, her stomach roiled. She'd feel safer if she had watched the device installed in the colony rather than watching it walk away where it could be lost or stolen.

There were other matters to deal with, though. "Were those containers you traded all filled with citrus?"

Ty turned to his station and tapped on the console. "According to the manifest, it's mostly fruits, some vegetables, and a few hundred pounds of protein bars."

How could he stand there and speak so calmly about stolen food? "I suppose the black-market value of that haul is enormous."

"Yes, it is." Espinoza sat in the captain's chair. "With that haul, we could live like royalty for years." He leaned toward her. "But you would know all about what that was like, living in a palace most of your life."

The air of sarcasm threatened to cut like a knife.

Geron didn't live in a palace. However, she did realize the Bane family home on Keveron, and even Geron's personal cruiser, were far more lavish than most commoners could ever dream of. She'd never really thought about it before. It was just the way it was.

Another tingle ran up her arm, like the shackles constricting even in their absence.

She flinched and shook her head to clear it. Espinoza was trying to deflect from the problem at hand.

Dania looked out at the stars. "I brought us here because this trajectory matched your flight plan, but why here? There aren't any trading outlets." And most criminals stayed in clusters. Their motto was *safety in numbers*, or something ridiculous like that.

The speaker sounded, and the doctor's voice filled the room. "Cal, can you come down here?"

Espinoza paled. "Is something wrong with Alanna?"

The doctor snorted. "Yes, she's a horrible patient. She's worse than you."

Espinoza smiled. It changed the structure of his face, his eyes. Dania warmed inside, but she wasn't sure why.

The captain stood. "I'll be right there." He headed for the door and stopped, glaring at her. "There are things in the galaxy that are lightyears more important than making money, lady." He turned away. "If you could get that through your head, you might make yourself a better cop."

Things more important than making money...like taking care of the pretty navigator?

This captain made no attempt to hide where his favors lay. The crew was a liability he probably wasn't even aware of. Dania just needed to find a way to use that to her advantage.

IF CAL STAYED there with the enforcer much longer, he'd probably punch a wall...or worse. They'd all agreed not to tell her where the food was going, that she needed to see the transaction as a crime, but a crime for good. Doc seemed fairly certain this information would unravel that obnoxious enforcer rigidity.

With that one-track mind of hers, though, Cal wasn't sure she'd ever be able to accept that the law wasn't always right.

For some odd reason, he needed this to work. He wanted her to believe in them.

In their mission.

Maybe even in him.

Obviously, they still had a lot of work ahead of them.

Dania blocked his path. "I'm going with you."

He raised a brow. "You are?"

"I brought your navigator back to the ship. I want to make sure your doctor cares for her properly so my efforts were not in vain."

Cal smiled as he headed down the hall. This was one

thing that was going really well, and it hadn't even been part of the official plan. "It's nice to see you and Alanna are getting along."

Dania stopped short. She stared Cal down, and he could only dream of the maniacal thoughts running through that thick enforcer skull.

She started walking again. "Your navigator has some curious talents. I'd like to find out more about them."

That wasn't really unexpected. Dania's expression had hardened when Alanna had called up the jump circle.

Jumpers were rare in the galaxy, but they weren't illegal, as far as he knew. Maybe Alanna's gift could buy them all some more time. "It seems like you two have been talking a lot, too."

Dania seemed to consider that. "The conversations have not been unpleasant."

Which would make them—dare he suggest—*friends?*

Cal kept walking. He wasn't sure if an enforcer was even capable of that kind of emotional attachment.

The door to the infirmary slid open. Across the room, Alanna sat on her bed and grinned at him.

"I thought you'd been shot?" Cal asked.

"Clean wound." Doc fastened a bandage on Alanna's arm. "One graze to the torso, and the shot to her arm went right through. She was lucky."

Alanna rolled her shoulder. "Hurt like the dickens, though."

Cal grimaced. He needed to keep Alanna onboard. He hated to admit how much they all depended on her jump ability for their escapes.

She liked to get off the ship once in a while, though,

and he couldn't blame her for that. Everyone needed to take a breath of fresh air from time to time.

The unfortunate truth they all needed to remember was that what they did for a living was dangerous. They could all get hurt at any time, as Alanna, Ethan, and even Doc could attest to.

Doc wiped his hands on a white cloth. "I am okaying her to return to light duty. No lifting, and I think it would be best to avoid navigational jumps for a while."

Alanna's mouth fell open. "Why can't I do jumps? I don't need two arms for that."

Doc sighed. "There is no research on the effects of recent surgery on jump capability. There are too few people with that kind of power."

Dania shifted her weight. Her lips thinned. Had jumping been added to the king's list of crimes? Impossible, since the king could jump ships himself, and ten times farther than Alanna could. Maybe her ability just made the enforcer uncomfortable, since all registered jumpers were royal.

Doc threw the towel into the recycler. It popped out the other side, folded. "I'd like her confined to the ship as well."

"What?" Alanna stood.

Doc held up his hands. "You're hurt. I know we're short-staffed, but I'm seriously considering keeping Ethan in bed, too. I shouldn't have let him leave the ship as it is. Now you both need some rest."

Cal dragged his fingers through his hair. He'd hoped to get Ethan back to normal duty. They really needed a full complement once they reached Kirato. If he timed it right, maybe they'd all be back in the game by the time they got there.

All that citrus had an expiration date, though. The clock was ticking, and he needed to be prepared, just in case.

The plan had always been to bring Dania to the surface for the last trade. But that was when she'd been in hand-cuffs. Now that she was free, Cal wasn't sure how to manage this and keep all their heads intact.

Being shorthanded, though, might be the perfect excuse.

He turned to her. "It's time to start earning your keep."

The enforcer looked confused. "What?"

"Like Doc said, we're shorthanded. I'm going to need your help with our next mission."

She frowned. "Why can't you wait for your crew to heal?"

"Waiting is not a luxury we can afford." Espinoza called up a viewscreen. "This is where we're headed."

He pointed to planet Kirato's orbit around its sun.

"There is a small window of opportunity when it's safe to drop into orbit. In about thirteen hours, the sun will be in direct alignment with the long-range communications station on Elbus Three."

Dania walked over to the screen. "So?"

Cal pointed to the spatial representation, showing her the line of sight. "This leaves the colony on the planet in the dark communications-wise for three weeks."

She stared at him, obviously not understanding. That was because she didn't think like a smuggler.

"With communications down, we can get in, do what we need to do, and get out before anyone can squeal and bring the enforcers down on us."

Dania balked. "You're going there to trade the illegal food."

Yeah, this was when she'd probably blow a fuse. "Yes."

Her eyes flashed. "I will not be part of your larcenous dealings."

Cal turned from the screen. He shouldn't have expected another outcome.

It would have been nice if she'd agreed. They could have landed on the planet like one big, happy family. He would have told his crew he was sorry for doubting them and happily agreed that even enforcers could change.

They still needed her on the surface, though. Cal had agreed to that much. They just had to make sure no one died before their point had been made.

He eyed the bandages on her arms and grimaced, remembering the sounds of the trappers' screams and the smell of charred flesh.

Dania was every bit the same monster as the enforcer who'd killed Cal's father. Death was nothing more than an easy way to erase problems for them.

But Cal had seen Dania take small steps in the right direction, and if Ty was right, seeing Kirato would be enough to finally push Dania into realizing that the universe's laws shouldn't be so rigidly defined.

Dania took another look at the screen, shook her head, and walked to the center of the room.

He couldn't have timed that better if he'd tried.

Doc nodded, and Cal took a deep breath.

He trusted Doc, but the only thing that was certain was that one way or another, the enforcer was about to be royally pissed off.

Cal threw Dania a blanket. "Here."

She caught it and stared at the dark fabric. "What's this for?"

Cal hit the blue button on the wall. Doc could have done it, but Cal was still officially wanted for murder. This would just be one more charge to add to his list, and one less that Doc would be burdened with.

A spray of white light fell over Dania.

She reached out, and the shimmering field buzzed. She drew away, looking at her fingers. "What is this?"

"It's a specially calibrated force field, made from some of the medical equipment. We figured, without the Palian steel, you'd probably be able to walk right out of our detainment cells."

She narrowed her eyes, looking down at the blanket. "Do you really expect me to sleep on the floor?"

Really? He'd locked her in a six-by-six box and she complained about sleeping on the floor? "You'll need to get over it. You can't have free run of my ship."

"We've already discussed that I will not kill you today."

"Yeah, *today*. I don't want to wake up one morning and find out you've changed your mind."

She balled the blanket in her fists. "Fine. I will not kill you, or your crew, tomorrow, either."

Espinoza smirked. "If I thought I could trust you, we wouldn't be talking through a force field."

She sighed, dropping the blanket to the floor.

Alanna eased off her bed. "I'll stay with her."

Dania's head jerked up, and her lips parted.

Alanna grabbed a blanket and rolled it up, placing it on the end of a cot. "I know I wouldn't want to be alone here all night."

"What am I?" Doc asked.

"A guy," Alanna said.

Cal smiled as he slipped out of the room. This was actually good. The enforcer seemed to have taken a liking to Alanna. His navigator might be the ticket into breaking through the enforcer's titanium exterior.

Doc met him outside. "I'm a little surprised that worked on the first try."

"That's why you are the master of all things."

Doc pulled a small gun out of his waistband. "This is for a last resort only. I can't be sure, but I think it will pack enough punch to take Dania out, even if she calls up one of those crazy magical shields."

Cal slipped the gun into the holster above his boot. "Thanks."

Hopefully, he would never have to use it—for more reasons than he cared to analyze at the moment—but he knew they were all living on borrowed time with that woman. She could snap at any time, and if she did, he'd have to be quick. Maybe quicker than he really wanted to be, if he were being honest with himself.

His gut twisted, but he knew he'd need to be the one to shoot first.

The enforcer wouldn't give him a second chance.

DANIA PACED HER TINY PRISON. Did Espinoza really think he could get away with trapping her here? She sent a burst of energy into the shield, but it bounced back, stinging her.

The doctor turned a dial on a panel in the wall. "I've studied the pathogens in your blood and the way they resonate when you center your energy. This force field is calibrated to change constantly to keep ahead of your magic." He looked up at her. "It might sting a little more each time you try to get out. Sorry about that, sweetie."

There was that word *sweetie* again.

So, once more, she was trapped. And they'd done it so easily. Embarrassingly easily. "I suppose you will sell this technology to the highest bidder the first chance you get."

He shook his head. "I have nothing against enforcers. I think laws are good, and people should always try to do the right thing."

"Yet you've imprisoned me."

He adjusted the dial again. "I just think the enforcers can get carried away sometimes."

Alanna kicked her feet like a child as she sat on the edge of her gurney. "He's right. For instance, Cal shouldn't die just because someone thought he killed someone."

Dania lifted her chin "I agree."

The woman's eyes widened.

"However, he still has to die for his other crimes," Dania continued.

Alanna stopped swinging her feet. "Do you really think the only punishment for any crime, no matter what, should be death?"

"It doesn't matter what I think. That's the king's law." She strolled to the opposite side of her prison, studying the way the light resonated as she approached. "Was your previous penal system any better?"

Alanna lowered her gaze. "Maybe not, but death as the punishment for everything seems a little harsh. Some crimes are no big deal."

"Breaking the king's law is always a big deal."

"What about children?" Doc asked. "Kids aren't always even capable of understanding they've broken a law."

Alanna wiped her palms on her thighs. "Have you ever killed a kid?"

"Executed," Dania corrected.

She wouldn't have them insinuating that she'd done anything wrong.

Then again, the cries of that mother when Dania had pried her adolescent son from the woman's arms, the sound of the family wailing as the boy had screamed, twisting on the dirt trying to put out the flames as Dania's fire consumed him...

Her stomach lurched. She nearly fell to her knees.

What was wrong with her? That had been a clean execution. The boy had admitted guilt.

"Would you at least concede that maybe there should be levels of punishment?" Alanna slipped off the gurney and approached the shimmering wall between them. "I mean, you can't say all crimes deserve death."

Dania looked away. The smell of charred flesh wafted over her, the memory as fresh as the day she'd passed judgment. That child had trespassed on another's property. He had done so once. He would do it again.

But would that have been so bad?

The lights dimmed.

"Time to get some sleep, ladies," Doc said.

Alanna curled up on her gurney, facing the force field. She smiled without a hint of malice. "Goodnight, Dania."

Dania turned away, rolled the blanket into a ball, and used it as a pillow.

Her stomach clenched as the memories of hundreds of punishments flashed through her mind.

Every single one of those people had committed crimes. They all deserved to die.

Didn't they?

———

Lights flashed in her eyes, blazing against the white walls of the medical center. Dania blinked as the doctor knelt beside her.

The shimmering walls of the force field were gone. Across from her, the sheets were folded neatly on the gurney Alanna had slept on.

The doctor smiled as he tapped her cheek. "Rise and shine, sweetie."

She sat up. "Why do you keep calling me that?"

"Would you rather I called you *cold-hearted bitch?*"

She supposed not.

He stood. "We're heading down to the planet. The captain still wants you to come with us."

He did? Dania had made it clear that she wouldn't help them.

"Why would he want me to come? Does he want me to keep a running tally of his crimes?"

Dania tried to sit up and found her hands bound in thin, silver restraints. She raised a brow to the doctor. Was he serious?

She held up her wrists. "These aren't Palian steel."

"No, but studying your blood has been fascinating. I reengineered these just like I did the medical shield. You still have full access to your power, but if you try to use it..." He scrunched up his face. "Let's just say it will be quite unpleasant."

Had he thought the Palian steel had been a walk through a garden simulator?

She lifted her chin. "I don't think I've seen you commit a crime yet, Doctor. I may have been inclined to let you walk away." She held up the bindings again. "But this would be considered a crime against the enforcers, and thus your king."

He held up his pointer finger. "Only if my actions retard you from doing your duty." He walked to the other side of the room and picked something up off his desk. "Since you have full access to your powers, you can do your duty at any time. It's your choice whether or not you are willing to go through mind-numbing pain to get the job done."

Dania's lip twitched. That was an interesting interpretation of the law, which, while being inconvenient, she had to admit had merit. This doctor was apparently more intelligent than he'd initially seemed.

"If I have already agreed not to kill you today, then why do I need the restraints?"

"Captain's orders. Apparently, he doesn't want you passing judgment on anyone on the surface, either."

If they'd all simply abide by the law, they wouldn't be placing themselves at risk. Why these people failed to understand that was beyond her.

As they walked down the halls, Dania tested the integrity of the bindings, releasing small bursts of power at spaced intervals. Each time, she was hit with a sting of increasing magnitude.

The doctor's clever programming was both intricate and effective. She'd probably think through the revolving patterns eventually. For now, though, she'd have to endure whatever larceny she witnessed, cataloging each illicit act so she could return at a later date to dole out punishment where punishment was deserved.

They stepped off the ship onto a dry, sandy surface. The heat of the sun seemed like a punch after the more moderate temperatures on the ship. However the fresh air, despite the heat, was welcome.

The area was cleared for landing dozens of ships, but the *Star Renegade* stood alone, centered in the enormous circle lined with structures that appeared to be made of tan mud bricks, each with flattened dirt walking paths between them, and three larger openings that one might consider roads if they'd had more modern paving.

Espinoza adjusted a small metal device attached to his belt, and the shining metal cases holding their spoils rose from their cargo bays and floated over their heads, blocking out the sun.

Dania did a quick count. There were more than the original thirty she'd been aware of. Apparently, these thieves had been collecting their illicit goods for quite some time.

Ty and the doctor walked on either side of her, following Espinoza toward the larger cluster of buildings. Two small, dirty faces peeked through the windowless opening in one of the buildings.

One smiled. "It's the *Star Renegade!*"

A tone sounded, and the streets came alive. Children ran out, hugging Espinoza around the waist.

"Doc!" A dark-haired child not more than four feet tall jumped into his arms.

The doctor ruffled his grimy mop of curls. "Look how big you got."

"I'm seven!" The child held up six fingers before Doc placed him down and the little boy ran away.

"Your child?" Dania asked.

Ty snorted, and Doc pursed his lips at him. "No, sweetie. No kids for me. I just set a broken arm for him once."

It was odd, though. These people seemed to be celebrating this ship's arrival. Who celebrated the arrival of criminals?

One of the houses they passed had crumbled, leaving the insides exposed. It looked like someone still lived there.

Dania paused. Kirato was noted in the king's records as being a thriving trade center. Why was it so desolate and its buildings in such disrepair?

Espinoza dropped back and walked beside her. "Sad, isn't it?"

Sad wasn't quite the word she would have chosen. "What happened?"

Espinoza leaned his head back, letting the sun shine on his face. The slightest hint of stubble shaded his jawline. He was younger than she'd expected, maybe a year or two older than herself. Far too young to be hunted for so many crimes.

He turned his light blue eyes on her. "The outer rim colonies are feeling the hit of the war raging between the Banes and the Carteks."

That made sense. This colony was very close to the Cartek border. The Carteks had been known to lie in wait, stealing what they could.

Dania circumvented a hunk of stone that may have been part of the adjacent wall.

Espinoza held her arm as she stepped over some loose gravel. "With fewer traders willing to come this far out, the prices of simple necessities, like food, have become out of reach for most." He kicked some of the debris out of their way. "These people are using all they have just to survive. They can't afford to keep things in good repair."

Bile rose in her throat. These people were starving, and this criminal was about to sell them food, probably at an astronomical profit. He'd probably spew lies about supply and demand.

She tested the restraints again, more than ready to remove his head right now, but the sting lashed back at her.

She'd get them off eventually, though. She was wrong about this man. He was every bit the criminal she'd thought.

A woman in long pants with a rip up the side of her hip ran to them, clutching a child to her chest. "Are you Espinoza? Is your doctor here?"

Doc stepped forward. "What's wrong?"

The woman held out her child, a girl of maybe six years. "My little Katie. She's sick!"

The child's eyes bulged from their sockets and deep, red sores riddled her arms. Her head lolled to the side, as if she were moments from death.

Dania's gut clenched. She couldn't allow this. She wasn't a healer like Alexander, but maybe she could extract whatever was wrong, just like she'd pulled the invasive particles from the engineer's back.

She turned toward the doctor and raised her bindings. "Take these off me."

"No way," Espinoza said.

She spun to him. "I've already promised not to hurt you."

"What about the rest of the people on the planet?"

Dania looked into the child's absent gaze before turning back to Espinoza. "All right. I promise I will not execute anyone on this planet today."

The captain groaned. "You had to slip that 'today' in there, didn't you?"

Dania closed her eyes. This man needed to understand that there was just so far an enforcer could bend.

She opened her eyes and leveled her gaze. "That's the best I can do."

He stared at her, a thousand scenarios swirling through

his eyes. He needed to understand that she was serious, though. This was just a child. An innocent!

He turned away. "Fine. Take them off."

As the shackles fell to the ground, Dania placed her hands on the child while Doc ran a scanner over the girl. Dania searched for something to remove, just as she'd done with the engineer, but everything she found seemed to be a part of the child.

The doctor pulled on Dania's shoulder. "Stop."

"Why? We need to help."

"This isn't a poison or a virus that you can remove." He held up the scanner. "This is scurvy. She doesn't need something taken out. What she needs is vitamin C."

Dania reeled back, gaping at the mother. "Why don't you give her supplements?"

Tears streamed down the woman's face. "We haven't seen a supplement trader in years."

Ridiculous. No child on her watch was going to die from something as avoidable as scurvy.

Holding out her arms, she called to her prince's power. She warmed, soaking up his gifts before she levitated, floating up to where the canisters hung over their heads.

Finding the same canister that the trader Glenn had shown them, she willed it open and filled her arms with oranges.

After sealing the container from the sun's heat, she lowered herself to the ground. Dropping all but one of the fruits, she broke through the peel and held it to the girl's mouth. She called up more of her power, pushing every last drop of the vitamin C into the girl's bloodstream.

The mother wiped tears from her eyes. "Thank you."

Dania handed her the rest of the oranges. "Make sure she eats more as soon as she is conscious."

"I will." She choked back a sob. "A thousand times, thank you."

Espinoza smirked at Dania, folding his arms.

She stood. "What?"

"You do realize that you just distributed stolen goods, right?" He quirked a brow. "I do believe that's a crime."

Dania's nose flared. "This is a special case. It is not illegal to save a child."

"Even by distributing stolen goods?"

Dania hesitated. The law was clear. The distribution of stolen goods, for any reason, was illegal and punishable by death.

She looked at her palms, opening and closing her hands. Her programming should have stopped her. She should have realized what she'd been doing.

The mother folded the child in her arms as a man helped her collect the fruit. They smiled at each other, small lines forming around their eyes as if they'd shed far too many tears.

What Dania had done was wrong, but that child might live to her next birthday due to Dania's crime.

She should hate herself for forsaking her king, but she wasn't sure she wouldn't do it again.

Her chest grew heavy, a pain pressing in. How could she enforce the law if she couldn't abide by the laws herself?

CAL COULD BARELY BELIEVE IT, but a single tear had formed at the edge of Dania's eye and dripped down the side of her face as she watched the family walk away. She wiped the dampness from her cheek, then stared at her fingertips, as if this were something foreign to her.

If everything Doc said about what the Banes had done to her was true, maybe emotion was a new experience.

Ty nudged him with his elbow. "Still think this was a mistake?"

"That remains to be seen."

The enforcer looked up and around, seeming to take things in with a new set of eyes.

With any luck, she'd go back home and report to that blasted prince she loved so much and tell him that these people needed help. And hopefully, he'd care enough to do something about it.

Cal placed his hand on Dania's back. "Come on."

She turned her nose up at him, that flare of anger returning to her eyes.

He sighed. He'd hoped the kinder, gentler Dania would

stick around a little while longer. He guessed that was simply not meant to be.

"It's okay," Ty whispered. "We'll just do what we always do."

Cal shook his head, considering her unbound wrists. Hopefully, they'd all live to see the next sunrise.

Skirting more rubble, they made their way past the houses and headed toward the largest building in the colony.

It had been nearly six years since Cal had first stumbled through here. He'd been delirious from dehydration after stowing away on a cargo ship, hiding after being falsely convicted of murder. Despite the risk, these colonists had taken him in and given him a home. They'd shared what little they had with a stranger, asking for nothing in return.

Cal cringed, realizing he was doing the one thing he'd sworn he'd never do to these people…bringing the enforcers down on top of them. At this point, there was no turning back, though.

Cal dearly hoped, for the first time in his life, that Ty was right and he was wrong.

A lone man exited the mud-caked structure, wearing a once-white, now gray-stained robe and a turban-style head-covering hiding the edges of his thick black beard.

His gaze locked with Ty's, and a wide smile spread over his lips. "My boy!"

Ty took a deep breath beside Cal. It had been over three years since Ty had left Kirato. At the time, the kid had no intentions of returning. He probably never expected to miss his adopted parents so much.

Ty held up his palm. "Hey, Stanley!"

The kid was acting like coming home was no big deal,

but Cal knew better. Stanley's hospitality and enthusiasm were infectious, and hard to resist.

The old trader had been a good friend to Cal, hiding him in this very building when the authorities had swept through, looking for their murder suspect. Now, Cal was walking an enforcer right up to his doorstep. Hopefully, when Stanley saw her uniform, they wouldn't all get shot on site.

Stanley's wife, Amelia, pushed past her husband, wiping her hands on her apron.

"Tyler!" She ran toward Ty, her rounded form bobbing slightly in her wide skirts. "How's my boy? You look skinny. Aren't you eating?" She kissed both his cheeks.

"I'm fine, Mel."

She tapped his shoulder. "You better be." She turned to Cal. "And how's my handsome Calvin?"

Cal gave her his best grin. "Good to see you, Mel."

"Peter." She squeezed Doc's cheeks. "And how's the humble doctor?" She didn't wait for a response before turning to Dania. She looked her up and down. "You are not Alanna."

"Obviously," Dania said.

Dammit. Couldn't she be polite for just a second?

Stanley pulled his wife back, his gaze glued to Dania. "I trust this is an old-fashioned Halloween costume."

Cal looked down. "I wish it was."

Stanley and Mel had come in contact with far too many enforcers not to recognize that her uniform was the real thing, even with the missing arms. Cal should have insisted on new clothes for her, but with her initially in handcuffs, and then flying through the air like she did, there was really no hiding what she was.

Mel folded into her husband's arms. "Are-Are Alanna and Ethan okay?"

"Yeah, they're back on the ship, recovering," Cal said. "Actually, Dania saved both their lives."

The couple gaped at her.

"Why do they keep staring at me like that?" Dania took a step toward them. "You aren't criminals, are you?"

Cal pulled her back. "You made me a promise, remember?"

"But are they criminals?"

"No," Cal said with more force than he'd intended. "They're traders. Nice, legal traders. Good people, and you will treat them with a thousand times more respect than you give me."

She turned back to the couple. "My apologies. I should not have assumed." She placed her hand over her heart. "Your king appreciates the hard work of the good people in the galaxy."

Mel's gaze flicked nervously between Dania and Cal before she stepped forward, smiling. "Well, any friend of Calvin's is a friend of ours."

She shifted awkwardly, eyeing Dania's hair. Frowning, she glanced at Cal.

He knew the question that they were smart enough not to ask. Dania's hair had faded. It was even more blonde now than it had been last night. And it didn't move on its own anymore, not even when she'd hovered in the air like it was no big deal a few minutes ago.

"I suppose this is just a social visit." Stanley folded his hands. "No business?" His eyes darted to Dania again. Stanley knew enough about the universe to keep all his dealings under the radar, even refusing the food, if they had to, to avoid detection from the enforcers.

What was going through his head right now? He and Mel had opened their home to Cal, giving him more trust than he deserved. Now Cal would have to explain why he'd let the angel of death walk up to their front door.

Deep down, Cal wanted to tell them to run, but after she'd just saved that child, Dania seemed more open than ever, and they'd come too far to turn back now. He needed to ease some of this tension, though.

Cal put his arm on Stanley's shoulder. "Let's just do what we normally do."

His friend eyed the containers flying overhead. "Are you sure?"

No. But Cal nodded anyway.

Stanley stopped, staring into Cal's eyes. "I trust you like a son. You know this, yes?"

Cal wanted to hug him, tell him that he would never put him or his wife in harm's way. The words wouldn't come out, though, because he wasn't sure they were true.

Ty put his hand on Cal's shoulder. "Hey. We're good." He looked at his adoptive parents. "We promise, it's all good." He locked gazes with Stanley. "*I* promise."

Amelia flashed a dazzling smile. They both trusted Cal, but their trust in their little boy was something altogether different. "Then we must start making some cakes," she said. "I will make double, and you bring them back to Alanna and Ethan for me. Yes?"

Ty beamed. "I would jump off a ship in the middle of space to get to one of your cakes, Mel."

She ruffled his hair. "Then I will get baking while you boys play."

Stanley pulled Cal away from the others. "Please tell me that's not a real enforcer."

"She's promised not to kill anyone." *Today*, but Cal decided to leave that part out. "Ty is pretty certain this one is different."

Stanley considered Dania. "She looks like the ones the slavers take. The ones who are beaten and broken." He motioned around his head with his hands. "The hair is not alive."

Yeah, her hair was looking more normal by the second. Cal needed to talk to Doc about that. Hopefully that didn't mean she was even closer to death that they'd thought.

Cal tapped his friend's back. "Let's not worry about that right now. I have a few tons of merchandise hanging up there that I know you'll be excited to see."

Stanley grinned through his thick beard. "We are always excited when our Calvin comes home with gifts." The older man put his arm around Cal's shoulder and pulled him farther toward the building. "We need to talk."

Yeah, Cal bet he did. He turned to Ty and called, "Your job is to make sure she keeps her promise."

Ty put his arm around Dania's waist. "Any time I get to spend with my good buddy Dania is like a bonus."

She scowled at him. Good. If she was fending off Ty, maybe she wouldn't notice they were about to stroll into a den of sin.

Stanley folded his hands as he walked with Cal. "They called me, told me about a beautiful woman floating in the sky, giving children fruit." He stopped walking. "I'd hoped they were joking."

"I can explain."

"I very much hope you can."

Cal dragged his fingernails through his hair. Sand had caked against his scalp, as it did every time he'd come here since the rain machines had stopped cycling. He desperately needed a shower.

He looked back, where Dania stared at Ty indignantly as he pointed to the side of the building. Knowing Ty, he was probably trying to tell her it was priceless art.

"Ty did something stupid," Cal began.

"As Tyler always does. He's impulsive, that one. I warned you."

Yes, he had. "He's also a damn good pilot. Better than me."

"But his piloting is not the issue."

Cal wished it was that simple. "Ty got wrapped up with Dania. I was trying to untie the knot when a ring of slavers dropped down on us." Cal licked his lips against the dry air. They instantly caked, worse than before. "I should have left her there. I just couldn't."

Stanley tapped Cal's back. "Chivalry is not dead for Calvin Espinoza."

Cal laughed halfheartedly. "She threatens to kill me every ten minutes."

"Yet you are not dead."

Behind them, Doc was now pointing at the same wall. Dania folded her arms, glaring at them.

"I'm not really sure why we're not all dead yet."

Stanley grinned as Doc burst into laughter. "Maybe she likes you?"

Cal guffawed. "That monster is not capable of liking anyone."

Although the tears for the child and her apparent fondness for Alanna made him wonder…

"Don't be so sure." Stanley started walking again. "Slavers break enforcers. I have no idea how, but I have seen the aftermath. They're a fraction of the beings they once were—meek and shattered." He pointed back at Dania. "The hair on the broken ones looks like that. Like the silver dye has worn away. She may still be able to fly through the air, but she is still weakened. You probably saved her life."

"I don't think she looks at it that way."

He rubbed his beard, watching the spectacle near the wall. "Maybe in time, she will. After all, she hasn't killed those two yet."

Cal would take even those little wins, at the moment.

The cylinders moved overhead, disappearing behind the mortared fence. "Time to go to work."

Stanley dabbed the sweat from his brow. "Do you have a way to contain your new friend, should things go bad?"

Cal felt for the small gun Doc had given him. "Yeah. I just hope I don't have to use it."

"That makes two of us, my boy."

They followed the cases into the center courtyard of the U-shaped building Cal used to call home. Cal felt for the weapon again as Ty and Doc followed them in, Dania walking between them. Scattered around the compound, workers bent down over their tasks, many working on machinery lining the walls.

Dania's eyes widened as workers used blast torches to remove serial numbers, while another group repainted several land vehicles a different color. Her hands clenched and unclenched before Ty distracted her by starting one of his classic senseless babble routines. Cal had seen the most focused people in the galaxy fall victim to his first mate's silver tongue. Hopefully, this time would be no different.

Ty pulled Dania over to the people painting the all-terrain vehicles, of all places. Cal had no idea how he would sugarcoat that obvious sign of a cover-up.

Dania looked over her shoulder at Cal. Her lips pressed to a thin line.

His heartbeat quickened and he checked the gun one more time. These people were friends. Family. He'd protect them if he had to. The trick was not dying in the process.

CHAPTER 22
DANIA

TY PULLED Dania toward five men and one woman changing the color of three vehicles from white to black. The identification plates were worn clean, except for the first, which a second woman was etching new numbers onto. Dania's skin prickled with the need to stop her.

Ty held out his hands. "Look at this authentic outer-rim colony craftsmanship."

She nearly spat at him. "I'm not a fool. These people are trying to conceal stolen goods."

He waved his finger at her. "Careful there. Less than an hour ago, I believe you were seen by several hundred people helping to distribute said stolen goods."

She spoke through clenched teeth, doing her best to keep her promise not to slice this smuggler in two. "I had a good reason."

Ty grabbed her by the shoulders. She flinched, stunned.

He looked deep into her eyes. "Maybe, just maybe, these people have just as good a reason as you did."

"I find that highly unlikely."

"But can you say it's impossible?"

Impossible, no. But she wasn't a criminal. Criminals worked for themselves. For profit. They preyed on others for their own gain. Dania was sure these people were no different. There was never a reason to break a law.

She flinched. *Almost never.*

"Ty! Doc!" Espinoza called them from across the yard. Dania followed to where the cylinders of stolen goods were lined up in the center of the courtyard.

Espinoza looked her up and down as she approached. "You can either help or stand back and keep out of the way."

Dania swallowed the bile building in her throat as the last of the containers drifted to the surface, kicking up dust as they hit the ground. Espinoza was the worst kind of criminal, milking the poor who had nothing, all to line his pockets with cash, probably to spend on useless trinkets and whores.

Several citizens wearing the soiled rags she'd seen on so many of the townspeople when the *Star Renegade* had landed approached with small woven bags. Espinoza smiled, shook their hands, and placed several fruits and an assortment of other foodstuffs from multiple containers into each sack. More people approached, including several children...all with bags.

A line formed as more colonists arrived. Ty, Doc, Stanley, and Amelia joined Espinoza, working like a practiced unit, filling bags expediently as more people piled into the square. A crowd formed, but none pushed. It was all so... orderly, as if they'd done this hundreds of times.

Dania moved closer. Each bag got a bottle of pills— maybe medicine or supplements of some kind—and several pieces of fruit. Everyone got oranges. One container had bags of grain. One had contraband even worse than the oranges: spot-frozen beef and chicken, one of the most expensive food products available. Her hands trembled. That meat needed to be taken back to the food stores where it could be distributed where needed!

Ty gathered several handfuls of the meat and placed it into a child's sack. "Say *hi* to your dad for me."

The girl curtsied, holding out her tattered dress. "I will. Thank you, sir."

Espinoza shook a man's hand before giving him a bag. A woman hugged him, thanking him and telling him what a good person he was. The next woman in line received two bags, and none of the others complained that she'd received more.

Dania blinked as those who received the food left the square.

There was no one collecting their coin. No one was even making note of who had been given what.

A deep ache formed in her chest. She stood frozen as more and more people filed in. She rubbed her chest, but nothing would thwart the ache until the last bags had been handed out.

As Espinoza closed the container nearest him, Dania stumbled forward, her knees weak.

She pointed to the people leaving. "You just gave all that food away?"

He tapped the lid of the container. "Pretty much."

"But you risked your life and the lives of your crew to get it. That food was worth a small fortune."

Espinoza straightened, pushing out his broad chest. "As we've been trying to tell you, there are certain things that are worth breaking the law for."

Dania stared at him, gaping. The world spun around her, and she fought to steady herself.

Espinoza pushed away from the container. "About three years ago, the royal family called this colony a loss. They left these people here to die."

Dania startled. "That's not possible. The Banes protect everyone in their domain. They don't pick and choose."

Espinoza looked over his shoulder. "Stanley, when was the last time you had a royal tradesman here?"

The merchant tapped his lips. "About two years ago."

Dania's chest tightened. Could it be true?

No. Certainly, Prince Geron has no idea this had happened. He was many of the things people said he was, but he'd never allow his people to suffer.

She straightened, shaking off the doubt and facing Stanley. "This has to be a mistake. When I return, I will inform the royal family of your plight."

Espinoza scoffed. "The royal family doesn't give a shooting star about the people out here, and I'm not sure they ever have."

Dania's chest seized. Acid shot into her throat, and she nearly dropped to her knees, retching. She shook her head. "No, I-I can't believe that." But she'd seen it with her own eyes. This planet was in ruins.

"Believe it." Espinoza turned from her and called to Stanley. "Let's bring the people back."

"What are you doing?" she asked.

Espinoza opened the containers back up. "We have plenty more. We ration at first to make sure everyone gets something, and now anyone who needs more can come back and get it."

"Nothing goes to waste." Ty filled bags with oranges and set them to the side.

And nothing should. Food was a basic of life. The king deemed it necessary, and starvation was illegal. No one was supposed to go hungry in his domain. Ever.

Dania picked up a bag. "Can we give more to the family of the girl who has scurvy?"

Doc held up two overflowing bags. "Already on it."

A little girl walked up and opened up her bag to Dania. Dirt stained the child's skin gray and matted down her hair. Dania grabbed three oranges and placed them in her bag.

The child licked her lips, looking at the protein bars. Dania added those as well.

"Thank you," the little girl said before backing away.

A strand of hair flew into Dania's face, and she tucked it back. She couldn't remember anyone thanking her for anything before. She'd seen people thank Alexander for healing, but when Dania left a colony, people were usually wailing and crying.

The child turned at the gate and waved at her. Dania warmed inside—a not-all-that-unpleasant feeling—and waved back.

When the last of the extra food had been handed out, Stanley reached for the bags of oranges Doc had set aside. "I will get these to Katie's mother."

"Wait." Dania held out her hand. Those oranges were worth more than one of those vehicles they were painting. She couldn't trust them with just anyone.

Cal gently put down her hands. "We can trust Stanley."

The merchant backed away from the fruit and smiled, placing his hands on Dania's shoulders. "I understand trust is hard to earn. Out here, especially, we learn to look into people's hearts." He pointed to her chest. "I can see you have a good heart, and I hope you can see the goodness in mine."

A lump grew in her throat, making it hard to swallow.

Was she sick? She massaged her neck, but it wouldn't go away. She found that she *did* trust this man, and she barely knew him.

What she'd seen told her he was a criminal. She should be executing him, but for some reason, she didn't care about the automated vehicles, or any of the other illicit items scattered around the square. All she could see were the people smiling and hugging each other as they left with basic necessities that her king had denied them.

She sniffed and blinked back tears she hoped no one noticed. Maybe there wasn't such a clean line between right and wrong. If called to judge this man, or any of them, she wasn't sure she'd be able to find them guilty, even though they'd plainly broken the law.

Espinoza placed his hand gently on her back. "Let's go."

She held her head, the world spinning as he led her back to the ship.

TY POINTED out the crumbling terracotta-like planters lining the streets, explaining how lush and beautiful the plants that once grew along the sidewalks used to be. Unlike Cal, who'd only hidden here for a short time while trying to figure out how to remain invisible in a galaxy when there was a price on his head big enough to buy a small moon, Ty had grown up in these streets.

He was one of the many kids trained to run goods to the merchant ships in orbit, back when all the dealings on this planet had been legal, and profits were good. Now, most of those kids, like Ty, had fled for new lives. Cal wished he could have done better by Ty, but the kid—now a man, he guessed—knew he'd been signing on as the pilot for a convicted murderer.

Doc tugged Cal's sleeve, slowing his gait as they walked back to the *Star Renegade*. Ty and Dania continued ahead.

"Is the plan still to dump the enforcer here? Because now might be the time to do it," Doc said.

Cal shook his head. "I'm not sure anymore."

Ahead of them, Ty stopped, showing Dania a painting

on the wall that looked like it had been created by children. The colors had faded over the last few years, but Cal remembered delivering those paints. They'd cost him nearly a month's worth of wages, but the smiles on those kids' faces had been worth ten times the weight of the paint in citrus.

Dania reached out, tentatively touching the artwork. Cal wished he could see her face.

"Her hair is even more blonde now than it was this morning," Doc said.

"Yeah. We also noticed it doesn't move like a million crazed moonworms anymore. Do you know why?"

"Theories only. Like I said, there is no medical history on enforcers." Doc wiped the sweat from his forehead. "I took another reading on her this morning while she was still asleep. She had about forty-nine percent of the pathogens in her blood as in the first sample I took. They're dying off exponentially."

"Is that good or bad?"

Doc shrugged. "I'm seeing a direct relationship between the decrease in pathogens and her not only looking more human, but acting more human."

"What do you mean?"

He pointed back to the square. "When was the last time you ever saw an enforcer stand there and watch people distribute stolen goods without blowing a gasket? Let alone help them with their own hands?" He looked back to Dania and Ty. "She's changing right before our eyes, and I'm starting to wonder if those pathogens are some sort of biological hypnotic."

Cal leaned back. "Do you actually think all of the enforcers have been hypnotized?"

"I don't know. It's a long shot, but I remember working the underground on Kemper Station when a princess showed up in full battle armor with about three dozen enforcers in tow." He shivered. "At one point, she turned her head to the right quickly, and all the enforcers did, too, at the exact same time. When she started walking, they all did, too. And they started on the same foot. It was like they were robots or something." His lips thinned. "At a bare minimum, it might be a form of mind control."

Hypnotics, mind control—it all seemed crazy, but no more crazy than finding out that an elite alien enforcer was devolving back into a human.

Were all the enforcers human? If so, that meant they weren't their own race at all, but something manufactured by the royal family.

Ahead of them, Ty held his hands out to the side, and Dania laughed.

Dania.

The enforcer.

Laughed.

Ty said something else, and she laughed again, holding her hand to her chest. It all looked so normal, so *human*.

Could Doc be right?

More importantly, could Ty have been right? If they'd broken this woman out of her fog, would she be able to see the *Star Renegade's* crew as people with purpose, and not just criminals? But did that even matter? If the Banes really *were* monsters, would sending her back with this new information even make a difference?

It still could work. If she ranked as highly as Doc said she did, maybe she could make them listen.

Maybe. It was a long shot.

A *very* long shot.

But a long shot was more than they'd ever had before.

Cal had thought Ty was out of his mind when he'd gone after the enforcer, but now she might be the secret to their salvation.

Dania laughed again, her eyes sparkling as she glanced back at Cal.

Could they really be this lucky, or were they falling for the biggest con of their lives?

A TINY CYCLONE of sand whisked past Dania's feet as they returned to the smuggling ship. She rubbed her shoulders as a chill iced over her despite the desert-like heat. She'd left the ship that morning ready to add to the list of crimes this crew was already more than guilty of, and she hadn't been disappointed.

Until she'd committed a crime herself.

Would Prince Geron excuse her for disseminating pilfered food?

Would he understand that these people were hungry?

The goods were stolen in origin. That was almost a certainty. But the crew hadn't actually sold them. The law did not require the exchange of money, though, so they had in fact committed a crime.

She had committed a crime.

Another chill sliced up her spine as they neared the ship. Her gaze fogged, and she blinked to clear it.

"Are you okay?" Ty asked, leaning closer.

Dania pushed him back, but not as hard as she normally would. "I'm fine."

But she wasn't fine, and she wasn't quite sure what to do about it.

Alanna's eyes widened as she stepped off the landing platform and approached them. "Dania?"

She stopped. "What is it?"

The navigator squinted in the bright sun. "Your hair looks funny."

Dania tilted her head. That was an odd statement coming from a woman who'd artificially colored half the strands of her own hair pink. However, the woman's brow furrowed with concern.

Dania grabbed the ends of her hair and pulled the strands forward. Her heart fluttered when the locks lay still between her fingertips, rather than shifting with primordial heat. She blinked twice, hoping it was a trick of the sun shining off the edge of the ship's hull. She flipped the ends of her hair over, then plucked a lock from her other shoulder. Her hair was not the vibrant, glinting opal of the enforcers, but a dull, mundane blonde.

She spun toward the doctor walking up behind them. "What have you done to me?"

He held up his hands. "Whoa there, tiger. Nothing."

"Really?" She held out fistfuls of her hair in each hand. "Then what is this? You took my blood, but did you inject something into me at the same time?"

He narrowed his eyes. "It doesn't work that way. It's kind of a one-way needle."

"Then why is my appearance changing?"

The doctor's face blurred. She shook her head to clear it.

He hazarded a step closer. "Maybe we should take you to the med bay so I can get you checked out."

She pushed him away, nearly stumbling as she did so. "Why? So you can lock me in another force field? So you can make me sleep on the floor?"

He shook his head. "I just want to take some readings to make sure you're okay."

"The last time you took readings, this happened." She held out her hair again.

The doctor glanced at Espinoza and then back to her. "Dania, you're not like the rest of the crew. I'm not accustomed to working with enforcers, but to me, it looks like something's wrong, and I'll need to do some research to fix you."

She balked. "Fix me? You *did this* to me."

"I just want to help you. I promise, no needles unless you say it's okay. I will explain everything I'm doing."

Alanna's hand appeared on Dania's arm. "Hey, I'll go with you. I'll stay with you the whole time, just like last night."

Dania's heart twisted. This woman, for some reason, she trusted. The men were a threat.

But why? She could slice them all in two with the will of her mind.

Her sight blurred again.

"Dania?" Alanna's hazy face came into view. "Please. You don't look good."

Maybe it was this planet, or the intense heat, but she knew they were right.

Something was wrong with her, and at the moment, she had no other choice than to trust the criminals.

CHAPTER 25
CAL

BACK ON THE SHIP, Ethan walked toward Cal with a slower-than-usual gate, but with the same fire in his eyes that had nearly gotten him thrown off the ship numerous times. "I thought the plan was to leave the enforcer on the surface and make a run for it? I had the engines pumped and ready."

Cal kept walking. "You were supposed to be resting. In case you forgot the mind-melting pain, you were hit with a particle distributor."

"I'm serious." Ethan grabbed him as he tried to walk by.

The engineer winced, like even lifting his arm hurt.

Cal wished the people on his crew would learn to take it easy when they were injured.

Cal looked at the hand on his arm and raised a brow in warning until Ethan dropped his grip.

"Stuff happened out there," Cal said. "And it looks like she might be sick. Those colonists can't help her." Of course, Cal wasn't sure that Doc would be able to help her, either, but she had a better chance with the tenacious, self-

223

taught genius than she had with a real doctor in the colony, someone used to treating normal human injuries and sicknesses.

"I get that, but she's still a ticking time bomb."

Cal poked Ethan's chest. "You were the one with Ty when he came up with this star-blasted scheme."

"That was before she started threatening to kill us all."

"She did save your life, or at least saved you from permanent spinal damage."

Ethan stared at the wall. "Yeah, I know. I'm still trying to wrap my head around that." He took a deep breath. "So, what's the new plan?"

Good question. Cal looked back to the med bay door. "Right now, I think we're still trying to build trust. She's agreed that I didn't kill Filluck Palogivan."

"Yeah, but she also said she might still have to kill you for it."

Yeah, she *had* alluded to that. He needed to remember to keep getting her word not to kill him each morning. "But today, *she* committed a crime."

Ethan balked. "What?"

"She gave out stolen goods by accident and then about an hour later, she did it again, knowing full well what she was doing."

"And you think that's because she's sick?"

"Doc doesn't think she's sick. He thinks that she *was* sick, but now she's getting better. She's becoming human again."

"Can we afford to take this chance?"

Could they afford *not* to?

Cal put his hand on Ethan's shoulder. "We're heading

to Hitus Four. If things look bad, we can drop her off there.”

“It’s not as safe as here. Here, we’d get a week’s head start before she could call for help.”

“I know.” And missing this opportunity would probably keep Cal awake at night.

It wasn’t just his own life on the line anymore, but the crew’s. This would probably be their one and only chance at changing their death sentences to something less…*final*. If it worked, Great! If it didn’t, they were no worse off than they were now.

As long as they didn’t get themselves caught in the process.

This was a chance worth taking.

He was the captain, but he needed them all to be a part of this decision, even if they only voiced their opinions and Cal made the final call.

He placed his hand on the entry pad, and the doors to the med bay slid open. Dania sat on a gurney, her eyes on the floor as Doc ran a laser scanner across her forehead. Alanna sat beside her with an arm around the enforcer’s shoulder.

At this point, it was quite possible that they were all still alive because of Alanna. She was more than a ship’s navigator. She’d added a softness and sense of direction, and maybe even decorum, to the crew—something they very much needed.

Dania looked up as the door slid closed behind Cal. Her skin was pale by human standards, but more like someone who’d been on a ship for years without any exposure to natural light, rather than the pearly glow of the enforcers.

“Feeling any better?” Cal asked.

"No." Dania lifted a glass of bright green liquid to her lips.

Trying to tell her that she looked healthier, when the sight of her own face probably scared her to death, probably wasn't a good plan. Maybe deflecting to the more prudent issues would be better.

"How do you feel about what happened today?" Cal asked.

Dania handed the glass to Alanna and rubbed her temples. "There were so many laws being broken. I started to lose count."

She looked down. She seemed to be contemplating, as if it was strange for her to lose count.

Maybe this was good. Maybe this was more humanity coming out.

Cal slid his fingers in his pockets. "There *were* a few things happening that some people might find questionable." Okay, maybe more than a few things. That didn't really matter at the moment. "But I'm more interested in how you *feel* about what you saw."

"Confused." She lowered her hands. "Because I understand why. Those colonists are desperate, and it's no fault of their own."

Her whole body spasmed, as if hit with a massive chill. She held on to the gurney until the episode passed.

"What you did was illegal, but I can't say that it wasn't good." Dania folded her hands on her lap. "I can't sit here and judge you for breaking the king's laws when there was no other way to save those people."

Cal, Alanna, and Doc stared at each other with wide eyes.

That was a huge admission for an enforcer, one he was certain she wouldn't have been capable of a few days ago.

Dania sniffed, and a drop of water splashed to the floor tiles. Another tear?

Her hands covered her face. "I can't stop thinking of how many people I may have passed judgment on who weren't really guilty. Or maybe they were guilty, but the degree of their crimes didn't warrant death." Her hands dropped to her abdomen. "I-I think I might… My stomach."

Alanna jumped off the gurney and handed Dania a bucket. "Here you go." She rubbed the enforcer's shoulder. "It's going to be okay."

Doc waved Cal to the side. "We've given her some electrolytes, but that's not going to fix the root cause of all this."

Alanna continued to rub Dania's back. "Try to take in a deep breath, and let it out slowly."

Doc initiated a sound barrier, cutting them off from the other side of the room.

"What's up?" Cal asked.

Doc called up some information on a computer screen. "The count of pathogens in her blood is down to forty-four and a half percent. That's four and a half percentage points lower than this morning. They're declining faster than her body seems to be able to handle." He turned from the screen and looked at Cal. "They have to be the cause of her inability to see reason when she first got here, and the drastic change to what we see now."

And the remorse—all very human things that the Banes somehow had found a way to suppress.

Doc looked at Dania through the slight haze of the

privacy filter. "The sickness, though, isn't just her being disgusted with herself. The pathogens have become part of her, and now I can tell you with even more certainty that her body has synthesized with them. When those pathogens run out, her internal organs are going to start shutting down one at a time."

Well, that didn't sound good.

Cal's stomach churned. He'd thought they'd helped her, but now this. "How long does she have?"

"It all depends on how long the rest of the pathogens last. I just don't know."

Cal could see the wheels turning in Doc's mind. A slight hint of a smile twitched at the edge of his lips.

"Can I take for granted that you've figured all this out?"

Doc snorted. "Of course."

"You aren't thinking of going all Frankenstein and rebuilding her, right?"

"In a way, yes, but not that extreme." He called up a few more screens, and data flew by as Doc relayed information like Cal had even a fraction of an idea of what he was talking about.

Cal held up a hand, stopping him. "Can you just cut to the part about what you need from me?"

"Time. And some new toys."

Across the room, Dania retched into the bucket.

"It doesn't look like she has that much time."

"She doesn't. That's why I need time to think. And I'm going to need supplies—the kind that are probably going to take some creative procurement."

"You mean illegal."

"Illegal supplies are the most fun to get."

So much for heading toward the placid colonies of

Hitus. Those kinds of supplies would probably mean heading out to the remote sectors.

Tears streamed down Dania's face as Alanna helped wipe the enforcer's mouth.

Dania looked so helpless...so normal. Guilt cut into Cal's gut, knowing that he'd had a part in doing this to her. It was the right thing to do, but knowing she was hurting made him want to punch something.

Alanna finished wiping Dania's mouth and tossed the dirty rag into the recycler. "It's okay. This happens sometimes. It's no big deal."

But it probably was to Dania, if she really couldn't remember ever being sick.

Alanna cooed something to the enforcer as she helped Dania lie on the gurney.

"Make a list," Cal said. "Whatever you need, I'll figure out a way to get it."

Doc bit his bottom lip as Alanna covered Dania with a thin blanket. "You need to know that she still has a crazy amount of power coursing through her. I mean, nowhere near as much, but she can still kick all our asses without even lifting a finger."

"Meaning we'll have to make it look like we're trading legally, even if we're dealing with pirates again."

"Bingo." Doc rubbed the stubble on his chin. "This had to be hard on her. She's confused and lost. She might decide to kill us all, just to prove to herself that she still can."

Great. Just great.

However, after seeing her cure the child, and how she'd reacted to giving out the food, it was obvious she wasn't the automaton that had first walked onto their ship. This was still a once-in-a-lifetime opportunity to get an enforcer on their side. On *everyone's* side.

Cal didn't have Ty's overly-optimistic hope that she'd completely clear their names. Cal knew that would never happen, but she'd already admitted that she'd executed people whose crimes probably didn't warrant death. If she mentioned this to the Banes, would they listen?

If she could convince them to change the law, Earth's holdings wouldn't have to live in fear of the people who were supposed to protect them. This could stop thousands of little boys from losing their fathers for no good reason.

This was a chance worth taking.

They just needed to keep Dania on the path to recovery without her finding another reason to execute them all.

DANIA CLUNG to her pillow as Alanna brushed back her hair like she was a child. Everything that made Dania what she was told her to shove the woman away for the insolence. Yet she allowed it, over and over, as this woman pet her like a dog.

She couldn't remember anyone outside of her sponsor, or maybe Alexander, touching her like they cared. And never this long, and with such pointed attention on only Dania and not themselves.

Dania could imagine being scolded for allowing herself to look weak, especially in the eyes of these so-called criminals. But she didn't care. The bigger question was, though, *why* didn't she care?

Espinoza left the room, probably amused by Dania's weakened state, and the doctor returned to her bedside.

"Is she going to be all right?" Alanna asked.

He looked into a portable data screen. "Yes. Actually, she's getting better by the minute. Given time, she might be normal again."

"Normal?" Dania whispered.

He nodded. "What is your earliest memory? Your first recollection as a child?"

There were many, most dealing with her and Alexander getting into trouble with the queen, and Prince Geron scolding them, and snickering about it when he'd thought they couldn't see.

But the earliest memory? "I remember opening my eyes, and bright lights. A white room, and my prince smiling at me. I was afraid, and he held out his arms and held me."

"How old were you?"

Dania eased up on her elbows. "I'm not sure. We talked to each other, so I couldn't have been too young."

"What about your parents?"

Dania blinked, surprised by the question. "Enforcers don't have parents like humans do. We have sponsors."

The doctor motioned to the data screen. "According to the royal archive records, the king gave you to his son. You don't remember anything before that?"

The king—*gave* her to Geron?

She shook her head. "My memories are all of my prince."

"Huh." He walked across the room. "I don't see any sign of your memories being altered or erased altogether. Then again, with what they did to you, the mass alteration of your cellular structure..."

Dania sat up the rest of the way. Her head spun, and Alanna helped her. "What are you talking about?"

The doctor's expression softened. "Your name was Dania Rain. You were the daughter of a merchant before you were sold to the royal family."

Her chest tightened. "What?"

"It went on record as an adoption, but they paid a not-so-small fortune for you."

Ridiculous. Just because she could not remember did not mean she'd been sold. "Lies."

He shook his head and handed her the data pad.

She sifted through the information before raising her gaze to him. She used a few codes to trace the information back to the source data, and the doctor was correct. The records originated in the archives. "Hacking into the royal record archives is illegal."

"I know, but I thought you deserved to know where you came from."

None of this seemed right, though. She would have known if she had parents. Then again, she'd never had reason to question. None of the enforcers had parents or families. They had their sponsors. From the very beginning, there had been nothing but Geron. And, of course, Alexander.

She looked up again. "Is there any record of an adoption of a boy at the same time? About the same age?"

He blinked back what seemed like surprise at the question. "I was only tracing back your DNA. I can look, though, if you want."

Would it make a difference? She'd always known Alexander was not her biological brother, but growing up together had made them closer than most enforcers. It didn't really matter where he'd come from.

She shook her head and handed the data pad back to the doctor. "I didn't know any of this, but it makes no difference. The Banes are my family. Prince Geron has always cared for me."

"While he mutated your genes and turned you into something unnatural."

She shifted, and small aches twinged through her. The doctor said she was getting healthier, but she had to disagree. If this was being human, she wanted none of it. "If he changed me, he made me better."

"But for his own purposes. He may have disguised it well, but he took away your individuality."

"He made me stronger."

"Maybe, but at what cost?"

Dania wiped her brow with the back of her hand.

The child on Kirato suffering from scurvy had winced in pain. She would have died if Dania hadn't intervened. A month ago, Dania may have walked right by the child. Helping innocents was Alexander's programming, not hers.

A chill ran over her. Alexander's *programming*. She'd always known she'd been programmed to lead Geron's enforcers. She'd been programmed to punish the lawbreakers. She'd been programmed to kill.

She'd always had trouble understanding Alexander's sometimes inefficient need to help others, but it was *programming*, so she'd needed to accept that.

She'd never thought about what *programming* meant. They'd said it was what helped her to be everything Prince Geron needed.

Yes, he'd made her stronger, but had he also erased the part of her that maybe wanted to be a little more like Alexander?

Another child's face popped into her mind. Dirty, cherub cheeks stained with tears as Dania grasped his wrist, yanking him into the air—and the screams of his mother as she cried for mercy while the other enforcers held the woman back.

Miguel had ended up executing the mother as well for trying to intervene. Her bloody, broken body had fallen atop that of her son, a reminder to the rest of their colony what happened when you broke the king's law.

But what had that child done?

The crime melted into hundreds of others, all dealt with by exacting the only punishment sanctioned by the king. Once a criminal, always a criminal. The only way to make the galaxy a better place was to eliminate the source of crime.

But hadn't the crew of this ship made the galaxy a better place with the spoils of their crimes?

Her ears rang. None of this was right. Nothing made sense. These people were confusing her.

She pressed her temples between her palms.

The ringing heightened, tearing through her skull.

This was all wrong. The doctor had done something to her. She needed to execute them all and get back to her prince. If there *was* something wrong with her, he was the only one who could fix her.

"Dania?" Alanna rubbed her back.

Warmth spread through her as the woman's voice pushed away the confused thoughts.

The tenacity in Dania's shoulders waned. Her blood still tingled, but her body calmed, as if finding safety for the first time in her life.

She tried to push it away. She was anything but safe. Yet her body was hard to convince.

The doctor shined a light in Dania's eyes. "If your head is bothering you, I can give you a local pain reliever, but at this point, I need to clear you. From a medical standpoint, there isn't anything wrong. You were overrun with pathogens, but your body is fighting them off."

His cheek twitched, and Dania couldn't discern if he thought that was a good or a bad thing.

Dania hugged her shoulders. "Are you saying I'm all right? How can that be true?"

"I think you're feeling normal, human things that maybe you've never had the capacity to feel before. From what I can tell, your hair and your eyes are returning to their original pre-pathogen color. I really think the silvery coloring was the result of exposure to something."

"Exposure? I have not been exposed to radiation or anything like that, if this is what you're insinuating."

"No, but you have been exposed to the Banes. They're an alien race, and the power they wield makes enforcers look like second-rate magicians. It's possible that just being around them affected you in ways human medicine can't explain."

So, there was hope for her, then. "This means that my hair will go back to normal when I get home, and that these uncomfortable feelings and pains will go away when I get back to where I belong?"

He looked away. "Well, yes, but I think that maybe you should take into consideration that you never belonged there in the first place." He held his palm out to the door. "Anyway, for now you're free to go."

Dania balked. "I am?"

"Absolutely. The captain thinks you acted admirably today, and he asked me to invite you to our crew dinner tonight."

Dania narrowed her eyes. "Is that a euphemism for something?"

"Only if you mean good company, fun conversation, and delicious homemade food."

Dania rubbed her hands across the tops of her legs. Alanna had been bringing her food to whatever place Espinoza had decided to chain her up at any given time. She'd never expected to be invited to join them for a meal.

Alanna nudged her shoulder. "You should come. It will be fun. Everyone can get a chance to know you like I have."

Get to know her? Had she gotten to know Alanna between promises of granting her a quick death when the time came?

Alanna smiled at her, and there was no animosity there, no slight change in body temperature to show that she was lying.

Odd, how something as simple as a smile could put her at ease. Everything about these people was a surprise. A conundrum she couldn't decipher. They should hate her, yet they'd invited her to join them for what sounded like their personal bonding time.

Even odder…Dania *wanted* to attend.

She trembled at the sign of weakness, then pushed the feeling away. Kinship wasn't a bad thing. No one ever tried to stop her and Alexander from being close. Of course, Alexander wasn't a criminal.

Dania rubbed her hands together and grimaced as grit balled up on her palms. Odd that she cared more about the dirt on her hands than the crimes of the people surrounding her. "I'll need to wash up first."

"Sure." Alanna jumped off the edge of the cot. "You can come to my room."

Another sign of hospitality towards someone they should consider an enemy. These people made no sense.

Alanna talked about the ship as they walked through the hallways—what modifications they had made and explaining some of the dark, burnt patches Dania had noticed earlier. In two instances, they'd been caused by the engineer, Ethan, experimenting with substances that had exploded. In the third case, the charred mark actually was the result of a firefight when they'd been boarded illegally on a trading run.

Again, there was no change in Alanna's temperature. She was telling the truth like someone with nothing to hide.

Maybe it was because she actually didn't have anything to hide?

Inside Alanna's living compartment, the navigator stayed in her main chamber, reviewing star charts while Dania stepped into the shower. The warm streaming water eased over her skin, oddly soothing after cleansing in decontamination stalls all of her life.

She stepped out of the chamber and looked back as a few drops fell from the faucet and splashed to the floor. What other luxuries did humanity have that had been hidden from her all this time?

The water streamed down her hair and shoulders, puddling beneath her feet. She couldn't recall being wet before. Kever sanitization facilities contained fine particles of sand, not water.

A slight chill touched her skin as she walked into the main chamber, her feet slapping against the tiles.

Alanna's eyes widened. "You-You're naked."

Dania looked down at her body. "Was I supposed to

shower clothed? Would the water have washed my uniform as well?”

“No.” Alanna laughed, grabbing a thick, white bundle of cloth from a panel in the wall. “Here, dry off with this.”

Dania stared at the rough fabric.

Alanna cocked her head. “Haven’t you used a towel before?”

Dania shook her head.

Her smile was sad, but sweet. “It’s okay. It helps you to dry off. You rub it all over yourself, and it soaks up the water.” She pointed at the floor. “And be careful. The water might make the floor slippery.”

Dania dropped the towel to the floor and used a push of her power to rub the fabric over her wet footprints. As Alanna said, the water disappeared into the fabric. Archaic, but effective.

Smiling, Alanna handed Dania more folded fabric. “I don’t have a recycler, so you can change into these clothes until we get your uniform cleaned. We’re close to the same height, but it will probably be a little loose on you. Some people like clothes loose and comfy like that.

She was…giving Dania her own clothes?

“I’m going to jump into the shower.” Alanna grabbed another towel and tossed it to Dania. “Use this one to dry yourself off. I’ll be out in a snap.”

The towels did a remarkably good job removing the water from her skin. She rubbed her hair over and over, though, and the tresses still hung in thick, wet clumps.

A slight chill grazed her skin, and Dania eased into the clothing Alanna had given her: a thick, brown jumpsuit that hugged her thighs but hung loose around her chest. The fabric was lighter than her uniform, yet warm.

Alanna returned. "Hey, it looks good."

The woman was already dressed. Dania was happy to see her hair was wet as well.

Alanna took a small canister from a shelf and sprayed a fluffy, white substance into her hands before working the material into her hair. "Do you want some product?"

Dania stared at her. The woman held out the canister like Dania would know what *product* was. Her stomach clenched again. This was another world…so many things that seemed so simple to Alanna, so normal.

Her cheeks heated, and she looked away.

Alanna walked up. "Hey, it's okay. Look." She sprayed the canister into her palm again, rubbed her hands together, and then smoothed them through Dania's hair. "This keeps your hair from getting frizzy and makes it lay nice after you extract the water."

"Extract the water?"

"Sure. Come here." She tugged Dania to the corner. "Stand still."

She pressed a button on the wall, and they were both basked in red light and heat. Alanna's hair lifted. A fog drifted up from her hair, and when the lights winked out, her chin-length tresses hung neatly around her face.

Alanna laughed. "You look so stunned."

The woman pointed to a mirror. Dania's own hair hung in well-ordered waves draped over her shoulders. Her hair was that odd, creamy tan color, and it seemed strange that it hung without moving, but it looked appealing, like some of the well-dressed merchant women she'd seen walking through space stations.

Dania had never really thought of her appearance. She simply wore her uniform every day, and her hair shifted into whatever form it wanted at will. She warmed, knowing that she could decide what her hair looked like now.

Smoothing her palm over her stomach, she smiled. The brown coloration in her jumpsuit was oddly comforting after wearing the pearlescent white all her life. The warmth inside her spread…an odd, but agreeable sensation.

She turned to Alanna. "Thank you."

"You got it. Ready for dinner?"

She nodded, and they headed out.

A small flutter alighted in Dania's chest. She'd had many group meals before with her enforcers. They discussed battle tactics and special orders from their prince. A meal without an agenda was something new, and she quickened her pace, wondering what might be discussed.

Again, Alanna gave an explanation for the nicks and pocks in the walls, and the replaced panels in different parts of the ship. They'd certainly done a lot of maintenance on the vessel.

Alanna's presence, and even her voice, was oddly soothing. It reminded Dania of carefree conversations with Alexander, but this felt more like kinship, like being in someone's company simply because their presence pleased you, rather than the close proximity of being sponsored by the same prince. It was a peculiar feeling, but a nice one.

Dania slowed her gait. She shouldn't get used to this odd, misplaced comradery. There was no point. No matter what the doctor tried to make Dania believe, there *was* something wrong with her. The only way to truly heal and renew her strength was to reunite with her prince.

"We're like one big family here," Alanna said, finishing a thought that Dania had missed.

Her heart clenched. The crew did seem to care for each other.

It was...*nice*.

Dania imagined Prince Geron's open arms welcoming her back, and she shivered.

For the first time in her life, she felt like she had something to lose, and she wasn't sure why.

CAL SET a few plates on the large table in the center of his private meeting-space turned dining-room. He hesitated, placing the additional plate next to Alanna's seat. It had been a long time since they'd had a guest at their table. Never in his wildest dreams had he imagined himself serving an enforcer.

What would his dad have thought? His mom?

He looked at the portrait of the three of them hanging on the wall beside the kitchen door. He'd been twelve years old when the picture had been taken, and they'd just come back from a trip to the ship design expo. A few weeks later, his dad was dead.

Cal rubbed his eyes as a slight ache developed over his brow. So much for his pledge to keep a million miles between himself and the enforcers.

Ethan paced the far wall, rubbing his chin. "I'm still on board with trying to convince the enforcer we're all innocent. You know I've always been on board with that. But letting her walk around free? That's just asking for punishment." He stopped and looked at Cal. "What if she went down to the storage lockers and started poking around?"

Ty leaned back in his chair and put his feet up on the end of the table. "Then we just better make sure she doesn't poke around."

"I'm serious," Ethan said.

"So am I."

Cal pushed Ty's feet off the table. "Do you mind? People are going to eat here."

The doors split open, and Doc walked in. "I guess I'm not late." He looked at each of them. "Did I miss something?"

"Ethan's afraid the enforcer might snoop around and find something."

Doc walked across the room. "If she snoops around, it wouldn't take her long to find any number of things that could get us all killed." He opened a drawer and grabbed a few handfuls of silverware. "We all knew the risks of bringing her on board."

"I get that." Ethan held out his hands. "But I thought we were dumping her on Kirato."

Cal set a glass on the table. "We need to start showing her the same charity that we show the colonists, or anyone else we share our spoils with. One dinner won't hurt us." At least, he hoped it wouldn't.

"I agree," Doc said. "If anything, it will give us a chance to find out a little more about her. If we can get her to let her guard down, that is."

Ethan shoved his hands in his pockets. "I guess I'm getting cold feet. I'm a little fond of breathing."

Cal bit back a smile. A few years ago, back when the *Star Renegade* still only had a crew of two, Ty had won a game of poker against Ethan. When Ethan couldn't ante up, he'd offered to fix their hydrogen converter to pay off his debt. Cal had never been one to pass up a free maintenance job, so Ethan had gotten to work.

But when someone else showed up wanting to collect from Ethan, they hadn't been as interested in Ethan working off his gambling losses. When it became obvious that they'd been ready to take their spoils out of the engineer's hide, Ethan had pleaded for help, saying the exact phrase, "I'm a little fond of breathing."

Of course, at the time, Cal and Ty were more worried about themselves than a loser who couldn't pay off his debts. Still, they'd had to take off—with Ethan still on board—before they got holes punched in the side of their ship for something they hadn't even done.

It hadn't all been bad. The guy ended up being a competent engineer. He'd become an important part of their crew, and despite following Ty around no matter how insane some of his ideas were—like trying to convince an enforcer they were all innocent—the guy did normally have a respectable desire to keep breathing, so Cal understood his hesitation.

Dania was still a big unknown, no matter how human she'd become. In this case, caution wasn't a sign of weakness. Ethan was being smart for a change. Which was strange, since Cal had suddenly become reckless.

He knew, deep down, that Ethan was probably right, and they should have left her on Kirato. That had been their best, and maybe only chance of escape. But the stakes seemed so much higher now. Like it could really all be worth the risk.

Cal glanced up to the picture on the wall.

His father's hand on Cal's shoulder. The smiles on all their faces.

The all-too-familiar pain formed in his throat.

Enforcers were cold, calculating killing machines. They'd proven that over and over. But Cal had to agree with Doc. The longer Dania was away from that prince, the less demonic she seemed. A month ago Cal would never have thought it was possible, but this enforcer had changed.

Maybe not completely, but she seemed to be on the way to recovery. This wasn't something they could ignore. If Dania could be saved, could the others be saved, too?

He tensed, remembering an armada of enforcer ships encircling the king's cruiser in the alpha sector a few years ago. The flotilla seemed to go on forever.

The *Star Renegade* was a little ship with a small crew. They couldn't take on those kinds of numbers, especially since none of the enforcers knew they were being brainwashed.

He needed to concentrate on the one he *could* save. They'd taken her too far to turn back now.

His mom used to tell him that a stone thrown in the water made a small circle around it, but that circle grew larger and larger until the whole pond had been influenced by its splash. The story never really made sense to him until now. The galaxy was a pretty big pond, but someone needed to have the audacity to throw that stone.

Cal leaned against the edge of the table. "We're heading back to the main trade zones to get some things Doc needs. By the time we get there, we'll have had some more time to get to know each other and really drive home that we aren't the space scum she thought we were." Cal looked at each of them, hoping to find the courage he wasn't sure he'd find inside himself. "Once we get back to civilization, if she still wants to find her star-blasted prince, then we'll take her there." Hopefully, that would be enough of a splash to start those circles spreading.

Ethan held up both his hands. "Please tell me you're not thinking of dropping her on the Banes' doorstep."

Cal shook his head. "I'm not a fool. I'm not going within a hundred million miles of Keveron. We can be nicer about where we drop her off, though, rather than leaving her stranded for two weeks in the outer rims."

Although Mel would have taken it upon herself to make sure Dania had gained a little weight while she was there. The woman sure loved to make sure no one ever went hungry.

He walked toward his kitchen. "Believe me, I still have every intention of hightailing it out of there and leaving as much space as we can between her and us once we decide to part ways."

Cal's stomach twinged, and it had nothing to do with the aromas wafting in from the kitchen. He'd never dreamed he'd have so much apprehension about throwing a stone.

The door split open, and Alanna wrapped her knuckles on the side of the wall. "Knock, knock. The girls are here. Time to be on your best behavior."

Ethan grinned. "Alanna, everything about you puts me on my worst behavior, you know that."

"Don't remind me." She placed her hand over her heart and inhaled. "Cal, whatever that is smells heavenly."

The enforcer inched through the door behind her. She glanced around the room, almost looking meek.

Almost.

Cal smiled. "Hello. Welcome."

She'd changed out of the soiled white uniform and into one of Alanna's tinkering coveralls. The light brown fabric fit tight around her middle, and loose on top. Her hair was even darker now that she'd showered, hanging in graceful waves to her shoulders.

She looked like any other girl…a *very beautiful* any other girl.

Cal forced his gaze away and took a deep breath. He needed to remind himself that this wasn't an ordinary passenger.

He glanced up at the picture of his parents again. Their eyes seemed to focus on him, judging.

For the first time in his life, he wished that the photo wasn't there.

Dania looked at him, then at the table.

Cal had to stop himself from pulling out her chair. Instead, he held out his hand to the extra place setting. "Would you like to take a seat?"

She hesitated.

"It's okay." Alanna drew her to the table.

Dania took Alanna's normal seat right beside Cal.

His grip tightened on the back of his chair. That was going to make things a little more awkward than needed.

Alanna shrugged and took the other seat beside Ty while Ethan and Doc took their regular seats opposite them.

Ty smiled at Dania from the far side of the table. "You haven't eaten until you've tried Cal's home cooking." Ty flashed Dania the grin that had gotten them out of a million tight places. Of course, that same grin had them running for their lives a few times, too.

Dania cocked her head. "You actually have a kitchen?"

"This is an older ship," Ty explained. "The galley wasn't operational when we first picked her up. I cannibalized some parts from junkers and got the stove and oven operational just for fun. I never really dreamed anyone would actually use it."

Cal watched for a change of expression. He'd often wondered if Ty had any hard feelings about Stanley giving Cal the *Renegade* after Ty had worked so hard refurbishing her. The kid had kicked dirt and thrown things at first until Cal had made him an unexpected offer: a position as first mate.

Only seventeen, the kid had stared at him like he was summing up if Cal had been serious, before Ty dusted off his pants and accepted. He'd probably looked at this ship as a ticket off Kirato, and as long as that happened, Ty didn't care who was in charge.

Taking a deep breath, Cal went back to the kitchen and prepared two plates of food. He placed the first in front of Dania, and the second in front of Alanna. "Ladies first."

"I take offense to that," Doc said.

Cal smacked his shoulder. "You wait like the rest of the dogs." Cal pulled together two more plates, moving as quickly as he could. The tension in the room had raised the heat a few degrees. Either that, or Cal was just sweating through his shirt.

This was just dinner, like any other night. He had to push it out of his mind that they were sharing their table with a former mass murderer—one who could turn on them at any moment.

Cal balked. Ethan and his big mouth were in that room with Dania. And Cal wasn't there to monitor him.

He bolted back out, nearly tripping. He placed one plate in front of Ty and the other in front of Ethan.

He stared his engineer down. "Eat."

Ethan frowned, tilting his head. "When have I not eaten?"

Doc held up his palms. "Where's mine? Is this punishment for the *ladies first* comment?"

Cal shook his head. "I'll be right back."

So far so good. He pulled two more plates together. Now, if he could just keep them eating, maybe they could all get through this night in one piece.

Taking a deep breath, he gave Doc his plate and sat at the end of the table with his own. When he looked up, the enforcer's eyes were narrowed on him.

"Why are you serving the crew?" Dania asked. "Aren't you the captain?"

Cal pressed some simulated butter into his mashed potatoes. "Yes, I am, but these people work hard for me every day. The least I can do is make them a special meal once in a while."

"Cal cooks for us at least once a week." Alanna cut up her chicken. "It's not always this elaborate, but it's always delicious."

Dania frowned at her plate before taking a bite of her food. She startled before swallowing. "Is that real poultry?"

There was no use denying it. "Yes."

"From Earth?"

He smiled, folded his arms on the table, and leaned slightly toward her. "How about you stop worrying about where it came from and enjoy it?"

She set down her fork and mimicked his folded arms, leaning in. Her eyes had darkened from the pale crystal hue to a bluish green. "You kept some of the stolen food."

Here we go. This was the part where she'd probably start threatening to execute them all again.

He looked down at his plate of illegal, but very delicious contraband. It was obvious what was going on here. There was no point in lying.

"I keep a portion of every supply run we make. It's usually enough to make a few good meals."

Mostly because he loved it. Some of his greatest memories of his mother were helping her harvest vegetables from their self-sustaining eco-garden, and her explaining how to properly prepare meats whenever they were available in the markets.

They'd been poor in the grand scheme of things, but his mother had always made sure there'd been food on the table, no matter what. Mom had taught him that food was an important part of their heritage, and a loving home always had food to spare. That was probably why cooking out here in space seemed so important. These people were his family now, and he wanted to provide for them whenever he could.

Cal looked at his plate. It wasn't overflowing like his mom's dinners, but he did his best.

He looked up. "I try to do this as often as I can to show my appreciation for all their hard work."

"And the rest of the time?" Dania asked.

Cal stirred the melting butter-like substance into his potatoes. "The rest of the time, we eat good, old-fashioned freeze-dried ration packets and meat sticks, just like everyone else in the galaxy."

Ty poked a chunk of chicken into his mouth. "But this is sooo much better."

"Cal is a great cook," Doc said. "We eat like royalty."

"With stolen food," Dania whispered, glaring at her plate.

"Yes." Cal leaned back. He probably shouldn't have hoped she would appreciate the significance of a great meal. "This far out, only the rich can afford real meat."

So occasionally, Cal and a few others intercepted their orders. It wasn't nice, but wealthy people always stockpiled enough for a few months.

"If their shipment doesn't arrive, the merchants who can afford to eat like this in the first place just order another supply run." Cal set down his fork. "I make sure that the colonies that normally go without get the same treatment as the merchants on the larger supply stations and resort worlds. The poorer colonists are people, too, and they deserve the same non-synthetic food once in a while." As did his crew, but Cal kept that part to himself. His people knew where his heart was.

Dania continued to glare at her plate.

"Isn't wasting food a crime?" Alanna asked.

Dania looked up. "Of course."

Alanna pointed at the enforcer's plate with her fork. "Then you better eat that before it gets cold. Two wrongs don't make a right, my mother used to always say."

Dania pursed her lips before taking a bite. After a moment, her eyes brightened. "I've never tasted such flavoring on poultry. On Keveron, meats are usually bland."

"I cook it all myself," Cal said. "I use spices from Earth and the Severus moons. It gives it a great zing."

She seemed to consider that before she started eating again.

"Do you eat a lot of meat where you come from?" Alanna asked.

It probably wasn't the best icebreaker, but it would do.

Dania wiped the edges of her lips with her fingers. "My prince always makes sure we are well fed. We get protein supplements and large servings of vegetables, but meat is reserved for special occasions, even for the king."

"Why is that?" Ethan asked. "I mean, I'm sure the king can afford it."

Careful, Ethan. They didn't want to get her all riled up.

Dania glanced at Alanna before focusing on Ethan. "It's just the way it is. I don't think any of us ever thought to question it. We simply eat what we're given."

She lowered her gaze as if considering that. What was going through her mind?

"What's the king like?" Alanna asked.

Cal gave her a cold stare. She was going to press about the king too? Ethan might not have known better, but Alanna did.

"What?" Alanna asked. "I'm curious."

Dania shifted, still surveying her plate. "I don't really know him well. I simply guard my prince when he stands by his father's side." She seemed to think it over. "The king seems direct. Straightforward." She hesitated. "Maybe a bit impatient."

Everyone's forks stopped moving.

Doc darted a glance at Cal. What enforcer in their right mind would admit the king was impatient?

Easy answer. One who was not in her right mind, or one who was running low on mind-altering pathogens.

"What about your prince?" Alanna stirred her potatoes. "Which one sponsors you?"

They all knew perfectly well which one. Hopefully, this didn't remind Dania that Cal was public enemy number one.

Dania smiled. "I have the honor of serving Prince Geron."

Before being charged for killing the guy's best friend, Cal hadn't even heard of Prince Geron. He wasn't high on the list of royals. There was a High Prince who would be the next king, and a secondary, and a princess. Geron must have been somewhere below them on the royal totem pole.

"What's he like?" Alanna asked.

Dania's eyes sparkled. "He is wonderful. A good man. It's a pleasure to serve him in the king's name."

What did that even mean?

Cal tensed as Ethan leaned across the table. "Isn't he some kind of a playboy? Doesn't he get in trouble with whores and things like that?"

Oh, crap. "Ethan!"

Dania placed her fork down. "Geron does enjoy his pleasures. There's nothing wrong with that."

Ethan smirked. "They say he's an embarrassment to the royal family."

Dania's smile faded.

Cal glared at the engineer. "Enough!" Hadn't Ethan just said he was fond of breathing? "Dania's our guest. Be respectful."

Ethan lowered his eyes, probably realizing he'd put them all on shaky ground. "I'm sorry. Cal's right. That was rude."

Dania ignored him, pushing her untouched potatoes

with her fork. She seemed lost, as if trying to remember something she'd forgotten, before looking at Cal. "What are your intentions now that you've given all your spoils to the colonists?"

Obviously, they'd have to trade a little more to make up for their losses. What was she fishing for?

Cal sliced off a hunk of chicken and dipped it into the pseudo butter pooled in his mashed potatoes. "We're traders, so we're going to be doing some trading." He pointed his fork in Doc's direction. "We need to head out to Sector Z8 to get some things the Doc needs for a project he's working on."

And hopefully, he'll be able to fix you, and you'll run home to your playboy prince and convince him to stop executing people for forgetting to say gesundheit after someone sneezes.

He glanced back to the picture of his dad. This had to be the craziest scheme they'd ever come up with.

Dania placed her fork down. "Sector Z8 is filled with outlier worlds known for larceny."

Cal swallowed his chicken. "Very true, but they're also great places to find hard to get supplies."

She arched her brow. "You mean illicit supplies."

Cal sat back. "Yes, you can buy a lot of prohibited stuff there. But it's not all illegal. There are a lot of folks in those trade centers who are just trying to make a living."

"Not many."

"No, but there are some. Our goal is always to find them." That, at least, was true. "We'll pick up a few things along the way with the intent to trade for something better, and repeat the process until we have enough good stuff to pay for food again."

Cal shifted his weight. Hopefully, she'd understand that

to make enough money to purchase food out here, sometimes you had to buy and trade in unlawful goods. If he could get her to recognize that the ultimate goal was worthwhile, they'd be a step in the right direction.

Whether or not she was capable of seeing past the crime, though, was the question that would decide all their fates.

He set his hands on the end of the table, ready for her to blast him about all the illegalities of his life, but instead, she picked up the fork and mounded her potatoes like a child playing with her food. When the pile was as high as her serving allowed, she used the fork to cut down the sides, creating a perfect pyramid.

Alanna glanced at Cal, then started mounding her own potatoes. "I used to do this all the time as a kid. It drove my parents crazy."

Dania laughed. "Mine, too." The smile melted from her face. She shook her head. "No, that's not right." She stared at the mound as if it were something foreign.

"Everything okay?" Alanna asked.

Dania worked her lips a few times. "I've-I've never eaten potato before."

All points to the contrary. "Are you sure?" Cal asked.

Dania didn't even look up. "No."

A stream of juices from the chicken trailed toward the base of her creation as Dania stared at the pointed mound.

The crew remained silent as she tilted her head and then smashed the makeshift pyramid. Obliterating it from existence.

Her cheeks reddened and she placed her fork down.

Alanna leaned toward her. "Are you okay?"

Dania shook her head and whispered something in Alanna's ear.

Alanna wiped her mouth and stood. "Well, this has been lovely. Thank you, gentlemen, for a nice evening."

Lovely? Nice evening? Cal raised a brow at his navigator.

Alanna stared back. She darted her eyes to Dania and then back to Cal.

Okay, he wasn't completely understanding her signals, but something was up. Cal knew better than to not trust a woman's intuition.

Alanna turned to Dania. "Are you ready to turn in for the night?"

"We have room J4 all set up for her," Ethan said. "She'll be snug like a bug in a rug."

Or snug like a bug under twenty-four hour surveillance with a top-of-the-line security system. But hey, same thing. Cal took a sip of his drink.

"Thank you." Dania stood. "This has been..." She looked down at the ruined potato pyramid. "This has been...nice." The inflection was odd, like she meant it, but was *surprised* that she meant it.

She followed Alanna out, and the door slid shut behind them.

Ethan let out a breath and sat back in his chair. "I never dreamed potatoes could be so stressful."

Doc glared at him. "Screw the potatoes. Did you seriously disrespect a member of the royal family right in front of an enforcer?"

Ethan scrunched up his face. "Yeah, probably not one of my smarter moves."

That was the understatement of the century.

Ty sat forward. "But he's alive. I mean, Dania flinched, but I think she kinda agreed with you."

Cal folded his hands in front of his plate. "So what does that mean?"

Doc stared at his water glass. "It means she's getting more human by the second."

"That's not a good thing?" Ty asked.

Doc sighed. "It is and it isn't. She's dying."

"What?" Ty and Ethan said at the same time.

He looked at them both. "The Banes did something to her. Her body is so badly damaged that she can't survive without them."

Ty laughed. "I can tell by the look on your face that you think you can fix it."

"*Think* is the important word there," Cal pointed out. "Doc has theories, not proven facts."

"I'd take Doc's theories as fact in most cases," Ethan said.

Doc pushed back his plate and rubbed his hands. "If I'm wrong, she's dead."

"*Are* you wrong?" Cal asked.

Doc shook his head. "I don't think so."

The door slid open, and Alanna stepped back in.

"Sorry about that." She returned to her chair, eyeing Dania's plate. "I have a sister who used to get overstimulated once in a while. Dania had that same look on her face."

Cal nodded as she slipped into her seat. He'd sent her first pay stipend home to the navigator's family to pay for her sister's medication.

She looked back to them all. "I figured it would be better to help Dania decompress a little, because if my sister got too upset, we only had to worry about her throwing a tantrum, not frying everyone to a crisp."

Well, that was a sobering thought.

"Where is Dania now?" Cal asked.

"She's lying down. It's been a huge day for her. She's exhausted."

Ethan smiled. "And if she as much as sneezes, I'll know about it."

"The security is all up and running?" Cal asked.

Ethan pulled out a data pad from his pocket and held up a video of Dania lying in bed.

"Is Ethan really the best person to monitor her?" Alanna's cheeks flushed. "I mean, what if she takes a shower or something?"

Ethan held his hand over his heart. "I'm deeply hurt. You know you're the only one I want to see naked."

Alanna pursed her lips. "Keep dreaming."

"Focus, people." Cal filled Alanna in on Dania's current medical situation.

Alanna sat, drumming her fingers on the edge of the table. "Dania isn't the same person. I can attest to that. I mean, she didn't even threaten me today."

Ethan snorted.

"I'm serious."

"We know what you mean." Doc pointed to Dania's plate. "Does anyone else think she was reliving a suppressed memory?"

"I had the same thought," Cal said. "I'm just not sure what to make of it."

"I do." Alanna folded her arms in that *men-are-all-buffoons* way. "She's becoming more like us."

Ethan massaged his temples. "Us, with enough fire-power to eradicate a small moon."

Alanna scoffed at him before turning to Doc. "Do you really think you can save her?"

Doc steepled his fingers. "I have to admit, it's only a theory. What I'm proposing is creating tiny synthetic pathogens. No one has ever done anything like this, but…"

"This is the kind of real-world experimentation bull that got your name on the king's execution list to begin with." Cal didn't mean to dredge up the past, but they all needed to understand the risks.

"Yeah." Doc grimaced. "And contrary to Ethan's high opinion of me, I have been wrong once or twice."

Two years ago, Doc had accidentally killed a kid when a treatment had gone awry. That's what had brought the might of the enforcers down on him. Luckily enough, the *Star Renegade* had been prepped for takeoff before the enforcers had landed that day. And Cal had been on the lookout for a medic. Or, in this case, something like a medic. It had been a win-win for both of them. It wasn't like Cal wasn't already on the run for his own crimes.

Alanna rubbed her hands across the tops of her legs. "So, is this one of those things we're going to vote on? Because I want to try to save her."

Cal tapped the edge of his plate. "It's risky." On many levels. "We can save her, and she could still turn us in."

Ty held out his hands. "Or, we can save her, and she appreciates it, and saves us all right back."

Ty was always the eternal optimist. Cal wished it could always be as easy as things seemed in his first mate's head.

"We could also send her home now," Ethan pointed out.

"That way, we know she'll survive, and maybe she can convince them to cancel the execution orders."

"Before the Banes turn her into a machine again?" Alanna stood. "I'm telling you guys, what came on board that first day was a monster. Right now, she's a person. A confused, lost person. If we send her back there…" She shook her head. "If we're going to do that, we might as well let her die."

"Maybe we should let her decide?" Cal still wanted Dania to be that proverbial stone, but Alanna had a point. Was it right to free her, and then send her back where she might be turned into a living machine again?

Doc rubbed his chin. "I'm not sure she's capable of deciding for herself yet. Like Alanna said, she's confused. Everything is new to her."

Which was a problem in and of itself. She could snap at any minute.

Cal glanced at Dania's plate. None of them wanted to suffer the same fate as her mashed potatoes.

Ty stood. "All in favor of letting the good doctor try to save the enforcer say *aye*." He held up his hand.

So did Alanna and Doc.

Ethan stared at the tabletop. This ship wasn't a complete democracy. Cal could still say *no* and drop Dania off at the nearest star system. But giving up wasn't really a part of who he was anymore. There was still a chance that Dania could make a difference, and part of him wanted to see if Doc really was the mad genius Ethan believed he was.

Cal raised his hand. "Aye."

Ethan nodded. "Okay, sounds like a party. We're all used to running for our lives, anyway, right?"

THE LIGHT above Dania's bed flickered once. Twice. A third time. The fourth time, she sat up.

How could a ship in such disrepair elude the enforcers for so long?

She stood and paced the small room. Alanna's living space was larger than the one they'd given Dania, but that made sense, since she appeared to be the equivalent of an officer in this odd larcenous operation. In fact, they all did.

Dania snickered, imagining Prince Geron preparing dinner for his enforcers, let alone serving them with his own hands. Their prince was a good man, but *humble* was not a word anyone would use to describe him. In fact, humility was not something any Bane or their enforcers would aspire to. Humility made one appear weak.

Dania stared at the door. Why would the captain have invited her to that meal, knowing he'd appear spineless in her eyes? She'd already agreed that he hadn't killed anyone —anyone that she was aware of, at least.

Of course, he was still guilty of a myriad of other

crimes… Crimes Dania was no longer sure she'd be able to punish him for. She wasn't sure how to feel about that.

She took a step closer to the door and placed her hand on the switch plate. The door slid open.

They'd left it unlocked?

She peeked out, but the hallway was empty.

Interesting.

She stepped back inside and closed the door. Even though she'd made it clear she wouldn't judge this crew for what they'd done, she was still an enforcer, and this was still a smuggling ship. The captain wouldn't be foolish enough to leave her completely free.

Her gaze carried over the stark white walls. Other than the flickering light, the room showed no signs of wear. It was quite possible she was the first occupant.

A dark speck in the corner caught her attention. Yes— there, a pin camera.

Military grade, of course. Highly illegal in the private sector.

She closed her eyes and followed the energy of the feed through the wall and to a computer station in a room on the far side of the ship. Additional signals led to a laser-triggered alarm, tainted with the same DNA structure of the copper-haired engineer.

If Dania had left the room, rather than simply looking out, the warning system would have activated, letting the crew know she was no longer in bed.

So, she was not completely free after all.

She couldn't blame Cal for being careful. She was still an unknown to them.

Trailing her fingertips along the wall, Dania caught her reflection in the mirror and frowned at her honey-colored hair. At the moment, she was an unknown even to herself. What if the doctor *had* done something to her?

Pacing her newfound prison, she pulled at the edges of her hair. This discoloration was the most obvious sign of the sickness that had overtaken her, but not the only one. Looking to the mirror again, she turned away, unable to stomach the odd color of her irises.

If she were home, she'd be sprinting to her sponsor, begging him to fix this.

No…he'd have seen her need, maybe even felt it, and he'd have come for her. Geron took care of all of his charges, not like some other sponsors, who left their enforcers for long periods, leaving them open to the attacks that she was supposed to have been thwarting when she'd ended up on this ship.

A shiver ran up her spine, remembering Matara. The girl could be anywhere by now. If she were even still alive.

Dania couldn't imagine being that young, losing her power, and feeling the strain of distance from her sponsor.

The strain of being overcome by humans.

Of becoming *less*.

Dania flexed her hands and stared at her palms. The doctor had made it seem like she would adjust and get better over time, but this would only get worse.

Taking a deep breath, she lay back on the bed. She didn't get the impression that the crew had any intention of harming her or otherwise selling her to the traffickers. So what was their plan, then? Why invite her to dinner? Were they trying to sway her opinions of them?

That was difficult, when the signs of their illegal pursuits were everywhere. Like the camera aimed right at her bed.

Still, she couldn't hate them, despite who they were. Which was another level of concern all together.

Dania closed her eyes and sent a small tickle of power into the camera, setting the frame to still and then locking the image. Anyone casually checking the feeds would believe she was sleeping.

She stood, held out her hands, and felt the reverberation of the energy flowing through the lasers going across the door. This system would be a little harder to thwart than the camera. If she disengaged the laser, the mechanism would read that the system had been breached, and the alarm would sound.

Alexander was always the one to deal with more technical problems like this. He was more patient. He would think it through and consider it a challenge to find a way to circumvent the invisible curtain keeping her inside.

Patience had never been Dania's strong point. Moving to the side of the door, past where the infrared energy hummed, she held her palms up to the wall.

This was foolish in her current state, but she couldn't be sure of the captain's intentions for her. She needed clarity, and clarity could not be achieved while trapped in a room.

Pressing against the wall, she imagined the millions of particles within. The tiny specks of matter fought her for a moment before humming with a resonance all their own. As they dispersed, she stepped through the shifting particles of the wall and into the hallway, then let the atoms spring back to their previous forms.

She released the power and stumbled into the opposite wall. The hallway blurred.

What she'd just done should be child's play. Jumping

through walls had gotten her and Alexander in trouble with the queen on several occasions when they'd been children. Dania had never felt ill afterward.

She blinked until her vision cleared. She'd always wondered how it was possible for an enforcer to be taken and enslaved. She'd been weakened in battle before, but even then, she could have easily taken on countless humans.

This, though, was something different. Alexander had warned her about expending too much energy, and then the Palian steel had stolen even more. She couldn't remember ever having such a small amount of power flowing through her.

She opened and closed her palms as her hands came into focus. Her skin had started to turn a pinkish color, similar to Alanna's.

Her stomach clenched. So much had changed. Too much.

She'd never been vulnerable in her life. This wasn't who she was, and she needed to get herself well. Using the wall to brace herself, she looked down the empty hallway. A hunger gnawed inside her that couldn't be quenched with stolen food. She needed to feed as only an enforcer could.

Holding flat against the edge of the wall, she inched down the corridor, concentrating on the empty space, waiting to hear voices or footsteps.

There were none.

Either the crew had retired for the night, or they were still gathered around the table, enjoying their spoils. She should have hated them for their frivolity, but she still found it hard. Food must be difficult to get out this far in space, no matter who you were.

Growling, Dania punched the wall. Why was she feeling a kinship to these people? These feelings went against her programming and negated all her training.

She flinched at the word *programming*.

Like Alexander's programming to help people, Dania's programming should guide her to make sound decisions. Why wasn't it helping her now? Why couldn't she find a concise thought, a clear direction, as she always had?

Dania held the sides of her head. Whatever this was, she needed to fix it before it got any worse.

She sidled around a corner and found an emergency climb-way. Holding tight to steady herself, she descended the ladder. Cooler air swept across her cheeks as she stepped out onto a dark platform. The echo of her shoes warned of a wide-open space before the lights flicked on.

She held up her palms, ready for attack, but nothing challenged her. A light flickered in the corner before the globe burst, casting the area in darkness again. The rest of the chamber, though, held rows upon rows of freight canisters. Some looked familiar, the same coloring and size that had transported the food to the colony on Kirato.

Hopefully, they were the same canisters, returned to the ship empty.

She turned away and moved through the room. It was more likely that those canisters were filled with more illicit goods. If they were, though, she didn't want to know. She'd seen such goodness from these people. She didn't want to believe they could do anything more against the king's wishes.

An orange beacon pulsed in the back of the room. She made her way toward the light, illuminating the words *E-Com-4*.

Narrowing her eyes, she pressed the red square beside the door, and it slid open. The lights inside flared on and panels came to life. Dania took in the odd, outdated, and faded equipment. It seemed to be an ancient communication station, one not linked to the ship's systems. But why?

What reason would there be to not link your communications to the efficiency of the interplanetary networks?

Her stomach sank, and she looked back to the containers. The interplanetary network was monitored and run through filters.

Older Earth communication, while slower, were nearly undetectable to the king's technology. These systems had been deemed illegal by the Peace Accord. They should only exist in museums...and in ships that might want to avoid detection.

This was yet another crime to add to the list. Dania wanted to return to her room before she found more illegal wares, but this discovery sparked of opportunity.

This console was, by design, not linked up to the ship's communication system. It was as blind to Cal as it was to the crown. Despite the obvious advantages to smugglers, they probably used this as a backup for emergencies as well. And right now, Dania had an emergency.

She slipped inside and closed the doors. The controls were archaic. The edge of the dials were encased in...stars, was that plastic? She shook her head, wondering how humans had ever made it into space.

The system came to life, and an old-fashioned microphone rose from the center of the console. A computer screen that appeared to be encased in planetary-quality glass came from inside the wall and moved toward her.

As children, she and Alexander had played with archaic

machines like this. The controls were far more complicated than modern equipment, but the puzzle of sorting through the design had always been amusing. She set a mild encryption, the same scramble that she and Alexander had come up with when they'd exchanged messages from each other's rooms at night when they should have been sleeping. Dania only hoped he'd recognize it.

She leaned close to the microphone. "It's Dania. I'm ill and weak. Please tell me how to heal myself so I can finish my mission."

She dared not say more. A larger message might be picked up by communications security.

If she could treat herself, Alexander would know how, and he'd help her no matter what. She coded the message to his call signature, and hit *send*.

Now, she needed to wait.

She rubbed her face and sat back. She couldn't remember a time feeling this fragile. Since her very first memory of reaching out and taking Geron's hand, she'd felt safe, sure, and always strong.

In the past few years, her strength had grown exponentially, and now she stood at the prince's side as his general. She was not one to be toyed with. She deserved every ounce of respect given to her.

This weakness, though, made her wonder. Was she really anything without her sponsor?

A tone sounded, and Dania straightened. Alexander must have been sitting at a communication station, waiting for her, just in case. That was very much like him. For once, his predictability fell in her favor, rather than being an annoyance.

She opened the line. Static hummed across the screen

as the ancient equipment struggled to decipher the message from so far away.

Dania's hands shook. Deep down, she knew Alexander wouldn't be able to help her, but she needed to try. Going back to the very doctor who might have triggered this illness was the last thing she wanted to do.

The static dissipated. Dania waited for Alexander's ice blue eyes and warming smile to give her comfort.

Instead, a deep blue uniform came into view as someone else sat before the screen.

Definitely not Alexander.

Dania gasped as she took in the green and blue shimmering skin and dark green gaze of the last person she'd expected to see…

Her sponsor, Prince Geron.

The man who'd asked for Cal's head.

SHE TREMBLED, stunned, but she should have expected this. If their prince had given an order to let him know if she contacted anyone, Alexander would have been compelled to comply without question. He wouldn't even have been able to warn her.

Geron stared at the screen. He must have been far away and not yet able to see her.

Dania reached for the screen and ran her fingers over the glass. She didn't realize how much she really needed him until he was there in front of her.

Geron's eyes widened. He reached for her as she'd reached for him before drawing his hand from the screen and speaking to her in his own language. *"Dania, you look awful. Are they not feeding you?"*

She nearly laughed. Always the dutiful sponsor, worrying about her needs. "Yes, Ada. They're feeding me, but not what I really need."

Every cell in her body vibrated at hearing his voice, even from so far away.

His lips thinned. *"Catching the trappers is not worth losing you. Come home immediately."*

"I'm not with the trappers. I'm with a smuggler."

She shouldn't tell him about Cal. She may regret letting even that one hint of where she was slip.

Her prince's eyes narrowed, and a wave of calm spread over her, as it always did anytime she looked into his gaze.

She could tell him anything. He was her prince. He was everything to her.

Dania took a steadying breath. "I'm with the smuggler Calvin Espinoza."

Geron's nose flared. *"The man who killed Filluck?"*

Dania shifted her weight. How could she explain why Espinoza wasn't already dead for his crimes?

She couldn't lie to her sponsor, but maybe leaving part of the story out would be the best. "I've discovered a file."

She reviewed what she'd seen, and the royal encryption that had kept the file safe until it had reached her hands. She waited for a reaction, but his eyes seemed cold. Distant.

"Who would have sealed those files?" she asked. "They clearly show that Espinoza was not the murderer."

Geron stared at her for several moments. She took another deep breath, reminding herself that this was only the time delay.

The wait seemed longer than normal, though.

"How did you open these files?" Geron finally asked.

"I used your decryption codes."

"Without my permission?"

A chill ran over her. Why would she need permission?

Wasn't that why he'd given her the codes to begin with, to use at her discretion?

"I only did my duty, Ada."

Her chest tightened. If this were an interrogation, if he were a human under suspicion of a crime, she'd already be planning his means of execution. Geron's stance, his change of voice… Everything about him prodded at her training to detect a lie.

That was ridiculous, though. Geron never lied. Especially to her.

It had to be something else, and she needed to find out what before the biting in her stomach grew worse.

No matter how many of her internal sensors flared, she couldn't accuse him, nor imply one of the people charged with keeping law in the universe had committed a crime. She needed to place her words carefully. "Does this mean you knew the files had been sealed?"

He rubbed his eyes. *"I do not know who sealed the files, Dania."*

She released the breath she'd been holding, and the ache subsided.

Of course he didn't know. It was ridiculous for her to even consider such a thought. A prince, committing a crime… It was unheard of.

She did have to relay what she'd found, though. "You need to know that the recordings clearly show Filluck committing crimes."

The elongated silence shoved a new wedge into her ribcage.

Geron's finger tapped the table in front of him. *"Actions seen through security footage taken out of context do not necessarily show truth. Either way, that would not make it okay for him to be killed by an insignificant human."*

But...wouldn't Filluck have had to be executed for his crimes?

Geron's eyes darkened. *"It was foolish of me to approve this mission knowing you'd be gone so long. Come home. Now."*

Her heart twisted. "Were you aware Filluck was involved in illicit activity?"

Her prince looked down. *"I admit I had suspicions."* His gaze returned to hers. *"I was going to confront him about it, but Espinoza killed him before I had a chance."*

"Cal didn't do it."

His head tilted. *"Cal?"*

She stiffened. Had she called him that?

Geron waved his hand in the air. *"It makes no difference. Calvin Espinoza has already been found guilty."*

"I told you the recording proves his innocence."

The prince's eyes bored into her. *"I have heard enough. You need to come home to be fed. You are not well, and you are not thinking clearly."*

"I admit I'm not well, but on this one thing, I'm clear. I need you to look at the recordings."

He stared again. How much of this was the time delay, and how much was actual anger?

"Please, Ada."

He closed his eyes. *"Fine. Send them."*

Good. She concatenated the file and sent the data along the open stream.

Her prince was a good man. Once he saw the recordings, he'd come to the same conclusion she had. He'd clear the murder charges, and then they could discuss the rest of the charges, which were, unfortunately for the crew, quite incriminating. She needed to handle this delicately.

He stared low at the screen. His lips thinned. *"Why have you sent the file with spatial encryption?"*

That was an odd question. There was only one reason in the universe to use spatial encryption...to hide one's location.

His gaze lanced hers. *"Send me your location."*

"I need you to watch the recording." Small steps. First she needed to clear Cal.

His nose flared again. *"Send. Me. Your. Location."*

Dania's stomach roiled. Her skin crawled. She wanted to send the location.

No. She needed to. Her prince had demanded it.

So why did she hesitate?

A pressure built inside her, and her hands twitched toward the controls.

Had the doctor done something to her, or was he correct, that her body needed her royal sponsor like most species needed air?

Things would change when she went back. She wouldn't care about anything but the law.

"Dania?"

She shut her eyes, as if doing so would hide her from his gaze. She had no choice but to comply, but before she agreed, she needed to get this information to him. "You need to promise me you'll watch the recordings."

"I already told you I would. Are you questioning me?"

"I-I..." She what? Didn't trust him? No, that wasn't true. She trusted him implicitly. He'd never given her a reason not to trust him. Ever.

He slapped the desk before him. *"This is all the more reason to get you home as quickly as possible. Send me your location immediately. I will come for you myself."*

Dania considered the yellow knob on the console. With one press of a button, she could stamp their spatial location on the star map. He'd know exactly where the *Star Renegade* was.

Was that the right thing to do, though? "Please promise you will watch the recording with an open mind."

The stare again. She wasn't imagining it. He was angry. He'd never been angry with her. Not even when she and Alexander had set fire to the linens in his mother's receiving hall.

He leveled his gaze on hers. *"I will watch the recording you sent me."*

Good. Her heart lifted. A smile spread across her face, relief flooding her.

Geron was a reasonable man. This would start a dialog. He just needed to see what she'd seen.

"The location is coming." She hit the button.

When the light flashed on the other side a few moments later, sweat formed on her brow.

A satisfied expression crossed Geron's features.

Her chest clenched. A flood of panic swept over her.

But why? Geron would never hurt her.

But what about the crew? They had, in fact, committed crimes, and Geron was charged with upholding the king's law, and that law, no matter what those tapes proved, was very clear.

Her stomach soured.

What had she done?

The prince looked up. *"Do not warn the crew. I do not want them changing your location before I can get to you."*

And what would happen once he got here? "Y-You don't need to come for me. I'm fine."

He shook his head in the same way he had all those years ago, after they'd put out the fire. *"Spoken like someone who has not looked in the mirror in some time. You need me more than I think you realize. I am not losing you. I am coming."*

He ran his fingers over the screen. Dania closed her eyes and imagined him touching her, breathing life back into her dying body. She needed this. She needed *him*.

But when the screen went blank, a chill ran through her.

He *would* watch the recordings. He'd promised. He would see that he was wrong, that Cal hadn't murdered anyone. The truth would finally be known. Nothing else mattered.

Standing, she blinked.

Something else *had mattered* to her. But what?

She rubbed her temples. It was so strange, how she'd feel fuzzy sometimes after speaking to Geron, like she'd been so swept up just by being in his presence that parts of their conversations would simply melt away.

No matter. He was coming. She'd done what she'd needed to do.

Everything would be made right once he arrived.

She made her way back through the warehouse chamber, past the circumspect containers, and climbed the ladder back to the deck where the crew quarters were. Reaching the top, she leaned against the wall, steadying her breath.

A simple climb shouldn't have winded her. Maybe she should have tried to contact Geron sooner. He was right that she needed him. It was foolish of her to think she was so strong she could be away from her sponsor for so long.

Would this be seen as a sign of weakness, though? She'd been assigned a mission and couldn't complete it.

No. She would complete her mission. Right now, she just needed rest. She'd accept the hospitality of the bed she'd been offered, and sleep.

Until her sponsor came for her, that was the most she could do to make herself feel better.

Yes, sleep was all she needed.

Everything would be fine once Geron arrived.

A TONE BROKE through the haze of wispy clouds hanging lazily around a sunset off the Hawaiian Islands on Earth. Not that Cal had ever been to Hawaii—or Earth, for that matter. The vision was a common one, available for free in virtual reality centers. The scene popped into his dreams often. He'd always wondered if the islands were as beautiful in real life as the sims made them out to be.

Another tone.

He rolled over and squinted at the holoclock beside his bed. It was barely six a.m. No one on this crew ever got up before eight. He must have been dreaming. He rolled back over and remembered the warm breezes and reflection of the sun in the water.

Another tone, followed by banging.

The emergency breakers engaged, and the door screeched open.

Cal rolled over and squinted at the silhouette of a man standing in his doorway, backlit in a blurry, white gleam from the hallway. He rubbed his eyes. "Ty? Someone better be dead."

"We might all be dead."

Cal sat up. "Lights." The room illuminated twenty-five percent. "What's going on?"

"Someone dropped a pin last night."

Cal rubbed the back of his neck. "Impossible. No one is careless enough to do that."

"I'm telling you, boss, someone dropped a pin and cascaded our location."

Cal jumped from the bed. "Cascaded our location?"

Ty nodded. "Someone knows exactly where we are."

Cal grabbed the pants draped over the chair and pulled them on. "Did you move the ship?"

"Of course. I woke Ethan first. He's tweaking the efficiency, making sure we're burning hard and clean, but we're still on a straight line. Anyone with any sense of knowhow is going to be able to track us."

Cal pulled on his shirt. "Did you wake anyone else up? Question them? Maybe this is all just a mistake?"

But Cal knew it wasn't a mistake. His crew knew how dangerous a pin was. None of them would send a pin through a transmission, encrypted or not.

Dania had sold them out.

He pulled on his flight jacket. "Where's the enforcer?"

"I've got Alanna watching her in the lounge."

Cal flinched. Dania was the least likely to hurt Alanna, but Alanna was probably also the easiest one for the enforcer to manipulate. "How in the blazes did Dania get out of her room?"

"Who knows?" Ty held up his hands. "The door wire wasn't breached, and the camera showed her in bed all night."

Cal was done with underestimating this woman, or trusting her in any way, for that matter.

"Does Alanna know that Dania dropped a pin?"

His lips thinned. "You know Alanna. She said that Dania has changed, and she wouldn't do anything like that to us."

Cal moved into the hall. "Yeah, well, this wouldn't be the first time Alanna was wrong about someone." He shook the lingering fog from his eyes. "Is there a reason I'm the last one you woke up?"

Ty shrugged. "I didn't wake up Doc yet."

"Get him up. We might need all hands on deck."

Ty hit a comm pad on the wall as Cal kept walking. "Doc, rise and shine, princess."

Doc groaned. "What time is it?"

"Too early. Get some caffeine and meet us in the lounge. We might need that big brain of yours."

"Is this one of those *we're going to die* situations?"

"Definitely."

"Okay, I'll be right there."

Ty caught up to Cal. "What you are you going to do? I mean, she's weak, but she could probably still take your head off."

Cal stopped and glared at him.

His first mate held up his hands. "Hey, I'm just reminding you, because you have that look on your face."

"I don't have a *look* on my face."

"You do. It's that same look you had when you punched Ethan for letting that Festian cave boar out of its cage."

Cal started walking again. "I'm fine."

But punching something might feel pretty good at the moment.

The *Renegade* shivered under his feet as they made their way down the hall. Either Ethan was pushing her to her limits, or the ship could feel the weight of doom hurtling toward them.

The speed was good, but Ty was right. They needed to change direction or they'd be easily tracked. Of course, that meant slowing down. He didn't want to lose any momentum until they knew whether or not they were dealing with the worst-case scenario.

When they reached the lounge, Cal slapped his palm on the control panel. He squeezed between the doors, not waiting for them to open completely.

Alanna sat across from the enforcer, a line of dominos spread out in front of her. Alanna gaped at him, holding a tile in midair, about to place it on the board.

Cal stormed toward Dania and slammed his fist onto the table, scattering the tiles. "What did you do?"

The enforcer pushed back her pieces, not meeting his gaze. "What I needed to."

"That's a load of meteor rock and you know it."

The door opened and Doc slipped in, rubbing his eyes. Ty leaned toward him, whispering into his ear.

Alanna covered her mouth. "Stars, Dania, did you really do it?"

The enforcer raised her gaze. She opened her mouth as if to say something to Alanna before closing it and looking down at the scattering of tiles on the table.

Cal took a deep breath and clenched and unclenched his fists. "Would you at least do me the courtesy of telling me where you sent the pin?"

She looked up at him, her posture lax. "I'm sick."

Doc pushed forward. "I told you that you aren't sick.

This is called withdrawal." He knelt beside her. "I know you find this hard to believe, but the royal family did something to you. Your body is addicted to these pathogens. I can help you, though, if you let me."

Her hand shook on the edge of the table. "You can't help me. Only my prince can fix this."

Alanna gasped.

Cal's head spun, and he realized he'd stopped breathing. "You called your prince? The one who wants my head on a pike?"

She straightened slightly. "Yes, but I told him you were innocent."

"Yeah, I bet that went over well."

"I sent him the files I decrypted. He said he will watch them."

"And you believed him?"

"Yes, of course." She smiled with all the innocence of a child. "Once he sees the evidence, he'll come to the same conclusion I have."

Cal shook his head. "You are seriously delusional, lady." He started to pace. "I know you don't give a damn about the rest of us, but I would have thought you would've been a little more hesitant about putting Alanna's life in danger."

Dania cocked her head. "Alanna is the least guilty of all of you. I would hope that he'd…"

"What, grant her leniency? What is the punishment for committing a crime, Dania? What is the punishment for *any* crime?"

She lowered her gaze. "Death."

Cal leaned on the table and looked down at her. "And you've just told the royal family exactly where we are."

She seemed to turn that over in her head. Horror crossed her features. "B-But he's not coming for you. He's coming for me."

Doc rubbed his face. "I should have expected this. The prince still has too much control. She probably can't even fathom what's about to happen to us."

Cal loomed over Dania. How could she be so blind? "Do you actually think he won't kill every person on this ship, even if we give you up freely?"

The color drained from her face. She opened her lips twice to speak, but the words didn't form.

Cal slammed his fist on the table, shaking the tiles again. "Ty, lock her up in the reinforced cargo locker."

His first mate's eyes widened. "Are you serious?"

"Deadly serious." Cal turned to Doc. "Build one of those force fields on all four sides to make sure she stays there."

Dania lifted her chin. "You're imprisoning me again?"

"Yeah, well, you've proven that you can't be trusted." He turned to Alanna. "I need you on the bridge. We need to start jumping in another direction or they're going to find us."

Alanna stood. "We can't outrun a prince."

Cal stomped toward the door. "Maybe not, but we can sure as hell try."

CHAPTER 31

CAL

THE BRIDGE PULSED with a soft white glow. At least someone had been able to turn off the alarm so Cal could think.

Ty grimaced, looking into his screen. "This is not good."

"Talk to me," Cal said.

"Something is coming up fast on the sensors. It's either really big, or it's a lot of somethings."

"Either one is bad news. Where's Alanna?"

"Here." She ran through the door and dropped into her chair. She winced, fingering her side.

"You okay?"

Alanna shifted in her chair uncomfortably. "I'll have to be. Don't worry about it."

But he did worry about it. She was injured. So was Ethan. They should both be in bed resting, not stressing out in another race for their lives.

He looked out the window. They could jump and maybe hurt Alanna, or they could slow down and turn, or they could make a full arc and hope the prince wouldn't notice and pass them by.

And then Cal could wake up and join reality.

The ship jolted.

Cal turned to Ty. "What'd you just do?"

"I changed trajectory by point two degrees. I mean, it's not much, but it gives us a chance."

A chance wasn't enough. This crew was about to die because Cal had made a bad decision and hadn't dropped the enforcer off on Kirato like they'd originally planned.

Cal knew better than to think they'd be able to change her. Enforcers were the one horrific constant in the galaxy.

Ty cursed under his breath and changed course again. "They're following."

Alanna removed her hand from her side. "I can jump us."

But what would it do to her? "No, you can't," Cal said.

She glared at him. "Do you have a better idea?"

Cal rubbed his face. He wished he did. Things were bad enough. He didn't want to put anyone in danger if there were any other good options. "A small jump, just to take us off this course. If it hurts, stop."

Alanna flicked her wrist, and the blue navigation circle appeared. She turned the dials in the air.

"Okay. Here we go." Alanna cringed as she poked her fingers into the center of the magical gears.

Cal held his breath as the world stretched, turning pinkish-purple.

This had to work. If they'd ever needed good karma, it was now.

His stomach lurched before the color whisked away, leaving deep black space speckled with stars before them.

"Where are we?" Cal asked.

Ty looked at his screen. "About fifteen meters from

where we were, but who cares? We're headed in another direction."

"Engines are at full throttle," Ethan shouted over the comm.

Finally, some good news.

Ty whooped, throwing his fist in the air. "The *Star Renegade* slips through their fingers again!"

Alanna flopped into her chair, holding her face in her hands.

Cal walked over and squeezed her shoulder. "Hey, you did it. Are you okay?"

"I-I think so." She raised her glossy eyes to Cal. "I don't think I have another jump in me. I'm sorry."

"It's all right. You did good."

Hopefully, now they could find a small planet to hide out on and get everyone well again. This was one of those golden opportunities to use the emergency supply store and lie low for a while.

Cal returned to his chair.

The stars twinkled in the distance. Thousands of galaxies, some explored, some not. He used to look up at the sky as a kid, wondering what it would be like to go into space.

Despite stowing away in cargo containers for his first few trips, interplanetary travel had been everything he'd dreamed. Until people had started chasing him.

There was still an element of magic in looking out into infinity, though. Space was so big, so vast. Knowing you were smaller than a grain of sand in the big scheme of things made the toils of humanity seem so trivial.

"No!" Ty growled through clenched teeth. "No. No. No. No. No!" He punched the side of his console.

"What?" Cal asked.

"We have incoming!" Ty shouted.

Sweat beaded on Cal's brow. He tightened his grip on his armrests, staring at the clear pathway of stars before him. "Are we still at full throttle?"

"Of course!"

"Don't look back. Just keep pushing." It was wishful thinking that they could outrun the prince without Alanna, but until they were caught, there was always a chance they might get away.

The stars before them blurred.

Cal leaned forward. "What is that?"

The blur intensified and then boldened, the colors darkening until a massive behemoth of polished glass and metal appeared out of nowhere.

"They have a jumper!" Ty banked the ship up.

Cal's head whipped back as Alanna cried out, sliding across the floor.

Ty leveled the ship off. "We're good. I can fly circles around anything that big."

Another smaller ship appeared, then another. The second fired two long range blasts from its gun turrets.

Ty swiveled around the shots. "Whoa!"

A clear path appeared before them again.

"Throttle it!" Cal called.

"Ethan, do we have the power?" Ty yelled into the comm.

"Go, go, go!" Ethan yelled.

The ship hummed beneath them before shooting into the stars, leaving the larger, bulkier ships behind. This was why the *Star Renegade* had never been captured. With this crew of brilliant misfits at the helm, the little ship defied physics and any other laws of space they'd come up against.

Alanna pulled herself up to her station. "They're not following."

Cal smiled. "You bet your ass they're not following."

Ty paled, looking into the smaller screen on his console. "Wait."

No. It wasn't possible. "Wait for what?"

Ty pointed in front of them. "There."

Another ship materialized, or maybe the same ship—the big one.

Ty growled, spinning the *Star Renegade* full circle, only to run into another ship. Two more popped into existence on their left and right. Ships kept appearing until they were surrounded like a fish in a bowl. The *Renegade* was still moving, but the royal ships matched them pace for pace.

They were trapped.

"Break comms. Lock everything down." Cal turned to Ty. "Options?"

His first mate stared as the largest cruiser came closer. "I...um..."

Alanna rested her full weight on her console. She panted, holding her side. "I can still jump us out."

"You can barely stand." Cal pushed up from his seat. "Can we squeak between them and keep changing course?"

Ty shook his head. "They've got a jumper."

"But so do we," Alanna said.

Yes, Alanna was good, but she'd never jumped so many times injured like this. Risking her wasn't an option.

The screens before them flickered, and the feed showing the advancing ship morphed into the face of an enforcer with their signature opalescent hair, cut short with the exception of longer spikes on top, and silver-blue eyes. His pale gray uniform looked like he never sat down, ate, or even moved as he glared into the camera.

"I thought I told you to lock everything down?" Cal asked.

Ty fiddled with the controls. "We did. The comms are off. This shouldn't be possible."

The enforcer lifted his chin. "Vessel call sign SR87795682 dash GH841, you have been charged with…" His eyes narrowed, looking off the screen. He pursed his lips before he returned his attention to the camera. "You've been charged with more crimes than I care to note. Prepare to be boarded."

Ty sat back. "Do I have your permission to give him the finger?"

Cal snickered. "You might as well. It certainly isn't going to get any worse." He reached across his console and hit the override lever. "Taking controls."

He pushed forward, banking up and over the ship. The face on the screen, rather than showing surprise, looked bored before the feed stopped, and Cal could see out the window again.

"Throw a broad sweep of thermal lasers over their bow," Cal said, pushing down into open space.

"That's not going to do much more than *tickle* a ship that size," Ty said.

Cal hit the comm. "Ethan, Doc, if you have any kind of heavy munitions hidden down there that I'd normally be pissed off about, I'd love to hear it."

Alanna held the sides of her console as she looked into the screen. "Something long and nasty-looking just shot out of one of the smaller ships."

"We have some very active rotation signatures coming in hot from the rear," Ty said. "It's artillery, but I'm not sure what kind."

Did it matter? "I'll take a wild guess and say it's the kind that blows you up."

Heavy rounds made no sense, though. The whole reason those ships were here was because of Dania. Had the high and mighty enforcer somehow become expendable?

Cal grunted. That would be inconvenient.

He banked the ship right, still throttling toward open space.

"They must have tracking sensors," Ty said. "The artillery turned with us."

Of course it did, because bad luck just followed them everywhere some days.

A flash of blue light flared up in Cal's peripheral vision. Alanna stood, her fingers spinning the lighted gears.

"Alanna, no!"

Her gaze met his before she tapped her fingers into the circle.

Cal flew back into his chair. The bridge around him blurred. A hum filled his ears as the ship rattled around him. This wasn't a little jump. This was a full-on hop. The kind that the ship would need to recover from. The purples and pinks faded to black as they blasted back into regular space.

"Three minutes!" Ty pressed a button and a timer started counting back. That was how long their trail would last before the particles dispersed too much to follow. If the royal ship's jumper was good enough, they'd be here by then. If not, they were home free.

Alanna stumbled, holding her head with one hand and her side with the other. Cal needed to get her to Doc as soon as possible. But he needed to get the rest of them safe first.

"Screw the cooldown," Cal said. "Start us moving."

Ty nodded, taking back the controls.

Cal jumped from his seat and caught Alanna just before she hit the floor. "What did you do?"

"I think I saved your rear end."

Cal smiled. "Maybe, but I had the situation under control."

She laughed, wincing. "Sure, you did."

Okay, maybe he didn't have it *that much* under control. Still… "You didn't have to hurt yourself."

Blood soaked her uniform. Cal had no idea how jump power worked, but he knew anyone with two recent munitions wounds should have been resting. Alanna looked like she'd just lifted weights or run full speed through a space terminal.

He brushed back her bangs with his fingertips and eased her the rest of the way to the floor. "We're going to have Doc patch you back up, but no more heroics from you. You're supposed to be the smart one."

The door slid open and someone entered.

"Smarter than Doc?" Alanna asked, her voice just above a whisper.

"You're definitely smarter than me." Doc moved further into the room and knelt beside her. "I'm just really good at making people *think* I'm smarter."

"How'd you know she was hurt?" Cal asked.

Doc shrugged. "One minute, we were being boarded, the next minute, everything turned purple. I figured our girl wasn't following doctor's orders." He scanned a laser pen across her forehead.

"You told me to take it easy." She groaned. "Jumping isn't like calisthenics or anything."

Doc play-slapped her shoulder. "That's why they call it jumping, girl. It always takes a lot out of you." He looked at Cal. "Next time, remind me to ban her from the bridge entirely."

Cal smiled. The truth was, though, that she had saved their hides. Again.

Ty squinted into this screen. "You gotta be kidding me."

"Now what?" Cal stood.

"Boss, they're relentless. We've got incoming."

So much for their three minutes. "Okay, people, let's…"

The lights flicked out. The consoles around them powered off.

"Ty, what did you do?" Doc asked.

"Wasn't me."

The bridge trembled beneath Cal's feet. The walls hummed like someone was running a vacuum.

"What is that?" Ty asked.

The hum heightened, and the yellow button on Ty's console flashed three times, lighting up the dark like a pinhead sun.

Cal's hands shook. "Ty?"

Cal heard three taps, then three more. Ty must have been trying to stop the light from blinking.

It wouldn't stop, though. It kept flashing—the only light in the darkness of space. Ice flooded Cal's veins. Darkness could make you feel alone, even surrounded by friends.

"The warning is real, this time," Ty said. "It's the proximity alarm."

"Can anyone see what's out there?"

Ty's face glowed in the triple-flash of the light. "Nothing."

Cal jumped when something banged against the door to the bridge, then banged again.

"Were we boarded?" Doc asked.

"This fast? Not likely." However, they were dealing with enforcers. For all he knew, they could beam themselves onto other ships like they had in the old *Star Trek* fictionals.

The door slid open a few inches. A dull, bluish haze seeped in from the hallway.

Ethan's shadow appeared in the light. "Everyone okay in there?"

Heat flooded Cal's veins. "We're fine. Why aren't you downstairs getting me power?"

Ethan manually pulled the doors the rest of the way open. "We got nothing. We were hit with some kind of energy-sucking weapon. Everything is down."

"Life support?" Cal asked.

Ethan took in an overzealous breath, then released it. "The backup batteries are working like a charm." He tapped his foot on the floor. "Gravity is good, too."

That was the first good news in a while. "How long will the air last?"

Ethan gave an accentuated grimace. "It's only a backup. I don't really know."

A voice filled the room. "Vessel call sign SR87795682 dash GH841, I am no longer amused. If you look out any exterior viewing port, you will see eight star hoppers and a royal cruiser circling you. If you attempt to skip space again, you will be destroyed."

"He's bluffing," Ty said. "They're not going to fire with Dania on board."

The voice snickered. "An enforcer can live in the vacuum of space. Can you?"

A rock formed in Cal's throat. "How can he hear us?"

Ty shook his head. "He shouldn't be able to. Comms are down."

"Not for a royal extraction force. We are boarding," the voice said.

Static filled the room. Ty grabbed Cal and pulled him to the floor with Doc and Alanna, out of the sight of the camera system—probably a good call.

Ethan dropped beside them. "I think we need a new strategy."

Alanna leaned up from the floor. "I don't need power to jump. Let me try again."

The dark, wet patch on her uniform glistened as the yellow light continued to blink.

Cal pulled her back down. "Rest up. You've done all you can."

Ty looked over his shoulder at the screen and then returned to the huddle. "Okay, so what's the plan?"

They all turned toward Cal. As usual, they were depending on him and his crazy-good instincts. Too bad at the moment those instincts had left him floating in space without an oxygen tank.

He glanced at the huge hulk of a ship filling the window. They were all about to die. The only question was, would they surrender or go down fighting?

CHAPTER 32

DANIA

A DEAFENING BOOM rattled the ship. Dania called up a small shield around her as she was thrown back, hitting the side wall. A hiss filled the chamber before a dull thump echoed through the emptiness as the emergency airlocks engaged.

The lights flickered again.

Was there anywhere on this ship not riddled with electrical problems?

Not that there was anything in the vicinity to look at. Her cell was exactly what the captain had claimed. The spaces were not much more than enlarged stainless steel storage lockers, hers with an advanced revolving energy field to keep her inside.

Once she was free, she'd need to look into this new technology and find a way to thwart it. Anything that could hold an enforcer must be deemed illegal and destroyed or there would be anarchy.

A wave swept over her, like a smack that stung her skin, carried through her body, and came clear out the other side. *What in the name of the king was that?*

It had to be some sort of a weapon, or a slap of power from a very irate prince.

The engines stopped humming. The lights winked out, and this time, they didn't flicker back on. The slight hum of energy surrounding her room and keeping her inside dissipated.

The ship was disabled. She was free.

A chill skated over her skin. Dania's enforcers would board now. Within the next hour, she'd be herself again.

She took one step toward the door, then hesitated. Was that what she really wanted? If asked to pass judgment on this crew, would she do it? *Could* she?

She shivered, realizing once she fed, she would find everyone onboard the *Star Renegade* guilty of at least smuggling, and they would die for their crimes...maybe even Alanna if no one noticed or took interest in her remarkable gifts...but even this information might not be able to save her in the face of Bane fury.

The ship jolted and a loud bang echoed through the halls. Dania fell to her knees, placing her hands down to steady herself.

That wasn't a weapon. Something had hit them.

They'd probably been bumped by an enforcer ship drifting too close. It was a tactic she'd used herself before boarding a condemned vessel. It confused the crew, left them wary, unstable, and ripe for the slaughter.

Dania jumped to her feet. Whatever happened, she was to blame. There would be no mercy for these people, even if Geron had watched the recordings she'd sent him. What was she thinking?

She *hadn't been* thinking.

A new chill swept over her.

On Kirato, she'd given a child food.

The girl had thanked her and then smiled, waving goodbye to Dania.

That's what life was supposed to be like. People should care about each other. Help each other.

But that's not what enforcers did. They didn't nurture. They punished.

It was foolish of her to think there was any other outcome to this day. The crew of the *Star Renegade* wouldn't get to plead their case in one of Earth's courts. The enforcers were about to come in with primordial power blazing. The entire crew of this ship was about to die.

She couldn't let that happen.

Holding out her hands, she called up what was left of the power swirling inside her. Primordial energy swelled up and burned from within. The power pulsed on the edges of her skin until she'd called everything she had… all that was left of the strength given to her by her prince.

It was more than she should summon at one time. But weakened as she was, she needed every bit of her remaining energy to make a difference.

Any other day, she wouldn't worry because the one person who could save her if she overextended herself was in one of the ships outside.

But that same person had done something to her. Something unforgivable. When she'd looked in Geron's eyes when he'd intercepted her transmission to Alexander, she simply hadn't cared about this crew anymore.

Dania clenched her teeth. That wasn't true. She *had* cared, but somehow Geron had managed to erase her worries, controlling her even from that far away.

The doctor had been right all along. She wasn't a person. She was a puppet.

Holding out her arms, her feet rose off the ground.

Her gut clenched. Nine years of conditioning told her this was wrong, that she should sit back and let justice be done. But there was no justice in the execution of this crew. This, she was sure of.

A tickle of warmth moved over her, a touch she knew all too well.

Geron?

Her sponsor's essence swirled through her. *I am here. I am coming for you.*

Bile rose in her throat again. She pushed him out. She would not be erased again.

His confusion flooded her, followed again by his warmth and his love.

And worst of all…understanding. *It's all right, Dania. I am here. It's over.*

She wanted to open herself to him and accept all he had to offer. She wanted to fold into his arms and have him tell her everything would be okay.

But then he'd *make it* okay. He'd change her back, make her like she had been.

Part of her still wanted that…but she couldn't. She wouldn't let the people on this ship die because they stole to feed others. No one could make her believe this galaxy would be a better place without anyone on this crew.

Tears streamed from her cheeks as she pushed her sponsor away.

The warmth in his power left, momentary confusion turned to anger.

I'm sorry. She choked out a sob. *I wish I could make you understand.*

But he'd never understand, and she was about to make an enemy of the last person she'd ever thought she'd betray.

CHAPTER 33

CAL

THE YELLOW LIGHT flashed in Ty's face, leaving him pasty and sickly-looking in the darkness. "There's a surge of power coming in," he said.

Cal dropped into his seat. "A weapon?"

"I'm not sure. It's almost like a transmission."

The main viewscreen flickered. The lights on the deck blinked once before rising to full illumination.

Cal jumped up. "Did we just get power back?"

"Not everything," Ty said. "Some computers, lights, and minor ship functions. No engines. No weapons."

The ships circling them faded into the flicker on the screen. The static lessened. A form appeared, muddy at first, and then cleared into the shimmering, light blue and green face of a Kever National in a navy blue uniform with royal insignias. The haze in the air about the Kever nearly glowed. His skin seemed reflective and shiny, like the enforcers' silvery-opalescent hair. The being contemplated the edge of what appeared to be something similar to a stick of licorice before taking a bite, ignoring Cal and the crew.

Did he not know the transmission had opened?

Cal stood, facing the screen. They were skunked no matter what they did, so he might as well see what they wanted. "I couldn't help but notice we hadn't been boarded yet."

The Kever flicked a glance in his direction and took another bite of his snack. Apparently, the *Star Renegade* was not important enough to interrupt his meal. Either that, or the Kever regarded them the same as he regarded the furniture, and he was making a point of letting them see it. Knowing the Banes, both options could be true.

After the third bite, the Kever licked his lips and centered his gaze on the screen. "Calvin Espinoza."

Cal shivered. There was no use denying it. "Yes."

"You have something of mine. I want it back."

Cal released the breath he'd been holding. The only thing he had that a Kever would be interested in was Dania, which meant he was being addressed by Prince Geron of the Imperial House Bane.

Geron wasn't high in the royal pecking order, but Earth had still bowed to his father. No smuggler ever wanted to be stared down by a Bane for any reason.

Still, they hadn't been boarded, as the other voice had promised. Had this turned into a negotiation? Could they have scanned the ship and found out that Dania was weakened and held within Doc's revolving barrier?

That technology was something new they hadn't seen before. Maybe they were afraid Cal would use it against them, or they could be afraid Dania might get hurt.

Cal scanned the deck, looking into the horrified expressions of his crew. They'd all known something like this was a possibility when they'd signed up. Smugglers eventually got caught, and the price on Cal's head was pretty high.

Of course, they'd brought this on themselves by bringing an enforcer on board. That would probably go down in the *Star Renegade* history as the dumbest thing they'd ever done.

If they lived long enough to make an entry in the ship's diary.

At the moment, Cal needed to do as much damage control as possible. He reset his footing, trying to look more confident than he felt. "I'm willing to talk this through."

Geron stared at Cal for a moment before snorting a bored laugh. "I want my enforcer back. Now."

The words *or what* itched on the edges of Cal's lips. Why hadn't they boarded and just taken her?

"I'm willing to give her to you," Cal said.

Doc looked to the floor. Cal knew his medic wanted to try to save her. He wished he could have given him the chance, but now he had to trade her life for theirs.

Cal cringed, remembering the sweet look on her face as she'd mounded her potatoes—the joy in something so simple as playing with her food.

He gritted his teeth. This shouldn't have hurt so much. She'd sold them all out.

So why did he feel like he was betraying one of his own?

He closed his eyes. She wasn't one of his own. But the others were. And they were his responsibility.

Cal looked back to the screen. "I'll hand-deliver her to your ship."

"Cal, no!" Alanna cried.

Ty jumped out of his chair, shaking his head. They knew as well as Cal did that stepping onto that royal cruiser was a death sentence.

Cal kept his focus on the screen. "You'll have your enforcer, and you'll have me. All I ask is that you let my crew go. They had nothing to do with this."

The prince's eyes narrowed. "That ship is wanted for smuggling and gun trafficking."

Gun trafficking? He glanced at Ty. His first mate didn't look up, but Ethan flinched.

Great. Just great.

Hopefully, those guns ended up in the hands of colonists who needed to protect themselves, and not the people looting the innocent.

Cal held out his hands. "Those are my terms."

The prince's smile was acidic enough to melt the paint off the walls. He stared for a moment more before tilting his head. "No."

A tone sounded behind the prince. He looked off to his right. Two enforcers, silver-white manes of hair flowing like they were underwater, ran from one side of the ship to the other.

The transmission went dead.

"What's going on?" Cal asked.

"I don't know, but something is definitely happening." Ty leaned toward his monitor, squinting like he'd forgotten his glasses. "I-I think we have power."

His screen beeped. Alanna's screens lit up, as well as the panels on the wall.

Ty gaped. "Yeah, we have power. Not a lot, but we've got essential systems up and running."

A blast of light flooded the room. Cal stepped back,

shielding his eyes. "What in the stars is that?"

"*Star* is a good equivalent, boss. The readings are telling me that a miniature sun just appeared between us and that ship."

Still holding his hand up to the light, Cal turned to Ty. "A sun?"

Alanna leaned over her station, still clutching her side and looking like she might fall out of her chair at any moment. "I'm showing a sun, too. It makes no sense."

This day kept getting crazier. "Do we have full power? Engines?"

Ty shook his head. "No engines. Just systems."

A tone sounded, and Doc typed something into the wall. "Umm, Dania's gone."

Cal looked over his shoulder. "What?"

Doc tapped a few more places on the screen. "She's not in her cell. Maybe she got free when the power went out?" He tapped on the screen again and then stepped away, squinting at the bright light hovering between them and the royal cruiser. "Cal, she's not on the ship."

Not on the ship?

The light lessened, the intensity easing back. Cal leaned closer to the screen as the brightness cleared, revealing a glowing woman with long, blonde hair floating in space.

Cal gripped his control panel. What had she done? "Is she alive?"

Doc tapped on the wall screen again. "Her heartrate is slower than my last readings, but yeah, she seems fine."

Alanna looked into her console. "That glow around her, it's like a bubble. If these readings are correct, it's like an oxygen shield."

And a slower heartrate wouldn't use up the oxygen as

quickly. That must have been what the enforcer had meant when he'd said they could survive in space.

What was she doing, though? Was she trying to get back to that star-blasted prince?

A swirl of energy spiraled in the area between her and the prince's ship, like the several yards of space immediately in front of her blurred into a solid circle.

Cal grimaced. She could be doing almost anything out there. "Can we back away?"

"Negative," Ty said. "We're still surrounded, but the royal cruiser just retreated a few yards."

They were backing away from their own enforcer?

Three more suns popped up, but they faded more quickly, leaving three more enforcers floating in space, as well as two single-person fighter planes. They didn't advance.

"Cal?" Alanna said. "Those ships have a weapons lock on Dania."

Cal shivered. They were locked on Dania because enforcers *faced* their targets. Soldiers stood in front of what they were protecting. Right now, Dania was facing the royal cruiser—her prince—and she looked like she was more than ready to kick ass.

No matter what, though, the last place he wanted to be was this close to a fight between a bunch of beings with insane galactic power.

Cal turned to his crew. "Get us out of here!"

"We have no engines," Ty said. "We're still trapped."

One of the enforcers, a woman with glowing white hair floating about her, held up a hand and shot a beam of energy at Dania. The blast bounced off the swirling shield and dissipated into space.

"They gotta be testing her," Ty said. "I've seen enforcers throw ten times that much power."

But not in space. Still, those other enforcers were probably fully charged, where Dania was weak.

The other two enforcers raised their hands, and two more bolts headed for Dania. They both bounced off, the one on the right shooting back toward the *Renegade*.

"Incoming!" Ty grabbed his console.

Cal fell back as the ship jolted. "Ethan, are we okay?"

The engineer pulled himself off the floor and tapped a few buttons on the wall beside the screen Doc had worked on. "Yeah. The hull is intact. But we lost the sync navigator."

"Is that a problem?"

Alanna shook her head. "Not if I have a clear line of sight."

At the moment, though, they didn't have a clear line of sight, unless what she wanted to look at was a royal execution squad. Another bolt of energy bounced off Dania, shaking their ship.

"Guys, we need an exit strategy." Cal eyed the dashboard. He could override Ty's control again and transfer piloting to himself. Of course, that would require engines, which they didn't have. "Suggestions?"

Alanna frowned into her screen. "Ummm..."

"I see it," Ty countered.

Cal's stomach sunk. "You see what?"

"That." Ty pointed across him to the far left of the window.

Cal leaned closer to the glass. Just beyond the leftmost fighter ship, the blackness of space swirled, small at first, but then becoming larger. The small ship drifted toward it before the pilot engaged its engine and headed back to the cruiser.

Dania still floated between the *Renegade* and the other ships, her arms out to her side, her legs slightly apart. She didn't move. Not that Cal could tell, anyway. She just hung there like a ghost.

He looked back to the swirling mass of nothing. Was she doing that?

The ship shuddered. The yellow light started to flash again.

"What's going on, people?"

"The proximity alarm is going nuts, and I already told it to ignore the ships." Ty stared at the black, swirling space. "Alanna, what's your take?"

She shook her head. "You don't want to know what I think."

All three of the floating enforcers winked out. The other two ships flared their engines.

The hairs on Cal's arms stood on end. Anyone in their right mind would run from an enforcer, but what did enforcers run from?

Cal's fingers tightened on the grips of his chair. "I would really like to know what you guys are thinking."

Their ship lurched. The cruiser started to drift toward the right, away from the anomaly.

But wait a minute… "Are they moving or are we moving?"

Ty scrambled with the controls. "We are."

Alanna pointed out the window, where the swirl had defined. "It's another black hole!"

The two small ships flew toward Dania. Bright red starbursts shot from both fighters, aimed right at her.

Cal wiped the sweat from his brow. They were helpless,

caught at the edge of a black hole's grip, and Dania was the only thing standing—or floating—between the *Renegade* and that prince.

And her own people had just opened fire.

He had no idea why she'd changed teams, but if anything happened to her, they were dead.

"Can we shield her?" Cal asked, but the blast had already hit Dania head on. The light around her dwindled before brightening again. The *Star Renegade* drifted farther toward the black hole. "Ethan, I need engines!"

His red curls stuck to his temples as he shook his head. "We barely have power. There's nothing I can do."

CHAPTER 34
DANIA

DANIA BOLSTERED her air shield bubble and stared down the ship throttling through space toward her. She opened herself and connected with the pilot just before she met First Lieutenant Shivana's gaze. The large woman's frame filled most of the cabin and she looked right into Dania's eyes before she bombarded her former general with another round of munitions.

Dania steeled herself, casting the artillery back toward the ship at minimal velocity, giving Shivana time to move her craft out of the way.

It was foolish of her. Shivana wouldn't show Dania that kind of mercy. Still, Dania couldn't harm one of her own people. Shivana was only following orders, as any good soldier should.

Shivana banked right, just as another ship flew past the blasts, firing larger rounds at Dania's shielding. The artillery rocked her barrier, sending a lashing jolt through Dania's core. Pain seared across her skin.

Those were grade three rounds...much heavier munitions than were needed. She reached out and felt the familiar waver of Miguel's power from within the ship. Either he had a grudge, or he'd been ordered to take her down no matter the cost.

She deflected a second volley, and a third ship joined, shooting rounds between Dania and Miguel...cautionary fire not meant to harm either side. Whoever that was, they were trying to thwart the attack. There was only one among her enforcers who'd stand between Dania and destroyer grade munitions.

Alexander.

Was he out of his mind? He'd be punished for going against their prince.

Unless Dania's friend hadn't been given a direct order to stop her. He might be acting on his inherent need to protect his general. Either way, the others would punish him for this impertinence.

Both combat crafts fired heavy rounds at Alexander's ship. Dania threw up a small barrier, enough to knock the artillery off course, then drew the power back into her palms.

She quaked as the missiles slammed into her defenses and spun off course. If those rounds hit something, they'd still explode. They should have been using shorter-range lasers. They were safer in tight battle.

But this wasn't Dania's command. Whoever was giving the orders didn't seem to be concerned with collateral damage.

The shielding around her wavered. Behind her, the *Star Renegade* pitched as Dania's power buckled. The ache in her shoulder deepened. She couldn't hold the smuggling ship away from the vortex and deflect these attacks for too much longer.

She needed to find a way, though. It would be several minutes before the black hole she'd conjured would be ready to use for travel. Until then, it would tear the *Star Renegade* apart if they were sucked inside.

Her arms burned and her eyes grew heavy. She needed sleep.

More so, she needed her prince to restore her energy supplies.

Dania blinked away the thought and tried to gulp the ache in her throat away. Recharging her primordial energy was no longer an option. She'd turned against her prince. He'd never share his power with her again.

A shot clipped Alexander's right wing. Dania threw another shield in his direction. One shot bounced off, but the other got through. She recoiled as the back edge of her friend's main injector column exploded.

His ship couldn't take much more.

Closing her eyes, she pressed a thought toward him: *Return to the ship. Don't risk yourself.*

His voice filled her mind. *Only if you come back with me. Stop protecting those smugglers.*

Dania shivered. Within the welcoming walls of her prince's star cruiser was peace, bliss, and freedom from all her worries. Once she was returned to her normal self, she'd be able to let the *Star Renegade* go...allow the criminals to meet their deaths, as all criminals should.

Returning to that cruiser was what she *should* do—what everything she'd been brought up to know and trust told her was right. Still...

She glanced back at Cal's illegally modified smuggling vessel. Her hands trembled.

Calling up the singularity had been a mistake. She was

far too weak to tame the natural energy of the universe *and* defend against her enforcers at the same time.

The *Star Renegade*'s hull buckled and dented from her invisible fingers holding them back from the black hole's pull. In this state, the ship would come apart and be crushed in the mouth of the vortex, and she'd be to blame.

The other ships banked up and over the cruiser and came toward them again, one flying toward Dania, the other toward the Star Renegade.

The ache in her limbs intensified. Closing her eyes, she pressed out more power, but the rings around her wrists where the shackles had been burned; a phantom reminder of the illegal steel's presence.

How much of her power had the bindings drained away? Was she still as strong? Was she even a general anymore, or was her power no greater than any of the enforcers under her command?

Enforcers who *used to be* under her command.

She threw out a wall between the *Star Renegade* and the attacking ship. Shivana's craft bounced back like hitting a pillow. That was only a short-lived barrier, though. Shivana would get through, and Cal's ship didn't have enough power to get away.

This was a no-win situation for any of them.

Standing against her prince would not be forgiven. She'd made a fateful choice, and she'd have to learn to live with that for however many more breaths she took before the black hole that she'd meant to be their salvation crushed them all.

The vision of her sponsor's ship phased in and out of sight.

A warmth spread over her, like a hug from beyond a foggy veil.

Geron.

She opened herself as a small trickle of her prince's power shot from the ship and swirled up around her, healing the ache and making everything okay.

It was a tease, the promise of all he still offered.

Her hands trembled. Her body craved more—a need deeper than any other.

Her prince was right there, within sight. All she needed to do was give in, relax, and let him take her back. She lowered her hands an inch, and more warmth spread through her.

This was right. This was how it was supposed to be.

But was this really what she wanted anymore?

Her mind screamed *'No!'* but her arms wanted to reach out and embrace her old life. Embrace *him.*

The two assault crafts hovered, one on either side of Alexander's ship.

Shivana's weapons were poised on Dania. Miguel's were still locked on Alexander. Miguel had never been fond of Alexander. Still, she knew this wasn't personal. His orders had come directly from Geron, and Miguel would have no problem with carrying them out.

In one, simple show of force, her prince had given her an ultimatum. Return to him, or pay the price—not only her life, but Alexander's.

And once she was gone, they'd probably destroy the *Star Renegade* as well.

Maybe if she returned, she could get Geron to finally listen. She just needed to get him to hear her out before he returned her power and took away her freedom to think, her freedom to choose.

Dania still didn't believe the crew deserved to die, but fighting was too much, and she had nothing left to give.

She lowered her hands just as Shivana's artillery banks sparked red.

The blast from the First Lieutenant's ship slammed into Dania's chest. Her shield wavered, then winked out.

She gasped, her lungs burning from the low oxygen. She wouldn't be able to take another blast.

Miguel's ship fired a volley in Alexander's direction. Her friend's ship turned, but the disabled wing and damaged injector slowed his retreat.

Dania's heart sank. The glow of the munitions turned from yellow to orange. Death blows.

Alexander's ship didn't raise its shields.

Her chest clenched, as if her heart had exploded.

"No!" she cried, but her voice didn't breach the small bubble of atmosphere she'd conjured around herself.

"I'm coming back!" she screamed into space. "I surrender!"

Miguel fired again.

Alexander was her only true friend. They'd grown up together, gotten in trouble together, and always found their way out...but together. That was what he'd been out here trying to do—to save her from herself, just like he'd done for as long as she could remember.

She couldn't let him die for it.

Flicking her left wrist, she shoved the *Star Renegade* from the mouth of the black hole. It wasn't much, but it would give them more time.

Taking a deep breath of the last cubits of air around her,

she held out her hands, calling everything left inside her and throwing a barrier of energy between Miguel's missiles and Alexander's ship.

Dania, don't! Alexander's voice brought tears to her eyes.

He knew as well as she did that this was the last of her strength. She'd told him once that she'd die for him, and she'd meant it.

She caught one last glimpse of his ship as she drifted toward the vortex.

He was better than her in so many ways. He deserved to be the one to live.

CHAPTER 35
CAL

CAL HELD on to the edge of his chair as the *Star Renegade* spiraled out of control. "What the blazes just happened?"

Ty shook his head, blinking like he could barely see. "I have no freaking clue. It's like we got hit with a bat."

At least they were moving away from the black hole. "Ethan, any good news about the engines?"

"I got engines. Power is the problem." The engineer looked over his shoulder, his hair a damp mass of curls. "Boss, we don't have enough juice to run everything."

The ship lost momentum before they started to shake again. The stars shifted, but in the wrong direction.

Cal's grip tightened on his armrests again. "Are we going in reverse?"

Doc swiped through screens on his panel. "We're getting drawn back to the black hole."

Ty stood, pulling on two levers on the control panel. "Ethan, divert everything to the engines."

"*Everything?*"

Ty wiped his brow. "We won't need lights or air if we get sucked in there."

Ethan gaped, looking to Cal.

If there was another idea, he'd take it. Ty was right, though. They were out of options. "Do it. Give Ty every speck of power we have."

Ty's face reddened as he pulled on the controls, but the ship continued to move backward, tilting to the left. "Ethan!"

The engineer pulled at his hair. "Everything but the power and air in this room has been diverted to the engines." His hands fell limp at his sides. "It's just not enough. It's like the propulsion centers aren't even there."

One of the enforcer ships fired on Dania, and the soft glow around her faded to almost nothing.

Why were they attacking their own person? Weren't they here to get her back?

Alanna covered her mouth. "I'm not getting a reading on Dania anymore." Her eyes reddened as their ship rattled again. "I think she was protecting us, holding us out of the black hole's gravitational pull."

And without her, they were all royally screwed. Dania had probably intended to use the cyclone as a portal like she had last time. Before, though, she'd been with them to keep them from being ripped apart. Now they were alone and at the mercy of one of the most destructive forces in the universe.

Ethan cursed under his breath. "We have major structural damage on the right side of the ship. If we take another hit, we're going to start venting air."

Great. "Can you seal it?"

The ship rumbled, pitching up.

"Not without supplies and a crack ton of time."

The arced set of the engineer's ginger brows iced Cal's veins. Nothing scared Ethan. The guy was a borderline mental case.

Alanna twirled a circle of blue light in the air. "I can't get a lock. There's no way I can jump us."

She lowered her hand, and the gears of light winked out. Alanna took two steps toward the window.

"Cal?"

She pointed to the stars, where Dania's wilted form lay limp, nearly lost in the void of space.

The navigator's eyes filled with tears. "That glowy shield around her is almost gone. She's not going to be able to breathe out there."

A weight formed in his chest. Dania had looked so beautiful at dinner. Normal. Maybe even a little awkward and scared. Last night, he would have done everything in his power to save her.

He'd watched her grow, become more than he'd dreamed an enforcer could be. He wanted to see this through as much as Doc and Alanna, but now he needed to concentrate on what he could control, and Cal had four people on this ship counting on him to survive.

He pushed away the sympathy, the innate need to help others that always crept up at the worst times. "She's an enforcer. She'll figure it out."

His gut twisted before the words had left his mouth. He wanted to help her. Dammit, he'd traipsed through the galaxies trying to save her. But at the moment, he wasn't even sure how to save himself.

Alanna stepped toward him. "She helped us. We can't leave her out there."

Was she freaking serious? Cal pointed at the growing mass of swirling space outside the window. "Excuse me—black hole, imminent death, and barely enough power to keep us out of being turned to space dust. What do you expect me to do?"

In the distance, the light around Dania winked out. Cal's chest clenched.

Yeah, she'd turned them in, but his crew was right. She'd been defending them in the end.

If there'd been any way to save her, he'd have done it. But it didn't look like that was an option anymore.

The ship rattled again, and something screeched.

"What was that?" Cal asked.

Ethan tapped on his panel, then looked at the ceiling. "The secondary comm juncture just ripped off."

This black hole was going to eat them one bite at a time.

Cal looked at each of them. His crew. His friends. His family. They'd been through hell and back, and now they all stared at him, waiting for Cal to save them.

But how? They were the smart ones. All Cal had going for him was luck, and even that had been running pretty scarce these days. The good thing was, when they worked together they were resourceful enough to make luck into reality.

"I need everyone to focus." He pointed out the window to the swirling mass of space. "Is there any chance of breaking free from that thing?"

Silence pressed in on all sides, giving him his answer.

Cal rubbed his face with his palms. Sometimes the hardest decisions were the ones that had only one answer.

"We're just wasting what little power we have. Cut the engines."

"*What?*" they all shouted.

"We'll get sucked in," Ty said.

Cal pointed back out the window. "There's no escaping that thing. Either we stay out here and get ripped apart, or we take our chances inside."

The stars shone brightly in the distance. Space held an ethereal beauty that Cal needed to remember to enjoy more often.

If he got the chance.

He took one last look as his crew. "It's been a pleasure." He nodded to each of them before focusing on Ty. "Buckle in. We've done this once. We can do it again."

"You do realize Dania was on board last time," Doc pointed out.

Cal glared at him but chose not to answer. He knew the risks. They all did.

Ty took a deep breath and sank into his seat. "Okay. I guess let's get ready to break the space and time barrier." He pressed several buttons on his panel.

Cal turned to Ethan. "Can you give us just enough punch so we go in head-first?"

Ty snorted. "The boss has definitely lost his mind."

Maybe he *had* lost his mind, but if they didn't make it out of this alive, he at least wanted to look into the mouth of the beast that killed him.

Ethan pressed a series of buttons on the wall. "Sorry, but it looks like that thing will be swallowing us however it wants. I've got nothing to give you."

In the distance, the royal cruiser backed off. Two specks of light sped from the massive vessel toward them. The tracking didn't have the light signatures of missiles or any artillery Cal had seen. They could only be ships.

"Are they seriously attacking us?" Cal asked.

Alanna leaned closer to her screen. "I don't think so." She pointed at the glass. "Those lights are engines firing in reverse, but they're still moving toward the hole at high velocity. It looks like they're caught in the pull of the vortex and trying to break free."

Yet the *Renegade* was only feeling a quarter of the singularity's pull, while the royal cruiser was right in the black hole's suck zone. They had been pushed to the side, maybe by Dania before she'd lost consciousness. They were still far too close, though.

The space around the massive cruiser wavered and darkened like it had taken shape and come alive. The darkness split into three tendrils and reached out like hands, grabbing the fighter crafts from space and drawing them back toward the ship. The third tendril reached for the *Star Renegade*.

Cal leaned forward. "What is that coming at us?"

The tendrils opened, looking very much like fingers.

Ethan grimaced. "I'd take a wild guess and say that's the hand of a really pissed-off prince."

Cal had a choice: be plucked from the jaws of death by a prince, or take his chances with the most destructive force in nature.

His nose flared. He'd seen the 'mercy' of the royal family. He and his crew had a better chance with the black hole. At the moment, though, his ship was caught between the two of them.

Cal rubbed his chin. He needed to think this through;

but first, he needed to understand what he was really dealing with.

He leaned back in his chair. "It's only energy. The prince is manipulating space, but how?"

Doc typed into his panel. "It's like he's solidifying the lack of matter...making something out of nothing. It's impossible."

Cal clenched his armrests. The giant hand widened, ready to grab them. Whatever this was, it was solid. If it is was solid, it could be destroyed. "Hit it with a particle beam."

Ethan shook his head. "We don't have enough energy to turn the ship. I sure as heck can't give you a particle beam."

Cal clenched his teeth as the hand reached them. He glanced at Alanna. "You can't get a lock to jump us safely, right?"

Her eyes widened. "No. There is too much interference."

"Then just jump us anywhere."

She shook her head. "We could end up in the black hole."

Or they could end up somewhere safe. They had a fifty-fifty chance. If the prince got them, they'd be executed. "Do it."

Her fingers trembled, but she still called up the ring of blue light and started spinning the gears.

"Here we go." She scrunched her face and tapped the center of the floating circle.

Space stretched. Cal's stomach heaved, but he closed one eye to steady himself. Someone slammed to the floor—

Doc, maybe. Light blasted out on all sides before they stopped.

Cal took a breath. "Where are we?"

Alanna blinked. "Shoot! We only moved a few feet."

"What?" A few spans away, the giant hand closed down on the empty space where the *Renegade* used to be.

Technically, they'd gone nowhere, but they'd gone just far enough.

The ship rumbled. The stars started to stretch out again.

Cal looked over his shoulder. "Alanna, are you jumping us again?"

"It's not me."

Ty spewed out a colorful collection of expletives.

"What?" Cal asked.

Cal's first mate pointed out the window. The ship tilted, leaving them peering down the gaping maw of an enormous swirling vortex of red, blue, yellow, and green.

Alanna had moved them out of the way of the attacking prince, but closer to the black hole.

The lights gleamed, beckoning, promising joy like a twinkling tree on winter solstice morning.

Until they started to spiral.

Alanna screeched.

Loose pieces of the ship and personal items took flight. Something slashed against Cal's face, followed by something larger. "Can anyone stabilize us?"

Ty answered, but the rattling of the ship covered his words.

The lights outside blended into one solid wall of white. They hung limp in space before dropping into another vortex of blue and black.

Someone retched, and something warm and wet hit Cal's hand. The stench of vomit filled the room. At a bare minimum, that meant he wasn't the only one still alive, and for now, he'd take whatever good news he could get.

The ship banked right, and the vortex turned red, then blue, then yellow before they dropped into normal space again. The navigational computers beeped in warning, flashing their inability to locate their position.

Cal blinked away the glossy sheen blurring his vision as they careened toward a massive wall of scrap metal in the distance. The sensors on his console swirled through databases, unable to identify the metallurgy.

Of course they couldn't. They'd just dropped out of a black hole. They could be anywhere, and that junk could be a million years old.

He tried to inhale, but his lungs refused to fill with air. Flashes of light exploded before his eyes. He needed oxygen. He needed to breathe. But...how did you do that?

His mind whirled. He knew he needed to fill his lungs, but his brain refused to comply.

The ship listed left, still careening toward the debris field.

His chest ached, and his vision blurred before his body twitched, remembering.

He drew in a deep breath, then another.

A dull hum filled his ears. Ty and Alanna lay over their stations, unconscious. Doc lay crumpled in the corner, his neck at an unnatural angle. Ethan moaned, trying to push himself up off the floor before collapsing back to the tiles.

Cal blinked away the last of the fog as the yellow light started flashing on the pilot's panel, illuminating Ty's lax face.

The massive hunks of metal hung like a wall in the distance, confirming that this time, the flashing wasn't a shorted fuse. It was an honest-to-goodness proximity warning. The mind-numbing blast of the alarm followed, and bright lights flashed around him.

Still, the crew didn't stir.

Taking another deep breath, Cal typed in his override codes and took the helm from Ty's station. He engaged the thrusters, but nothing happened. He pressed the button again and again as they advanced on the wall of metal.

Cal considered the massive hunk of debris filling his screen. Ethan had said they couldn't take another hit to the hull, and now Cal was staring at a giant metal mallet aimed right at them.

They'd come so far—survived an attack by a royal cruiser, and the throat of a black hole. He wasn't about to let them die on impact in some sort of cosmic junkyard.

He scanned the bridge, looking for something…*anything* to help them. Without power to the engines, though, there wasn't much he could do. Unless he could find something that didn't need an outside energy source.

Hydraulics.

Hydraulics didn't need power to work. It was a long shot, but a long shot was all he had at the moment.

He opened the emergency panel on the wall and rerouted some of the oxygen to the hallway and hydraulic storage area.

He waited, breathing heavily, before the other compartments turned from red to green.

Thank the stars something was finally going in his favor.

Sprinting from the bridge, he slid down the ladders to the lower decks.

The ship lurched. The artificial gravity sent him stumbling backward. Cal grabbed on to a side panel, pulling himself up like scaling a hill rather than walking down the hall. The hull thumped against something, and he froze, but there was no telltale hiss signaling the venting of air. He still had time.

How much, he had no clue.

He dragged himself forward, and the ship shifted in the other direction. Finally, fate had joined his team! He darted through the hall, now running downhill until he reached the main cargo bay.

A new set of alarms went off. Deeper and louder, as if he needed more of a reminder that they were about to die. Something squeaked, like metal scratching against the outer walls.

They'd reached the debris field. He was out of time.

GRABBING a manual crank from the emergency panel, Cal pried open the doors of the primary cargo bay.

Inside, seven hydraulic lifts still held freight containers overhead. That might be just enough weight to save their lives. All he had to do was get the machines to release their payloads. Then—he hoped—the ship would drift in the direction the weight had dropped, pushing them enough off course to float right past the debris.

It was only a theory, and he wished he had Doc's big brain to back it up, but for now, he could only rely on his instincts.

He sprinted to the first lift and slammed the heel of his hand onto the big blue *release* button.

Nothing happened.

"Come on!"

Cal stumbled back. His head pounded as the alarms screamed overhead. The last thing he needed was all that star-blasted noise!

He made his way to a control panel and disengaged the

speakers. He needed to think. There had to be something in there to help.

And there it was…like a beacon of hope…an old-fashioned yellow card hanging off the edge of the last machine. *Safety Protocols*. He scanned over the first paragraph. *To make sure none of the cargo drops accidentally…*

Screw *accidentally*! What if you wanted to drop it all on purpose?

The screech against the hull deepened. If the *Star Renegade* rolled—if that hunk of metal out there hit the damaged side of the ship—they were done for.

He read further. *Safety, safety…more stinking safety…then, finally…*

'*It is unadvisable to hit the red, then blue security buttons in a gravity-present setting, as this will cause the immediate retraction of the levitation planks. Be sure to disengage artificial gravity before…*'

That was it!

The ship rumbled about him. He looked closely at the machine. "Buttons, buttons…" He leaned around the side. "Where is the star-blasted red button?"

Then he realized there was a blue button, and a yellow button on this machine. The yellow looked reasonably new…probably replaced with spare parts.

He punched the yellow and then the blue. The base of the lift over his head started to retract.

"Yes!" He punched his fist in the air before jumping to the next machine.

On this one, he found the red and then the blue. Pressing both, he moved on to the next machine, then the next, and the next.

He stepped back. The scraping against the hull turned to a rumble. The ship started to spin.

It was rolling to the right, to the damaged side of the ship!

"Come on!" he screamed at the lifts.

This was his only chance.

How many times had this crew saved his hide? If he got out of this alive, he swore he'd spend more time with Doc and Ethan. He'd learn more about the ship, about engineering, and any of the other insane random stuff Doc knew about. He'd make sure he'd be a worthy captain, and not just a lucky son of a fading star.

The first lift dropped its cargo. The container smashed to the ground, exploding on impact. White goo sprawled across the deck—dead center—not enough to make the ship list.

His heart rattled in his chest. He started looking for anything else to use as ballast.

Another rasping screech echoed through the cargo hold, followed by a pop.

Cal's chest cinched as a hissing sound filled the chamber.

The air!

Sweat instantly drenched his shirt as the airlocks slammed down, sealing him off from the rest of the ship. That would give his crew some time—if any of them were still alive and conscious.

The air chilled around him, worsened by sweat. His hands started to ache. If he didn't find a way out, he was as good as dead.

He pushed the thought away. He still had one goal: save the ship. Getting out of this room was secondary.

Red lights flashed on the next lift and then the next as each apparatus dropped its containers on the deck. The cartons smashed down, the boxes hitting others and starting a chain reaction, plowing row after row of cargo toward one side of the ship.

The next dropped its cargo, knocking into another lift that fell over into a wall of shelving.

Cal choked on the freezing air. If he lived through this, Ty was going to kill him for making such a mess.

The ship creaked like prickly fingers were scratching on the outside of her walls.

The *Star Renegade* tilted in the direction of the spilt cargo, and Cal stumbled to the port window. Metal screeched against metal as the *Star Renegade* listed, scratching the wall of debris before jarring loose.

Cal leaned as close to the glass as he could and breathed a sigh of relief as they left the debris behind them.

They were free!

The damage had been done, though.

Nuts and bolts took flight, soaring across the room and slamming into the wall. They jammed into a small hole, plugging it partially. A slight weave of energy shimmered around the aperture as the ship's emergency shielding tried to seal the breach. It was probably the only reason Cal was still alive, but like everything else on this ship, it was failing, and the hiss of evacuating air and falling temperatures told him he had precious little time.

He picked up a plate of sheet metal, but it flew out of his hand and slammed against the hole.

Still, air hissed away into the vacuum of space.

The metal air shields sealing him off from the rest of the

ship creaked. Cal gritted his teeth. Those doors worked on the limited supply of backup power. Which meant that if the hole in the ship widened, those barriers would give way, putting the whole ship at risk. He couldn't do this alone.

He hit the comm button. "Ethan! If you can hear me, I need you to send any possible power to the emergency air shields of the main cargo deck."

Cal waited, but there was no response. Stars, he hoped they were still alive up there.

Moving into the center of the room, he took a deep breath. He'd seen every member of his crew ferret themselves out of ridiculous situations by keeping calm and thinking things through. This was yet another puzzle. Cal just needed to figure it out. Unfortunately, this time, he was on his own.

The hiss sliced through his ears, promising a slow, frigid death. He shivered. Would he freeze first or pass out from lack of oxygen?

No! Think like Doc... Clear your head and look at the problem.

The ship listed again and he stumbled, tripping into the pile of goo that had fallen from the first container. He tried to regain his footing, but his boot caught on the edge of the mound. He toppled over the pile and slammed into the hard, bumpy surface.

Holding his forehead, he stared at the glob of spilled cargo as his head spun.

That material had been liquid when it had fallen to the deck. Why was it so hard?

He ran his hand over the glassy surface. What in the name of Venus was this stuff?

He scrambled to the broken container and looked at the markings. *Polymer Sealant.*

That shouldn't have dried that quickly...but maybe the cold had sped the process. Could Cal get that lucky?

His fingers trembled as he reached into the broken shipping carton, looking for more. Every drop was a hardened ball.

He slammed his fist against the edge of the container. This wasn't fair! He needed to...

A small bit of the polymer under his fist chipped off. It glistened as it hit the floor, then fogged over and hardened.

The material was still wet underneath where the chill hadn't hit it. He just needed to get to the part that hadn't reached the air yet.

He slammed his fist into the mound. His knuckles bled, but the polymer didn't budge.

His eyes grew heavy.

No, no, no, no, no! He blinked hard. "Don't go to sleep, Cal." He drew in an icy breath.

Okay, this was an impossible situation. Normally, he'd look to Doc, and his resident genius would pull something crazy out of a hat. Cal stood slowly. His legs buckled, and he steadied himself.

Mind over matter, Cal. Your feet are there, even if you can't feel them.

Doc always had a bag of tricks. He'd use things a normal person wouldn't think of. Cal scanned the debris. In the corner, a red plus sign caught his eye—a medical kit.

He stumbled forward, falling three times before ripping the box off the wall. The contents fell out. Wisps of paper caught air and drifted toward the hull breach. Bandages, pain killers, a laser scalpel, burn ointments.

Come on! There had to be something in there he could use.

A blue packet rolled out. The words *Hot Pack* scrolled across the front in big letters.

"Yes!"

Cal cracked the package open and squeezed the two pouches inside. They snapped, and glorious heat met his fingertips.

He ran the packs back to the mound and pressed them against the polymer. If he could just get it to melt, he might get enough to seal the leak.

Lights danced in front of his eyes, like little will-o-the-wisps in the stories his babysitters used to read him as a child. Maybe the people who'd written those books had nearly suffocated to death.

His lids started to close, and he jerked himself awake.

No! There was still a chance his crew was alive. With the emergency air shields down, there would be no way for them to get into this room to stop the leak. And if those doors gave way, the rest of the ship would be in danger. Cal was their only hope.

He pulled the pouches away, but the solid polymer stood firm, mocking him.

"Dammit!"

He nearly threw the pouches but kept it together enough to tuck them into his boots. The sweet warmth rushed to his toes.

He needed something hotter. Something that could cut through polymer.

Cut through…

His gaze fell on the laser scalpel.

How stinking daft could he be? His hands shook as he

grabbed the chilled metal instrument. He flicked off the safety, pointed at the mound, and pressed the trigger. A small beam of light shot out. The polymer started to shine, then melt.

His eyes started to close again. His head dipped, and he caught himself before dropping the scalpel. A small puddle had formed in the polymer. It wasn't a lot, but it would have to do.

Using the edges of the busted container, Cal scooped up the polymer and raced it across the room.

The edges started to dull in the cold air. He tried huffing his breath on it, but he had barely enough warmth to keep *himself* going.

Making it to the hole, he pried off the slab of sheet metal and poured the goop right over the nuts and bolts. When the main glob of the goo started to lose its glossy sheen, he shoved the rest into the nooks and crannies with his fingers.

The hissing stopped.

Cal stared at the repair, holding his breath. He needed his luck now more than ever.

The hiss started again. Cal growled and punched the wall.

"K-Keep it together, C-Cal," he muttered. "This is g-going to work."

Stumbling back, he lasered another glob and added it to the rest of the repair.

The hiss stopped.

He knew better than to trust that, though. He staggered back to the polymer, lasered another blob, and added it to the already hardened mound over the breach.

He waited, gripping the wall around the patch.

Only silence greeted him. The repair was holding.

Choking out a relieved laugh, he slipped to the floor and held his head.

He'd promised his crew a better life, a place where they wouldn't be judged for their past crimes. He hadn't intended on them running for their lives eighty percent of the time.

Nor had he ever expected to feed them all to a black hole.

Or to nearly suffocate them.

Right now, the only one he was reasonably certain was alive was Ethan. The engineer had moved right before Cal had run from the bridge.

Cal closed his eyes and shivered, remembering the odd angle of Doc's head as he lay motionless on the ground...a brilliant mind, laid to waste.

A good friend.

Not to mention, he was the only one who may have been able to help the others if they were hurt.

Cal rubbed his face. What had he brought them all to? And for what?

He could have holed them all up on a hidden colony somewhere, and they could have lived long, happy lives on the spoils of a single good smuggling run. Instead, they'd followed Cal and his ridiculous delusions that one little smuggling ship could make a difference.

They certainly hadn't changed anything, and now they were dead in space. Alone.

Maybe Cal should have let the prince grab them. At least he could have offered them a quick death. He lolled closer to the floor.

The light on the security camera in the corner blinked

on. The lens scanned the room, stopping on him. Cal took a deep breath of, well, nothing.

"I'm almost out of air," he told whoever was on the other end of the camera.

A vent on the far side of the room creaked. A hum filled the chamber.

Cal blinked. His chest ached. Sitting upright, talking, even thinking was too much. Hopefully, whoever was manipulating the camera could find enough supplies to survive. He had nothing left to give.

Closing his eyes, he slipped to the floor and gave in to the darkness.

THE FLOOR HUMMED beneath Cal's cheek. A deep ache surged through his temples, changing to a vicious drumming. He pressed on the cold floor but couldn't lift himself up.

"Cal!" Ty's voice blasted through his brain like an assault on the pirate frontier. "Come on, Cal!" There was a scratching noise, like Ty had tapped the speaker. "Are you sure this thing is working?"

"Totally," Ethan's voice rang out. "Wait. I think he just moved."

Cal glanced up at the camera still pointed at him, but the drumming behind his eyes forced him to close them again. He tried to say Ethan's name, but it came out. "Etberrthaven."

"What? Cal, are you there?"

Cal opened his lips. "Tyee-eterhaben-thhhh."

He took in a deep breath, and his eyes bolted open. There was air!

He drew in another breath, and another. Tears dampened his cheeks.

"Awwww." Ty's voice again. "We're super happy to see you too, boss."

Cal tried to curse at him, but it came out "Fuuussssstthoooo."

There was some murmuring between the two of them, like someone held their hand over the microphone.

Cal sat up, coughing. He held his chest, taking in another long drag of the sweetest stagnant recycled air he'd ever smelled in his entire life. "Wh-What's w-wrong?"

He couldn't imagine it was any worse than being caught in a cosmic junkyard goodness-knew-where, with questionable polymer sealant plugging a hole in their ship.

A sigh hung heavy over the speaker. "Cal, you need to get up here," Ty said. "Can you walk?"

Cal squinted up at the camera. He rubbed his temples before pulling himself to his feet. He blinked, taking a moment for his eyes to fully focus. "The airlocks are still shut."

"Roger that. We're still showing a hull breach, but the pressure reads fine. What did you do down there?"

Cal glanced at the makeshift repair. "I used the polymer in one of the cargo containers."

A thin film shined around the edges of the patch. The polymer bubbled out in places, but it seemed to have fully hardened.

"Boss, that's genius," Ethan said. "I'm impressed." There was a tapping, like he was checking readings on a panel. "As long as the pressure has stabilized, the doors should open."

Cal looked at the patch again. "Will the polymer hold?"

"At least for a few hours. I'll check it as soon as I can."

Cal rubbed his forehead. "How about you check it now?"

"Cal..." The sound of Ty's voice chilled him more than losing pressure and atmospheric control.

Cal grabbed the wall. "What is it?"

When Cal had run from the bridge, Alanna had been slumped over her panel. Doc had been twisted in a heap on the floor...

Ty's voice broke. "Boss, you need to get up here."

Cal's chest burned more than when there'd been no air. He sprinted for the door, and his legs gave out. He stumbled, tripping over some of the broken containers.

He glanced up at the camera. Why wasn't Doc yelling at him, telling him to take it slow and explaining all the possible bad effects of nearly freezing and suffocating to death?

He knew why, but he'd hoped he'd been wrong. His chest seized and he coughed, stumbling forward.

He had to be wrong. Doc was fine. So was Alanna. He'd make them dinner tonight. Their favorites. And a cake. Doc loved cake.

By the time he got to the door, Cal's eyes burned. He opened the panel and engaged the controls. The system blinked twice, checking the pressure, before it beeped and slid open a few inches.

Cal stared at the door, then looked back to the camera. "It didn't open."

"We barely have enough power for air circulation at this point," Ethan said. "Once you get up here, we can shut off the cargo bays. I've already shut down areas six and two."

Area two...where the medical bay was. Why would he shut that down?

Cal grabbed the edges of the doors and growled, pulling them apart. His muscles trembled, and he grunted before they finally opened just enough for him to get through.

Each stomp of his boots echoed as he sprinted down the hall. The way before him blurred, but he ignored it.

Whatever this was messing Cal up—space sickness, oxygen deprivation—it didn't matter. Doc could fix it. He could fix anything.

Sweat stung his eyes as he hauled himself up the service ladder to the upper decks. They just needed to get through this latest snafu. Then he and his crew would glue this ship together using tape if they needed to, and Alanna could jump them out of there.

They'd be fine.

Like they always were.

He stopped at the entrance to the bridge. Whatever he found inside, he had to deal with it. He was the captain. He needed to be strong, no matter what.

He placed his hand on the control button and the doors slid open.

Ty and Ethan jumped to their feet, their faces pale and drawn. The throbbing in Cal's head grew louder.

Someone sniffed.

Alanna—thank the stars!

She knelt on the floor, her head lowered. She clung to Doc, holding his head against her chest, rocking him.

"You're going to be okay," she whispered. "Everything is just fine. You'll see."

Cal tried to take a step, but he couldn't. Doc's hand lay limp beside Alanna's hip, his skin pale.

Ty gulped, then turned away. Ethan met Cal's gaze, then looked at the floor.

Now Cal knew why the medical bay had been shut down. They wouldn't be needing it anymore.

Alanna sniffed. "Remember when we were on Kirato and Amelia was trying to get you to try her sand crab stew?" She smoothed back Doc's hair. "You promised you'd eat some next time." She closed her eyes and swallowed. "You can't let Mel down like that. She'll never forgive you." Alanna pulled him closer. "Come on, Peter. Please don't do this."

Cal flinched. He hadn't heard anyone on this ship call Doc *'Peter'* in ages.

He glanced back at Ty, but his first mate just shook his head.

Ty's eyes reddened. He grimaced before he spun his entire body and looked out the window, folding his arms around himself.

The pounding in Cal's head increased. His vision skewed.

He was supposed to protect these people. They were his responsibility, his family. How could he have let this happen?

The yellow light on Ty's panel started flashing again.

Cal snapped. "Shut that damn thing off!"

Ty blinked, looking at the light and then at Cal. "I think there's actually something out there."

Ethan turned to the panel on the wall, the one Doc normally used. He looked relieved to have something to do. "He's right." He tapped a few buttons. "There's… There's a carbon signature, and life signs."

Cal squinted, holding his head. "Life signs?"

Bursts of light exploded in front of Cal's eyes. No one else reacted, so he tried to blink them away.

Ethan nodded. "Yeah, I got a heartbeat. I mean, it's barely there, but..." He held his palm out to the panel. "There you have it."

Ty whispered under his breath. The banging in Cal's head covered most of it, but it sounded like *holy ducks and spit*. Cal doubted that was what he'd said.

"Boss?"

Cal clawed at his temples. "Yeah, what?"

Ty turned toward him. "I think it's...Dania."

Alanna screamed. They all turned to her.

She stared back at them, wide-eyed. "He moved!" She leaned Doc down, wiping the hair from his forehead. "Peter?"

"Honey." Ty walked toward her. "He's gone."

"No!" She shoved Ty back. "I'm telling you, he moved!" Her eyes glistened.

Cal lowered his hands. "Alanna..."

"No!" She pulled Doc back onto her lap. "Screw you! I know what I felt."

Cal lowered his chin to his chest. Alanna had been lucky enough not to have to see too many people die.

Bodies evacuated all their waste. They relaxed, barely looking human at times, and they also twitched. She needed to understand that death pangs were a thing.

Cal knelt beside her and put his hand on her shoulder. "Alanna, listen to me."

She glared at him, and his chest tightened.

Of everyone in this crew, Alanna was the one who always kept emotion at bay. She was the optimist, but also the realist. Cal needed to remind her of that. Now was the worst possible time for her to hang on to what could never be.

Doc's body jolted. His eyes sprung open. Both of his hands rose like he was clutching something, and his mouth opened in a soundless scream.

Cal fell back.

"What's happening?" Alanna held her head.

Doc drew in a huge, loud breath, then started to scream.

Land mines started exploding in Cal's head. He crawled to the side and vomited.

Dammit! His crew needed him, and all he could do was…

The blast of a weapon discharge rocked the bridge, the sound reverberating in Cal's skull. Struggling against this new, deeper assault, Cal blinked and looked up.

Ethan stood a few steps away, holding a gun pointed at Doc.

And Doc wasn't moving anymore.

ALANNA SCREAMED, holding her head.

Cal brought himself to one knee. "Wh-What did you do?"

Ethan sidled back and dropped the gun. "I-I stunned him. I saw Doc do that once when someone was freaking out like that on Kemper Station." He drew his fingers through his hair. "Geez, did I kill him? Please tell me I didn't kill him!"

Cal dragged himself over to them. Doc's chest rose and fell in shallow breaths.

"He's breathing." Cal guffawed, holding his head. "Holy cats, he's breathing!"

Alanna leaned down and kissed Doc's forehead.

Another wave of nausea rolled over Cal. He ignored it. Doc was alive!

"Umm, guys?" Ty pointed his thumb over his shoulder. "If that really is Dania out there, she doesn't have much time. I mean, I'm thrilled Doc is okay, too, but..."

"Dania?" Alanna jumped to her station. "Is it possible?"

"She must have gotten sucked into the black hole just like we did."

Alanna's fingers fluttered over her console. "Life signs?"

"Slight heartbeat." Ty turned and started pushing buttons.

Ethan fiddled with Doc's console, sniffing and wiping his nose. "I think this says she's hibernating. Is that a thing? Can enforcers do that?"

Cal held back a smile. Even after all they'd been through today, they still jumped to action like a solidified unit, ignoring the tears still wet on their cheeks.

One problem solved, and they moved on to the next one.

Cal looked back to Doc. He probably needed medical care. The thing was, none of them had a stinking clue how to help him.

Doc was breathing, though. That was a first step. Cal supposed there wasn't much more they could do until he woke up again.

"I think I can grab her if you can get us close enough," Alanna said.

Ty fiddled with the controls. "I've plucked smaller cargo out of space. We can totally do this."

Cal leaned against the wall, trying to keep upright. "I thought we didn't have any power."

"Oh, we have power," Ethan said. "We're just sending it all to life support."

"You *are not* shutting off life support."

Ethan waved his hand in the air. "Only for a minute or two."

The booming inside Cal's head intensified, and he

squinted against the harsh light. "Definitely not. It might not come back on."

They all stared at him, and then Ethan and Alanna looked at Ty.

"Will you be able to get life support back on?" Ty asked.

Ethan rubbed his chin. "Maybe."

"*Maybe*?" Ty asked.

Ethan straightened. "Yes. I'm ninety-five percent positive." He glanced at the buttons on the wall panel. "Maybe eighty-five percent."

Alanna turned from her station. "Ty, Dania saved us from that royal cruiser. We can't abandon her."

Ty tapped on his control pad. "I have no intention of leaving her out there. Let's snatch ourselves an enforcer."

Dammit, Ty!

Ethan whooped, pressing buttons on the wall. "Let's do this!"

Each flash of the bright buttons sliced into Cal's brain. He held his head, breathing deeply as another wave of nausea hit.

Cal tried to stand, but he slid back to the floor. "Ethan. Do not turn off life support. I forbid it."

All three of them stared at him again. Why did they keep doing that?

Ty held up a hand. "All those in favor of deeming the captain unfit for duty say *aye*."

They all said *aye*.

"You can't do that." Cal winced, clutching his gut.

Ty smiled. "I'm pretty sure there's a rule book somewhere that says if the doctor is incapacitated, then the first mate can relieve the captain from duty for medical reasons."

Cal tried to straighten. "I'm fine."

Ty flipped a button on the panel and an alarm blared through the room. Cal dropped to his knee as the room spun around him. He held his hands over his ears, trying to keep his brain inside his head, where it belonged. His stomach roiled, and he vomited on the deck again.

He stared at the puke as it spread across the floor. They were right. He wasn't okay. But that didn't mean they should shut down life support.

He looked up. "You'll be risking all our lives to save one person."

Ty pointed out the window. "If it was me out there, or Doc, or Alanna, you'd do it."

Cal balked. He was right. Cal wasn't about to admit that, though.

Ethan cocked his head. "Or me, right?"

Ty raised a brow at him.

"He'd save me, too right?" Ethan asked.

Everyone turned back to their stations.

Ethan's lips twisted. "Gee, thanks, guys."

Ty sat at the controls. "Give me power, Ethan."

The engineer moved to his own station. "Sure. 'Give me power, Ethan.' 'Make sure life support comes back online, Ethan.' 'Save the day as always, but if you're floating in space, sorry, Ethan, you're screwed.'"

Alanna snickered. "I'd *think about* saving you."

A smile burst across Ethan's face. "That's because I'm so irresistible, baby."

She rolled her eyes and returned to work as Cal leaned against the lower maintenance plate. He pressed a button over his head, and a circular sanitation unit slid out of a panel near the floor, cleaned up the mess, then returned to its cubby in the wall.

The last thing he needed was one of them slipping in his puke and hitting their heads. Two incapacitated crew members were more than enough.

Ty brought up the main control panel. "How do Dania's readings look?"

Ethan switched to Doc's station. "Weaker than before. We need to stop screwing around."

"Don't rush it," Cal croaked. "Don't put the crew in jeopardy." He rubbed his sore throat.

"Noted." Ty didn't even look in Cal's direction. "Now shut up and get over whatever the hell is wrong with you. I'm really looking forward to your lecture on how reckless I've been lately." He turned to the others. "Shut down the life support, and stay alert. We might only get one chance at this."

The lights flickered. Cal's hands tensed on the deck below him. He'd just been in a room without life support. He'd lived through the cold. Just barely. His hands and feet throbbed almost worse than his head.

What if Ethan couldn't get the air back on?

"Power transferred to the engines and the grappling hooks," Ethan said.

Ty pulled on the controls and the ship banked right. "Let's go get our girl."

"I see her," Alanna said. "Take it in slow."

Cal crawled to Doc. The medic's chest still rose and fell in short breaths. Doc was a damn lucky son of a water driller. Cal pressed his palm against the doctor's head. He seemed cool, but not cold. He wasn't sure what that meant, though.

"Got her!" Alanna announced.

Ty squinted at his panel. "Bay four is the smallest. Pull her in there and then flood the space with air."

Flood a cargo hold with air?

Cal tried to sit up, but the room spun again. "We don't have enough oxygen to spare."

Once again, Ty didn't turn. "Shut up or I'm going to have Ethan shoot you."

Cal flinched when Ethan turned to him and smirked. He wanted to jump to his feet and make them all see reason, but he couldn't do more than sit and hope the room stopped spinning.

"Done," Alanna announced. "Snug like yesterday's contraband."

"Closing and sealing bay four," Ty said.

"Bringing life support back up." Ethan tapped on the wall. The lights lowered. "Oh, crap."

Cal grabbed the wall behind him. *Stars, no!*

Ethan snorted. "Just messing with you. We're fine."

The lights came back on.

One of these days, Cal was going to throw that guy out an airlock.

"Flooding Dania's compartment with air, and bringing the rest of the critical systems online." Ethan's fingers flew over the panel. "And...done!" He spun. Eyes wide. "I did it!"

Cal grimaced. "Why do you sound so surprised?"

Ethan shrugged.

Dammit! He'd hoped Ethan had been kidding about not being sure he could get life support back on.

Ty stood and frowned, looking down at Doc. "Anyone know anything about doctor-stuff?"

"I had first aid training in high school," Alanna said.

"I guess that's something." Ty looked at Ethan. "Give me light air in the corridors, and full air in the med bay and bridge." He looked at Cal. "Alanna and I are going to get Dania. We'll meet you in medical." He started walking.

Cal shook his head. "You should keep her in the cargo bay. Tie her up until we can figure out how Doc contained her."

Alanna pulled a med bag on her shoulder. "She saved us, Cal."

"She also led the prince straight to us. And she created the black hole that got us stuck here. She could have gotten us all killed. We could *still* get killed. We don't even know where we are."

Ty fastened a gun at his hip. "True, but you know me. I go with the flow." He turned to Ethan. "If Cal gives you any trouble, you *really do* have my permission to shoot him." He left the room. "On stun, Ethan!" he called through the door.

Alanna chuckled as she followed.

Ethan squatted beside Cal. "Are you going to be a good boy? Because I could really use help getting Doc onto a gurney." He cracked a smile. "But shooting you sounds like a lot of fun, too."

Great. He was barely sure he could get *himself* onto a gurney.

Ethan tapped him on the shoulder twice. "Hold tight. I'll be right back."

Cal blinked, glancing out the window. The stars outside were radiant and comforting, but brighter than home. The last time they'd gotten choked down by a black hole, they'd ended up on course. This time, nothing out there looked familiar.

Cal cringed. Maybe Ty's gut reaction had been a good one. As crazy as it might seem, they all might need Dania to get out of here, wherever *here* was.

Still, Ty's consistent lack of caution should be a concern for them all. Someone needed to be the voice of reason, and as usual, it ended up being Cal. He just needed to find a way to make them all listen to him again.

"Here we go." Ethan pushed a mattress on wheels onto the bridge...not quite an official gurney, but not a bad retrofit.

Doc had made himself a miniature hospital over the past couple of years, and the man's tinkering had saved a few of their lives on more than one occasion. Now, hopefully, they could do their genius mad scientist the same favor.

Cal helped Ethan lift Doc onto the mattress. His head pounded, and he closed his eyes to the brighter illumination in the halls.

"We can probably lower the lights out here and save some power," Cal suggested.

Ethan nodded. "I agree."

He stopped, opened a panel, and typed in a few codes. The lights dimmed, and several deep blue floor tiles illuminated their path.

Cal breathed a sigh of relief and opened his eyes again. It didn't make the headache go away; it just made it possible to see without it feeling like someone was blinding him with daggers.

He glanced at his engineer as they pushed the gurney

down the hallway. "You were the only one to side with me when we found out Dania was a general."

Ethan grunted.

"You know deep down that she's dangerous."

Doc's arm slipped off the side, and Ethan placed it back on the gurney. "I'm not a fool. I know what she's capable of."

Cal leaned forward as they maneuvered Doc around a corner. "She turned us in. We were getting attacked by her prince's ship. We have no idea why she really called up that black hole."

Ethan placed his palm on the med bay door panel, and it slid open. "What's your point, Cal?"

"I need someone else to back me up on this. That woman is a massive liability, whether or not she pushed our ship out of harm's way."

Cal wanted to believe differently. He wanted to believe she'd changed. But with her ricocheting from one side to another at a second's notice, they couldn't take this threat lightly.

Ethan pushed the gurney inside. "I agree."

There was an odd edge to his voice, like there was more to that sentence.

The medical bay lighting hit Cal like an avalanche of blinding white. He stumbled back and hit the floor.

His head pounded, and he rolled on his side and retched, but there was nothing left inside him. He collapsed, leaning his forehead on the cool tiles. Perspiration dripped into his eyes. The lines of sweat cut his skin like a knife, stinging and biting.

They were lost in the middle of nowhere.

The hull was breached.

His crew had turned on him.

And his brain pulsed in his head like it was imploding.

Maybe he'd died in that vortex and this was Hell. He couldn't imagine anything much worse.

Ethan's boots appeared beside him. "Sorry, boss."

Cal pushed himself up and shielded his eyes with his hand. "For what?"

The barrel of a gun came into focus.

"Wait!" Cal cried.

The flash seared through his pupils.

The boom echoed in his head, pounding in slow motion.

Everything went numb for a blessed two heartbeats before his head hit the floor and the harsh light finally faded to black.

A TONE SOUNDED, cutting through a deep, murky swamp.

Voices spoke in the distance.

Laughter boomed, slicing through Cal's mind, then faded.

Another tone. Muffled voices.

Footsteps.

Someone tugged on Cal's arm. Was it real? Maybe.

He fought to open his eyes, to speak, but nothing obeyed.

Time was an odd thing, ticking away.

Why did people say clocks ticked, anyway? Clocks hadn't ticked in hundreds of years. Odd, how people clung to the past, without even thinking about it. The past was like time, and time was fleeting.

Fleeting... What did that even mean? Fleets of ships?

The tone heightened, closer, and light shone through his eyelids. Cal willed them open, and he blinked.

Doc smiled down at him. "Good morning, sunshine."

He adjusted something at Cal's bedside. "How do you feel?"

Cal blinked. "Wh-What?"

The med bay came into partial focus.

Cal blinked at Doc again. "You-You were... Blast it, I don't know what you were."

Doc's lips thinned. "Ty and Ethan called it *dead*. Alanna says they were both just star-fried." He leaned closer. "At the moment, I'm more worried about you. Can you feel your toes?"

"My toes?" Cal wiggled them. "Yeah."

"Good. They tell me you were blasted at point-blank range with a distance-calibrated stun gun. Effective, but it toasted your brain for a few days." He adjusted a clear pouch of liquid hanging beside the bed.

"A few days?"

"Yup." Doc stopped fiddling with the bag. "You're pretty lucky. Ethan has been here checking on you every few hours. I've been trying to convince him you aren't dying, but I don't think he'll believe it until he sees you up and talking."

Cal blinked again and the room spun a little. "Ethan... He-He shot me."

"That's what I hear."

"Why?" Cal closed his eyes as he laid his head back. Cal had fallen, and the next thing he knew a gun was in his face.

Doc pushed a machine to the edge of the bed and checked a reading. "Well, according to Ethan, you were somewhat delusional, and you sounded like you were going to give Ty trouble about Dania."

What? "I was not delusional."

Doc picked up a thin metal cylinder. "He also said you were a stumbling, puking mess—which Alanna and Ty both confirmed, so I tend to believe him."

Cal eased up off the bed as heat rushed through his veins. "So he shot me?"

Doc pointed the cylinder at him. "He tried to stun you. Which would have been a great idea, except he grabbed a gun calibrated to stop someone at a distance." He put the metal tube in his coat pocket. "As I said, at point-blank range that could have killed you. It was a good thing Alanna thought to give you oxygen and fluids until they were able to revive me."

Cal held up his arm. A long, clear tube came off the bag, leading to Cal's inner elbow. "Alanna did this?"

"No. That's a magnesium drip. Luckily, I had some on hand to run some experiments with."

Cal blinked, still trying to focus. "Magnesium? Experiments?"

"According to my research, intravenous magnesium is an effective treatment for migraines." He lifted a brow. "Are you in any pain? Do you feel like you might puke?"

Cal shook his head.

"Good. Then I guess it's working." He looked over to another bed. A faint shimmer hung around the mattress like a curtain, or maybe a shield.

"Dania?" Cal asked.

Doc nodded. "She's still sedated. I wanted to talk to you before I woke her up."

Good, at least one member of his crew was taking the threat seriously.

Doc's gaze grew unusually serious. "They all tell me I

woke up and started seizing before Dania got on board. Is that true?"

Cal rubbed the back of his neck. "Yeah, it was right before they pulled her inside. Why?"

Doc sucked his teeth, tapped on a data pad, and showed Cal an x-ray of a head and shoulders.

"As usual, I have no idea what you're trying to show me."

Doc pointed to the spine. "Look at that."

Cal groaned. It looked like any other x-ray. What was he supposed to see? "How about you tell me what I'm looking at?"

"There are a whole lot of technical, very long words for what this shows, but basically, my spine looks like it was broken in several places and then got soldered back together."

Huh? "I take for granted you aren't talking about *actual* solder."

"No. My spine repaired itself."

Cal stared at the x-ray. "That's not possible, right?"

"No, it's not." He lowered the data pad. "I hate to side against my girl Alanna, but I think Ty and Ethan were right. I should be dead. At the bare minimum, I should be paralyzed."

Cal sat up. "So, what does your incredibly big brain tell you?"

Doc pointed at Dania. "That she did something. Enforcer healing. That's the only possible solution."

"She wasn't on board."

Doc smoothed back his hair. "I'm not complaining. I certainly like being alive, but something weird is going on."

He turned away. "Anyway, the lack of my demise is the *good news*."

"There's bad news?"

Doc faced Dania's bed, folding his arms. "I'm not sure I can save her anymore."

Cal balked. "What?"

"Remember those pathogens?"

Cal glanced at her. "Yeah."

"They're nearly gone. I think that's why she busted out of our brig and tried to stop her prince from shredding us to bits. There's nothing to suppress her from thinking for herself. I think she might be a real person now. Conscience and all."

"But she turned us in. She sent him our location."

"Yes, but while you were asleep, we all watched the recording of her conversation with that prince." Doc looked back at her. "She tried to convince him to look at the evidence that exonerates you."

Cal stretched his back against the mattress. "I'm going to guess that he didn't."

"Yeah, that would be my guess." Doc pressed a few buttons on the wall. "Look at this."

A split screen opened on the panel. On the left was Dania, hair frazzled and a confused look frozen on her face. On the right, the Kever prince who had demanded her return.

Doc pressed a button. "His majesty was speaking in Kever, so I you're listening to a translation."

Dania gulped on the screen. *"Were you aware Filluck was involved in illicit activity?"*

Whoa. She'd cut right to the chase. Even with how far she'd come, Cal hadn't expected her to be so direct.

The prince looked down. *"I admit I had suspicions."* He lifted his eyes. *"I was going to confront him about it, but Espinoza killed him before I had a chance."*

Yeah, rat bastard. Nice excuse.

Dania lifted her chin. *"Cal didn't do it."*

Cal leaned up in his bed. "Whoa. Wait."

Doc stopped the recording.

"What did she just call me?"

"Ah, so you caught that, too? I thought the same thing. All this time, she's been dehumanizing you by using your last name."

Cal rubbed his chin. "Probably to make it easier for her to kill me."

Doc flipped the switch. "You ain't seen nothing yet."

The prince tilted his head. *"Cal?"*

She balked, blinked, and turned to the side.

Interesting. So it *had been* a slip of the tongue. How long had she been thinking about him by his first name, rather than his last?

The prince waved his hand dismissively. *"It makes no difference. Calvin Espinoza has already been found guilty."*

No surprise there. That was how all Kevers thought. The king's idea of guilty and innocent was far too rigid.

Dania shifted in her seat. *"I told you the recording proves his innocence."*

And she was still pushing it? Cal glanced over to where Dania slept behind the energy curtain. An enforcer wouldn't do that. They would have accepted the prince's decision as law.

The Kever's eyes darkened to a glare that made Cal grip the edge of his bed. *"I've heard enough. You need to come home to be fed. You are not well, and you are not thinking clearly."*

Cal held up his hand. "Hold on."

Doc stopped the recording.

Cal stared at the screen. "Did you hear what he said? Come home to be *fed*?"

"Creepy, right? I'm starting to think about twentieth-century horror films."

Cal frowned. Just what did these aliens do to the enforcers? What had he meant by *feeding* her?

Cal shivered and waved for Doc to restart the recording.

On the screen, Dania took a deep breath, like a child trying to gain courage in front of an angry parent. *"I admit I'm not well, but on this one thing, I'm clear. I need you to look at the recordings."*

The prince's eyes widened slightly.

Damn, Cal might have buckled under that glare if it had been him. The interesting thing was, that the evidence made no difference. Yes, it proved he was innocent of murder, but he was guilty of smuggling and a myriad of other more minor offenses, but any one of them condemned him to death. So why push to remove the murder conviction?

Dania's cheeks glistened. Were those…tears? *"Please, Ada."*

The prince closed his eyes. *"Fine. Send them."*

Dania started pressing buttons.

Cal sat back. "I guess this is when she sold us out?"

"Nope," Doc said. This is where it gets pretty interesting." He pointed to the screen. "I think, right here, that she decided that she doesn't trust him. It's a huge step for her. Watch."

The prince's lips thinned. *"Why have you sent the file with spatial encryption?"*

Cal straightened, his heart suddenly racing. "She encrypted it?"

Doc held up his finger for Cal to listen.

The prince's glare returned. *"Send me your location."*

"I need you to watch the recording." Dania's response was quick. Again, like a child struggling for any possible advantage in an uncontrollable situation.

The prince's nostrils flared. *"Send. Me. Your. Location."*

Cal's hands dug into his sheets. Dania knew better than Cal did what kind of power backed up that harsh command.

She seemed to struggle to get a breath. *"You need to promise me to watch the recordings."*

"I already told you I would. Are you questioning me?"

Yeah, she was, and Cal could barely believe what he was watching.

"I-I..." Dania stammered.

Tell him that you don't trust him, Dania. Tell him that you want to be free. You want to. I can see it in your eyes!

The prince slapped the table in front of him. *"This is all the more reason to get you home as quickly as possible. Send me your location immediately. I will come for you myself."*

And that should have been the red flag. A prince meant death. She should have known that.

Dania looked down at something beneath her screen, maybe part of the console. *"Please promise you will watch the recording with an open mind."*

That wasn't going to happen. Ever. The prince was hiding something, and she was too afraid of him, or still too much under his power, to see it.

The Kever still looked like he wanted to peel the skin off someone's bones. *"I will watch the recording you sent me."*

But when? Probably not before he planned to kill them all.

Dania smiled, releasing a breath. *"The location is coming."*

She reached forward, and with the press of one button, sealed their fates.

A shit-eating grin appeared on the Kever's face. *"Do not warn the crew. I don't want them changing your location before I can get to you."*

"You don't need to come for me. I'm fine."

At least she'd given one last effort. By then, it had been too late, though.

"Spoken like someone who has not looked in the mirror in some time. You need me more than I think you realize. I'm not losing you. I'm coming."

Interesting. He actually looked like he cared about her, but it was probably more like an admiral worrying about losing a well-armed warship...a tool necessary for battle... than losing a person.

The screen went blank.

"So, do you see?" Doc said. "She actually tried, and in the end, she only sent our location because she still had faith that he'd watch the recording."

"But that recording wouldn't matter. As she's been so fond of reminding us all, we're guilty of other crimes. He would have killed us anyway."

Doc folded his arms and considered her. "We showed her the evidence in those recordings, and that was the start of her waking up and realizing that the law wasn't so cut and dry." He turned to Cal. "Maybe she thought it would work with her beloved prince as well." He started pacing, tapping his pointer fingers against his lips. "The guy promised he'd watch the recording, and she's programmed to believe him unconditionally. I think at that point, she still had hope."

"And then realized her mistake when he attacked."

"Yeah." Doc rubbed his chin. "She was almost awake from her daze during this conversation. She fought him, but he still got her to back down."

"But she had to know she was signing our execution orders."

"She did. Until right here." Doc set the time monitor back on the recording to the point where the prince had slapped the table. "There's a long pause here, right before he says that he'll watch the recordings."

"Your point?"

"Look at Dania. She isn't even moving."

He was right. Cal had thought it was a glitch in the recording. "Hypnosis?"

"I don't know, but after she stared at him, she seemed to forget that he'd kill us all." He leaned back. "I don't even know where to go with that information, but the base of my pathogen hypothesis still seems to be holding. Going into this conversation, she was starting to break out of her haze. She was trying to make him happy, without getting us killed." He pointed to the Kever's face on the screen. "He did something to her that set back her recovery, but as soon as she wasn't staring at him, it started to subside again."

"That's a long shot, even for you."

He shook his head. "I don't think so. When you pointed out to Dania that Geron would probably kill Alanna, she looked surprised. Horrified. Maybe even remorseful." He jutted his chin in Dania's direction. "I believe that was when she started back on the road toward humanity again, and she continued to evolve through the night while she was locked up." He walked over to her bed and placed his palm on her forehead. "I think everyone is right. She *was* trying to save us in the end."

Cal took a deep breath and let it out slowly. "So, we finally got her on our side, but she's not going to live long enough to tell anyone."

Or if she did, and she got anywhere near that prince, he could sway her thoughts and undo all their work.

Cal rubbed his face with his hand. So much for them throwing a stone into the galactic pond.

Doc turned back toward him. "I need to wake her up, soon."

Cal massaged a growing ache in his temples. "How long until her organs start breaking down from the lack of pathogens?"

Doc smiled at him and raised his eyebrows.

"What? You think I haven't been paying attention?"

Doc laughed, before the smile eased from his face. "I think it will happen pretty fast. I originally speculated she had a few months before the pathogens were all gone. Now that she's free, I imagine she'll start to experience complications within a few weeks or so."

Cal sat up and let his legs dangle off the edge of the bed. "If we have that long, we can still get you those supplies."

"Did the mighty Captain Cynic just jump on board with trying to save the enforcer?"

Dania's lips were slightly parted, and her dark blonde hair hung in sloppy waves about her face. She looked so peaceful while she was asleep. Normal.

Ten years ago, when that enforcer had killed Cal's dad

and walked away, leaving Cal holding his father as he'd bled out in the street, Cal had pictured all their kind as cold-blooded monsters.

In many ways, he'd been right.

He'd never considered the possibility they were being controlled.

Yes, the enforcers were an army of thousands, and the *Star Renegade* was one ship. But for this one enforcer, they could make a difference.

He wasn't ready to completely trust her. He'd be a fool if he did, especially if the prince could still press her buttons from a distance. But they'd come too far to give up on her now.

He met Doc's patient gaze. "Let's see if Ty knows where we are. I promised to get you the supplies. I'll make good on that if I can."

Cal eased off the edge of the mattress and took a tentative step.

Doc grabbed his shoulder. "Take it easy, there. You've been in bed for a while."

"I'm fine."

It was only partially true, but if they wanted to try to save the enforcer…if they wanted to save *Dania*, the captain needed to be on his feet.

Besides, Cal needed to find Ethan and punch him in the face for shooting him.

CHAPTER 40

DANIA

DANIA GRIPPED the white blankets pulled tight across her waist, yet her hands still trembled. A sour twist formed in her stomach. She wanted to discount the doctor's words as the ridiculous ramblings of a criminal, but she knew better.

When he placed his hand over hers, she jumped.

"Are you okay?" he asked.

An odd question, since he'd just told her she was going to die.

Alexander had always reminded her of her mortality, but she'd brushed it aside as a useless fact, one not necessary to keep in the front of her mind. She'd always thought she'd die in battle for the glory of her prince. It was every enforcer's dream.

But to die here? On a human ship? Dishonored?

Death was supposed to be quick. Anything slow, Alexander would probably have had time to heal. She never considered the possibility of fighting an invisible enemy... something inside her own body.

Her fingertip traced the pattern in the blanket. "If I'm

understanding correctly, my organs are going to fail one after another, unless I return to my sponsor."

"But going back to him isn't your only option." He walked over to a tray and picked up a glass tube with thick, red liquid inside. "I've been studying your blood. I'm not sure I can completely stop the degradation, but I can slow it down."

Slow it down? "How?"

"I think I can make synthetic pathogens that your body will respond to similarly as if you'd been re-infected by that prince."

Re-infected. Like there was something wrong with her, like she was sick. And yet, without the pathogens, she might die.

What the doctor didn't understand was that she didn't need a treatment. She needed her prince.

Dania cringed and shook away the thought.

Whenever she'd been weakened or hurt, her instincts had told her to return to Geron. He had always been there for her. He would always make whatever the problem was better. But at what cost?

Her skin itched with the need to run, to return home, to be whole again. But was this her own desire, or Geron's?

The doctor set the vial down. "I'm willing to try to help you, but you need to understand that this is purely experimental. I'll be working off my theories only, and we still need to see if we can find the supplies."

"These supplies... Were they the reason your ship had plotted a course to the pirate sector?"

He pursed his lips. "Well, most of what I'd need might be a little hard to find at more reputable trade stations."

So, in order to help her, they would have to deal with

illegal traders. Which meant if she wanted to be saved, she'd have to be a part of more larcenous activity.

She thought of the little girl dying of scurvy, and the hope in the parents' eyes as Dania had handed them the oranges.

Maybe this crew was right. Maybe there could be good reasons to break the law.

The doctor leaned against the side of her bed. "So, what's the decision? Do you want us to drop you off, ping your prince, and then disappear? Or would you like to take a stab at freedom?"

She clutched the blankets tighter. "You're giving me a choice?"

"That's the great thing about the *Star Renegade*. We all get a choice. If the crew hadn't chosen to save you, we wouldn't be having this conversation."

They'd chosen to save her, even after she'd put them at such a risk? If she stayed, though, they'd be at even more risk. Geron had invested nine years in her. He wouldn't give her up so easily.

The doctor nudged her shoulder. "Come on, girl. I say give it a go. Besides…" A smile broke out on his face. "I love a challenge."

Dania took a deep breath.

If she went back to Geron, she'd live. She'd be able to return to the life that she understood, the life where everything made sense. Not like this new world where there were confusing choices.

She flinched. She wanted those choices. She wanted to be free.

Still, everything inside her screamed to run home, like

all her cells knew what they needed, but only her mind had doubts.

If the doctor was right, then these feelings weren't her instincts, but Geron's doing. This was part of her programming...to return to him when her power waned, or if she was injured.

Staying with the humans meant she might die, possibly painfully, but her choices would be her own. She could decide what was good and bad, rather than being told what to think and following orders unconditionally.

She scrunched her eyes shut and steadied her breathing. She'd done such horrible things in Geron's name without even an afterthought. Killing was her duty. She'd needed to eradicate evil from the galaxy, no matter what.

The *no matter what* part might haunt her for the rest of her life.

The colonies didn't praise the enforcers' good work. They were horrified. The people bowed because they had no choice, not because they loved their king.

Dania couldn't be a part of that any longer. She refused.

She thought about the little girl she'd saved from scurvy, and smiled. Maybe she could save more children, even if it meant breaking a few laws? She winced, pain surging through her.

"You okay?" Doc asked.

"I just thought about committing a crime, and..." She scratched at her arms. "It hurt...inside."

"That prince is holding on for dear life, but it should get better and better as all the pathogens work their way out of your system."

She drew in a deep breath. The pain wasn't that bad. She could get through it.

Dania snickered, shaking her head.

Her chest clenched as her eyes fogged with tears. Was she really sitting here, talking herself into experiencing pain in order to commit crimes…even crimes for good reasons?

She remembered pulling a boy from his mother's arms years ago, and the mother's shriek as her child had received his punishment. Dania wasn't a defender of the law. She was a puppet. A monster.

She wouldn't kill children anymore. She couldn't execute otherwise good citizens for minor offenses. It wasn't right, no matter whose laws supported her.

Pain flooded through her again. She gritted her teeth.

She was supposed to uphold the highest standards, and she would. But she needed to be the one to choose what those standards would be.

"I've made my decision." She steadied herself with another deep breath. "I'd rather live a few more months free than become what I was." She straightened as much as the tight blankets allowed. "I'm not going back."

Her stomach twisted, and her hands started to tremble again.

She'd spoken those words aloud. Her fears, her trepidations, her doubts weren't just thoughts anymore.

She'd openly defied her prince, a crime punishable by death.

Dania smiled.

She'd just become the criminal element she'd been hunting her entire life.

CAL PACED in front of the gray starburst blast stain on the aft lounge wall. Someone had drawn a smiley face in the middle of the clear, oblong center of the discharge pattern.

Probably Ethan.

Cal pursed his lips. They'd lost their entire cargo that day, and almost lost their lives, yet the engineer had made a joke out of it. Cal should have sprung for the paint and cleaners to get rid of all those blast marks, but it had always seemed more important to stock up on protein sticks and vegetable supplements.

He stopped and stared at the small green star twinkle over the smiley's left eye. That little addition was new—probably Alanna's artwork.

His navigator had joked once that the blast marks gave the ship character. Maybe they did. They were a sign of survival, and maybe that twinkle-eyed smiley face was just a celebration of being alive.

What none of them understood, was what an incredible responsibility it was to keep them all that way.

He spun toward his crew, who were all lined up on the far side of the table, looking like rejects from the ancient *Last Supper* painting. Doc sat on the end beside Alanna, Dania in the middle, and Ty on the enforcer's left. Ethan sat on the opposite end, sporting the well-deserved black eye Cal had given him.

They were a motley crew, but they were his. Even Dania at this point, whether he liked it or not.

The enforcer folded her hands in front of her and stared at her fingers. She was the elephant in the room, but Cal wasn't sure how to tackle the renegade enforcer issue yet.

"What's the status on the hull breach?" he asked no one in particular.

Ethan drummed his fingers on the table. "I'm not an exterior maintenance guy, but it looks pretty good. The hull pressure is fine."

Ty sat back. "Alanna and I added more of your magic polymer since the seal seemed to hold. As soon as we can land somewhere, I'd like to replace the whole panel, but as long as no one is shooting at us, we'll be fine."

Ethan scoffed, and Ty glared at him.

The engineer was right, though. There was always someone shooting at them.

Cal turned to Alanna. "When can we get back to normal space?"

She shifted uncomfortably in her chair. "Well, that's a bit of a problem. Without knowing where we are, I don't know where to take us. If I make a guess, and I'm wrong, we can go in the wrong direction and it might be weeks before we even realize it."

Dania lifted her gaze. "I can help with that."

Cal scratched behind his ear. "Without magic?"

She flinched. "No."

From what Doc had told him, Dania probably didn't have much of that crazy enforcer power left. It would be hard, but they all needed to start treating her like a normal person.

Doc reached around Alanna and tapped the back of Dania's hand. "I don't think you should exert yourself, anyway, sweetie. You need all your strength to heal."

Dania closed her eyes and nodded. It looked so...*humble*. Hopefully, it wasn't an act.

Cal turned back to Alanna. "What's your best guess to safely get us home?"

She held up her hands. "Three months?"

Ty slapped the table with his palm. "We don't have enough supplies for three months."

"It's worse than that." Doc stood and put his hands on the enforcer's shoulders. "Dania doesn't have that long. I hate to say the clock is ticking, but it is."

Dania drew her hands closer to her chest, yet she didn't pull away from Doc. *Interesting.*

Cal rubbed his face. It might take them three months to get home, but Dania probably had a few weeks before her dependency on those stinking pathogens started killing her.

Doc grimaced as he returned to his chair. His gaze darted about, his mind probably whirling with possible ways to get out of this situation.

Hopefully, in a few hours, he'd narrow his thoughts down to a few plausible scenarios and get back to them with a solution.

Cal paced, dragging his nails through his hair. Dania still could, at any time, decide she wanted to live and find a way to bring that blasted prince back on top of all their heads. This was a real danger—one that they all needed to face.

Dania lowered her head, as if she knew his attention was on her.

Cal stopped pacing and folded his arms. "The last time I gave you a room to sleep in, you broke out and dropped a pin that nearly got us all killed."

Doc leaned forward. "So, what? You're going to lock her in the cargo bay again?"

Dania didn't look up from her hands.

Alanna put her arm around the enforcer's shoulder. "Cal, that's not right."

Cal shook his head. The cargo bay hadn't even crossed his mind. It would probably take too much power from other systems to set up a perimeter down there. The problem was, he didn't know what to do with her.

Doc raised his hand. "I can put a shield around her room just as easily as I can put one around a holding cell. I can even do a full circle around her bed if you want." He glanced at Dania. "But we need to start working on trust."

Cal didn't have trust in a lot of things, but he did have trust in Doc.

Ty looked down the line of the crew. "All in favor of letting Dania stay in a room say *aye*."

Cal pushed through the door before the sound of the last 'aye' faded, including his own.

As long as Doc could keep her confined while the rest of them slept, he really didn't care where Dania was quartered; and he had to admit, treating her a little more like the crew would probably help in the long run.

The lights in the hall flickered—something else to fix. It

seemed like no matter how many steps ahead they got, something always managed to push them back.

Before turning the corner, Cal looked down the hallway toward the closed lounge door. He'd agreed to help the enforcer. It was the right thing to do.

Still, the thought of her on this ship, walking around like the rest of the crew, made him want to punch something.

He'd spent his whole adult life trying to avoid the enforcers and upending everything they stood for. Screwing the system seemed like the right thing to do, like the only way to honor his father's good name.

He started walking again. Was taking Dania in honoring his father's name?

Maybe. Only time would tell.

All he could hope was that wherever his dad was, he was smiling at him with pride. That was all Cal really wanted.

He stepped onto the bridge and took in the vast array of unfamiliar stars scattered around hunks of twisted metal—the remains of goodness-knew-what. The *Star Renegade* could have been pulverized into space junk like that, but they were still here because they were survivors. They'd get out of this like a team, as always.

However, now they were a team plus one very big wild-card. Cal wanted to jump onboard Team Dania, but he couldn't forget what had brought them all to this star-forsaken place.

Doc might be able to help her, and she may be a valu-able ally, but Cal had thought this before, and she'd betrayed them.

He rubbed his face. No matter what Doc concocted,

Dania would always belong to that prince, and Cal wasn't so sure that once they got back to regular space, she wouldn't run back to him with her tail between her legs, begging for forgiveness. Especially if her symptoms worsened.

The yellow light on the dashboard flashed again. Cal checked the extra sensors, and when they came up clear, he tapped the light three times, and it stopped blinking.

Yeah, the ship was broken, but some things, like this light, actually gave the *Renegade* charm. Like the blast stains Alanna was so fond of, some things just didn't need to be fixed. They made things comfortable. Familiar. Home.

The stars twinkled in the distance. Any one of them might be a familiar sun, lost in an array of so many others.

Cal tapped his fingers on the edge of his console. It was easy to be lost, and not so easy, sometimes, to find yourself, or to make up for past sins. Cal knew that better than anyone.

The yellow light started to flash again, and Cal grinned, relaxing his posture.

He called up the cameras in the lounge. The crew had moved to the circular table, where Ty was dealing out a deck of cards. Everyone picked up their hands, but Dania stared at the cards on the table. Doc showed her how to pick them up and spread out the cards so she could see them.

If she was serious about wanting to be free, living on this ship would be a long list of firsts for the enforcer.

Yeah, it was a risk, but every supply run they made put their lives in jeopardy. This wasn't any different. Cal had opened his doors to her, and they'd stay open—unless she posed a threat.

Ty shoved Ethan, and Ethan held up his hands. He'd probably been caught cheating.

Nothing new, just another friendly card game on the *Renegade*.

Dania put down a card, and they all cheered. She looked up at them and smiled.

The enforcer…*smiled.*

Cal eased into his chair and tapped the yellow light three times. There was one thing that remained clear no matter what sort of mess they got into: this crew was his family. He loved them. Even Ethan.

He glanced back at the screen. He needed to believe that smile was genuine. The alternative was unthinkable.

Of course, he probably had worse things to worry about. That prince had gotten a good, long look at the *Star Renegade*, and by now, everyone in the galaxy was probably looking for them.

The light flashed yellow twice, then orange.

Cal stared at it. Had he seen that right?

Yellow, yellow, orange.

Yellow, yellow, orange.

He patched a communication through to the lounge. "Hey, Ty, the light is flashing up here again."

"Just tap it three times."

"Yeah, I did, but now it's flashing yellow twice and then orange. You told me to call you right away if that ever happened."

Silence hung in the air. On the screen, Ty looked at Ethan. "That's not funny, Cal."

That didn't sound good. "It wasn't meant to be funny. What does it mean?"

Yellow, orange, orange.

"Now there's two oranges."

Both Ethan and Ty cursed. "We're coming!"

Now what?

Cal leaned closer to the glass. They were completely clear of the debris. He couldn't see anything out there.

Ty and Ethan stormed through the door first. Doc filed in behind, followed by Alanna and Dania.

Yellow, orange, orange.

Ethan flipped several switches on the wall. "Killing the power on all decks but the bridge."

"What?" Cal said. "We just barely got the power up."

Ty reached his station. "Killing the outer hull shields in three, two, one."

"Stop!" Cal reached for him, but he'd already thrown the switch. "What are you doing?"

Yellow, orange, orange.

"We're being scanned!" Ty looked over his shoulder. "Everyone, get seated. We're about to become just another piece of floating debris." He glanced at a panel on the wall. "Cutting the rest of the power now."

The lights went out.

"Here goes life support," Ethan said, and the always present gentle rumbling beneath their feet ebbed away.

Cal tensed. With all of them in that room, they probably had about ten minutes before they ran out of air.

Orange, orange, orange.

Ty held his finger to his lips as the light flashed in his face.

Orange, orange, orange.

So many questions hung in the air. But even Ethan sat in the dark, not moving. Not speaking.

Yellow, orange, orange.

Ty pointed at the light and gave a thumbs-up before holding his finger to his lips again.

This was crazy. They were already dead in space. Now they were dead-er. What if they couldn't get the power back up?

Cal shook away the thought. They were in no shape to fight. Hiding was a good call, no matter the outcome.

Yellow, orange, orange.

Alanna's teeth chattered, and Doc held his hand over her mouth. Her eyes were wide as the light flashed. Doc pulled her closer into a hug. Cal could see her shivering from across the bridge. Ty folded in on himself and Ethan shoved his hands in his pockets.

Yellow, yellow, orange.

They were well past the uncharted sectors. How in the stars were they being scanned?

Yellow, yellow, yellow.

There it was: the normal, beautiful broken light.

Ty released a breath. Doc let go of Alanna.

Ty flicked a few switches and a soft glow rose in the cabin. "Getting cold in here."

A puff of white formed in front of his face as Cal laughed.

That was nothing. They had no idea what cold was until they'd been stuck without environmental controls for as long as he had.

"On it." Ethan started tapping the panel.

The floorboards started to hum.

"Are we clear?" Cal asked.

Ty stared at his screens. "Yeah, we're good."

Cal sighed, straightening. "How was that even possible?

We're in the middle of nowhere. Who has scanners that reach that far?"

Dania rubbed her shoulders, shaking off the chill. "Enforcers."

Cal shuddered, holding his breath as the crew turned and stared at her.

"It's Geron." Dania's gaze lowered to the floor. "He knows we're out here, and he'll never let me go."

A NOTE FROM THE AUTHOR:

I hope you loved book one of *Star Bandits: Uprising*!
Ready for more intergalactic adventure?
Keep scrolling for a sneak peek at book two, or if you're a
true smuggler at heart,
Click here to pick up your copy now!

Want to hear updates on future books and any other stuff that's going on? Sign up for my newsletter here.
https://www.subscribepage.com/s2b4f1_copy4

ACKNOWLEDGMENTS

Normally, when I sit down to do acknowledgements, I need to scroll back through YEARS of files. Star Bandits is no different. My original pitches for the series are dated July 2018. The actual outlines for all five books are dated June, July, and August of 2019. Crazy, right? A whole year later!

But I have no regrets. Star Bandits is my first foray into space opera, and I wanted to get it right. As Ethan would say, "Patience is a virtue!"

Dania stepped off the platform onto Midway Station on November 1, 2019 and I finished book one on December 8, 2019. That was where the fun began, and here is where I can start thanking people.

First, I need to give a shout out to R. Hamilton, who very patiently kept me on track while making sure I had a solid plot for five books, and how to line up the character journeys. I'm not sure I wouldn't have dropped into my own black hole if you hadn't been looking over my shoulder.

There was some trial and error in book one. Dania originally was a homicidal death machine, and while I do miss how horrible she was, I understand how she might have been a little "too much" in my first drafts of this novel. Thank you, Sharon Hughson and Shaila Patel for helping me tame her down to be scary, but not *too* scary.

Readers! Readers are super important. I put out some feelers to my fan base, and a lot of people offered to read and comment on the later drafts. I plucked a few names out of a hat (or a random number generator—same thing) and I'd like to thank Robin Kenny, Louise Haring, and Lori Lenox for stepping up to the landing platform and sending me your feedback.

I fretted over these covers, and placed the art in the talented hands of Julie Nicholls of Covers by Julie. Thank you Julie, and... MORE KIND-OF-SHINY WHITEISH OPAL FLOATING HAIR!

(Yeah, she definitely put up with a lot.)

I've mentioned before that I'm comma-deficient. Which is why my editors are wonderful, patient people with an eagle eye. Thank you Scarlet West, Amy McNulty, and Tandy Boese. You guys totally rock!

Of course, thank you to my family for their support, and readers like you for your fantastic feedback, and very much appreciated reviews. Yes, I do read your reviews, and it always means a lot when someone takes the time to tell others how much they enjoyed my work.

Thanks again for reading, and we'll catch up again soon in an unknown galaxy far, far away!

—Jennifer

See more great books by Jennifer M. Eaton

ABOUT THE AUTHOR

Jennifer M. Eaton hails from the eastern shore of the North American Continent on planet Earth. Yes, regrettably, she is human, but please don't hold that against her.

While not traipsing through the galaxy looking for specimens for her space moth collection, she lives with her wonderfully supportive husband, three energetic offspring, and a duo of poodles who run the spaceport when she's not around.

During infrequent excursions to her home planet of Earth, Jennifer enjoys long hikes in the woods, bicycling, swimming, snorkeling, and snuggling up by the fire with a great book; but great adventures are always a short shuttle ride away.

Read more from Jennifer M. Eaton

www.jennifereaton.com

bookbub.com/authors/jennifer-m-eaton

goodreads.com/Jennifermeaton

facebook.com/Jennifer.m.eaton.3

twitter.com/jennifermeaton

instagram.com/jennifermeaton

pinterest.com/jennifermeaton

PREVIEW OF STAR BANDITS UPRISING, BOOK 2: RENEGADE THIEF

CHAPTER 1 DANIA

Being human wasn't so bad, except for always worrying about getting killed.

Dania sat beside an array of supplies as Alanna leaned through a large hole in the wall of the *Star Renegade's* cargo hold. The woman seemed to go about her business, unharried by the inevitability of an angry prince catching up to the ship and murdering them all.

Maybe that was because that angry prince wasn't actually after Alanna. That wouldn't save her, or any of the crew, though.

Dania considered the makeshift patch on the far wall of the cargo bay, a remnant of their last encounter with Dania's former sponsor. A few weeks ago, the captain had nearly frozen and suffocated to death in this very chamber, and he'd used a mystery polymer to seal a hull breach—saving himself, and probably the ship. He was resourceful, as were all the humans on this crew.

Alanna backed out of the crevice. "All done."

"That was fast."

"I'm getting better at this." The woman beamed. "It's nice to have the help, too. Thanks."

Dania shrugged. "All I did was hand you things. I wouldn't actually be able to do any maintenance."

Alanna eased onto the floor and took a drink from a water flask. "I couldn't either when I first got here." She wiped her mouth on her sleeve. "You should have seen me. I was such a mess."

Dania doubted the woman had ever been 'a mess' in her life.

Alanna looked up into the hole. "Anyway, I discovered through necessity, that I like to fix things, and I'm pretty good at it, most of the time."

Dania's chest clenched, and she looked down. Her only friend, Alexander, had been good at fixing things, too. He'd loved discovering how machines worked, and making them better.

Dania's warm smile melted from her face. The last time she'd seen Alexander was through the glass of a fighter craft. He'd begged her to come home moments before Prince Geron had opened fire on him.

She'd thrown a shield up to protect him before she'd passed out and been dragged into the black hole that had stranded her and the *Star Renegade* crew here...wherever *here* was.

The ache in her heart deepened. She may never know if Alexander had survived that day. If he hadn't, Dania wasn't sure if she'd be able to live with the guilt.

Alanna stood. "I'm sure that we'll find something you're good at too. It makes living on a ship more interesting when you have a job to do."

Dania nodded, but the truth was, the only thing she'd ever been good at was killing people. Those skills weren't quite transferable to shipboard life, unless the captain wanted a bodyguard.

Alanna held up a jar of polymer. "This is just enough to add to the edges of Cal's seal. We might as well use it up."

"I thought you and Ty had already reinforced it?"

Alanna walked over to the hull breach and poured the material over the existing makeshift repair. "Yeah. Twice." She leaned back wiping her brow as the gray-white material flowed into the pits and grooves. "I just wish there was a way to heat it all up at the same time to make sure there aren't any more micro-leaks. The maintenance torches only melt sections, and I'm never sure they seal together."

Heat? That shouldn't be too hard.

Dania grabbed an angled plate and held it up to the seal. "I think I can help with that."

Centering her focus on the plate, she pressed power into the metal.

At least, she tried to.

She frowned, staring at her hands. This should be simple. Child's play.

She gritted her teeth, searching for the few traces of glowing primordial energy still flowing in her veins. A slight tremor erupted in her chest, before flowing out to her hands. She drank in the vibrating energy before pressing the heat into the metal. Air currents ran to her, filling the molecular space between her and the steel, insulating her skin as the plate turned molten red, then cooled back to silver.

Dania's vision wavered and she held her head. The plate

slipped to the floor, leaving behind a hazy, but solid reinforced patch.

Alanna leaned closer to the repair. "Wow! That's a handy trick. I think we've found your calling."

The room spun and Dania fell back, clutching her temples.

"Oh my gosh!" Alanna's blurry face appeared in front of her. "Are you okay?" She disappeared from view. "Peter, I need you in the cargo bay. Dania's sick again."

Again. Dania grimaced. How could she live the rest of her life as the weak link? She was raised to be an enforcer. A leader. She didn't know how to be anything else.

The room skewed again, and the doctor's kind face appeared.

He shined a light into her eyes. "What were you guys doing?"

Alanna explained how Dania had melted the polymer. Their voices sounded like they were underwater.

"I'm okay." Dania tried to sit up, but slumped back down. "Maybe I'm a little tired."

The doctor came back into Dania's view. "Does using your abilities usually sap your strength like this?"

Dania closed her eyes, wishing the answer was different. "No. What I did should have been simple."

But it wasn't. And each day simple tasks seemed harder and harder.

The doctor finally came into focus. "You need to try to limit the use of your power until I find a way to replenish your pathogens."

Pathogens.

Dania cringed. The doctor insisted that her prince had infected her body with tiny microbes that changed her body. He claimed that she'd been human before she'd been an enforcer, and she now needed those microbes to survive. He thought he could replicate them with the right supplies. Of course, they'd need to find their way back to civilized space, first.

Dania nodded, but she wasn't really sure what she was agreeing to. This news was more of the same, and none of this bode well for her when they didn't even know where they were in the universe, and which way to travel to get home.

A loud tone sounded from the overhead comm system.

"Heads up, people!" Ty's voice shouted. "We're about to be scanned. I need everyone out of those cargo bays and in the center of the ship in ten. Nine. Eight..."

"Come on!" Alanna grabbed Dania's arm, and the doctor took the other. Dania scrambled to keep up, but the humans mostly dragged her into the hall and dropped her on the floor. Alanna hit the controls, and the doors shut before she huddled up against Dania, and the doctor put his arms around her from the other side.

The speakers continued with Ty's voice: "Three. Two. One. Here we go..."

The lights winked out. The chill sunk in quickly, faster than it did in the upper levels. They needed to spend less time in the cargo areas until the incessant scans stopped.

Dania knew they wouldn't stop, though, not until Prince Geron found her. These people were protecting her for no better reason then a human code of ethics that told them it was the right thing to do.

Dania hoped their odd morality didn't lead to all their deaths.

The doctor drew her in tighter, and Alanna pressed

closer from the other side. This kind of contact had repelled her at first, but she understood the need for body warmth when the cold of space reached through a ship, looking for lives to erase.

The captain worried the power might not come back on each time they shut down to avoid detection, and with good reason, with the amount of damage this ship had seen since Dania had come on board.

This was the fourth time they'd been scanned over the last two weeks, but Ty and Ethan's strategy must be working, because no ships had dropped out of the abyss to kill the crew and drag Dania back to her prince.

Discovery was inevitable though. If they didn't get out of there, if they didn't find safe harbor, they would be found. And once her prince restored her to her former self, there would be nothing she could do to save this crew.

CHAPTER 2 CAL

Ty's face glowed with each flash of the confounded orange light. Cal might have nightmares about that color for the rest of his days. Oranges were supposed to be a blessing, a tasty treat and a cure for certain diseases out in the dark expanses of space.

Why Ty had programmed such a wonderful color to mean "death is looking for you," Cal would never understand.

They'd been dealing with a short that made the light blink yellow for a long time now. Yellow was a proximity alarm. No big deal, normally. Orange flashing was bad. Very bad. They'd all learned to hate orange.

Now, more than ever.

"Life support?" Cal whispered.

Ty simply held his fingers to his lips.

Could a long-range scan even hear Cal's whisper? He wasn't so sure about that. However, it wasn't just anyone out there looking for them, but a full blown, angry, probably vengeful prince. With the Banes, anything was possible.

Ethan shivered, glancing up to the still flashing light.

Orange. Orange. Orange.

It seemed like every scan, the orange flashing lasted longer, like the blasted prince was picking something up, wasn't sure, so he swept the area a few more times, just to make sure.

Cal looked out the viewport into the still unfamiliar stars. *I guess this is what you get when you liberate a prince's prized possession.*

Still, he wouldn't change anything.

Orange. Orange. Orange.

Dania had been a monster when they'd bought her on board. Now she was just like the rest of them. Wanted by the government, and on the run.

He drew in a deep breath, and the room spun, the thinning air not providing enough oxygen.

Across the room, Ethan grimaced and folded in on himself, protecting his hands from the encroaching cold. They couldn't keep shutting down life support like this. One of these days, it wouldn't come back on.

Orange. Orange. Yellow.

Ty held up one finger, and they all breathed a sigh of relief. The scan was still close, but moving away. That meant air, and blessed heat, would soon be back.

Cal hoped.

The *Star Renegade* was an old ship, and she wasn't meant for this kind of abuse.

Orange. Yellow. Yellow.

Ty's teeth glowed in the ochre light as he held up two fingers. Cal nodded.

Alanna had said it could be months before they found their way back to civilization. And they didn't even know which way to go.

Yellow. Yellow. Yellow.

"Clear!" Ty called.

Ethan jumped to his station and started pressing buttons.

Ty triggered the ship-wide comm. "Heat and oxygen coming your way, guys, hold tight."

The chill started to itch up Cal's back. "Ethan?"

"Working on it!"

The floor started to hum. Cal exhaled as the vents pushed in beautiful, life giving recycled air.

Each of them slumped into their chairs, drawing in deep breaths.

Cal rubbed his cold hands on the tops of his jeans. "How long can we keep this up? Are we playing Russian Roulette with the air?"

Ethan shook his head. "We're fine." But he glanced at Ty, who looked away, avoiding Cal's gaze.

Sometimes, what these guys didn't say was more important than what they *did* say.

The truth was, they were sitting ducks out here.

Cal hit the comm. "I want everyone to warm up, and then meet me in the lounge." He was done with floating out here, waiting to get caught. They needed to take control. *He* needed to take control. Luck wasn't going to get them out of this one.

———

Cal sank into the seat at the head of the large table in the lounge. "We need to do our best to stop shutting the systems down."

"Tell us something we don't know." Ty leaned back in his own chair.

"We can't keep hiding forever. We need to get out of here." Cal turned to Ethan. "When can you get the engines working to full capacity?"

The engineer smoothed back his curly copper hair. "Tomorrow."

Everyone stared at him.

"Why are you guys always surprised when I work miracles?" Ethan held out his hands. "Hey, it's me, remember?"

Ty folded his arms. "So you did something by accident, got incredibly lucky, and fixed it?"

Ethan laced his fingers behind his head. "Hey a miracle is a miracle. The *how* should never be questioned."

"Fine," Cal said. "Are you sure we'll have engines back online tomorrow."

He nodded. "You can have them tonight if I don't sleep."

The last thing they needed was a tired engineer when they might need him the most. "Statistically we have a few more days until that scan hits us again. As long as we're long gone, and don't have to shut off life support anymore, we're fine. So everyone sleeps tonight." Cal turned to Alanna. "If we're up and running, how long to get home?"

"Still the same as I said earlier. Maybe three months. I don't even know which direction to go."

Dania kneaded her hands. "I can help with that."

"I told you, no more black holes," Cal said.

Dania opened her mouth to speak, but Doc touched her arm. "Honey, you nearly passed out heating something up. As your doctor, I am putting you on permanent light duty until further notice."

"Until further notice? Then that wouldn't be permanent," Ethan said.

"Shut up, Ethan."

Ethan held up his hands again. "Why is everyone always telling me to shut up?"

"What are the other options?" Cal asked.

"I told you I can help." Dania stood up and walked to the center of the room. She closed her eyes, and then pointed. "Home is that way."

Cal glanced around the room. "Are you sure?"

"Yes." She walked back to her place and slumped into her chair. Her eyes reddened before she closed them and looked down, letting her long, blonde hair cover her face.

Alanna put her arm around the former-enforcer's shoulder. "How do you know?"

Dania folded further into herself. "I'm sick, and every fiber of my being is screaming to run home to my sponsor." She pointed again. "He's that way."

Ethan held up a tentative hand. "Does anyone else think it is a really bad idea to head toward the homicidal prince?"

"I'm not saying we should fly directly toward him." Dania straightened, looking at each of them as she spoke. "The chance that Geron is sitting right on the border of known space is slim. I suggest going in that direction until one of us, or the computers, recognizes where we are, and then quickly go in another direction."

Cal rubbed his chin. "If we're heading toward him, and he scans this junkyard, will the scan intercept us?"

She shook her head. "It's not line of sight. It's projected. The enforcers read the singularity I created before it collapsed, so they know where we went. They just don't know if we survived."

Cal nodded. It seemed like only yesterday when the prince had surrounded the *Star Renegade*. They were as good as caught, but Dania had used her enforcer abilities to create a black hole that sucked them out of civilized space and dumped them here, in the middle of nowhere.

If that scan would skip right over them, though, that would be a big boon. Still, Cal would rather be free and clear. "What will it take to make him stop scanning?"

She rubbed her forehead. "He won't stop looking for me until he finds my body."

Cal closed his eyes. He knew that would be the answer. He'd just hoped there would be a simpler solution. Shooting a cadaver into space wouldn't save their hides this time. At this point, their best course of action was to get out of this fish bowl before they got hooked.

"All right. Dania, go up to the bridge with Alanna and point the way home. Alanna, take us back in small jumps just so we make sure we don't accidentally appear on Geron's doorstep."

"I can't," Alanna said.

"You can't?"

"Well, I can, but I don't think we should." She looked at Ethan and Ty. "No one seems to know for sure what that polymer Ethan bought is. It might hold, but then again, it might not. Jumping puts a lot of strain on the hull in the best conditions. With a breach…"

Cal rubbed his face. "Yeah, I get it." He looked at Ethan. "You didn't get a metallurgy analysis on that stuff?"

The engineer narrowed his eyes. "I'm not even really sure what a *metallurgy analysis* is, and for the price I paid, I don't think they really had a whole lot of information."

Which also meant they were trusting their hull integrity on some sort of glue that for all they knew might be rigged to explode.

"I should probably put a containment field around that deck," Doc said.

Cal nodded. "Good call. Take anything you need from storage." Cal turned to Ethan. "Let us know when the engines are running." He stood. "Everyone else prep for immediate departure as soon as Ethan gets those engines online."

CHAPTER 3 CAL

Cal let the door to the lounge close behind him. Without Alanna jumping them, their chances of getting out of this in one piece decreased far more than he wanted to admit. He couldn't dwell on what couldn't be, though. He needed to figure out what they could do to get out of this mess alive.

"Boss?" Doc pushed through the door and entered the hall.

"What's up?"

"I'm worried about Dania."

"Of course you are. You're the doctor. It kind of goes with the territory."

"Well, in this case I'm worried about how tired she got when she was helping Alanna. I told her not to use any of her powers, but it seems to be instinctual." He sighed. "It would be like asking Ethan not to be annoying. He couldn't do it. It's just part of who he is."

Cal held back a snicker. Poor Ethan. "What's your point, Doc?"

"Dania told me that what she did shouldn't have tired her out so much."

"Well, we expected this, didn't we? She's been getting weaker all along."

"Yes and no. Not like this." He scrolled through a hand-held tablet. "You know how I hate to be wrong, but I think I underestimated when the problems would start." He looked up. "I'm afraid it might be her lungs, or worse."

Cal bit back a curse. "What do you need?"

"Once we get to regular space our first stop needs to be sector Z8 so I can get the supplies I need to try to help her." He stopped scrolling and put the device into his pocket. "I was serious when I said she's like a junkie. She knows that the pathogen load inside her is bad but she still wants it. Her body craves it, but in her case, she actually will die if she doesn't get it."

"I get you loud and clear." Cal continued down the hall. "We're doing our best to get back to civilized space. We can't really do anything until we get there."

Cal paused. That sounded pretty cold, even to his own ears.

He turned back to Doc. "I promise you, we're not giving up on her. As soon as we can get to sector Z8, we'll do our best to help her." And he meant it. She hadn't been here long, but she was here by unanimous vote. Dania was no longer their prisoner, but a member of their crew, for as long as she wanted to stay.

His chest clenched as he realized he wanted that to happen. Another mouth to feed would be a problem, but at this point, the ship would feel empty without her.

Doc nodded and headed back down the hall, hopefully to work on that containment field. Maybe his big brain could find a way to solidify that seal enough that they could actually use Alanna's jump ability. That would be a huge asset right now.

Cal pursed his lips as he entered the bridge and slammed into his chair. He didn't like insinuation that he wasn't going to help Dania. Even if she put them all in danger, she still saved them all in the end. Helping her didn't mean that he trusted her, though. He'd never be stupid enough to trust her again. Although, deep down, he really wanted to.

The doorway behind him opened and Ty entered the bridge. "Hey, boss. Everything going good up here?"

"Sure, but you're late to the party. I've got the whole ship running like clockwork."

Ty snorted. "Yeah, a broken clock, maybe." He tapped a few keys on his panel. "Do you really think it's going to take us a few months to get out of here?"

"I don't have the luxury of thinking that. I'm pretty sure you're the one who pointed out we don't have enough food to last that long."

The light on Ty's panel flashed orange once.

Ice flashed through Cal's veins. It was too soon. They'd just been scanned that morning.

Silence hung thick in the room. Cal didn't breathe until he heard Ty let out his breath when the light didn't flash again.

"Must've been a glitch," Ty said.

"We can't have that kind of a glitch," Cal said. "The yellow flashing was bad enough."

"I agree. Do you want me to get on that first?"

With so many other things wrong with the ship? "Not unless it happens again. Our focus needs to be getting out here."

Ty opened up his panel and started pulling out the burned and melted wiring. Cal worked on some of the more simple repairs himself. He was getting better at fixing things, but he'd never know the *Star Renegade* as well as Ty. The guy had been fixing the ship up since he was a kid, hoping that his employer at the time—Stanley, back on planet Kirato—would give the ship to him once the rebuild was done.

Unfortunately for the kid, Cal had come along. Stanley and his wife had hid Cal for what seemed like an eternity while the enforcers chased him down for a murder he hadn't committed. And when it was time to leave, Stanley gave the ship to Cal.

Luckily enough, Ty was more than happy to take the position of first mate, and neither of them ever looked back. Well, except for returning time to time, repaying the colony's kindness with food and supplies.

Kirato had been cut off from the supply traders due to the war between the Banes and the Carteks. Which was also, in a way, how they ended up here. If Earth hadn't bowed to the Banes for protection against the Cartek's,

Dania never would've been on board, and they never would have been running from that blasted prince.

Cal still had nightmares—when he was able to sleep—about the prince's cold stare on the main viewing screen when he'd demanded Dania's return. Usually, Cal would laugh at that kind of ultimatum, but dealing with pirates and smugglers was far less complicated. Normal criminals couldn't blindside you with magical powers you have no defense against.

Still, Cal did his best to hide his fears. Although the growing circles under Ty's eyes made him wonder how many of them were keeping their own anxiety to themselves.

The *Star Renegade* had always been a place for open discussion. Cal genuinely wanted to know what was on everyone's minds. But lately, they'd been as silent as Cal about what had happened to them.

Maybe, after Cal's migraine episodes, they were too worried about causing more stress. He hoped that wasn't the case. He'd rather be plugged in than kept in the dark.

Ty, of course, had a way of knowing everything happening on the ship, with the personnel as well as the wiring. A fact that Cal needed to take advantage of more often.

"How is the crew holding up?" Cal asked.

Ty leaned underneath his panel with a screwdriver. "They've been through worse."

"Worse than being lost in the middle of nowhere with no way to get home?"

"At the moment, no one is in the immediate vicinity trying to kill us." Ty looked up. "I say this sounds like a vacation."

An alarm boomed through the deck, the sound echoing off the ceiling and walls.

"I was kidding!" Ty punched his chair. "Come on!"

Cal covered his ears, his entire body tensing, the horror of his recent headaches making him want to crawl in a corner and hide. Luckily enough, the pain didn't come. And he lowered his hands.

"What's going on?" Cal asked.

Ty cursed. "There's some kind of a leak in the engine room." Ty called up the comm. "Ethan what's going on?"

"Kind of busy right now."

Ty leaned closer to his monitor. "Radiation levels are rising. Ethan, get out of there. Now."

"And sacrifice the ship? No way. I can hold it."

Cal slammed his fist onto the comm button. "No heroics. We'll figure it out. Get out of there. That's an order."

Static filled the line.

"Ethan?"

Ty gulped. His eyes flashed at Cal.

"Ethan!" But Cal didn't wait for an answer. He jumped to his feet and ran to the door barely waiting for the panels to open for him.

He sprinted through the halls, red lights flashing and sirens echoing. The sound of Ty's boots slamming on the floor tiles behind him was barely audible over the blaring alarms.

Cal skidded to a stop at the end of the hall a few paces from the engineering room.

Alanna stood outside the door, pounding her fists on the glass, and screaming Ethan's name.

Still holding his screwdriver, Ty pried the panel beside

the door off and fiddled with the wires. "I can't get it open," he said. "The emergency locks have engaged."

"Then how do we get him out of there?" Alanna wiped tears from her eyes.

Ty grimaced, but he didn't say what they all already knew. There was no way to open that door. Not with a radiation leak.

Order your copy of Renegade Thief Now!